International acclaim for Julian Gough's

Juno & Juliet

"Grace and warmth . . . exude from *Juno & Juliet*. . . . It's the most brutally—
and hilariously—real depiction of Irish undergraduate and academic life
since *The Ginger Man*. . . . Sweetness is stubbornly maintained here, and
(with one exception) everyone—for once—lives happily ever after."
—*Los Angeles Times Book Review*

"Endearing."   —*Entertainment Weekly*

"*Juno & Juliet* achieves that all too rare synthesis of piercing observation
and the feelgood factor. . . . A modern, at times brilliantly ironic rework-
ing of the classical fairy tale, with nods to Shakespeare, Austen and
Beckett, Gough's novel is an intelligent look at the magical banality of
student life."   —*Literary Review*

"Utterly charming and hilarious."   —*The Independent on Sunday*

"Pungent. . . . A light romantic Irish comedy. . . . Gough is a clever
writer. . . . Witty phrases, and several that are thoughtfully provocative,
are [his] strength."   —*Richard Eder, The New York Times*

JULIAN GOUGH

Juno & Juliet

Julian Gough is the author of a satirical serial, the coauthor of a successful stage play, and the executive producer of a documentary; *Juno & Juliet* is his first novel. During the 1990s he founded and performed in the underground rock band Toasted Heretic, which has toured widely here and in the U.K. He lives in Galway, Ireland.

juno & juliet

ANCHOR BOOKS

A DIVISION OF RANDOM HOUSE. INC.

NEW YORK

juno & juliet

A NOVEL

JULIAN GOUGH

FIRST ANCHOR BOOKS EDITION, AUGUST 2002

Copyright © 2001 by Julian Gough

All rights reserved under International and Pan-American Copyright Conventions. Published
in the United States by Anchor Books, a division of Random House, Inc., New York, and
simultaneously in Canada by Random House of Canada Limited, Toronto. Originally published in
hardcover in the United Kingdom by Flamingo, and imprint of HarperCollins Publishers,
London, and in the United States by Nan A. Talese, an imprint of Doubleday, a division
of Random House, Inc., New York, in 2001.

The Library of Congress has cataloged the Nan A. Talese/Doubleday edition as follows:
Gough, Julian.
Juno & Juliet : a novel/Julian Gough.—1st ed. in the USA.
p.   cm.
ISBN 978-0-385-72161-5
1. Women college students—Fiction.   2. Galway (Ireland)—Fiction.   3. Sisters—Fiction.
4. Twins—Fiction.   I. Title: Juno and Juliet.   II. Title.
PR6057.O815 J86 2001
823'.92—dc21
00-041111
CIP

Anchor ISBN: 978-0-385-72161-5

Book design by Terry J. Karydes

www.anchorbooks.com

Printed in the United States of America
10   9   8   7   6   5   4

*"...[M]an has the advantage of choice,
woman only the power of refusal...."*

—Mr. Tilney on matrimony and dancing,
from *Northanger Abbey*
by Jane Austen

"I like to teach," Angela said.
"It's easier than learning."

—from *Couples*
by John Updike

juno & juliet

PART I

Galway

1

When Juno and I stepped off the bus in Eyre Square we were armed only with an enormous rucksack each and the scribbled address of a distant cousin. A blizzard of youth-hostel flyers immediately engulfed us, clearing only to reveal a blizzard of youths, smiling at us in French, Spanish, English, and Italian. Juno told them we didn't need a hostel, but thank you anyway. I told them we didn't need a hostel, so fuck off.

And there I think you have, neatly illustrated, the essential difference between her and me.

I had, to be fair to me, not enjoyed my journey much. The peace had held all through the morning's packing, but on the way out the door I managed to have an almighty row with our father. What was it about?

Ah, what are they ever about. It was about nothing. All the way up on the bus I had stomach cramps and a headache. A drunk behind us spewed against the back of my seat. Then he tried to make light conversation. The driver spent the entire journey with the radio on at full blast as he attempted, with an ever-increasing lack of success which would have disheartened a lesser man, to tune in to a country-and-western station that seemed to be making its last, faint, desperate broadcast from somewhere beyond the edge of the solar system.

Things rapidly improved once we'd got off the bus and through the blizzard. Pausing only to shovel fistfuls of flyers into the big yellow litter bins that disfigured the edge of Eyre Square, we headed for the nearest coffee shop. Apart from a couple of buskers and another drunk and a spotty boy with a clipboard who promised not to take up much of our valuable time and didn't, nobody bothered us for money, our names, or a kiss in the hundred yards to the G. B. C. Coffee Shop and Restaurant.

Some kind of record.

I should probably explain that Juno began to be beautiful around the age of fourteen and the process shows no sign of stopping. Her beauty refines and upgrades itself constantly. At the time this story begins, she has just turned eighteen and it's almost ridiculous how beautiful she is. No, it *is* ridiculous how beautiful she is. She's beautiful to the point where it might as well be a disfigurement. She's invisible behind it. It's all people see. Not just men. Everyone. That doesn't mean everyone's attracted to her. It just means everyone has an attitude, an opinion, before they know a damn thing about her. It's nobody's fault. It's the way we are. It annoys the hell out of me.

I should probably also explain that Juno is my identical twin.

We got a seat in the nook at the back. The coffee was lovely. My cramps and headache faded. We'd left home. I felt great. Eventually we paid up and went to look for the house of our distant cousin.

We found it.

2

The front door of 14 Bishop Casey Terrace swung open and we stepped trustingly into what might as well have been deep space. It was so dark I had the sensation of falling, and grabbed Juno. Seconds later, as our eyes adjusted, we found ourselves blinking in the centre of a kind of smoke-blackened igloo constructed entirely from plaster statues of Our Lady of Perpetual Sorrow, in assorted sizes, and large, framed pictures of Pope John XXIII. Turf dust covered every flat surface an inch deep. No light came through the shroudlike curtains. A tiny turf fire in the grate sent a little light halfway across the rug, while the small, sinister, glowing sacred-heart lamp on the far wall did its job of flooding the rear of the room with darkness. Our distant cousin was now close enough for us to count her teeth, even by that light.

Five. Three up on top.

She spoke in tongues, and vanished. I was terrified.

"What the hell was that about?" I asked Juno.

"She's gone to put her teeth in and put on the kettle," said Juno, who'd always been better at languages. "She hopes we had a pleasant journey."

The tea was actually grand and over the course of it our cousin slowly turned into a human being, although a very old, very religious human being with no sense of humour. That didn't stop her being very funny, it just stopped her from noticing the fact. We had to turn a lot of laughs into coughs, to the extent that she gave us both Hacks cough sweets, which she took with a creaking of bones from the top of the dresser, half a packet of them softened with age into a thick paste in their paper wrappers. They came in some obsolete, unrecognisable flavour, probably that of a long-extinct plant. Gobi Water Lily. Sabre-Toothed Parsley. We liked her. We even ate some of the sweets for her.

She had left Galway twice in her life, once to go to Lourdes (the Mecca of the Irish) and once to go to Sligo (the Sligo of the Irish). She thought both places overrated, which, given that Sligo has a global reputation as one of the three wettest, dullest towns north of Antarctica, was a pretty harsh judgement. I coughed enthusiastically and declined another sweet. A cat, half-blind with age, jumped up on the table and began to lick the butter. Juno coughed, and declined a scone.

We hadn't come to Galway to live with our distant cousin. We'd come to Galway to go to university and study English. We were just staying with our cousin until we found somewhere to live. She was lovely, and after five minutes even I liked her. Juno liked her instantly. Juno tends to do that. Living with our cousin was out of the question, though. Her house was a classic Galway terrace house, the kind in which Nora Barnacle and her countless siblings grew halfway up (bad diet, short people). The bottom floor comprised a small living room. The top floor comprised a small bedroom. That was it. Her periodic vanishings to the "kitchen" were only made possible by the almost total absence of light in vast areas of the tiny room. The "kitchen" was a gas cooker, installed strategically under the stairs long before we were born to ensure fatalities in the case of a chip-pan fire. Sadly, everyone had grown up and left or died of natural causes before the cooker could fulfil its destiny. Now it probably wouldn't bother, with only our cousin to operate it and nobody else to be trapped upstairs.

I shall draw a discreet veil over the defects of the sinister, pre-war plumbing. Suffice to say, everything lurked in a shed the size of a wardrobe in the tiny yard out the back. Before retiring for the night, we were introduced to the facilities, a stiff breeze caressing our ankles in the dark. We returned shaken, traumatised, but alive. Let us pass on.

We spent our first night in Galway in sleeping bags on the living-room floor, lulled to sleep by the reassuring hiss of gas leaking from the perished rubber tubes joining the antique cooker to the rusty cylinder, and by the comforting weight of cats lying drowsily across our feet.

"Night-night, Juno."

"Night-night, Juliet."

3

We awoke at what felt like dawn, though of course it was still dark in the living room. Our cousin was making us breakfast. By the time we'd thanked God that we couldn't see the state of the plates we were eating off and had eaten an enormous fry, our eyes had adjusted enough to see the state of the plates we had eaten off. They were practically trimmed in fur. We thanked her very much, enthusiastically declined to visit the chamber of horrors out the back, and headed rather urgently out into an explosion of light to look for somewhere civilized to piss. And, once we'd carried out our priority mission, somewhere civilized to live.

We had turned up in Galway a week and a half before the start of college to make sure we would have plenty of time to find a place. So had several thousand other people. These were the late arrivals. Many thousands more had already been in Galway for quite some time looking for places, with far from universal success. A lucky few had parents with the foresight to give birth to them in Galway, but even some of these were struggling. Galway is a small town with a large university. All that Thursday we saw people fighting for bedsits a wino's dog wouldn't tolerate. We saw flats that seemed hewn from the living mildew. We didn't see them immediately. First we had to queue. We saw cookers that would have left our distant cousin exclaiming, "How quaint! An antique!" We saw electric heaters that were obviously prototypes from the dawn of the age of electricity, and slightly before the dawn of the age of tenants' rights. We saw Mesozoic lino. We saw Precambrian carpets.

We saw armchairs with no arms. We saw tables with no legs. We saw young men fighting and dying in a senseless war over a few square yards of worthless ground, and the winners spending half their grant on the deposit.

We saw our lives flash before us.

We had to sit down.

"Jesus, this is awful," I said. I had begun to feel very far from home. Every place we'd looked at had been disgusting, expensive, and taken. Our parents didn't have any more money, I wasn't even sure how they'd gotten what they'd given us, and it wasn't enough. Our grants weren't going to come through for weeks, and all we had to last us until then would barely cover a deposit. If we could find a place. And then how would we eat? How could we buy books? Were we beaten? Was it over before it had started? Would I ever, ever, ever get away from Tipperary and my parents and my school and my life? I started to cry.

Juno held me as we sat on the wall of a tiny house in New Road that had been subdivided, with sturdy cardboard partitions, into five "bedsits," in all of which you had just about enough room to prove the description truthful by sitting on the bed, as long as you didn't try anything recklessly space-consuming while you were at it, like crossing your legs, or removing a hat. The last one had gone for a suitcase of used notes, a kidney, and some share options ten minutes before we'd arrived. We'd looked, wistfully, anyway. "Oh Juno, I'm homesick and I don't want to go home," I sobbed. Juno held me tighter. "Hey, 's OK, baby Juliet. I'm here." That's one of the nice things about Juno. She understands me no matter how little sense I'm making, and she never goes for an obvious joke at my expense. And when I feel like a baby she never stays tough. Me, I stay tough, I'm awkward when she's sad, I feel useless and I can't say the things I know I should. But she's good with me. She's really very good.

When I'd stopped crying we went back to our cousin's house. It was after seven P.M.; we'd been looking for a place since we'd picked up the new *Galway Advertiser* that morning. Our copy was in bits, the big "Accommodation Available" section was covered in scribbled phone numbers and directions and prices, we'd used up two phone cards and walked ourselves stumpy. Time to go home.

Our cousin gave us tea and sympathy and a red-hot tip. "I'm sure old

Mrs. Flannery has rooms to let, I'm sure of it. You should try her tomorrow, first thing. She has a house down by the docks, half-empty for months. I'm sure I have her address here somewhere, yes you must call on her tomorrow and enquire." Our cousin hesitated. "Ye might find her a little . . . old-fashioned." She frowned. "And she'd be a bit too religious for my taste, now."

We gulped. But we went.

4

We bearded Mrs. Flannery in her lair, armoured by our innocence. She lived in Renmore, a good mile from the docks, in a house that bristled with old ladies of uncertain function. They could have been friends, relatives, or servants. It was impossible to tell from Mrs. Flannery's erratic manner, and she didn't deign to explain. All through our interview they flitted in and out of the half-dark of the drawing room, bringing us fresh tea and bearing away the old cups. The tea was lovely. Biscuits were provided by swift, silent figures. Soon we were ignoring them with the same serene composure as old Mrs. Flannery herself.

Old Mrs. Flannery (so-called because of the existence of a young Mrs. Flannery, her daughter, a victim of coincidence or inbreeding) indeed had rooms to let. Not just that, the house down by the docks had been half-empty for months, not because it was uninhabitable (our first guess: Why else would a house be half-empty in Galway?), but because old Mrs. Flannery didn't believe in advertising, and anyone who'd heard about it by word of mouth had also heard the stories about old Mrs. Flannery and was afraid to go near her. We tut-tutted, people were terrible. I wondered if we'd get out alive.

She was crazy as a loon. She talked to us for twenty minutes about the worldwide Jewish/Communist conspiracy against Catholicism. She offered us more tea, which arrived instantly. She told us for a quarter of an hour about the profound evil of usury, and for ten minutes expounded on the satanic nature of the Bank of England. She passed the biscuits. Then, after a quick history of the Masons, she told us what fine young ladies we appeared to be, warned us against the heresies of Martin Luther, and gave us the keys to the house near the docks. The top floor was ours if we wanted it, forty pounds a week (Each? No, for the whole floor: two bedrooms, living room/kitchen, and bathroom). She was sorry about the rent, it had been thirty-five pounds but, thanks to the Jewish/Communist economic conspiracy against Catholicism, money wasn't worth what it once was. We made noises that indicated an understanding of the words said, without necessarily indicating an agreement with the sentiments they expressed. We were pretty good at these noises by now, after an hour's practice. Juno handed me the keys to put in my pocket and we left.

The place was great. We took it.

Thus it was that we snatched the finest flat in Galway from beneath the noses of an astonished world.

5

By the time university started, we'd settled in nicely and I was in love. I was in love with Galway, I was in love with our fabulous fourth-story flat, I was in love with our view of Galway from our flat, I was in love with buying Brillo pads; I was in love with freedom.

I would wake Juno or Juno would wake me and we'd get up and wander in and out of the bathroom and each other's rooms and shower and dress and eventually have breakfast together in the living room, looking out high over the harbour and the sea. The coast of Clare would shimmer in the haze across the bay (and much later, in the winter, would dis-

appear behind walls of rain, reappear, and disappear again). I never tired
of it, and I don't think I ever would have. We'd walk into town after
breakfast, buy the makings of dinner, explore the shops, talk a lot.

I began to know Juno much better in those conversations. It sounds
stupid, when she was my twin, when we'd lived in the same house and
often the same room for all of our lives. But how can you see something
that's always so close? My picture of her grew much clearer against an
unfamiliar background. I'd loved her absentmindedly. I began to love her
more.

Wait. Slow down. This makes me sound like I was full of love, that I
was a casual user of the word, that I was comfortable with the idea. Not
at all. I was full of confusion, anger, angst. The usual. I was just eighteen.
I wouldn't even have used the word. But looking back, I would call all
these things forms of love. For Juno, a respect gone wild, a kind of love.
For my freedom, a passion, a kind of love. For the view, an awe and fascination that didn't wear out, a kind of love.

At the time, I didn't believe in love. Juno believed in love. Believing
in it didn't protect her. Not believing in it didn't protect me. It was an interesting year. This is the story of it.

6

I was disappointed by the university, and vice versa. My
fellow students, my comrades in the classics, turned out not to be the
dedicated seekers-out of knowledge I'd envisioned. Not only did they not
seek out knowledge, but many of them hid when it visited. I went to a lot
of introductory lectures in the first week of my first term, even in subjects I knew I wouldn't do, or couldn't do because they clashed with
English or philosophy. Those two I knew I wished to do.

In all the introductories, as the lecturers explained the subject and the work that they would cover that year, I looked around me at my fellows. It was a sight to tear at the hardest heart. Anguish and horror ploughed furrows across their low brows as it sank in that they were being asked to read, and not just read but read books, and not just read books but read books with no pictures. By the end of the tougher introductories, whole rows of jaws had slackened in dull horror till they hung like ripe fruit above their owners' laps, swinging in the mouth-wind, dribbling a little now and then. The attached heads sank slowly between shoulders now drooping, postures melted and slumped like lead figures in an oven. They took it pretty badly. It was like watching evolution in reverse.

After the lecturer had called for any questions, and received no response from the ringing, shell-shocked silence, and left, they would crawl erect and drag their knuckles out of the theatre, quizzing each other fiercely.

"Are we to do all that in one year?"

"My God, so many books, surely we don't need them all, does he think we're made of money?"

"If she expects us to read all those she's mad, I'm already going to be doing history and archaeology, sure you'd want three heads."

They'd go to the canteen and I'd follow and hover, fascinated. The complaints never stopped, never slackened. The price of the meals, the taste of the coffee, the workload, the book list, semesterisation, repeat fees, bad holiday jobs, dole regulations. I'd drift from table to table, past clumps of frightened first-years and second-year couples and bearded survivors from another age who were repeating their final year for the second-last time. The only constant was the white noise of complaint. I gradually got the peculiar impression that they'd all been promised a three-year holiday in Disney World but had been brought here by cattle truck instead.

"This pizza's shite."

"I'd piss better coffee."

"Your man's a fuckin' eejit."

"Bogroll here's hardly worth fecking."

"I won't even get a job at the end of it."

"She won't give me her notes, the bitch."

"There's no paper in the toilets."

"He won't tell us the questions."

"It's too hard."

"It's too easy."

"It's too boring."

The constant whine of self-pity from the student body began to drive me frantic, like a mosquito in my ear. Who were these people? Why had they come here? How was it they were so offended by their own choice of life?

I'd so looked forward to leaving the cultural wasteland in which I'd half-grown up, and in my last year at school I'd fever-visioned a dreamy, sunlit university-state peopled by the brightest and the best. I'd half-lived there for the final school months, it had seemed more real to me than the town outside. To get to the university and find it had fallen into barbarian hands, that its halls were full of the very peasants and savages I thought I'd left behind, still talking about how their new shoes had split on the second day, and of the TV shows they'd missed, and the terrible price of twenty cigarettes . . . it was a bitter blow.

I still hadn't made it out of town. As I travelled, the town limits expanded ahead of me.

Then Juno met Michael.

OK. I know I should be modern and not really tell you anything directly, and imply everything, and be subtle and oblique, but I'm no good at that. If I feel I should tell you something, I'm afraid I'm just going to tell you it. Another confession: My vice is the Victorian vice of sentimentality, not the modern vice of irony. If I slip, it will be in the direction of old-fashioned sentiment. For this, I apologise in advance.

7

Juno met Michael Fowler in a disco. I know I should say "at a club," but you know I'm old-fashioned. Dance music was enjoying one of its periods of universal popularity when we arrived in Galway, and many of the clubs were so full of a sense of their own cultural importance that they could barely find room for the paying public. I couldn't take them seriously, and quickly got into the habit of calling them discos because it annoyed the more dedicated clubbers. I had a talent to annoy. They didn't expect it from me, which was useful. I didn't look like the sort of person I was. I had the same serene beauty as Juno, though I cooperated with it less. My hair was cut quite severely, while Juno's was long. Also, my posture was lousy, whilst Juno could have descended a spiral stair-case in an earthquake with the National Library on her head.

But in this disco, in the Castle one Thursday a couple of weeks into term, it was me that Michael Fowler first approached. I don't even re-member what he said. It was nothing offensive, just a tentative line that could have been read as a chat-up from the tone, or left as it seemed on the surface with no embarrassment. Nicely balanced. A request for a light? The time? It's gone. I forget.

I was rude or perhaps not rude, but very abrupt. His face registered a little pain but he took it well, and I felt a little guilty stab, damn, he didn't deserve that, as he turned away. You can tell some people are nice almost instantly, God knows how, but you can. He was nice. Juno stood up and took a step and halted him and gave him a light or the time, and they stood there longer, talking. Not a light, Juno didn't smoke. It must have been the time. When he moved off she sat back down and we talked about him for a while, Juno liked him, he was funny and fast, and then a song came on that we actually liked and we danced.

Later the lights came up, and the cave of deep bass and strobe-lit

statues collapsed back into a hall full of blotchy-faced boys and girls with
their hair stranded across their faces by sweat. As everybody tried to find
their coats and one another, Michael came over. He was funny and direct and unembarrassable, and the three of us left together. It was quite
obvious he wanted to sleep with Juno even before he said, "Christ, you
wouldn't believe how much I want to sleep with you, Juno."

Juno reached for his hand and looked into his eyes.

"And I'm afraid you wouldn't believe how little I want to sleep with
you, Michael."

Michael sighed and turned to me.

"Christ, you wouldn't believe how much I want to sleep with you,
Juliet."

I laughed. What was funny, and very disarming, was that he was
quite serious, but entirely aware of how he was coming across. It was a
strategy Juno and I were both familiar with, a kind of bizarre elevated
honesty that mocked itself, but he did it very well. Somehow it was
flattering, it was charming. It wasn't likely to work, but it was very entertaining.

The three of us walked back into town along the seafront, there was
a sliver of moon, it was lovely. Michael linked his arms with ours. I unlinked mine. Juno didn't.

"So you will sleep with me then," he said, delighted.

She unlinked her arm from his.

"No," she said.

"Ah well," he said, and they linked arms again. I coughed.

"Perhaps I should pretend I have to tie a shoelace, and fall behind a
bit," I said.

"You're a genius!" said Michael.

"No," said Juno.

"I suppose both of you together is out of the question?"

"Yes."

"Yes."

Michael sighed, and we walked and talked on.

There was a lot to talk about. Rumours of a ceasefire. The collapse of Catholicism. *Home & Away*.

At the door we said good-bye and then somehow we were all upstairs in our living room, I was making three mugs of coffee, and Michael was lying on the floor in front of the bookcase saying "wow" a lot and asking if he could borrow Juno's copy of *The Groucho Letters*. He took milk, one sugar.

At four in the morning there was still no sign of his leaving and I had a lecture at ten so I went to bed and left them to it.

I got up at nine and stumbled into the living room, where I assembled a breakfast of cereals without at any point opening both eyes at once. Juno's door was closed, no sign of Michael, no clue as to whether he'd stayed or gone. I munched meditatively. Curious emotions swelled in me, small, nameless, and contradictory. I had a quick shower and sprinted for University College Galway. (*Sprinted:* Old English student word, meaning "walked faster than usual.") The lecture was in sociology and politics, known in the Golden Tongue as soc and pol. Juno hadn't chosen it as one of her subjects because saying the word *sock* made her laugh. I burned with curiosity till lunchtime, when Juno wandered into the canteen through the usual swirl of glances, sat beside me, and took a spoonful of my apple crumble.

"It tastes like . . . Johnson's Baby Shampoo?" she said.

"Don't start," I said, "you'll turn into one of them. It's lovely, and it's very cheap. Sometimes they don't rinse all the washing-up liquid off the dishes, that's all."

Juno sighed. "There's nothing wrong with complaining when there's something to complain about."

"Oh Juno, there's *always* something to complain about, so don't start."

She took some more crumble, this time from the middle.

"Not bad. And no, he didn't stay over, I can tell you're dying to ask. With great difficulty I managed to get him out of the house at five-thirty. I like him a lot, but the persistence got wearing. And I did fancy him, yes, but if he'd got what he wanted last night I'd never have seen him again, and he's too entertaining for that. It would have been a waste. I'm meeting him at nine in the Crane, and I want you to come along."

I cocked my head. "Gooseberry?"

"No, if you're there it'll be a conversation. If it's just him and me it'll be judo. He's promised to show me some of his cartoons, you'll enjoy it, come."

"But you want him, don't you, at some stage?"

Juno stared into an ashtray full of tiny ripped-up pieces of polystyrene. "Maybe . . . no. He's not boyfriend material. But . . . I'd like to be his friend. I don't know if that's possible. . . . Come along."

"OK," I said. "I'd like him as a friend too."

8

The first obscene letter arrived that day by second post, while we were out. We didn't know it was an obscene letter at the time, but the later ones made it so. We just found it rather peculiar, maybe flattering. Yes, we did find it flattering, only the things that happened afterward soured that. The first letter was a nice thing to get, a puzzle, very shy. We thought it was embarrassment and shyness had led to the writer's leaving it unsigned. Perhaps it was, at first.

It was addressed to Juno, and one of the strange, mouselike downstairs tenants must have picked it up and left it on the hall table inside the front door, among the postal silt of all such buildings—the dusty junk mail and bank envelopes of long-departed tenants. We almost didn't see it, unaccustomed as we were to receiving mail, a standard small white envelope, nondescript. I'd been hoping for a postcard from a friend who'd gone to London. I glanced at the surface layer on the table and moved past, stepped back, picked it up, and handed it to Juno.

"For you. Nearly missed it."

A neatly printed address: Juno Taylor, 14 McDonagh Quay, Galway. She opened it in the hall, read it going up the stairs.

"Who's it from?"

"I don't know." She kept reading.

"Who signed it?"

"Nobody."

She handed it to me and unlocked our living-room door. I sat at the table and read:

Dear Juno,

I know that you do not know me, and I do not know you. Maybe you will think this letter is stupid. That's OK. All I want to say is that the other day when my life had got so dark and black I could not stand it anymore, I saw you pass, you shone. I followed you. I know I should not have followed you. I would have thanked you but I was afraid then. I want to thank you now. Looking at you, I cured myself somehow. Your beauty pulled me through. That is all. And I thank you.

The paper was ordinary, white, a single sheet, folded and folded then folded again to fit the small envelope. The black ordinary print of any letter written on computer. The look of the letters so ordinary. Times, I thought calmly. Times roman. The one you get unless you ask for something else. I carefully refolded the page along the original creases until it was a little white pillow of energy small enough to pack into its envelope. I turned the envelope face up. Stamp. Galway postmark.

"Juno, you do attract them."

"It's creepy."

"It's almost nice, for a creepy letter. Polite. Weird prose style, though. And whatever happened to illiteracy and green ink? The guy writes like a computer in love."

"If it's a guy."

"Come on, it's a guy. He writes like a guy, and you've never got weird shit from a girl. Guilty flirting or straight proposals, but not weird shit. Guy."

"If it was a girl, that might be why she wrote instead of talking to me."

"Nah. Guy. I'd bet money."

"The printing thing, it's scary. The not signing it."

"But there's nothing bad in it. It's not . . . threatening. Could just be someone shy, or with a stutter."

"It reads wrong. Could be someone crazy."

"Most crazy people are perfectly harmless. You've had weird admirers. So this is another one."

"Mmm."

"Maybe it's somebody foreign. Bad English. Doesn't know the social conventions. Thinks Walentine's Day is in Oktober."

Juno laughed. Stopped. "Our address. Whoever it was must have followed me home, oh God. Don't leave our door open anymore, not even going for milk."

"He, or she, whatever, doesn't sound dangerous. Except maybe to himself. Herself. Itself."

We called it Juno's Pervert after that. A figure of fun at first. A shy hermaphrodite. We'd spot it shopping.

"That's your pervert there, buying the *Telegraph*. Look at the look it gave you. Definitely."

And a startled old man would sprint from our interested stares, out of Eason's, bumping into tourists and blushing furiously.

"Look! It's buying the *Cosmo* with the sexual-obsession article! What a giveaway!"

And we'd stalk some poor woman to the checkout. Bookshops and newsagents were good for this game, every purchase a clue to character. After a week or two we'd forgotten the letter, except as an excuse for the game.

9

"And now everyone's annoyed with Freud for being such a beastly patriarch and oppressor and for being totally wrong about everything anyway. Well, you know, what a crock of fucking shit. He was a Viennese Jew, for Christ's sake, a fan of cocaine with a theory of the mind. He couldn't have oppressed the world if he'd tried. People seem to be mixing him up with a chap called Hitler. Freud's theories spread because everybody loved them, they were sexy theories, it was a new idea, near as dammit. A new way to look at ourselves, and Christ we love to look at ourselves. That's all any form of therapy is really, a socially approved system of self-obsession. An excuse for talking about yourself to strangers. Fucked-up people are paying someone money to listen to them talk about how amazingly fucked-up they are. They don't want to waste valuable time being cured. If they were cured they'd have nothing to talk about. They'd be somebody else. They'd have to get a new hobby. Golf or something. As for 'alternative' therapies . . . Jesus."

Michael Fowler pulled deep on his pint. Juno and I looked at each other, and raised simultaneous eyebrows. One got the impression that Michael had not had a good day. Our meetings in the Crane were by now a regular fixture of the week, and Michael's conversational style did have a tendency to incorporate the rant as a major stylistic feature, but today it was scarcely a conversation at all. He had come in, got his pint, sat down, ranted about Galway City Council, ranted about modern architecture, dismissed modern popular music in a cogently argued six thousand words, gone to the toilet, returned with his fly undone and launched straight into a rant about the sort of people who attend therapy, finishing up with his analysis of the popular appeal of Freudianism. He put his pint down and began again.

"The bloody Silva method. You know it? Using coloured pens on pretty scraps of paper, you write out embarrassing, twee, positivist Christmas-cracker mottoes that would make a Care-Bear puke, and you stick these vile, offensive slogans on every available surface, at eye level. I had a friend who attended a Silva course. Jesus. A sign on his fridge would be telling me that I was a happy and healthy person who ate only what I needed, while I'd be cursing and rooting around behind the vegetables to see where he'd hidden his beer. This was a guy who spent most of his day slumped across his work desk, stoned and giggling, under a big orange sign saying 'I am a happy, productive worker, enjoying doing the work I like.' I'd go for a piss and be told by the cistern that I was precious, valuable, unique, and in the process of deservedly achieving my goals as I pissed the shit-smears off the back of the bowl. Actually, I think he probably meant that one to be funny, he wasn't a complete moron. But you see what I mean? Therapy designed to make you feel OK about the way you are, while pretending to be therapy designed to make you a new, improved person. Most people aren't happy, healthy, productive people, and a bunch of little stickers won't make them happy, healthy, productive people. Most people are dreadful, fucked-up, useless people who should just be honest and stick a My Little Pony notelet on their bedroom mirror saying 'I am a dreadful, fucked-up, useless person, and I will never change because I like it that way.' Psychotherapy. Aromatherapy. Touch therapy. Colour therapy. Native-American wanking therapy. A bunch of excuses for buying new clothes, getting your back rubbed, and blaming your life on your parents and your star sign. Crap."

"Michael," said Juno gently, "what the hell is wrong with you?"

She took the hand that wasn't lifting the pint to his lips, and he shivered violently.

"Nothing. Everything."

"Well that narrows it down. Give us another clue," I said.

Juno frowned at me to take it seriously. Michael didn't seem to have minded, or noticed.

"A bunch of things," he said. "Sorry. I have been talking complete shite. It's nothing. I'm sorry."

The conversation slowly turned into an actual conversation, but he still wouldn't tell us what the problem was. I had a shocking idea, but I was afraid to ask in case I was right. There was an awkwardness that wouldn't fade, and when we all left early he didn't come back to the flat with us as he usually would for coffee and talk. Juno went straight to bed, on the thin excuse that we had a ten o'clock lecture on Blake the next day. I almost asked her if we shared the same suspicion, but I couldn't bring myself to. After she'd gone to bed I sat up for another hour in the living room listening to *The Hounds of Love* till the tape clicked off and I switched off the table lamp and sat a while longer by the window, looking out on a level with the high, bright, harbour lights at a fisheries vessel with tarpaulins over its guns, in close to our building, the width of the street away, its radar level with me, and behind it the long rusty bulk of a tanker, and across the harbour all the pretty little fishing boats named after wives and daughters.

10

UCG was built in the 1840s and the 1970s. The original, tiny, and beautiful campus was built in the 1840s, to instruct a select few in the classics. The vast bulk of today's university was built in the 1970s, to instruct the masses in assorted categories of engineering, science, commerce, and the liberal arts.

The original buildings were erected in stone by hardy empire-builders who believed in fresh air and a standard twenty feet of headroom, from boardroom to toilets. The offices and passages of the Old Quad were therefore cool and airy in the summer and almost uninhabitably cold in the winter, as the stone sucked the heat from your bones, and a combination of ground fog and low-lying light cloud obscured your view of the ceiling.

The modern buildings, in striking contrast, were designed and constructed entirely of glass immediately before the first great oil crisis.

Examined abstractly, objectively, with no clues given as to the intended function of the complex, you would have to guess that UCG was a vast heat-shedding experiment, a machine built on a tremendous scale to discover whether stone or glass could most efficiently transfer heat from the inside to the outside of buildings.

The modern buildings had the advantage there, in that they had far more heat available for transfer. The thermostats had been set high in 1971, and the secrets of their whereabouts, or how to alter them if ever accidentally found, were by now forgotten even by God. Slowly but surely UCG's oil consumption crippled our great Republic's balance of trade and brought the country to its knees, while downwind of the university, tropical plants blossomed in a swathe across the rocky wastes of Connemara, and carelessly discarded peach stones sprouted luxuriantly before they'd hit the ground.

Thus my thoughts as I snoozed through a lecture on Blake in the balmy heat of the Kirwan lecture theatre on a cold wet day in November. Professor Flannery Ryan, a fierce rabbit of a man, was blessed with a high, thin voice, a lisp, and, on this particular day, a startlingly deep cough. As he leaped from bass to falsetto and back, neatly avoiding most of the frequencies available to the human ear, but causing consternation among the local whale and bat populations, I rested my chin in my hands and thought about heat and architecture, and the night before.

Juno dozed beside me, oblivious to Professor Ryan's whistles and booms. She hadn't slept well, had eventually given up trying, and had instead read for several hours before falling asleep at dawn. This she'd told me over a shaky breakfast. We hadn't discussed Michael.

I thought Michael was falling in love with Juno. And I thought Juno thought so too.

The heating vent beside me suddenly snored a warm Sahara wind into being, ruffling my sparse notes. Professor Ryan gripped the lectern firmly and loosed a cough like cannon-fire. The benches trembled gently beneath the sleeping students.

"Who, then, exactly, is this 'prince of love'?"

(Cough, boom . . . echo . . .)

"This 'prince of love' who

> *. . . loves to sit and hear me sing*
> *Then, laughing, sports and plays with me*
> *Then stretches out my golden wing*
> *And mocks my loss of liberty.*

. . . Eh? 'And mocks my loss of liberty.' Eh? Hey? Yes."

He loves her.

11

Nothing happened for a while after that. I didn't talk to Juno about Michael, and she didn't talk to me. I didn't know how she felt about Michael, and, crucially, I didn't know how I felt about Michael. I couldn't bring the subject up because I didn't know what I'd say. I was, if I were to be honest with myself (something I was incapable of being at the time), terrified of my own emotions and quite in the dark as to what they actually were. I had a genius for hiding my feelings from myself, and I was working at the limits of my genius on this one. I knew that I believed Michael had begun to love Juno. I refused to think how that made me feel. If you'd asked me, I would have calmly denied I felt anything at all, and I would have believed that to be absolutely true. The day after the Blake lecture, Michael went to Dublin for a week to work on cartoons and layout for a theatre festival, their posters and brochure and adverts and everything, and the crisis was postponed. Great word, *postponed*. Hoisted higher, on a thinner rope.

The morning before he was due to come back, I was due to attend my first Modern English tutorial, in Room 315, Tower 2 of the Arts Block.

I woke early and wandered into the living room/kitchen wearing my favourite night gown, cotton and covered in pale yellow roses with black, shiny thorns on their long, delicate stems. Pouring the milk onto my cornflakes left-handed, because I was holding open Jane Austen's *Emma* with my right hand, I landed the milk in the bowl of the spoon, from which the milk curved back up again and lofted into my lap. Reflexively, my right hand moved, as though to stop pouring, while my left hand poured on. I thought to drop the book (a confused thought, that I could stop the pouring if I was unencumbered by the book), and dropped the carton instead, my hands and their actions utterly confused in my head by now. Milk everywhere.

Mopping up with toilet paper (first the table because it was flat and easy, then the carpet, then me), I studied the night gown. It wouldn't survive much longer. It was faded and thin and the seams were beginning to go. The hem had lost its stitching almost all the way around. I was shocked at how aged it was. I hadn't really looked at it for a very long time, just assumed it still matched my image of it as it was when new. It had been one of the first items of clothing I had chosen for myself, years before, and it had been far too big for me. My mother had not been able to talk me out of it, literally, for I had tried it on over my primary-school uniform. It was made in China, had "Night-Gown" on the tag, and came in no smaller sizes. I told my mother I would grow.

I wore it for a while, tripping on the hem, then it vanished for a couple of years, reappearing on the foot of my bed one day with no fanfare when I was big enough to wear it. I had squealed with pleasure and ran down to the kitchen and hugged my mother. "You grew," she shrugged.

I showered and dressed and threw the night gown in the wash pile and left the building. It was cool and foggy out; the tutorial was set for nine. Tutorials got all the awkward times, slotted in around the lectures after term had already begun, trying not to clash with people's other subjects. Juno's was at six on a Friday. She wouldn't be up till eleven today.

I loved the fog. Ships' masts disappeared up into it and I'd imagine them emerging into sunshine, and sailors in crow's nests up there, waving across to each other, smoking cigarettes in the sun, and the vanished world beneath their feet going on without them.

No, that's not true, I'm romanticising dreadfully here. I thought all that once and was immediately annoyed at myself for being so wet. Crow's nests? Hardly anything of any size even had a mast anymore. It's the mention and the memory of the night gown.

That night gown is now gone, as I knew that day it soon would be. All those years are gone with it, and while we can't weep for the years or we'd never stop weeping, we can feel a little sorrow for the things that don't matter, the toys and the clothes. That's safe enough. We can keep that under control.

I am trying to tell this story straight, but sometimes it gets coloured by what I'm feeling as I write. Sorry about that. It's only sometimes.

But I did love the fog, as I walked from the docks through Galway on my way to UCG. No shops open yet, no cars on the streets, the occasional figures on the far pavement lost in fog and thought at twenty past eight in the morning. I was perversely early because I loved the fog. Any later and the clattering of metal shutters and hosing down of pavements and extension of awnings and putting out of signs and arrival of deliveries and staff and managers and customers would have begun to begin, ruining everything. I liked the muffle of early-morning fog, the way the very occasional sound sank away completely and was drowned, leaving the pool of silence waiting for the next sound.

As I came over the Salmon Weir Bridge I stopped, and my footsteps stopped, and I stood looking over the bridge parapet into the white until I couldn't tell the roar of the blood in my ears from the roar of the weir.

A kind of ecstasy filled me then, or rather replaced me: I had disappeared. The world was fog, and I couldn't tell the sound of myself from the sound of the world. In the roar of the weir and the roar of my blood with my eyes open and the world erased, I vanished.

Such moments, when they came, were very welcome. I had a turbulent self and was glad to be relieved of its burden for however brief a timeless moment.

Eventually a taxi came by, headlights dipped, very slow, and the delicate kiss of light and movement released me. I returned to the world and walked on.

1 2

Over the bridge and past the invisible bulk of the cathedral, feeling it like an increase in gravity to my left as I pass it, and along University Road and across it.

Entering the university grounds now, keeping the low wall on my left, with all the trees in the world penned behind it. Not walking too close to the wall, though, because the sycamores overhang it a good deal, and as the fog condenses on the vast collective surface of their countless twigs and branches and the last autumnal leaves, it's raining pretty heavily under the trees.

Past dull buildings with interesting names. Past the Ladies' Club. Past the Terrapins. Past the Wind Tunnel.

On a whim, because I am early, I swing off course, walk parallel to the tennis courts, up the steps, and, hopping over the high lintel of the small open gate set into the large closed gate of the archway, I enter the Old Quad. I walk to the centre of it, and look around me. The grass fades into the fog on all sides, hints of the bulk of the surrounding buildings teeter on the edge of vision, I can't really see them but I can tell they are there. I pirouette. A small bird flies past me, low, at knee height, and startles me. From somewhere close by and seemingly above me, a big slurring voice begins to sing a half-familiar piece of opera. Half-familiar to me, half-familiar to the singer, he lurches to a puzzled halt, and a window slams before I can remember where I've heard it.

The gravel paths begin to crunch with arriving workers. I leave the Quad, nodding to the ghost porter who is swinging open the big gate as I slip through the gap. It's hard to speak when the world's this quiet.

As I walk towards the Arts Block and its towers, ghost students melt out of the fog and solidify into real students and the mood of the morning fades to white and vanishes. I enter the Arts Block as though I were modern too.

There's no fog in the building. Objects have edges. I take the lift to the third floor of Tower 2.

13

Room 315 was small, white, and empty. Fluorescent lights, on. Ten black plastic chairs. One long table. I walked to the window and looked out. I was disappointed not to be above the fog, though it was thinner up here. I could see the pale disc of the sun glowing dimly from quite a different quarter than the one I'd expected.

I was looking into the dim sun when somebody came in and dumped a pile of books and papers across the table. I spun around, ghost suns dancing in front of my eyes, the newcomer's face bleached and streaked and gone in the pileup of afterimages flaring and dying in the centre of my vision.

"Where's east?" I said, and a book tilted and fell off the table and hit the floor flat with a noise like a stomach being gently slapped. The static flared again as I blinked.

"There," he said, and pointed past me at the sun. "I think."

"Yes," I said as he slowly grew more detailed and more real. "It must be. Where the sun comes from." And I felt rather silly. "But I'd thought the east was over there, where the river comes from, when you can see it."

"No," he said, "I don't think so. I think the river flows south into Galway Bay, though the bay runs east to west and out into the ocean. One does tend to think of the Corrib as flowing west and out into the Atlantic but I don't think, on the maps, it does. Easy mistake."

I could see him now; he looked embarrassed at talking so much. His hand shot out. "David Hennessey, I'm taking this tutorial, I mean, giving it. I'm their new Modern English chap. I must say, I feel a terrible fraud. People have been calling me professor. Students, I mean. I've been doing Bellow and Updike and Nabokov with the third-years, and most of them look older than me and I can tell they don't believe a word I'm saying. One of the new boys is trying it on, they're thinking. I must knit myself a grey beard as a matter of the most extreme urgency. Can you knit?"

I didn't think he wanted a real answer, but he slumped into a plastic chair at the head of the table and waited till I said, "No, not really. My mother does."

He gave a gloomy nod.

"I'm Juliet Taylor, by the way."

He sprang out of the chair and shook my hand again, "Sorry, sorry, didn't even ask. I always forget names, so I've never really gotten into the habit of asking. Juliet Taylor. Jolly good. David Hennessey, well, yes." He sat down again. "I'll forget, but I forget everybody's. Actually, where are the others?" He looked at his watch. "Oh, early days."

I hung my coat on the back of a chair and took *Emma* and a notebook and pen out of the right-hand pocket. It had pockets like shopping bags, which was one of the reasons I'd bought it. The other reasons were that it was rather nicely cut, that it cost only five pounds in the St. Vincent de Paul shop, and that Galway had a rainy season that started with a bang in August and ran straight through till the following June. I carefully placed my novel, notebook and pen on the far end of the table from him, and sat down.

"Oh good, you brought *Emma*." He'd noticed my bookmark, a Maltesers wrapper three-quarters-way through. "How are you finding it?"

"Oh, it's brilliant, I think she's going to marry Mr. Knightley, at least I hope she does." I blushed furiously as soon as I'd said it. I was supposed to *know* these novels, I was supposed to be *studying* them, not treating them like Mills & Boons. I think she's going to marry Mr. Knightley. Oh God. But David Hennessey seemed delighted.

"You managed to skip that foul introduction, then? Thank Christ. It spoils the whole plot in two badly written pages. These bloody introductions to these bloody 'classic' editions that tell you the ending and just ruin the book. A law ought to be passed. It's outrageous. Anyhow I won't spoil it for you. Knightley, hey? No, no hints, my face will give away nothing."

I liked his smile, he did look rather young to be lecturing. A beard would have looked silly on him. A lot of the department did have beards. Professor O'Neill, the head of the department, had a pure white Santa Claus beard. Patrick Norris in Middle English had a black goatee. Donald Kruger (Modern English, though his accent meant you often had to take this on faith) from certain angles looked like a man drowning in hamsters. Even the department's Old English specialist Pamela Henderson cultivated a wispy moustache, which she would stroke fiercely as she read from *Beowulf* in a heavy Derry accent.

In fact, by the standards of the department, David Hennessey was extraordinarily presentable. He hadn't yet developed the bizarre, mannered, tic-ridden voice of the longtime lecturer, nor chosen from the array of twitches, stoops, and puzzlingly meaningless hand gestures that traditionally go with the job. He looked, in short, like a human being, and though he did talk too much it seemed to be from nerves, and he seemed to be aware of it. I suspected that, among friends, he would be a good balance of talker and listener. As the rest of the tutorial group began to arrive, he retreated into silence and began to arrange his papers. I recognised some of the others from lectures but didn't know any of them well enough to start a conversation. Some of the new arrivals mumbled to one another, while a last straggler straggled in, looked around for somewhere to sit, left, and returned with a chair. Everyone fumbled intently with biros without catching the tutor's eye until it became evident that anyone who would be turning up had done so. David Hennessey coughed.

"OK, well, I'm your tutor in Modern English, and my name is David Hennessey. I'm very bad with names, so if we all write our names on, ah, hideous scraps of paper and prop them up in front of us, we will be saved a vast amount of embarrassment later on. Well, when I say 'we,' I mean I will."

People tore paper and fumbled for pens. I wrote "JULIET" in neat capitals on a page from my notebook, and wondered should I add my surname beneath, seeing as I'd already told him it. As I hesitated, the girl beside me glanced at my sheet of paper and wrote "RACHEL" on hers. Seamus looked at hers, wrote "SEAMUS."

Jason wrote "JASON."

"KATHY."

"MAOLISSA."

"JANE."

"SIOBHÁN."

"TOM."

"TOM."

They looked at each other. The first Tom, annoyed and out of space, added "FITZMAURICE." The second Tom, triumphant, added "FOX."

"Everybody finished? Good. Well, as it said on the notice board, we're going to have a crack at Jane Austen today. Now I know not all of you have finished *Emma,* which incidentally is wonderful, so I hesitate to spoil the book by discussing it in detail before you've all finished it.... How many of you have actually finished it, by the way? Oh. I see."

Nobody had finished it.

"And how many have started it?"

Me, Rachel, and Tom Fox.

"Oh dear. Well, how many of you have, in a spirit of commendable perversity, started or finished any of Jane Austen's other books recently?"

I wasn't sure if I should put my hand up again so I didn't. Neither did anybody else.

"Hmm. Let's try to clarify this. How many of you have never read anything by Jane Austen?"

Six reluctant hands.

"Oh dear. Oh dear. I'm not here to insert a knowledge of Jane Austen's work into your heads via the ear. This is a tutorial, you understand, not a lecture. We are all supposed to *discuss* Jane Austen and her fine works, in particular *Emma,* which I recall asking you all to read on the notice, which I assume you read, telling you about this tutorial. We are meant to exchange views, to debate furiously the merits and demerits of her prose, to attack the plausibility of her plots, praise the clarity of her depiction of a male society from which she was so largely excluded, place her in her context and analyse her legacy. If you have failed even to bring sandwiches and a flask of tea to this Feast of Reason, then I cannot see how we can succeed in these modest aims."

He stood, and frowned. "If I was Robin Williams I'd stand on the desk and do this, but we're not insured for it and the ceiling's too low anyhow. You may imagine I'm standing on the desk, though. And lit beautifully." He cleared his throat. I felt an absurd urge to applaud, which I fought back.

"You have studied, filled in forms, undergone examinations, trials, ordeals, to win a place here. I have to assume you have within you a love for English literature, or at least a capacity for such love. I have to assume that you actively wish to read these great books and poems and dramas, and will rush to do so at the slightest encouragement. Therefore I am now telling you that I expect you to have read *Emma* by next week's tutorial. If you haven't read it by then, I would prefer you not to turn up. I have absolutely no qualms in expecting this of you, because I truly believe that the experience will enrich your lives. It will also enable us to have a meaningful discussion of the book at our tutorial, where everyone is equal and armed with the necessary knowledge to take issue with me and with one another as we tease our way through it and admire it from different angles in various lights."

He leaned forward and put his palms flat on the table, looking us each individually in the eye, one by one, even the shy Maolissa coaxed by the silence into reluctantly looking up from under his blond fringe. David continued.

"I do not demand that you master the jargon of literary theory. I do not demand that you bury yourself in the major critics. I merely expect you to read the works, which will tend to be novels of the nineteenth and twentieth centuries. You are no doubt attending, or failing to attend, lectures and entire courses where you can get away with regurgitating half-understood literary theory and a fistful of quotes from the eminent critics without having actually read the text, but in my tutorials that will be a hanging offence. Yes, I will throw an assortment of critical theories at you in the course of these tutorials, a variety of specific and general approaches to the works, which I will expect you to ponder, evaluate, and either accept or discard in the light of your own reading of the works. But the critics are, to coin a phrase, tools."

Jason sniggered. David, wearing a smile of surpassing innocence, carried on.

"The important relationship is between you and the book. I am interested in what you truly think, not in what someone else thought, nor in what you think I want to hear. I have perhaps an intimidating manner, but I tell you this, I will never think less of you for voicing an opinion, no matter how much I disagree with it, as long as it's your honest opinion and you have the courage to state it and defend it if necessary. You do not exhaust these works with a single truth. They can bear a great weight of conflicting opinion. We are each of us creating a fresh work as we read it into being. To read a good book well is perhaps the greatest, the richest and most rewarding thing you will ever do, short of creating a new life. On the more practical side, if any of you at any point do not have and cannot afford one of our tutorial texts for whatever reason, come to me either here or in my office and I will supply you with it. I have stacks of the cheapest possible editions of all of them, which I scatter about me like confetti anyway in my mission to bring civilization to Europe, so think absolutely nothing of it. It is fair exchange. I give you the book, you read it. We are quits."

He paused. I breathed out. He glanced at me, and then away, out the window into the golden mist. I followed his glance. A bird flew past the window, too close, in a shallow dive, then flicked onto a wingtip and down into the mist and gone. The mist was thinning. I looked back at David.

"Again, if there is anything you do not understand, please ask. These books may be written in what is technically known as Modern English, but Modern English has been around quite a while now. Both the words and the world have changed considerably. Some will have been written in your lifetime, but in an England or America unfamiliar to you. Much may be obscure. You are still very young. You are not expected to know everything. That's why you are here. Do not be ashamed of, do not hide your ignorance. Ask. I may not know, but I can ask in my turn. We will solve mysteries. We will lay bare truth. We will argue. We will learn. We will, I hope and believe, enjoy. For my sake, for your sake: Enjoy. That American-derived imperative form is a great addition to the English language. Ladies and gentlemen, I give you Jane Austen, P. G. Wodehouse, John Updike, Roddy Doyle, William Shakespeare, David Lodge, Vladimir Nabokov, Dick Francis, *Oliver Twist, Catch-22* and *The Great Gatsby:* Enjoy."

He bowed. Some of us began to applaud. He sat back into his chair. The spontaneous applauders were joined by the rest, nervous and reluctant, dragging the speed down. He waved us into silence.

"Just read *Emma* for next week, OK? Now, please do ask any questions you might have."

I slipped my hand into the air when it seemed no one else particularly wished to.

"I've heard of the others, but, um, who is Dick Francis?"

David Hennessey smiled. "Ah. Yes. Dick Francis . . . Well some of you are bound to know Dick Francis. Anybody?"

Halfway down the table Tom Fitzmaurice, a boy with a great frizzy head of brown curls, spoke, his voice cracking high on the first couple of words.

"He, he's a writer, well, ah, he writes thrillers. About horses."

He immediately looked as though he bitterly regretted opening his mouth.

"Yes." David smiled again. "Quite correct, he's a bloody fine writer of racing thrillers. My particular area of, ah, expertise, is that of genre fiction, the kind of books that are usually not considered literature at all. At this point in the century, however, you'll find some of the best and most vigorous writing is marketed as genre fiction. The literary novel is, in my opinion, suffering from a crippling self-consciousness. Too many options. It's paralysed by freedom. After *Ulysses,* after *Lolita,* after *Gravity's Rainbow,* no subject is taboo, no style too outlandish. It's been very bad for the literary novel of course. Absolute freedom is oppressive and always leads to a dreadful conformity. Can you tell free-verse poets apart? Can you tell abstract paintings apart? Can you tell contemporary literary novels apart, with their tiresome ambiguities, their massed ranks of unreliable narrators? I mean how many of you can say in all honesty that you prefer John Banville to Stephen King?"

There was a horrified pause, as though we'd been smilingly invited to grasp an exposed electric wire. Then Rachel spoke up beside me.

"But that's just populism, that's just saying it's good because it sells, it's good because it's mainstream."

David shrugged. "Shakespeare was mainstream. Jane Austen was mainstream. Dickens was mainstream. Modern literary fiction's gone down a dead end. By abandoning the mass audience it's cut off its own taproot, the spring of its vitality." He seemed to be enjoying himself now, as his unexpected attack on literature goaded the slumped students erect in their seats.

"So are you honestly saying thrillers are better than, you know, Booker Prize–winners?" said Jason, a pugnacious tough in a faded Fatima Mansions T-shirt that read, "Keep Music Evil."

"I'm saying a good thriller can be better than a bad Booker nominee. Not just as entertainment, but as literature. Of course, good genre writers are happy to be kidnapped by the literary establishment, by us. Which maintains the status quo. When Cormac McCarthy writes a truly great western, we refuse to call it a western. When Kurt Vonnegut writes a truly great science-fiction novel, we refuse to call it science fiction. *All the Pretty Horses, Slaughterhouse Five:* it must be literature really, because it's good. Circular argument. And ask any publisher—the Booker book is as tightly defined a genre as the western—"

"But you're contradicting yourself, you said literary fiction has no rules and now you're saying it's tightly defined," said Rachel, exasperated.

"Well, how would you define a literary novel?" David asked. "A novel of literary merit?"

"It's written . . . it's written . . . it's not written for money."

David nodded encouragingly, and said, "Dickens wrote for money."

"It's not just written . . . I mean . . . it aims . . . it tries to do something new." Rachel was struggling.

David nodded, and said, "All Shakespeare's plots were stolen."

"The style, the style is new—"

"The words are more important than the story," broke in Maolissa, formerly the World's Quietest Boy.

"Interesting . . . good, Maolissa . . . this is all good. . . . Seamus, you look like a man with an idea."

"It's really that, we agree that . . . there's a type of book from a type of publisher, and we call it literary fiction, so, it's how it's presented. It's an artificial construction, it's a social construct. . . ."

David nodded. "Good, interesting approach . . . but, well, Beckett's novels were first published by a French pornographer. Were they literature then? Or did they become literature later? Siobhán?"

"They were literature always."

"OK, good, we're getting somewhere. . . . But, looked at from another angle, can a book stop being literature? Nobody reads Galsworthy. He used to be literature. Has he stopped being literature?" Nobody wanted to go for that, it felt like a trap. We mulled it over suspiciously. David smiled and moved the argument sideways. "Is literary value something we discover inside a work, that's intrinsic to the work, or is it a label we stick onto the work, that we can always take off again if the fashion changes? Does the writer make it literature, or the reader?"

Maolissa raised his hand cautiously. "Whether it's literature or not isn't about the reader, or the genre either. It's about the ambition of the writer."

"Ambition, excellent point. But let's flip that on its head, to test it. Could a great work of literature be written by mistake? By an unambitious writer? Could you think you were writing a formulaic piece of junk and accidentally, for subconscious reasons, or through innate talent, write a great piece of literature by mistake?"

"Yes," said Siobhán, and "No," said Maolissa, and we were off. David unobtrusively stepped back from the argument and began to act as referee. Our arguments got better as our brains slowly warmed up with use. David held it together, kept the debate moving briskly, and subtly coaxed contributions from the mice at the margins. Even when their initial ideas were banal and, frankly, stupid, he treated them with respect, and we took our cue from him and did likewise. After a while a few of them flowered into quite respectable human beings with interesting views, especially surly Jason, who turned out to have an incandescent passion for Patrick Kavanagh, the poems and the novels. David's were the only tutorials I ever attended that weren't dominated by their tutor and perhaps two or three interested students.

I don't mean to give the impression that ten lives were changed in an hour. It wasn't like that. Life isn't.

But at the end of that first Modern English tutorial there was a vigour and a pride to the air as the group dispersed, and I moved to the window and looked out to see the fog had lifted, burned off by the sun.

Exultantly, I thought "Oh no, too gross, too crude, 'Look, the fog has lifted from the world.' Must nature be so obvious? Where is her Art? I would have done it better" and I felt like a writer or a god, looking down on the shimmer of the river through the trees, flowing in the wrong direction to the sea.

14

The heady rush of that first tutorial carried me giddily through the scholarly day. On Tuesday morning I was astonished to find it still hadn't worn off. I awoke glowing with rude intellectual curiosity, and raced into college. I was early for my lectures, I took legible notes, and at lunchtime I read about the Famine as I ate lasagne, each putting me off the other in a grisly, and indeed gristly, feedback loop of multi-sensory horror. That evening I stayed late in the library finishing a long overdue essay on Aristotle's *Poetics*.

When I finally crawled home, exhausted with virtue, Juno had already gone to bed. She seemed to be sleeping uneasily, I could hear her mumbling something through the thin door of her bedroom. The air was warm, but the stove was out. I touched it, cold, it hadn't been lit. A faint smell of burning in the air, though. Cigarettes? More like paper . . . both. I sniffed and shrugged. Cooker. One electric ring was on full. That was most unlike Juno. Michael must have been round, lighting cigarettes off the cooker again, and left it on. Spa. Pity I'd missed him. The downside of this newly virtuous life. I switched off the cooker and stood swaying with my face in the rippling column of heat above the ring, feeling its power fade. God, I was tired. My brain ached like a muscle. Bed.

In bed, I fell straight into an uneasy, unpleasant half-dream and dreamt I was trying to row to an island but the oarlocks were too loud and kept creaking and everyone was going to hear me and they wouldn't let me land, and the beach filled up with couples and they wouldn't let me land, and as the boat sank beneath me I sank into the cool silent dark and it was beautiful.

15

I walked into Juno's room the next day in my ordinary night-dress, not my night gown with the roses, and saw Michael's narrow back. His face was hidden in my sister's hair. Her back was to his chest. The tiny single duvet had slid down and half off them as they slept. They faced the wall, the two of them forming the same curve.

I stopped before the bed and stirred their mingled clothes with my right foot. I lifted Michael's jeans a little, grasping the belt with my toes. I let it go, and drew out Juno's shoe and slid in my foot. Wrong foot. I pushed it back, under his shirt, and turned to go.

"Juliet," said Juno.

I turned again, to see her twisting in his arms to raise herself.

"Juliet, we didn't, last night, there was another letter. . . ."

Michael was blinking and waking. He rolled on his back and looked past Juno at me.

"Juliet," he said, pleased and sleepy. "Morning. Juno, Juliet, morning."

Juno put her hand over his mouth.

"Shush. I want to talk to Juliet about the letter and everything. Stay."

She got out of bed in her Doris Day pyjamas and pulled the duvet up over Michael.

"Hey, my arm's dead," said Michael, lifting his left arm from under the duvet with his right hand, and laying the arm across his chest. "Look" and he lifted and dropped it a couple of times with his right hand. He attempted to swing it off his chest under its own power, to lay it by his side, but his control of the dead arm was erratic, and it buckled back at the elbow and the dead hand slapped across his face.

"Ouch," he said, "hurts. And pins and needles."

"Very good, Michael," said Juno. "Now put it away before you do any more damage." Michael laughed till he coughed.

I thought, They have private jokes.

In the living room/kitchen I sat at the table while Juno put on the kettle. "Michael!" she shouted, "coffee?"

"No, yes," dull through the shut door, "milk, one sugar."

Juno sat across the table from me. The kettle began suddenly to rattle as the element warmed and expanded. It was the noisiest kettle I'd ever heard. I glanced up at Juno.

"I got another letter" Juno said, holding my glance. "From the pervert. He really is a pervert. And he's definitely a he. It wasn't a nice letter. It wasn't like the last letter. It was . . . I was a long time waiting for you to come home."

"I stayed late in the library, that essay on Aristotle's *Poetics*."

Juno nodded, but I kept going.

"It was overdue, you know I had to get it done—"

"You couldn't have known," Juno said. "But I got upset, alone with it. I burnt it."

"I smelt the smoke when I came home."

"I burnt it to stop it . . . I washed the ashes down the sink. But it was worse, remembering, and not remembering, and thinking, Did he say that? Did he say that? I shouldn't have burnt it."

"Oh, Juno, I'm so sorry."

"I got into a bit of a state. I nearly went looking for you, but I was afraid to go out. And then Michael called." She shrugged.

"He loves you," I said.

"Yes," she said. "But we didn't do anything."

"It's OK," I said.

"Mmm," Juno said.

"No, it's OK," I said again.

Juno stood up and walked round the table. She sat in my lap and put her arms around me, like I used to do with her when we were very young and I was frightened by something on the television, or by something that I'd heard somebody say. I rested my cheek on her shoulder. I could smell my shampoo on her hair; we liked different shampoos, but she'd run out a few days before and had been using mine. I breathed way in. The smell of her hair the smell of my hair. This must be what it would be like to lie beside me.

"I would never hurt you," she said, very quietly.

"No, it's OK," I said. The kettle would boil soon. I could hear the noise changing. It was moving toward the quiet, low roar of boiling point, the tone deepening and widening.

"I don't mind," I said. "It's good. He's nice. You like him. I'm . . . It's good."

Juno turned her head a little toward me to kiss the top of my head. Her hair bunched and piled against my face as she turned. I inhaled again the sharp smell of the shampoo, harder.

"Thank you," said Juno. We were silent. "I wish he didn't love me," she said.

"Mmm," I said.

"It's . . . I don't think he's used to love. Even though he's been through college and everything and travelled and done all those things . . . he doesn't seem very grown up about this. He seems too happy. Is that stupid?"

"No," I said.

"He says he's never been in love, but Michael . . . how much should I believe? I mean, he does exaggerate all the time. . . . But I think he loves me. And I like him an awful lot. Do you think this is a terrible idea?"

"No," I said.

The kettle was boiling now.

"He was lovely last night," said Juno. "About the letter. I was nearly hysterical. He was . . . considerate. I didn't think he was that nice, you know? I liked him a lot, but I thought he was cold inside. Funny, but self-obsessed. Harsh. Funny but harsh. But he was crying. Shaking . . . he held me till I fell asleep. He wasn't . . . I didn't think he could be so nice. . . ."

"Kettle's boiling," I said. I lifted my head from her shoulder. Juno unwrapped her arms from round me and stood up.

"Oh, yes. Coffee?"

"No," I said. "Or, I will, yes. Thanks."

There was a tanker in the harbour, unloading oil by the huge storage tanks. Three tiny men stood on the deck, their arms in the air, waiting to receive the weight of the first of the rigid, hinged pipes that was swinging out from the dock into position over their heads, ready to be coupled to the valves through which the oil would be pumped ashore. I had watched it perhaps a dozen times before. I admired them, it seemed such real work. Some of that oil would heat buildings I passed through. They wrestled the pipe down to the big valve.

A spoon chimed off a lip as Juno made three mugs of coffee.

"They're unloading a tanker in the harbour," I said.

"Mmm?" said Juno. "Oh. I think I made yours a little strong."

"It's fine," I said as she put it on the table. I took a sip. "Fine."

16

The three of us walked to the Dramsoc auditions. Michael had painted the sets for their last production, and if they paid him for that tonight, he would be painting the sets for their next production too.

The auditions were held in the Aula Maxima, where the play was due, ultimately, to be performed. The Aula was a lovely old Gothic limestone barn of a building, straight across the Quad from the Main Arch.

As we approached the Main Arch from the tennis courts we could see the front of the Aula across the grass and gravel, at the far side of the Quad, framed nicely in the archway, its massive wooden doors surrounded by reddening creeper. We entered the archway, walked through and out into the Quad and the last of the day's light, across the grass to the steps of the Aula, arguing.

"You bastard, you gave me the impression you wanted help painting a set and now you're saying we're auditioning? You've set us up for an audition? Michael, I can't act."

"Oh, Juno said the same, and even if it's true you attach far too much weight to it. Have you ever seen student drama? None of them can act."

"But I don't want to act."

"Oh they won't hold that against you. You could walk in by mistake to do the dusting and you'd end up playing Hamlet. I'm afraid you're beautiful, and thus doomed to act. They'd rewrite a one-man play about a rugby-playing sperm donor to give you a part."

"Michael, you're not listening, I can't act, I don't want to act, I won't act, cancel the audition."

"Ach it's nothing as formal as that."

We were at the double doors. Michael swung the left one open and bade us enter. Juno entered, and he patted her bottom as she did so. I entered and he didn't. He entered, and I slapped his bottom hard. He gave me a hurt look, I gave him a sweet smile, Juno laughed and then looked contrite as Michael switched his hurt look to her.

"Poor Michael," she said, "beaten and mocked. It's hard, being an artist."

He grabbed her and growled, "A little more sympathy and understanding from the little woman, please. I fall upon the thorns of life, you know, I bleed."

"Not as much as I do," said Juno very quietly, and kissed him. They stood backlit and framed by the open door. Soft piano music played from somewhere. It looked ridiculously like a scene from a film. I felt sublimely ill.

Ironic applause came from the far end of the empty room. "Bravo! Magnificent, magnificent, Michael." I turned but could not see the speaker in the long gloom of the room, the stage in darkness.

"A wonderful entrance. It had everything." A tall, thin boy with a great swag of dark brown fringe jumped down from the distant stage and walked into the light. "Drama, passion, beauty," he continued as he walked toward us, "mystery . . . what did she say to you to make you blush so, Michael? So this must be Juno"—arriving in front of us, he shook her hand. "And Juliet?" He reached for mine, I grasped his, a handshake as firm and reassuring as a salesman's. "Delighted to meet you both. I've heard so much. I'm Dominic O'Connaire. I have the honour of being auditor of Dramsoc this year." An ironic bow.

We walked toward the stage. "I'm not here to audition," I said.

"I'm afraid Michael may have misled you," Juno said. "We can't act."

"Oh, none of them can," said Dominic airily. "We haven't had a decent actor in Dramsoc since the Emergency, isn't that right Gemma?"

I looked where he was looking and saw a girl sitting at a piano in shadow at the back of the stage. For a moment the thought, Oh there's a girl up there playing the piano, sat comfortably alongside the thought, And I must remember to ask what's that album they're playing, until with a mental double-take I realised that the music that had been playing softly since we entered wasn't a recording. Gemma looked up from the keyboard. Her face wasn't pretty, but was very alive, very strong, with high cheekbones, long dark hair, a severe spiked fringe.

"We had a good actor, but he died," she said. Nice voice, carried well. An actress?

We arrived at the stage. Dominic bounded athletically up and over the lip, avoiding the steps provided.

"A sad business," said Dominic, frowning down at us. "Got a good review in the *Irish Times* for a thing we did at ISDA. Singled him out. 'Tremendous, controlled performance. Seldom have I seen . . .' Ego burst." He looked sorrowfully at his shoes for a moment and seemed briefly lost to melancholy. "Seven hundred and seventy-six people signed up on Societies Day ['Free Murphy's,' explained Gemma], all pledging their immortal souls to Dramsoc, in their heart's blood. Three have turned up for the open auditions."

"You should have promised them free tequila slammers," said Gemma. Dominic ignored her again. I didn't like him. Then again, I didn't like anybody.

"We're waiting for the man," said Dominic to Michael.

"On the piss?" said Michael.

"Worse. On the wagon," said Dominic. "Probably can't tie his shoes with the shock. I sent the three laddeens away for a fag, they were annoying me with their wetting themselves and their stench of fear. 'But we don't smoke.' Well fucking learn, I told them. Ye're actors now."

Michael walked up the steps onto the stage with Juno, holding her hand. He nodded Dominic to one side. Dominic made a last attempt to look down my cleavage, sighed, and joined them. Juno crossed her eyes down at me as Michael and Dominic began to talk money.

I simmered gently. Gemma stood up from the piano and walked over to the stage edge. "He's a pig, isn't he?" she said to me. Dominic, with his back to her, oinked without turning around. I nodded. "Fag?" she said.

"Don't smoke," I said.

"Well, you can sit upwind," she said, walking down the steps and taking my elbow. "If I stay, I'll hit him."

"Again," said Dominic over his shoulder.

"Harder," she said over hers.

"Juliet," I said, "Juliet Taylor. That was lovely, the piano." We began to walk slowly toward the door.

"Gemma Mannion. I was making mistakes all over the place, but thanks anyway." She released my elbow to take a packet of rolling tobacco from her pocket, removed a packet of Rizlas, and began expertly to assemble a rollie. "Are you auditioning for Dominic's mad Republican version of *Cavalcade*, or the Synge?"

"I'm not auditioning for anything. I'm here with my sister and"—that trip of indecision when someone has dual roles in your life—"her boyfriend."

Her boyfriend didn't sound right, but neither did anything else.

"Oh, Michael." She smiled. "Yes, she seems to have calmed him down a lot. He was a mental bastard last year."

We looked back to where Michael stood on stage with his arm around Juno, talking to Dominic. They must have sorted out the money. Now Michael was gesturing broadly with his free hand, all of them laughing at his description of an exhibition opening he'd attended in Dublin. I could pick out the artists' names. He'd told me and Juno the story before. It was funny.

"Why, what did he get up to last year?" I said absently, still looking at him. We were standing just inside the doorway now, shadowed.

"Oh, you know," said Gemma, pausing to lick the Rizla. "Every kind of mad crack" and I could tell he'd slept with her, the evasion swept around the unspoken admission like a river round an island, just helping to define it.

"Yes," I said, "he's pretty wild alright." I looked back at Gemma and studied her more carefully. No, not pretty. Better than pretty. Interesting. Her face was alive, and her body seemed restless just standing, like a dancer waiting to go on. "Are you auditioning?" I asked.

"No," she said, and lit the rollie. "They don't bother auditioning me anymore. I end up in everything anyway."

"So that's the auditor of Dramsoc. No wonder nobody turns up for auditions."

"In . . . ," said Gemma, pausing, then emitting a cloud of smoke that emerged from the shadows to blot out half the Aula, ". . . deed."

"If he's auditor, what are you?" I asked.

"His girlfriend," said Gemma drily.

"Shit, sorry . . ."

"Don't worry. I'm thinking of resigning the position. He claims he only pretends to be a sexist arsehole to wind people up, and for the laugh, like. But for the life of me, I can't tell the difference between pretending to be an arsehole all the time and actually being an arsehole. I suppose I should have done philosophy."

I was still somewhat preoccupied with the biting of my tongue, and said nothing. From the stage, Dominic looked over at us. "No smoking. Out," he called.

"After you, dear," said Gemma, placing a hand in the small of my back as she took a deep, deep drag and released it straight up like a steamtrain blowing off pressure. Was that an actressy *dear* or a country *dear?*

17

Gemma and I walked out onto the stone steps and into the low autumn sun, the enclosed Quad holding surprising warmth. An unshaven derelict was sitting on the top step, slump-shouldered, staring into space, the bottle in his right hand, the cigarette in the other. The collar of his tweed jacket was frayed. Smoke from the cigarette swirled out of his mouth and drifted round his neck like a spiderweb scarf, then reappeared at the back of his head. The air behaved oddly in the Quad, enclosed and heated and protected from the world outside.

"Hello, Connie," said Gemma, and the derelict stood up, straightened his shoulders, and turned into a dignified man in his forties, maybe fifties, sporting a short, neat beard and wearing a favourite old jacket. I'm too quick to judge, I thought despairingly. He put his cigarette in his mouth to free his left hand, passed his bottle of Lucozade over to it from his right hand, and shook hands with Gemma, saying, "Gemma, delighted, sorry I'm late," the cigarette bouncing on his lower lip as he spoke. Smoke swirled up into his eyes, squinting them, as he looked at me.

Gemma introduced us. "Conrad Hayes, he's writer-in-residence. Juliet . . ."

"Taylor."

"Taylor. She's auditioning with her sister."

"Oh, right."

"I'm not really."

"Oh, that's a pity, you should. It's a very good experience for anyone, I feel."

"Connie's doing workshops with the auditioners. The basics."

"They're usually rather enjoyable."

"I'm not an actress."

Perhaps I said it rather forcefully. He took a step backward, slipped on the smooth step edge, and dropped his bottle of Lucozade.

Gemma pointed out fragments ("Can't risk the fingers, got a recital Saturday . . . bit over there by the Tayto packet"), while I helped him pick up the pieces, and he was absurdly grateful and humiliated.

When I'd piled all the sticky glass into Conrad's hands, we re-entered the Aula. Conrad cautiously tipped the sharp wet heap into a bin and then looked around helplessly, arms outstretched. His hands began to flutter like butterflies. Drinker, I thought disapprovingly. He brought his arms in to his sides and half-closed his fists, touched them to his hips, trying to stop them fluttering without being obvious. Poor sod.

"You should rinse your hands," I said. "Slivers of glass."

He began to walk toward a door at the back of the hall. "Locked," said Gemma.

He made a noise of annoyance. "I'll use my own place." He headed toward the double doors, stopped, and turned. "You really might like acting."

"No," I said, "may I wash my hands too?"

"Of course, yes," he said, flustered. I followed him diagonally across the grass of the Quad to the far right corner. "The grass isn't too wet? Your shoes?" he said anxiously, halfway across. "Too late now, I suppose."

"It's fine," I said. We walked in through the open door of the tower. He hesitated. "You have an office here?" I asked, impressed.

"An office of sorts, yes."

"Beautiful building."

"Cold building . . . hmm . . . my rooms are at the top, it's easier. . . ." He led me past the stairs along a corridor, a sharp right, then along another, longer corridor to a toilet with a quaintly skirted female figure on the door. "There you are," he said, and turned away.

"Don't you want to wash your hands?" I said.

"Oh, no, no, no," he said, taken aback. "This is . . . I'll wash them in my rooms . . . off my rooms. I'm used to . . . there's a washroom in my corridor. . . ."

"I shan't tell." I smiled.

He hesitated. "Well, my generation doesn't . . . can't . . . I've never been in a ladies' toilet," he said.

"Oh, they're amazing," I said. "Jacuzzis, attendants, water beds . . . if you're lucky a eunuch will anoint you with oils."

"In the present, ah, political climate, I'd prefer not to risk it," he said, and smiled back.

"Save you a walk."

"I'm old-fashioned," he said apologetically, and bowed to me and turned away. I went in and turned on the hot tap.

"So am I," I said to the mirror. Slowly and carefully I washed the stickiness and glittering fragments from my hands. Then I had a wee and stayed in the cubicle while thinking of this and that. Then I unlocked the cubicle door, washed my right hand, and returned to the Aula.

18

By the time I arrived back at the Aula, things were looking up. A good half a dozen people who couldn't act had arrived.

Conrad greeted my return warmly. "I thought you'd gone home." His breath smelt of whiskey.

"Dominic said you were on the wagon," I said.

"I was," he said happily, rolling a cigarette. "I gave these up too." His hands were rock steady.

"Can't do that in here," said Dominic, "fire regulations."

Conrad licked it, stuck it, and placed it behind his ear. "Fine, Dominic, fine."

Then the original three Dominic had told to take a fag break rolled back in singing with a bunch of new friends. They had obviously taken their break in the college bar and recovered their spirits there.

A quiet, skinny fellow wandered in and began to rig some lights. He dimmed the hall lights to try out a new lighting board with lots of knobs and sliding switches. The walls faded, and were gone.

We were in a space.

Suddenly, all about me was theatrical life. On the stage Dominic began auditioning those who'd acted before. Conrad began workshopping the basics of drama with the theatrical virgins, while Michael worked on the sets. You could smell the greasepaint, et cetera. It was the kind of bustling, flirtatiously theatrical atmosphere designed to seduce a young lady into giving her heart to the theatre.

I hated it.

I had always hated actors and acting. I had disliked very much the experience of acting in our school plays. Acting is a kind of lying with your whole self, and it can infect the self. I could neither understand nor share in the enjoyment of acting that many of the other girls felt. They had frightened me a little with their willingness to stop being themselves, with the joy they took in it. I could never lose myself. Even in the tiny parts I played, I could never stop being myself. I was afraid to stop being myself and would stand there, stubbornly, hopelessly me, imitating something outside of me. I was scared and a little contemptuous of those of my classmates who could abandon themselves, act another part. They seemed to get drunk on it, frightening me more, level after level of loss of control. For weeks after, they would seem to be acting their own lives.

Lurking in the dim light of the Aula then, I hated it, but I couldn't bring myself to leave. I hung around, without really joining in. When Juno was free I chatted with her. I helped Michael build sets till I hit his thumb with a hammer. I chatted with Gemma a bit. Mainly I watched Juno as she chatted, as she acted, as she lived. I saw her as though through the eyes of the others. I imagined what they saw when they looked at Juno.

Very beautiful.

Very still.

You could see anything you wanted in her.

I would look at her when we were fourteen, and I would see myself. She looked more real to me than I did. Our faces identical, our hair the same then, long and blond. I would hold her by the shoulders in our room and look at her as in a mirror. She joined in the game. I would stick out my tongue at her, and she would stick out hers at me. We would blink together and rock our heads from side to side in unison. She was very quick. I'd try to catch her out, and fail. Then she'd smile and I wouldn't, and the illusion would be gone. I'd look into her smiling face, no longer my face, and think, She's nothing like me. And feel desperately alone. Happiest days of your life.

I looked at her laughing across the hall. And felt desperately alone. How I hated her. How I loved her. It hurt.

Dominic stuck two fingers in his mouth and whistled, a shriek like a rabbit in a snare. "Everybody in the centre for this one. Chop-chop." As a dozen or so boys and girls assembled in the middle of the room, and I found a shadow and glued my backside to the wall, Dominic dragged two plastic chairs out onto the sprung wooden floor and placed them back to back, about ten feet apart, either side of the door. He walked back toward the stage, did the same with two more plastic chairs at that end, and returned to the centre of the wooden floor.

"Goalposts: We're going to play football. This is the football." He held up nothing. "There's no offside, no referee. I trust you to keep it clean and not to cheat. First to three wins."

He divided them into boys and girls. My heart shrank. "Boys versus girls . . . in the World Series . . . of Lurve," said one spotted dick. Dominic tried to steer me onto the floor. I was stuck to the wall like a suction cup.

"I'm not an actor," I said again, exhausted from saying it.

"It's just a game," he said.

"I don't play games," I said.

He left me.

The boys kicked off. I hated it. They passed the imaginary ball from wing to wing, balanced it on their heads, flicked it from foot to foot, danced past the tackles of the girls. There was some uncertainty and giggling at first, but the boys very soon got serious. The spotted dick scored, a hotly disputed header from a tight angle.

"I was right in front of you!" said Gemma. "How's that a goal? I was right between you and the goal." The boys shouted her down. The girls muttered among themselves, put Juno in goal, and kicked off from the centre circle. Michael tackled a shy and retiring pre-Raphaelite and won the imaginary ball, took it with him along the wing nearest me. Juno came out to meet him. Michael slowed, feinted left. Juno took the ball cleanly from Michael's toe, but he refused to acknowledge it and kept going, the imaginary ball tight to his feet, leaving Juno standing there, staring after him.

"Goal!" he said, dribbling it through the chairs.

"I can play this game," I said, and walked onto the pitch.

"What?" said Dominic. He and Conrad had been standing on the sidelines, unobtrusively talking, observing, and taking notes.

"I can play. This," I said. (As I had a sudden flash of memory. Watching *Match of the Day* with Paul and Aengus, them arguing about offside decisions while I prayed for Gary Lineker to score, so that I could watch him getting kissed, hugged, and fondled, in close-up and slow motion, by the rest of the team, again and again.)

I picked the ball out of the back of the net and walked to the centre circle, put it down, and walked forward. "Kick it to me, for fuck's sake," I said to the long drink of water nearest it. She feebly poked at air. The ball came to me, I cut straight into the box and slammed it sidefoot across the body of the keeper, who went the wrong way.

I picked it out of their net, walked back to the centre circle, and threw the ball at the chest of their least-effective-looking player. He dropped it, tapped at it, back vaguely toward his keeper. Michael ran across and intercepted it, tried to go by me. I stood straight in front of him. He went into me and was so surprised he stopped playing for a moment and didn't even try to recover the ball. I put my foot on it, made to go right, went left with the ball, left him standing. A huge red-haired ox of an engineer tackled me, and there was a moment of confusion as we both came out of the tackle with the ball.

I believed in mine more. I scored from the centre circle.

It got a bit heated and personal. "They've got more players!" the boys complained to Dominic. "Either she goes off or one of you comes on."

"Why don't you both join in," I said, "they need all the help they can get."

"Fair enough," said Dominic, and he and Conrad came on for the boys for the restart.

"Now they've got more," objected the long drink of water in my general direction.

"So what," I said.

Dominic tried to go past me on the wing. I tackled, took the ball, but he'd done this before, knew the tricks, saw through me, kept going, and all the eyes and players followed him.

I went after him, and I kicked the fucking legs from under him, from behind. "Foul!" "Card!" "Ref!" shouted the boys.

"There's no referee," I said. "Dominic trusts us." I turned the ball around the spotted dick and drove a rising shot into the roof of the net. "Three. We win."

I walked out of the Aula and went home.

19

Juno and I had been in the library every night for a week. We arrived early enough to get seats opposite each other at the same table, and we stayed till it closed at eleven at night. All our books and notes in a great pile between us.

Juno was studying history carefully and well, highlighting the key points as she slowly read a paperback on the Reformation, taking notes at the end of each chapter to summarize the argument.

I was studying her.

The familiar despair and paralysis had me. I would never get it done. I couldn't hold my attention to the page. What blocked me from doing what I had to do, what I even wanted to do? How could Juno find it so easy? I had my lecture notes on Yeats open in front of me, but I'd only read through two pages in an hour. Every change in the hum of the fluorescent lights, every crack of a fresh page turning, every whisper between distant friends ten tables away whipped my attention into a towering, helpless foam. The door to the stairs banged, and my thoughts jangled like cutlery dropped on concrete. Just another week to go, nothing done. When would I learn? Where would I find the discipline? And: Why was I, why was I, why was I wasting so much time in fruitless self-reproach

when all I had to do was *start*. Start *now*. Eyes down. Pick up the pen.
Read the words. Study.

> Yeats's love poetry. Realistic, personal. In 1903 Maud Gonne
> marries John MacBride.
> Disillusion?
> He celebrates his loss. Helen of Troy. She is beyond blame or com-
> ment. Complete change of style: topical, specific, prosaic, yet poetic
> and universal. Like the Greek myths. Deliberate parallels.
> Yeats, Joyce: new mythologies.

Just words to me, no sense. I threw down the pen and pushed away the
foolscap notes. All just words to me. I rested my chin on my forearm and
watched Juno over the low wall of books, watched her eyes darting back
and forth, back and forth along the long lines of the Reformation text, taking it all in. How could she do that? To the bottom of the page, turn over.
Scanning it in. Stop. Highlight a line in yellow. Move on. Her hair about her
shoulders waved a moment, the long blond ends drifting a lazy inch, and
then back, above the black table in the brief breeze as the door to the stairs
opened. Slam. She read on, impervious to disorder, immune, blessed.

I couldn't bear it, looked away. Why weren't we the same? I glanced
about me—countless heads, all lost in learning, or seeming so. Far down
and to the right another head looked up, a boy, dark hair, gold-framed
glasses, handsome. He yawned and stretched his head back and closed
his eyes a moment. Oh, look at me, I thought, startling myself. He took
off his glasses right-handed, and rubbed his eyes with the knuckles of
the left. Replaced them, returned to work. Disappeared among the rows
of heads, studying.

My eyes filled with tears. Juno, with the usual casual intuition,
looked up. Leaned over, whispered

"Are you OK? Want to talk? What's wrong?"

Infuriating, infuriating. I blinked them back and wiped them away
with a sleeve and said "Nothing. Headache."

She said, "I think I've two Paracetamol in my bag downstairs," and went to stand, but I said, "No," rather too loudly, and "no" again. "I can't concentrate. . . . I'm going to go clear my head." I walked to the door and through, slam, and ran down the stairs, making a hell of a clatter, and out of the library, picked up my coat and bag from the heap in the foyer, and out into the drizzle and cold air. Oh, lovely. She'd bring my notes home when she left.

I walked home by the canals, but there was no heron at the little weir.

When I exploded into the living room, I startled Michael, who was rummaging in the drawer by the sink.

"You're early," he said. "Where's Juno?"

"Still studying," I said, disappearing into my room and shutting the door. Well, no, slamming the door.

I threw my bag into the corner and dropped full length on the bed. Face into the pillow.

A tentative knock at my door. Slowly it opened enough to let Michael peep round it.

"Er, Juliet . . ."

"*Yes?*" through the pillow.

"I thought maybe, ah . . . you knew where the can opener might be."

20

I helped him find the can opener; I helped him find the saucepan.

In my best Australian soap-opera accent I said, "You're a *moron*, Michael."

"I can do it, I can do it. Once I'm past the tricky early stages, it's a breeze. Opening the can, that's where a lot of people lose it completely.

They fail to grasp that opening the can is possibly the most important step of the entire process."

He clamped the opener to the can.

"Too many people are dazzled by the details, lose sight of the basics."

He slowly ran the opener round the rim.

"This is where the war is won or lost. I've seen it so often, perfectly intelligent people—lawyers, doctors, hereditary peers—could buy and sell you, thinking, No, not the Ritz tonight, I think I'll stay in and have some baked beans, and two hours later there they are with their parsley, sage, rosemary, and thyme, but they've neglected the *basics*."

He tipped the beans into the saucepan, pushed the flap of lid down into the can, put the can on its side on the floor, crushed it flat with his heel, picked it up, and slid it into the small, almost-full plastic rubbish bag hanging by the sink

"And where are they then, Juliet, for all their wealth and intelligence and the perfect toast and every sauce known to man? *Fucked*, that's where."

He turned on the heat and sat in the green armchair, across the table from me.

"See? The rest's a formality. A child could do it."

"Describe Juno," I said.

He blinked. "What, physically?"

"No, the things you like about her. Why you like her."

"Whooo." He ran his palm across his chin. Stubbly noise. I liked it. We used to do that to our father when I was very young. "Tricky . . . where to start? . . . well, first of all, she *is* very beautiful"—a nod in my direction—"as you well know, but it isn't that or not just that, of course not. Lots of beautiful women in the world. She's . . . strong."

He was struggling, moving his hands about, trying to pick the right words. Taking the question seriously.

"She's very strong. I mean, ah, morally, she's a good person. I can trust her. And she's worth trusting. . . . This doesn't sound very appealing, does it? Sounds like I'm going out with a nun. Intelligent . . . Christ, I don't know why I like her so much. She's just not like anybody else. She's beautiful, she's tough as nails, she wouldn't have obeyed orders at Auschwitz. And she's an incredible fuck, I mean, I don't know, sorry Juliet, I can't explain it. I didn't want to love her, but I do, and I can't explain why."

He got up to stir the beans and add some black pepper.

"Is she . . . " I changed tack. "What do you think she sees in you?"

He looked over at me. "Why on earth are you asking these questions? Got a sociology essay to do on human bonding?"

I shrugged and smiled a none-too-impressive smile.

"Interested," I said.

I felt like an old wooden dam with too great a head of water backed up behind it. I felt an extraordinary, almost unbearable pressure, as though I would crack or split or burst if any part of me began to weaken. The smile was a risk. I held myself still.

He could tell I was serious.

"You're studying too much," he said. "You need a break."

"Tell me," I said.

He shrugged. Lot of shrugging going on. Happy Italian family. My eyes were hot in my head, but I held myself still. He was wearing black jeans and a T-shirt he'd made himself, white print on black cotton, a still from a film of the Nuremberg rallies, a night shot of the great search-lights roaring straight up into the black sky above the stadium. Under it a simple mathematical formula, a refutation of Keats: "Truth ≠ Beauty." Truth not equal to beauty.

"Tell."

He put two slices of bread in the toaster.

"My dog-like devotion," he said.

"No," I said.

He looked at me again. "You're right, it pisses her off. I can't help it. I try not to smother her. I know . . ."

Long pause.

"I realize that she . . . doesn't feel as strongly about me as I do about her. Hard, that. But I'm older, had never loved. Had farther to fall. I try to keep it in check. Then the danger's swinging the other way."

Sharp look at me.

"I try . . . this sounds ridiculous . . . I try to love her less. And then of course . . . you're on word of honour, girl. This is not for broadcast."

I nodded.

"Between us? Because it's difficult, not speaking . . ."

I nodded.

"All bastards love good women, helplessly. But it doesn't stop them being bastards. The love is real, but so's the bastardry. I feel so helpless when I'm away from her, in Dublin or in London. I hate how much I need her, really rage against it."

He was talking down into the saucepan now, stirring. Choosing his words more carefully than usual. He reminded me suddenly of David Hennessey, that high seriousness. Oh Michael you're deep after all I thought, only half-mockingly.

"So short a time, and I've been away a lot already, and that's going to get worse. . . . Did I tell you they might want me in London, set design on a pop-art musical, Roy Lichtenstein backdrops and cartoon characters?"

I shook my head.

"They saw the Dramsoc show that made it to the Fringe—shit show, good sets. Rang me out of the blue on Tuesday. Afraid to mention it in case it doesn't happen."

He brooded till the toast popped. I wasn't sure if he was going to go on. He was giving me an answer to a question I hadn't asked. He seemed to wish to justify himself, though I'd accused him of nothing. I had that in common with Juno. Our silences drew confidences, and confessions. Again though, Juno more than me. The sticks and the stones by the side of the road would tell her their stories if she stopped for a moment, and cry for the cyclops or Goliath at the end of it. What a talent for inducing guilt we had. What reproach in our silence. What a terrible gift.

I watched him as he found a plate, buttered the toast, poured the beans on, left the saucepan in the sink to soak. These banal and domestic actions didn't lessen him or make him absurd, and again I was reminded, strangely, of David in the tutorials.

Michael put the plate on the table, but remained standing. Clasped his hands behind his back.

"When I try to love her less, because she's not around and I know she loves me less than I love her, and it's too painful . . . other women offer me comfort. Women from my past, and new women. *But I don't fuck them.* Already I've ended up in . . . in the arms of one or two. But I didn't fuck them." He walked around the table and crouched by my chair, and I looked straight down into his face, my eyes darting from his mouth to his eyes and back, and I thought, My God, what question did I ask?

He held the arm of my chair, head not much below mine, weight forward, on the ball of the foot. "And I wanted to. But I love her, helplessly and stupidly and probably too much. I've ended up in bed with women I've liked very much, but I haven't fucked them. I've been pushed into bedrooms at parties; I've had to tuck my cock back into my pants; I've lain awake beside women I've wanted, with a short bar of iron between my thighs; but I haven't fucked them. I've ended up in these situations because I hate the stupid lovesick puppy I've turned into. I *want* to prove I'm free and I'm still me and I'm still a bit of the old bastard. But I can't do it. I kiss them a lot and talk about Juno."

My face was burning. I opened my mouth slightly to get more air.

"Sometimes I'm attractive, and sometimes I'm not. I don't know what controls it, but since Juno I've been radiating something, you know it's true, I won't fake modesty with you. When myself and Juno went down to Tipperary for the weekend, even her friends were coming on to me. And it's very difficult, and it's going to get worse."

His face seemed closer to me.

"When I love her too much, she retreats. When I love her too little I risk ruining everything. Some day I'll slip, and I'll resent Juno for my own infidelity and I'll resent the girl I've fucked and it'll be very bad for everybody."

I realised my face had been drifting closer to his, and I jerked back. He stood up.

"Thank you," I said, very formally. My face was so hot. I could feel sweat at the roots of my hair, at the back of my neck, at the base of my spine, between my breasts.

"Ach." He returned to his side of the table. "It's a relief to talk. I have to be so careful with her lately."

"I think it will be alright," I said, still formal.

"Hmm," he said, and sat down to his meal. "Let's change the subject."

We changed the subject, and Michael was funny and kind, and the bleakness slowly lifted and dispersed.

By the time Juno arrived home, we were laughing ourselves sick remembering the best bits out of Billy Wilder films.

"Juno! Good to see you! Do you remember the bit in *The Apartment* where Jack Lemmon's draining the spaghetti with a tennis racquet?"

I objected. "Billy Wilder didn't make *The Apartment*."

"Come on," said Michael, "of course he did. What's black and white and still funny? A Billy Wilder film."

"Your headache's better then," said Juno.

"Oh, yes," I said.

"What headache?" said Michael.

"I wasn't feeling well earlier," I said.

Juno said nothing. Oh God, I thought.

"It wasn't really a headache," I said. "I just felt terrible and I couldn't concentrate, so I left the library and I couldn't bring myself to go back."

"I brought your notes," Juno said.

"Oh, thanks."

She put them in the middle of the table. Michael stood.

"Coffee?"

Juno nodded yes. I said yes.

They went to bed early, after the coffee, and I put on music and danced round the living room, on my own. I danced thoughtfully rather than ecstatically, but I danced.

21

In the last Modern English tutorial of the year we pestered David Hennessey with questions and complaints about the exams.

Both questions and complaints were greeted with sighs. He seemed to have a lot on his mind, was almost snappy, appearing preoccupied sometimes with something that was none of our business. It was unsettling.

"Children, children, you are here to do exams. It's the point of the exercise. Don't *wince* Siobhán. I shall continue to call you children for as long as you continue to be childish. When the English exams were immediately *after* Christmas, students complained that the study spoiled their Christmas. Now they are immediately *before* Christmas, and students complain that they have no time to study. Personally I think the lot of you should be herded into the basement and executed and that we should start again with candidates who actually wish to learn, if any such can be found, but of course the department won't listen to me, so I'm stuck with you."

The levity seemed forced, masking a genuine annoyance with us. Several times over the course of the tutorial he spoke with an unusual sharpness and then expanded and exaggerated his ill-humour till it became self-mocking and the sting was removed from the initial remark. But it made for an uncomfortable hour, and by the end of it we were unusually subdued. He was enough his old self to seem to notice this and regret it. As we gathered our books and notes, he gestured the rising end-of-class conversational mumble back down to silence and said, "Before you go, I'm sorry if I wasn't entirely . . . supportive today. Events in my own life are occupying much of my attention at the moment and I'm afraid I was a little bit, ah, brusque with some of you. Please accept my apologies. I was entirely at fault there."

He coloured a little, paused, and pressed on.

"As this is our last tutorial of the calendar year, I'd like to say one or two, ah, embarrassing things that we can all forget over the holidays. Firstly, it's been a great pleasure teaching you this year, and in the case of 'The Great Hunger,' a great pleasure being taught."

This was a tutorial in-joke too complicated to explain, at which we all gratefully laughed as a way of shyly avoiding the compliment.

"Secondly, none of you need fear these exams. You've fine minds and a fine understanding of what literature is and how it works. Believe me, many of you will be surprised at how well you do. I have great confidence in you."

A brief pleased and embarrassed silence.

"Thirdly, may I wish you a merry Christmas and a happy New Year? And read *Heart of Darkness* and *The Great Gatsby* over the holiday; they're not long."

A chorus of mock indignation and some "Merry Christmas's," and the group dispersed.

I found myself beside him in the crush for the lift.

"Could I buy a *Heart of Darkness* off you, sir?" I said.

"Oh, lord, Juliet, don't call me sir. It makes me feel hideously old. If you're stuck for one, I'll give you one, of course." The lift arrived and he stepped back politely to allow the others in first.

"Oh, no, I don't mind paying, it's just that they'd sold out yesterday in the college bookshop and rather than traipse around town looking or maybe forget, I thought I'd ask you now and save time." I was over-explaining, and stopped myself, blushing crazily and feeling like a perfect idiot. The lift, full, descended, leaving us alone by the silver doors.

"Well, certainly, yes." He hit the button to summon it back up again. "I've a stack in my office, nice cheap Wordsworth Classic edition, nothing wrong with it. So you'd like a copy now?"

I nodded. "Unless you're in a hurry."

"Oh, no, not at all."

We stood in silence. The floor indicators showed the lift approaching us. I cleared my throat.

julian gough

The Up light went off and the doors clattered open. We each waited for the other to move. David waved me forward, and I entered the lift.

We ascended to the top floor of the tower and stepped out into the corridor of the English Department. I followed David around two corners to his office.

He opened the door, which hadn't been locked, and waved me in. Leaving the door ajar, he began looking.

"Heart of Darkness . . ."

Absentmindedly he indicated a chair, and I sat. The office resembled a large library in a small telephone booth. The computer was buried in books. The bookshelves round the walls were jammed to capacity, and tall piles of paperbacks occupied the corners of the room. From a stack of new books in the far corner, which wasn't very far at all, he extracted a copy of Joseph Conrad's *Heart of Darkness*.

"Here, yes."

He stepped back and gave it to me. I stood, took a note from the money pocket of my bag and made to pay him.

"God, no, don't be ridiculous. Take it. I've no change and they're so cheap, it's nothing."

"No, I must pay for it."

"Look, really, it's nothing. Buy me a coffee sometime."

"Now," I said.

"Pardon?" he said.

I stuttered slightly in my eagerness not to be misunderstood. "I'll buy you a coffee now, if you're not busy. It's not a, I'm not, it's, you look like you need one and you gave me this, so . . ." I shrugged. Thank God for the shrug.

He looked at me thoughtfully.

"Well, that's very kind of you Juliet. Thank you. I'm afraid I'm being collected by a friend in"—he checked his watch—"twenty minutes, but I'd be glad of a quick cup of coffee first, thank you. The canteen, I suppose?"

We left his office and made our way down to the canteen. He loosened up, unbent as we walked, began to seem younger than in the tutorials. By the time we sat with our coffees at an empty table in the large and, this early, only half-full canteen, I was almost at ease with him. Almost. I even dared to ask him what had been on his mind during the tutorial.

"My father is dying," he said, which rather put me back to square one, blushing and apologising and wishing I'd kept my mouth shut, or better yet, not gotten out of bed at all. He brushed it off.

"We've both known for some considerable time that he was dying, it's not a great shock, but the results of two tests came through yesterday and they're both bad. He has less time than we thought. I'm very close to him, I took it rather badly. Rather worse than he did, in fact. I shouldn't have taken it out on the class today, but their complaints seemed unusually petty, I was a little disappointed in them, and that didn't combine at all well with the mood I was already in. I wanted to get stuck into *Watt* and they wanted hints on the Middle English paper."

I apologised on behalf of the class, sounding depressingly pompous in my own ears.

"Oh, not your fault, and at least we got some discussion of the book in toward the end. Besides, it's understandable that you're worried. You're a conscientious lot, by and large. I should have been pleased you cared about the exams at all. Half of this year's take are probably going to fail at least one paper. None of you will, or not the regular attenders anyway."

I didn't particularly want to talk about the exams, and changed the subject. "Could you have had an office in the Quad if you'd wanted?"

He seemed amused. "Not since about 1969. Rather before my time."

"But people do have offices there."

"Oh, accounts, admissions, the building department. Only useful people, not us flighty academics."

"But Conrad Hayes has an office in the Quad, and he's in the English Department," I said.

"Conrad Hayes is a special case. He was appointed as a kind of writer-in-residence and as such has a special status, and quarters in the Old Quad."

"Alcoholic-in-residence," I said involuntarily, a phrase Gemma Mannion had used in the Aula.

He looked startled. "Well, yes, ah, he does . . . well, yes, he is an alcoholic. He used to be quite a fine dramatist though. Marvellous first play. Dreadful second play, but marvellous first play. *The Living*. I saw it revived in the Royal Court when I was even younger than I am now, I found it most affecting. It was quite a talent he ruined."

"What's it about?"

"Oh, sons and mothers. An uptight father. Everybody eloquently unable to communicate. The guilty secret, the usual. It's the same play Druid have been putting on under different titles for twenty years. A repressed rural family bottling everything up, all the better to uncork it in the third act. Heritage theatre, for the tourist crowd. They had a big success with it when they were starting off. Of course it's yet another rewrite of *The Playboy of the Western World*, like all Druid's stuff, but good of its kind, confident. He did it very well. He had a strong, clear, funny, original voice in that play. It says nothing but it plays like a dream. If only he'd found something worth saying in the subsequent twenty years."

"Has he written much since then? I mean, I'd never heard of him before I came to Galway. I've never seen anything by him."

"Oh he's written the odd thing. There's the second play, which is just shockingly bad, and a novel, God the novel, it's named after his ex-wife I think—*Sarah*, or no, *Sandra*; no, it is *Sarah*. My memory revolts against containing such information. Awful 'experimental' nonsense, quite unreadable. Worse than *Lost in the Funhouse*."

"That's his second play?" I said.

"Bless your ignorance, no. *Lost in the Funhouse* is a novel, and another man's drivel entirely, John Barth. Continue in ignorance of John Barth's *Lost in the Funhouse*, and you will lead a long and happy life."

I had, literally, kicked myself for making the mistake, not too hard a kick, but he seemed actually pleased I hadn't heard of it.

"The technical term for books like *Sarah* and *Lost in the Funhouse* is Utter Crap."

"So why's he writer-in-residence then?" I asked.

"Ah. Brilliant question. You could baffle a finer mind than my own with a question like that. I'll attempt to guide you toward the truth, though."

He paused and steepled his forefingers and looked comically stern and professorial for a moment, and I felt a surge of warmth towards him as I thought of how often I'd seen him look like that in the tutorials and not thought to think he might be born of mortal man and have a father he was fond of, private worries, private grief. He'd always looked so composed, so controlled, like this: gathering his thoughts, answering my questions, telling me things I didn't know. I felt absurdly like a schoolgirl with a crush, and I laughed at myself, Don't be silly, Juliet. But there was such a lot I didn't know, and I could feel the world expand as I listened to him. He seemed to have such a firm grasp of the goings-on of the whole, great, gaudy globe. I was only eighteen.

"Hayes . . . Do you really want to know all this about Hayes?"

I nodded yes.

"Conrad Hayes." Pause. "Writer-in-residence." Another pause. "God help us. You've got to understand that the universities of this world are as brutally exposed to the fickle winds of fashion as are the catwalks of Paris and Milan. Or perhaps a better comparison is with the stock market. Yes. . . . The University system is a vast, sluggish stock market of ideas, with various major centres of trade: Yale, Harvard, Columbia, Oxford and Cambridge of course, the Sorbonne. All the minor universities of the world take their cue from the great markets. If, and I'll speak of the wonderful world of English literary criticism here, Dickens's stock begins to rise in Yale, the other markets will follow suit. Dickens will return to the core curriculum. Dickens Studies will be offered in a dozen centres throughout the world. A Dickens Chair may well be instituted in the neo-brutalist, gold-glass-and-steel university of some nouveau-riche American oil town, and for a vast fee the board of governors of Hickslick, Illinois, will manage to poach from Yale the very man who started the whole Dickensian gold rush with his startlingly fresh approach to *Oliver*

Twist. His reputation secured by the amount of money he's being paid to take two classes every six months in what might as well be the wilds of Borneo, he can now relax. He need never make a fresh approach again, unless perhaps his eye is caught by some pretty girl or boy in the front row, and even then his approach is unlikely to be, and doesn't have to be, original. He can stop publishing. He can grow fat. That round of the game is over. Already some fiery-eyed revolutionary is riding into town, Cambridge perhaps, from, say, Italy, bearing aloft the strange device poststructuralism. Dickens ceases to exist. The word goes out from the markets: Ditch the author, invest in revolution. The academic hem shoots up six inches."

He took a sip of black coffee, and raised an am-I-boring-you eyebrow. I gave a please-do-go-on nod. He continued.

"Sometimes books are important, but authors are an embarrassment to be hidden in the attic when visitors call. Sometimes authors are so important there's no time left over for reading the books. Sometimes books are texts, and you can be hauled in front of a disciplinary committee for calling them books. Sometimes semiotics takes over completely, and the English language in its entirety vanishes. Frequently the novel is dead. Shakespeare is sometimes dead and sometimes God, but across the corridor in the philosophy department God is sometimes dead too, so Shakespeare watches his back at all times and gets Marlowe to taste his food for him. And every academic finds his career rising and falling in the wake of these great movements. The greatest living authority on 'The Ancient Mariner' is destroyed by the collapse of Coleridge Preferred. A bullish run on the Beats pushes a previously obscure Milwaukee professor to giddy heights. It's a marvellous game. Of course I'm speeding it up to make it interesting. Most of these shifts take years. But back a decade or so, there was a brief boom in Utter Crap. The Utter Crap market exploded overnight, if you'll forgive the image. Certainly it boomed very quickly, over a period of only two or three years. If it was pretentious and written on drugs, you could name your metaphorical price. There was a particularly virulent form of structuralism floating around at the time which worked brilliantly on plays and novels that had no plot and no character development. It was a bit of a write-off when applied to Jane Austen or Shakespeare or Henry James, but a lot of universities had invested heavily in this brand of structuralism and they had to use it on *something*. Negative reports were beginning to come in from the provinces. 'We have applied your theory to *Huckleberry Finn*, comma, and it appears to be nonsense, full stop. What should we do, query? Message ends.' Well, it was a full-scale crisis. The beast of theory has to be fed. If it wouldn't eat steak, there was obviously something wrong with the steak. Luckily, the solution was simple. Throw out the steak, and find it something it *could* chew."

He sipped his coffee again and I thought about how sad he looked when he was being funny, and did he do that deliberately to make the funny bits funnier by contrast, or was he really sad? I didn't know, I didn't know him at all. He put the mug down and looked past me.

"After a little trial-and-error, someone in Harvard came up with a strain of experimental literature running from about 1956 to the mid-1980s that kept the theory purring like a cat, and the word spread like wildfire. Across every campus in North America, coast to coast and right up to Quebec, you could hear full professors on the phone to their Utter Crap brokers, screaming 'Buy! Buy! Buy!' It was a good boom while it lasted. And it lifted Conrad Hayes to giddy heights. Both his second play and *Sarah* fitted the requirements of the age. Here was a man who could write Utter Crap for both page and stage! Academia wet itself. Some students revived his second play in Prague, and it proved so obscure that they were all arrested on suspicion of attempting to bring down the government. Huge kudos for Conrad! He was suddenly the fairy on the Christmas tree of fashion."

He waved at the illustrative reality which stood in a tub off to my left, shedding its needles already in the artificial December heat of the canteen.

"Prestigious reprints of *Sarah* and the second play ensued. Ironically, his good play was legally tangled up with a bad Irish publisher and didn't get reprinted. Nobody wanted it anyhow. It made sense. Anyway, offers of posts followed high-profile reviews of the reissues. Half a dozen writers were raised from the dead in this fashion, including a couple who'd actually been buried and who therefore weren't in the best position to take advantage of this upturn in their fortunes. Conrad Hayes, though, through the lucky circumstance of an expensive English divorce and an inadequate salary as a junior lecturer in Trinity, hadn't had the financial wherewithal to drink himself to death since *Sarah,* and so was alive to receive a generous offer from the University of Texas, which he accepted with a speedinesss that would have put men half his age to shame."

He paused.

"Am I boring you to tears with this? Conrad's life is a great source of departmental fascination and gossip, but I can't imagine it being of any great interest to anyone living a real life outside these walls."

"No, go on, I really am interested. It's like a soap opera with a real person, alcohol and America and everything. Failure and success. I'm interested in other people's lives." I felt so stupid. "I mean, everyone is."

"All right. The story continues. Conrad . . . did you know that Conrad's not, in fact, his name? He was christened Conor Hayes, was always known as Con, changed his name to Conrad for the first book, and later changed it officially, by deed poll."

"You know a lot about him," I said.

"Conrad Hayes . . . Conrad Hayes fascinates me. . . ."

"But you don't like him."

"No. He . . . *disgusts me* is a bit strong. I haven't been in UCG long, but I've learned a lot about him. I do not like the man at all. I shouldn't"—he smiled—"speak about another member of the department like that in front of a student, but I feel rather strongly about Conrad Hayes."

"What did he do that was so terrible?" I asked.

David said nothing.

"You don't have to tell me," I said.

David sighed, looked at his watch, gulped down some coffee.

"I should feel sorry for him. He achieved recognition too late, for the wrong thing. For the wrong reasons. When he got a good post, it was under false pretences, writer-in-residence in Austin, Texas. He'd been talking for years about his great unfinished work, sometimes a novel, sometimes a play, but it never existed. They found him out in Austin, saw through him very quickly. After a couple of classes they didn't even let him take classes. He was a wreck. He was kept on the payroll for a couple of years out of pity and because it would have been too cruel and embarrassing to make him face the fact that he wasn't writing and he wasn't capable anymore of writing. Then UCG got a vast European grant, and in a fit of hubris somebody decided we should have a writer-in-residence and Conrad heard about it and the University of Texas colluded with him to win the post and get him off their hands. Played a very sly game, pretending to try and hold on to him, and UCG got stuck with an expensive turkey. No one has the guts to admit they made a terrible mistake, so they stick him in the Quad well out of everybody's way and pretend to believe in his impending masterpiece and hope he'll drink himself to death. It's a mess."

He looked at his watch again.

"Probably best if you treat this chat as confidential. They get very touchy on the subject, and I'd find myself fielding self-important little memos from Flannery Ryan if he heard I was speaking ill of other members of staff, especially one he helped to appoint."

"You can trust me," I said.

He gave me a huge smile, much wider than the usual tight, controlled smiles I'd gotten used to. He seemed to have surprised himself with it. "Of course I can. Sorry."

I smiled and shook my head at the apology. "Why do you dislike him so much?"

He paused again. "He betrayed his talent. He betrayed himself. He didn't have to turn out like that."

"But you can't hate someone for hurting himself."

"Mmm. He named himself after Joseph Conrad, you know." And he pointed at my book.

"Really?"

"Yes. Did you have any Joseph Conrad on your Leaving Cert Course?"

"No, not my year. *Typhoon* was optional."

"Pity. He's good. Terribly serious, but good."

I grinned against my will. He raised an eyebrow and I shook my head.

"Well. Thank you very much for the coffee Miss Taylor, and now I must leave you, my friend is probably waiting." He rose to his feet. "Enjoy your Christmas, and I'll see you in class on January . . . twelfth?"

I didn't know. "See you then, sir." He winced. "And happy Christmas too."

He gave a funny little bow and left.

I finished the last of my coffee, cold now at the bottom of the white mug, and sat a little longer looking at the cover of *Heart of Darkness*, a beaten-up African steamship chugging away upriver, into a bank of fog.

22

The day before the first exam I went to a film. Not to the cinema, but to a College Film Society showing of *Wuthering Heights*, in a lecture theatre. "Revise without Studying!" said the posters. The moribund Film Society had been taken over that September by a group of high-spirited first-year English students, and in the week before the exams they had been running a successful and well-attended mock-educational Seven-Day Season of vaguely course-related films. I'd seen Kenneth Branagh's *Henry V* at the start of the season, instead of studying *Henry IV, Part One* as I should have done, a typically guilt-inducing evasion of my proper work. Even as I'd sat there I'd known that, had it been on my course, as it would be in a year's time, I probably would not have attended. For the subsequent five days I'd avoided study a little more subtly, with the books open in front of me, but now it was Sunday evening in the library. The first English exam was at nine the next morning. My other three first-year subjects filled out the following days of the week to the full and if I was unprepared in English, I was even less prepared in them. My head was throbbing and booming, on the verge of migraine, and my mouth tasted of metal. I stood and when Juno looked up I said quietly, "I'm going to see *Wuthering Heights*." She nodded, and apologetically indicated the neat stacks of notes in front of her. I shook my head, it's fine, and left.

On the concourse I queued between rowdy groups of engineering students who didn't have exams. The boys made crude remarks about Juliette Binoche and the girls made crude remarks about Ralph Fiennes.

I recognised some other first-year English students in the queue and was relieved to see that most of them looked anxious and depressed.

Then I'd paid and was in the theatre. I walked down toward the front and was hailed by Dominic O'Connaire.

"Juliet! Here!"

I turned to see him sitting with Gemma and Conrad, a dozen rows from the front. Oh, shit. But Dominic seemed pleased to see me. Extraordinarily pleased, given that I'd nearly broken his ankle from behind the last time we'd met. He and Gemma indicated the empty seats beside them. Double shitty-shit-shit. Oh well. I edged in, and Dominic bade me sit beside him. I could smell the drink coming off all of them. Ah.

"Revision or relaxation?" he said expansively. Of course, he was in science.

"Both," I said. Gemma said hello, and Conrad reached across both her and Dominic to shake my hand. He had a firm handshake, and my hand jerked in his as I remembered why we'd had no chance to shake hands before. Our hands had been coated in Lucozade and broken glass. Oh lord.

"Good to see you again," he said. "Pleasant surprise. I won't ask you, don't worry."

"What?"

"Have you changed your mind about acting."

"I'm afraid I haven't," I said, and returned my attention to Gemma and Dominic as Gemma said, "How's the study going?" and Dominic made a horrified face and said, "What a *question*, we'll be talking about the weather next."

"It's going OK, I suppose," I said. "I feel I've left everything too late and I'm going to fail everything, but . . ."

Gemma nodded. "Yeah, same here, and you never do. It's always the way. I suppose if we didn't panic, we'd never get anything done. Have you read this?"—meaning *Wuthering Heights*.

"Oh, yes," I said, "three or four times. It was on for my Leaving Cert. I loved it."

"Ah yeah, it's great. My sister's class did it last year, they all fell in love with Heathcliff. I've told them they wouldn't like him half so much in real life, but they just squeal 'No! No! He's lovely!' and fight over who should've played him in the film. Daniel Day-Lewis always gets a big vote."

I felt a pang as I realised I must be the same age as the young sister Gemma spoke so indulgently of—and a further pang when I remembered having exactly that argument with Juno in our room at home. I was too embarrassed to tell Gemma.

"Are you in second or third year?" I asked.

"Third. Final. I suppose I should be taking them more seriously, but I reckon the damage is done now. A bit late to be panicking. I decided I might as well take the evening off and relax. I'll give everything a last look-over when I get home."

I envied her calm. "And you're doing the play too?"

"Hah. Maybe. I must have been mad to say yes." Dominic gave a "Hey!" of protest, which Gemma blithely ignored. "Mind, it's shedding cast members like slates in a high wind. They all think Dominic's a lunatic. If any more go, I'd say he'll have to abandon it, so I might get out of it yet."

"Don't listen to her! They love me!" said Dominic. "Anyway, we can replace the bastards with more slave workers from First Arts after Christmas . . . I hope . . . shite on them, anyhow."

Gemma leaned over him towards me, putting her hand over his protesting mouth, to say in a mock-whisper, "I can't see him pulling it off. You can see what he's getting at, but it's way too ambitious, as usual. He wanted to put on *Nixon in China* in the College Bar last year, but only three people turned up for the audition, and they all thought it was some sort of one-man lunchtime comedy."

"I'm too good for this world," sighed Dominic's muffled voice. "Far too good. Wretched philistines."

Gemma removed her hand from his mouth and gave him a consoling pat on the head. The lights began to dim in the lecture theatre. I whispered "Good luck tomorrow" to Gemma, and she grinned at me. "And you," she said. Dominic ostentatiously shushed us and we sat back into our seats. Conrad hadn't joined in the conversation, and I'd been uncomfortably aware of his gaze all the way through it.

The film began.

It seemed very distant, quite lacking in passion, but I wasn't sure if that was the film's fault or mine. The characters distracted me by not being how I'd imagined them. My attention began to wander. The colour and light on the great screen began to seem abstract. A tiny moth in the projector's beam almost directly above me caught my eye and held it as he danced in and out of the light, too tiny and too far from the narrow source of the beam to interfere with the images on the screen. The moth swept into the beam again and again, in search of something. My head rested on the back of my seat as I looked up at him whirling frantically into the light, spinning free into the cool dark, and returning. Slowly he worked his way along up the beam, higher, tighter, brighter. Soon he'd be blocking enough of the light to be seen. It must be hot up there, in the first and brightest stretch of the beam, raw light from the hot projector's lens. If the film caught for a moment, it caught fire. All a moth could find at the heart of the light was death. Why did it love the light? Why did it seek out flame and death? What did it think it had found? I closed my eyes against the light.

Stupid with half-remembered philosophy and too many nights of tension and study, I fell asleep.

23

They woke me up when it was over and offered to walk me home.

"No, thanks, I'll be grand."

"It's no bother, we're going that way near enough," said Dominic.

"Meeting up with some friends down from Dublin, for the last pint," said Gemma. "Are you with us, or a Guinness?"

"No," I said. "Exam in the morning." I collapsed inside. Jesus. I'd forgotten.

They walked me home, the two men arguing all the way. Dominic seemed to be deliberately ignoring Gemma for some reason. A spiky trio. Gemma let me lean against her as we walked. I was so tired, I hardly spoke, I hardly listened. Soon I walked with my head on Gemma's shoulder, my eyes half-closed, in a lovely, dreamy rhythm over the bridges, the canal, and the river. Gemma hardly spoke either. Both of us must have half-nodded off, or have thought the other was leading, because we almost walked into a street lamp. We both stopped, abruptly, a foot short of it, and I woke and looked sleepily about me.

We'd all stopped.

"Gemma doesn't want to talk about girls and football," said Dominic sulkily. "I want to talk about girls and football. Is there one who understands me?"

"I think we've covered girls and football," said Conrad. "What remains to be said?"

Dominic howled at the moon. "Everything," he said. "We haven't begun." He threw his arms round myself and Gemma. Gemma sighed. Avoiding the lamppost, we moved on.

"Gemma doesn't believe in love," Dominic said, looking at me mournfully.

"I don't believe in football," I said back to him.

He turned to Gemma and said mournfully "Juliet doesn't believe in football." He pondered this, and sighed. "Will I ever be wed?" he said.

"I wouldn't recommend it," said Conrad, calmly walking alongside us.

"Ah, shut up, you," said Dominic. "Sure what do you know about women? You're just a bloody . . . worshipper."

"I did marry one," said Conrad mildly.

Dominic shook his head. "And you even worshipped her. Your wife, for Christ's sake. Now that's shite, Connie. You haven't a bull's notion about women, I don't care how many of them you've married. Sure nobody wants to be worshipped, Connie. Even Christ used to get a bit edgy after a long day of it. How can a woman fart or scratch her snatch in peace with you sitting around worshipping her all day? Sure no wonder Sarah had trouble with her nerves."

"But Dominic, I didn't worship Sarah. I'm not even sure if I liked Sarah."

"Ah that's all part of the same game, Connie. That's nothing to do with it, that's . . . thu . . . fff." Dominic took his arms from around our shoulders to gesture wildly, trying to get his point across. He spluttered and laughed as his tongue blundered. They hadn't sobered up noticeably during the course of the film. If anything, going back out into the cold air had kicked the drink back in. Or had they continued to drink as I slept in the flickering light?

Dominic was very obviously drunk, while Conrad gave the impression of being full to the lid with alcohol yet not really drunk, as though his metabolism had adjusted to a new normality. They were both quite obviously sliding along the well-oiled grooves of a familiar argument now.

"You'd worship anything, Connie. Marx. Bob fecking Dylan. James double-fecking bastard Joyce. You're always on the lookout for someone to let you down. I'd say the fall of the Wall had you dancing. You're the man with the portable pedestal, Connie." Dominic seemed almost serious now. "And you'd put anything up on it. Sure you'd worship God if you were stuck. And what harm, what harm, what harm. You like putting them up there because you love seeing them fall off. Fair enough. Whatever. Everything lets you down in the end because you want it to, 'cause it proves your shagging theory that the world is shit . . . which is bollocks . . . sorry, Gemma. Juliet."

Conrad was smiling and shaking his head.

Dominic waved a spare hand and continued. "But the worship of women, now, there's a thing that makes no sense. It's even more stupid than worshipping Marx, because at least Marx doesn't get pissed off with you and tell you to fuck off. Women don't want to be worshipped, Connie. And they're right."

We were almost at my door now. Gemma was resting her head on my shoulder. She groaned into my ear.

"No, no, no," interrupted Conrad, "you don't understand me at all. You're saying *worship* all the time. That's not it at all. You're too young to understand the tradition I'm coming from. I think I understand you . . . but I don't think you understand me. I treat women with respect because I come from a very solid, traditional, working-class background." (Why, I thought to myself dreamily, are writers always bursting to be working class? Nobody else is, not even the workers. They're all dying to win the Lotto and soar free on wings of gold.)

"Working class my arse," said Dominic, toning up the muscle of my suspicion.

"My father worked," said Conrad. "My mother had to too sometimes. We certainly weren't . . . well off. And I was brought up to respect women. To hold doors open for them. To think of them as ladies. To protect them. It was a culture, a decent and just one, that is now spat on by the likes of you." He seemed genuinely angry.

Dominic shook his head. "Opening doors and saying *ladies* isn't a culture."

"I have heard this so often," murmured Gemma in my ear. "Save me."

"No? No?" said Conrad, "a culture's a set of shared assumptions, of attitudes, and we used to have one in Ireland, a decent, hardworking culture, and I didn't agree with all of it, but it had a lot to be said for it, a lot, and now we have a generation of young bucks who have respect for the culture of Muslims, or the culture of blacks, or the culture of gays, but have no respect for the culture of their parents." I winced a little, the words struck a faint chord. Dominic tried to interrupt but Conrad waved a hand at him, one moment. "The young, they're concerned at the way the culture of the travellers is dying, or the culture of Polynesia, oh they're all rich, traditional ways of life. But they laugh at their parents and they've no time for their grandparents, because their attitudes and beliefs aren't a culture, a tradition, oh no, they're just sexist, racist, stupid, old-fashioned. Am I wrong? Am I wrong?"

"You are wrong," said Dominic.

"And how am I wrong?" said Conrad. We had arrived at my door. I gave it a push, in case one of the mouse people from downstairs had left it on the latch again, as was their wont, but they hadn't. I looked for my keys.

Dominic was fading. I'd seen the tiredness piling on as Conrad made his speech. "Oh, Connie," he said sadly, "you make it sound like there's a shagging war on and we'll have you out into the street. You make it sound like we're breaking up the pianos for firewood. We're all right, Connie. We're all right. There's no harm in us, Connie. There's nothing to be afraid of at all."

"Thanks for walking me home," I said. "I'd invite ye in but I'm knackered."

"Oh, that's all right," said Conrad.

"Are you sure you won't join us?" said Gemma.

"Thanks. Thanks. No."

In bed, I was asleep before the afterimage of the lightbulb had faded from my retina.

24

I entered the underworld of the exams and lived in the half-light of them for a week and a day.

The world seemed curiously far away for much of the time. I was aware of a light tension, not quite a headache, that defined my skull, and I was aware of the skin that wrapped my body. I felt very much inside my skull, inside my skin. The world seemed very separate from me.

I walked in each morning after a last burst of dawn study in the relevant subject, jacked up on caffeine, my blood tapping lightly at the back of my eyes every time my heels hit the ground, little pressure waves. Everything sounded further away than it was. A pile driver on the river behind the university drove huge concrete rods down into the riverbed as part of some European-funded university expansion program all through the first two days, and as the resentment and subvocalised complaints mounted into audible murmurs around me, I wrote serenely on. It was too far away to affect me. I was living behind my eyes. Everything I needed was there, or was of no use to me. I only vaguely realized that I wasn't usually like this, that this wasn't perhaps healthy. It was how I dealt with pressure, and if it wasn't the best way, well, there was nothing I could do about it now. The fact that much of the pressure I was enduring I had generated myself did not occur to me, as it never did occur to me.

Conversations with Juno for that week were strange, through fog. I sat exams, I studied, and I slept. Being spoken to felt like being woken up, forced to do something difficult. Michael gave up talking to me and walked around me carefully when he was there. Juno spoke sometimes but didn't expect answers, and that was alright. Only at the weekend, before the final day's exams, English again on a second Monday, was there a break long enough for me to emerge a little from myself into the world. Even then, I was only half out of the underworld. I was snappy and abstracted. Juno laid a trail of inconsequential conversational crumbs. I followed it, roughly, unhelpfully, like a hungry bear woken in winter. Poor Juno.

"The philosophy seems to have gone OK, then. People seemed happy enough."

"Mmm. Yeah."

"You were worried about the philosophy of art. Did he try anything tricky?"

"No." More seemed called for. "Easy enough."

"My second history paper was fine."

"Mm."

"Do you want a look at my Chaucer notes for Monday? You were saying you couldn't read yours."

The day I'd said that, at the height of my study panic ten days before, I couldn't have read my own name in lights.

"No. Mine're fine." I was forgetting something, what? "Thanks."

I had just spent two hours studying Middle English, and if I felt anything it certainly wasn't a desire to read any more about how funny, witty, and sharp Chaucer's dull, crude, longwinded *Canterbury Tales* were. Mainly I felt slightly nauseous, slightly hungry (not a good combination), and more than slightly impatient to get my period, which the stress of not studying followed immediately by the stress of studying seemed to be delaying an unconscionable length of time. I was now out of sync with Juno for the first time since the Leaving Cert, when exactly this had happened. Usually we were as regular and synchronised as two lifers in the same cell.

I bent over a little in my chair. The occasional gentle cramp went well with the permanent light stress headache. It was a small miracle I bothered answering her at all.

25

And then they were over. After Monday's Middle English paper I walked home without waiting for Juno to finish, and let myself into the building and climbed the stairs and let myself into the flat. Without bothering to get a towel from my room I put on the bathroom heater, pumped all my change into the meter for the shower, and stripped and stood under the warm, civilized water, my forehead against the cool tiles. I softened and loosened under the water, felt I was melting. With my eyes closed, I thought about nothing. Gradually my breasts ceased to feel as though they'd been stuffed with rocks.

I opened my eyes and tilted my head back into the path of the water and opened my mouth till it was filled with water and I was deaf, dumb, and blind. I closed my eyes and mouth and let the water jet from my mouth against the tiles. Suddenly and effortlessly the tension and the blood began to leave me and drain away under the coaxing of the warm water. Baptism, I thought. I stood there a while longer.

When I walked through the living room to my room, carrying the old clothes I'd used to dry myself, Juno was there.

"Hello," I said, disappearing into my room to get something clean to wear, "I didn't hear you come in."

Juno spoke from the living room. "Nice shower?"

"God, yes. How did you find the paper?"

"Fine. No surprises. Are you back among the living, then?"

"What do you mean?"

"Talking, asking questions. Smiling, unless my eyes deceived me just there." She stuck her head around the door.

"Come in, come in, sit down." I knocked the damp clothes off the chair and continued to dress. "Was I bad?"

"World of your own. You had Michael frightened to speak to you. He'd put the kettle on and offer to make you coffee and you'd give him the strangest look and not answer. He's been hiding in my room or staying well out of the way at his place for most of the week, not that I expect you noticed. Poor thing, try and put him at his ease when he calls round. Tell him you're back to normal and he's perfectly safe."

I'd been "Oh God"-ing and groaning for this. "Was I really dreadful?"

"Mm, yes, a bit. I'm well enough used to it, though. It unsettled the visitors mainly. Conrad and Dominic and Gemma all made *very* brief visits which you've probably forgotten, but I'd bet they haven't. Tourist figures are *down* for the flat."

"Was it worse than the Leaving?"

"Near enough. About the same."

"Oh, God. Sorry. I'm better now."

"Yes, I noticed. Don't worry about it. It's Christmas, home to good old Tipperary tomorrow."

I gave a theatrical shudder, but I didn't mean it. It would be good to see our mother, and I felt confident I could get through a Christmas without fighting with our father if I really put my mind to it, especially if I avoided talking to him. And there was the possibility that Paul might come home.

"Did you ring home?" I asked Juno. "Will Paul be coming?"

"No word last time I rang. Paul . . . who knows?"

We hardly knew Paul really, he was so much older and he'd left home so young. I hadn't seen him for two years, the last time he'd returned for Christmas. It hadn't been a great success. He still hated Tipperary and showed it. Our father took it personally. A couple of stupid arguments, an uneasy peace on Christmas Day, I'd spent most of the holiday in our room listening to the albums Paul had brought me. It was Paul who'd got me listening to Kate Bush, and to classical music. Sometimes an album or a book would arrive in the post from London and, later, San Francisco, often without the excuse of a birthday or Christmas, sometimes without even a note. He knew me well enough to know what I'd like, which can be hard enough when you live in the same house, but which shows real sensitivity and intelligence when you're guessing from an ocean away, and from memories of what someone was like when they were a child. Paul's presents to me kept pace with me as I grew older in a way that even my parents' presents didn't always. I liked Paul very much, in the distracted and casually intense way you can like an older brother, perhaps love him, without even thinking of him that often. I don't think I wrote even once to thank him for the albums and the books. Another nag of guilt every Christmas. I wanted to see him this year to say thank you, because I knew I'd love his present and that I'd never write to say so.

PART II

Tipperary

26

We caught a Ryan's bus home. It was packed with people that I half-knew—students, secretaries and civil servants, girls who would have been ahead of me in school and boys I'd last seen hanging out at the Market Cross when I was fifteen, four or five of them sharing a cigarette and sniggering as Juno and I passed them on our way home from school. The secretaries had had their hair done too often, until it looked as artificially over-alive as a snarling stuffed fox. The boy civil servants and insurance salesmen looked uncomfortable in tight shirt collars that rubbed raw the obligatory single boil on the back of each neck, the brave but feeble crusted remnants of their gloriously inflamed and eruptive youths. The students of both sexes just looked like students. Some of the girls said hello to me and Juno as we got on and walked halfway down the bus to find seats. The boys failed to catch our eyes, but I was very aware of the surreptitious glances. Pure, helpless hate boiled up in me, and when we sat down to wait for the bus to pull out I couldn't read. Why did Paul have to leave when these creatures stayed? But I looked at them again and slowly calmed down. Their lives were punishment enough. They were going home for Christmas with their laundry and their suits, and they looked terrible, sad and lost. Our brother was thousands of miles away because he wanted to be, and he was happy there, and I should be happy for him. I was. He'd won. It was OK.

I hadn't been home once since coming up to Galway. Juno had been home twice, on her own and with Michael, but I'd found excuses—essay deadlines, the library—and it had been quite easy not to go. Juno had brought home my summer clothes and brought back my winter ones, all listed out for her on a sheet torn from my philosophy notes.

I swopped places with Juno, who was reading history for pleasure, to look out the bus window as we drove through the darkening countryside. How bleak the fields were. The Galway fields, all stones and little black-thorn bushes growing sideways in the wind off the Atlantic, were bleak enough but had reason to be. They looked like a desert was taking them slowly, under a sky full of inexplicable clouds. Then the fields grew greener and richer, and the soil covered the rock, and we came over Portumna Bridge into Tipperary. Thick bushy hedges now, instead of dry stone walls. Lush, fallow winter pasture, instead of tilted slabs of rock with a little harsh grass on them.

But as the fields became larger, greener, and more prosperous, they remained empty and silent. The cattle all in winter quarters and no corn for the wind to send waves through. Big empty fields and the occasional farmhouse, curtains closed. Nobody walking or working those fields. Nobody with a gun, and dogs at his heel. Just the night falling on big empty fields. December.

The moon and the dark blue sky and the dark grey clouds low to the pink horizon flickered and dimmed and were buried under my sudden reflection as the lights shuddered on in a ripple down the length of the bus. A song I liked came on the crackling radio, and the driver retuned to a different station, very muffled and fading in and out as the bus revved to climb the low hills surrounding the town I was born in. It didn't feel like Christmas.

27

We stepped off the bus outside Kavanagh's Hotel. The street was crossed by a couple of dozen thin strands of Christmas lights. The Christmases of one's childhood are traditionally bigger and brighter than whatever Christmas you're enduring as an adult, but in my case I could quantify the decline. I remembered the Christmas the town council first hung Christmas lights across O'Connell Street, our imaginatively named main thoroughfare. I was five, and there were thirty strands, of mixed red, yellow, green, and blue bulbs. I counted them every time I walked down the street with my mother and Juno that Christmas, walking with my head back and our mother scolding me for not looking where I was going, and me not answering for fear I'd forget the number. Thirty strands, with forty and sometimes forty-one bulbs in each strand. As the years went by, bulbs broke or failed and went unreplaced, and entire strands would suffer mysterious disasters and go dead, not to reappear the next year. Now there were twenty-three strands, all with an assortment of bulbs missing and others gone for some reason dim. I counted the strands as we walked to the top of O'Connell Street before turning right into the narrower Well Street, at the end of which lay our family's home. Well Street was dark, with few streetlights, and our bags were heavy, and it was cold. We didn't talk till we reached the front door, when Juno said abruptly, "We'll have to get presents tomorrow." I put down my bag and found my key. "Oh my God, yes. Never entered my head."

The door swung open as my key approached the lock.

"Paul!" we said, and embraced him enthusiastically.

"My beautiful sisters," he said. "My God, you look wonderful. You're not little girls anymore. I'll have to burn the Barbie dolls I brought you."

We laughed and jumped around him and pretended to be babies while he picked up our bags with exaggerated groans and carried them into the living room.

"Look what I found," he said.

Our father grunted from his armchair. "Oh, more mouths to feed. I thought we were rid of ye."

I gritted my teeth a little, but I was too pleased at seeing Paul to let my father spoil it.

"Paul, Paul, give me my present, I want to weigh it," a reference to an old family joke about the value of presents, dating from when Juno and I used to weigh each other's presents on the kitchen scales as they arrived in the week before Christmas, as a poor substitute for opening them, which was forbidden until after dinner on Christmas Day. Whoever had the lightest presents would often end up in tears. One year my father gave Juno two bricks among her other presents, to annoy me. I cried when she weighed them on Christmas Eve, but Juno cried when she opened them on Christmas Day, and our mother stood up and swore at him in front of us all, which was very unusual and silenced everyone for hours after.

Paul lifted me up in the air and then lifted Juno up in the air.

"Presents of great worth," he said. "Oh, valuable presents these two. Who are they for?"

"No one," I said, blushing.

"Ah! You're blushing! You are somebody's present!" But he saw I wasn't enjoying the game and didn't pursue it.

"Where's Mum?" I said.

"She's gone out," said my father.

"I know she's out, where's she gone to?"

"She's out visiting the Brownes and trying not to get given one of their terrible cakes."

The Brownes were friends of our mother. Mrs. Browne had a love affair with cookery that wasn't reciprocated, and a number of distant, half-remembered Christmases had run aground on the rock of Mrs. Browne's Christmas cake. Eventually a rebellion led by Paul had brought about a compromise, and ended the tyranny. Now every year Mrs. Browne gave our mother a Christmas cake as a present, and every year our mother brought the cake home and put it in the dustbin with much swearing of the family to secrecy, and everyone was happy. I liked all these rituals.

Juno went to put on the kettle. There was a turf fire in the living room, and a small, real tree with the familiar decorations—dented silver balls with frosted top halves, silver-and-red streamers of tinsel moulted in places till you could see the string. The fairy on the top of the tree, a baby doll in a white dress our mother had made out of cardboard and a strip of net curtain, sat at the familiar uncomfortable angle, the glue that held on her head old and yellow and visible through the mesh of her net ruff.

Juno swung open the kitchen door to ask who wanted tea and a small gust of turf smoke came into the room and suddenly, and just in time, it felt like Christmas.

28

That night Paul, Juno, and I went to Connollys Hotel, Bar and Disco.

"Let's take in the best Tipperary has to offer," said Paul, and off we went.

It had been Connollys unfortunate slogan on their local radio ad for years, dating back to the days of the pirates, and a source of unending joy and sarcasm to Paul and his friend Aengus Cleary. They used to roar it, rolling home drunk together at half two in the morning after an evening in Connollys Bar, followed by a night in Connollys Disco, and a shared bag of chips from Connollys Illegal Chip-Van in Connollys Famous Car Park, the Biggest in the South. You'd never catch an apostrophe off a Connolly. A good Tipp hurling family, no time for soccer, the devil, the Brits, or punctuation.

"The best," Paul and Aengus would bellow, "the BEST Tipperary has to offer . . . take in the fucking BEST . . ." The drunker they got, the broader their brogue, till they were singing in pure Tipperary. "Deh *BESHT.*"

I'd hear them shushing each other below at the front door, dropping the key, entering the house with elaborate care, closing the door as quietly as they could, going into the living room, and turning on the radio full blast for thirty seconds before they could get it together to find the volume control and turn it down. *"Shush!"* *"SHUSH!"* "Jesus, the parents . . ."

If our parents woke, they never did anything about it. I don't think Juno ever heard the boys come home. She slept a lot deeper than I did, but I was sensitive to their coming home, I liked to hear it, I wanted it to wake me, so it did. Once or twice, careful not to wake Juno, I snuck downstairs to join them. They were pleased to see me, in an absent-minded sort of way. They asked me about school and my friends and my hated dance classes in a way that they never bothered to in our everyday encounters at breakfast and dinner and in front of the TV. It was as though we were all part of some underground community, meeting in the hush of the night, speaking in low voices, the last cigarette of the night going around, casually equal. It was only years later that I realized they were probably stoned out of their heads as they focused intently on my banal answers to their polite questions.

I loved it but I felt so dumb, in both senses, and young, in my stupid little pink going-to-the-bathroom socks which I tried to hide under my-self as I sat on the sofa. When I did say anything, the sentence would just come out so helplessly, hopelessly wrong that I could practically see it stranded in midair in front of me, dying in the silence. Eventually I would mumble something that sounded like an explanation or an apology or a straightforward goodnight but which didn't have any actual words in it and wasn't properly any of them, and I would sneak back to the cowardly safety of my room, my awful mumble ringing like a persistent tuning-fork tone in my ear, a blaze of embarrassment consuming me as I climbed the stairs in a rage of self-pity and fury at my youth and immaturity and stupidity, stupidity. Yet I still liked to hear them below me, murmuring, even after I gave up trying to join them.

As Juno and I accompanied Paul to Connollys then, I found myself almost giddy with excitement. I'd been to Connollys a billion times with Juno, but this was different. Look at me, going out on the town with Paul! I felt like singing, so I did.

"I could have danced all night, I could have danced all night. . . ."

I didn't know enough words. It was one of my father's favourites and I'd never really listened to it closely.

"You're in flying form," said Paul.

"Mm, yup."

And I was. All my melancholy had vanished—ping!—as the front door closed behind us. I did a giddy little dance and nearly tripped on the cracked pavement. I felt quite drunk, and we hadn't even arrived at the pub yet.

Paul pushed Connollys door open and waved us in. It was like putting your head in a kettle. The heat and steam and noise were overwhelming. I was—what's the word?—overwhelmed. Every exile on Earth seemed to have arranged to meet here, just inside the door, tonight, and most of them would appear to have arrived in the previous sixty seconds. The air juddered with back-slaps, roared greetings, howls of recognition and delight. Seamus! Jaysus! How'r ya! Moira! Feckit! Odysseus! C'mere t'me! Is it Napoleon, is it! Shake, man! Cain, begod! How's the brother?

All the returnees met up and exchanged histories in Connollys at Christmas and now to my shock I found I was a returnee. People greeted me, greeted Juno, greeted Paul, shook hands, offered drinks, refused money, piled coats, pushed over, and in a dizzy minute I was sitting at a table with a bunch of semi-strangers, a glass of Harp in front of me and another on the way. My protestation that I didn't like Harp, or glasses, had been as benignly overlooked as my proffered ten-pound note and my request for a pint of Guinness. Paul leaned over to calm me as steam leaked from my ears to aid the general smog. "They mean well," he said softly. "They're idiots, but they mean well. They probably don't even re-member beating the shit out of me in the Christian Brothers. If I can for-give them that, you can forgive them buying you Harp. I'll get you a Guinness later. Sit back and enjoy the comedy. It's Christmas."

So I sat back and calmed down and even drank some of one of my Harps before the flailing elbow of a new arrival swept them both into Paul's lap.

"Oh Jesus Paul, I'm sorry, buy you another. What was it?"

"Harp, but don't worry."

"Shit no, I'm not buying you that piss, Guinness is it, and what're your sisters having?"

"Hello Aengus, I'm grand."

"Hello Aengus, they were both mine and I'd have paid you to get rid of them, don't worry about it."

Aengus settled in among us, and the night began.

"God you're looking lovely, are you old enough for Guinness, grand, three then, I'm shagging loaded don't touch that, oh fuck it's murder at that bar let me get a breather first, is it English Paul tells me you're learn-ing, well that'll come in handy if you ever visit me in London, not that any fucker speaks it there anymore, did you hear the streets are paved with gold there, shagging right they are, but it's like lead, sure it causes terrible deformities, the people there have hearts the size of gooseberries and fierce short arms, every bastard in Soho must owe me a pint"

and having had his breather, he leaped up and squeezed through the scrum towards the bar.

"He's a dote," said Juno.

"He's a sexy dote," said I.

"Jesus, hands off Aengus, he's a friend," said Paul, alarmed. "And if I hear he's laid a hand on you, I'll kill him."

"OK, no hands," I said.

"Jesus," said Paul, mopping his brow, "you are joking, aren't you? Don't answer."

The night grew increasingly ribald, energetic, and drunken. Paul and Aengus vied to ply Juno and myself with pints. Juno found herself at the eye of a hurricane of male attention, and as I grew increasingly relaxed and less inclined to scowl at rubbernecked passers-by, so did I. I almost began to enjoy the attention, a very rare feeling for me. When James Power fondled my upper arm and playfully tousled my hair in his familiar creepy way, I told him to piss off rather than fuck off and didn't even stop smiling. Of course he took that as a come-on and did it again, brushing his forearm "accidentally" against my breast as he did so, and then I had to say "Fuck right off James, I mean it," and tread very hard on his instep to make absolutely sure he understood I meant it, but all in all it was a lovely, relaxed evening. By closing time I was pissed as a coot and up for divilment.

29

We swayed the very short walk from Connollys Bar to Connollys Disco, out the pub door and in a door six yards away, paid our money, found a table on the edge of the dance floor, and the night roared on. I leaned against Aengus.

"Tell me more about advertising," I said.

"I'm boring you," he said.

"No, tell me more. I love your voice. . . . It's all mixed up, all London and Tipperary." Either Aengus went red or the disco lights did, I wasn't sure and didn't care.

"Ah, they love me Irish accent over there," he said. "It's worth an extra ten K to me, no bother. They think I have a fiery Celtic creative soul. They know I can't be as thick as I sound, so they mistake their estimations in the other direction."

He said *thick* as "tick." And *mistake* as "mishtayk."

"What's K?" I said. He had to think back.

"K. A thousand. Thousand pounds. Forty K. Ninety K. It's a stupid way of talking about money real casual. Came from the City. I don't even know where the fuck I got it. I don't even know if it's fashionable anymore. It just slipped out 'cause I was drunk."

Thrunk. I wuz thrunk. I thought of saying something and thought better of it. "Let's dance," I said.

He hesitated for a moment, not sure if I wanted to dance or if I was merely identifying the tune. "Let's Dance" by David Bowie throbbed from the speakers. Someone should have slapped a preservation order on the DJ box as a Site of Special Historic Interest. Someone probably had. Was this DJ stored in one of the hotel freezers and only thawed out at Christmas? "Let's Dance" segued jarringly into "New Year's Day" by U2. Mother of God. It was a fucking museum with a mirror ball. We danced. I was having a great time.

Suddenly I felt a hand on my knee. On my *knee?* As I was *dancing?* I looked down to see one of the Gleeson twins grinning up at me, fag in mouth, head shaved to stubble, denim shirt, jacket, and jeans. They hadn't changed since they were ten. Chain-smoking their way through primary school, secondary school, reform school, and prison (rumour had it they lied about their age to get in), they had perfectly preserved their youthful figures, yellowed fingers, and, unfortunately, heights. Frankly, the two of them hadn't a height between them. It had been a very long time since they'd been able to head-butt anyone their own age in the face without the assistance of a stepladder, but they were still tiny objects of fear in the town, on the rare occasions they weren't in prison.

"Jimmy?" I said. "Johnny?"

"Johnny," said Johnny Gleeson. "Jimmy's gone for a slash. They let us out for Christmas." He leered up my skirt.

Juno and I had always had a soft spot for the Gleeson twins, partly because they were twins of roughly our own age and therefore somehow kindred spirits, and partly because they would steal things and give them to us when we were of an age to find that rather romantic. At ten they were giving us Toblerone, at fifteen they were giving us earrings, and on one memorable occasion they gave us a video recorder, which we made them promise to give back. They got caught giving it back and were given another go in reform school. We felt terribly guilty. They were one year older than us and neither had a half an ounce of sense. It was about the only thing they didn't have half an ounce of, mind you.

"Oh it's lovely to see you, Johnny," I said. I could never tell them apart, they were always wearing each other's clothes and they had identical prison tattoos on their knuckles.

"Where's Juno?" said Johnny.

"Over there, at the table by the pillar," I said. "Johnny, do you know Aengus Cleary?" but Johnny had already vanished among the dancing knees.

Aengus looked at me, faintly appalled. "You know Johnny Gleeson?" he said.

"Oh, Johnny and Jimmy are lovely," I said.

"They're fucking *psychopaths*," Aengus said.

I stopped dancing and began assembling furious words toward a reply.

"We'll agree to differ," he added in haste, hands raised in surrender.

I restarted dancing, but at a much slower pace than before, and wearing a pout that could have knocked out a pack mule. It took him till halfway through the Bryan Adams set to disarm the facial expression and bring me back up to speed. Then we realized what we were dancing to and returned to our seats.

"Oh, Joolz," said Juno, "you'll never guess." She was holding what could only be a Christmas present from the Gleeson twins.

"The Gleeson twins have given us a Christmas present," I guessed.

"Well, yes," said Juno. "They said we should open it together." She frowned. "In fact, they said we shouldn't open it here. . . . They wouldn't tell me why."

"Because it's stolen," said Aengus and I simultaneously.

I gave Aengus a startled look before realizing that he didn't actually know anything about our relationship with the Gleesons, he just knew a lot about the Gleesons.

"No," said Paul, "that's what Juno thought."

"Jimmy swore it wasn't stolen. Although I suppose buying it with their money is only one step away from theft, really. . . ."

"Ah sure, we ate the Toblerone," I said gaily, to the puzzlement of Paul and Aengus. "Open it."

Juno hesitated. The small, flat, extraordinarily badly wrapped present lay on the palm of her right hand. Juno lofted it slightly a few times as though weighing it. The wrinkled wrapping paper, striped with bands of crumpled Sellotape, much of it (by the fluff on it) sticky-side out, sat enigmatic on the palm, its white ribbon, oily with thumbprints, tied in no knot known to Scout, Cub, Guide, or Brownie.

Jimmy, or Johnny, whizzed by, seeming to my startled eye to pass beneath our table without stooping as he did so. I blinked.

"Hope you like your present," he Cagney'd from a mouth-corner as he orbited me. "Don't open it here."

And he was gone. They had always been shy.

30

Giggling like schoolgirls, Juno and I raced across the dance floor to the toilets to open our present. Giggling like a schoolgirl is never more *satisfying* than in the year after you've left school. The knowledge that no nun will ever again have the right to say "Stop that sniggering, girls" seems to triple the pleasure somehow. Actually that's probably just true for me, rather than a universal rule of iron, but for months after my Leaving Cert I couldn't pass a nun without giggling ostentatiously.

Anyway, still giggling, we entered the toilets. Every cubicle occupied, every mirror besieged. The air was beige with foundation as girls I half-recognised tried frantically to deal with the sweat damage sustained during "Summer of '69" in time to get back out for "(Everything I Do) I Do It for You." We were greeted distractedly by a couple of old classmates, one reapplying lipstick, one standing on one leg with a hairpin in her mouth.

"Mmm, m'no, mmm m'l't." She risked a smile at Juno, and the hairpin fell to the filthy floor. She glared at us. Obviously hadn't been a close friend.

The other girl gave a theatrical wave from about a yard away, and greeted us warmly without bothering to stop touching up her lipstick. "Juno! Just a . . . there . . . ? . . . yes . . . and Juliet, how are you?"

Juno told her. I couldn't be arsed, she'd never liked me anyway, and I'd always found her as brittle as our grandmother's right hip and as artificial as its replacement. She was one of the ones who'd acted in a school play and never bothered getting out of character. My memory refused to supply me with the part or the play. Julie bleeding Andrews in *The Sound of* bleeding *Music* no doubt. I bared my teeth as she passed me, and she chose to treat it as a smile. Sensible of her. I had a mad desire to snap at her like a dog and bark lustily to see how she'd react, but I fought the urge down. It was a bit too like our old school toilets in here for my liking. Connollys doormen wouldn't ask for I.D. if the entire cast of *The Great Escape* turned up with the contents of a kindergarten stuffed under their greatcoats, so a good half of the girls unsteadily swigging from their smuggled naggins of Smirnoff while they waited for a free sink to spew in were still attending our old school, and thus unpleasantly familiar to me. I felt nausea rather than nostalgia. It was a bit too recent for me to have romanticised it. Spots and braces. Homework. Dress codes. Ye gods. An unfortunate called Pam, whose mother was an alcoholic and who'd had to repeat fifth year, came out of one of the cubicles. She'd always liked me, God knows why.

"Hello Juliet" she said shyly. Her braces shone in the fluorescent light.

"Hello Pam" I said, and it was absolutely too much for me, I hauled Juno into the vacated cubicle and slammed the door on Pam's startled orthodentistry.

"Open the present, I'm going mad," I said.

Juno untied the Gordian bow and pulled off the paper. We stared.

"It's a *stamp* album," I said. "It's a . . . flipping stamp album. I think I'd have preferred Toblerone. And to think we made them give back that video recorder."

Juno giggled and said, "Well, it's the thought I suppose . . . and they *are* a bit dim . . . ," which was a charmingly uncharitable remark from her and made me think all the more highly of her.

She flicked the tiny stamp album open, and I said, "Well at least they've stuck in some stamps."

"Oh dear . . . ," said Juno, with the observational advantage of being slightly less drunk than me. "I don't think these are stamps . . . I think they're . . ."

31

"... Trips."

It is a tribute to the sheltered nature of my upbringing and to the sheer breadth of my ignorance that I did not know what my sister was talking about.

"Trips?" I said, vague images of foreign travel in my head.

"Trips, tabs, acid, LSD," said Juno impatiently, sounding like an unusually specialised drug dealer with a thesaurus, offering her wares. "*Drugs*, you idiot."

Now, I had read a lot about drugs, and I'd seen *Drugstore Cowboy* three times (for Matt Dillon) and *My Own Private Idaho* six times (three times for River Phoenix and another three times for Keanu Reeves, and I still couldn't decide . . . hey, I was young) and countless TV programs and news reports, but Tipperary and Galway were not exactly the drug capitals of Europe, and I'd never actually seen a Class A drug for real. I had the vague impression that "drugs" came in whacking great kilo bags of white powder with *Drugs* written on them.

"They're not *drugs*," I said. "They're *stamps*."

I peered at the stamp album again in the bad light of the toilet cubicle. It consisted of a number of small plastic pages, each with a number of small plastic pockets for stamps. In each pocket was a small paper square. I peered even closer. They were a bit small for stamps and all the same size. And they didn't have proper perforated edges. The first row of three were white with a blue globe on them. The next row of three were white with an Arabic squiggle on them. The next row of three were white with a cartoon explosion on them. I turned the page.

"Jeeeesus," I said.

"It's a selection box," said Juno. "They must be microdots." She pointed at three pockets, each containing what looked like a tiny ball of, well, snot.

I looked at Juno suspiciously. "How come you know so much about it?"

"Because I didn't skip religion when Sister Imelda showed us that video on drugs."

"Oh, yeah." I shrugged. I was still glad I'd missed it. Someone hammered on the cubicle door. "Fuck off," I said absently. I fished a square with a heart on it from its pocket and examined it. "Acid," I said. "Aciiiiiiiiieeeeeed . . ."

Now you will mock me for my innocence in what follows, but I blame it firmly on National Drug Prevention Day, the Press, the Guards, the Government, and Society. I had been bored to tears for years with the message that drugs, from hash and grass through acid and ecstasy to heroin and crack, were intrinsically evil and exceedingly dangerous. My experience had shown me that half the people I knew smoked marijuana in its various forms and that the message simply wasn't true. I'd smoked Satan's cigarettes a couple of times but couldn't inhale without coughing with embarrassing vigour for an impressive duration, so the full health-and-life-destroying joys of Reefer Madness had been denied to me. I'd drunk mushroom soup once at a party, too. It was meant to be magic-mushroom soup, but after two hours of sitting around watching MTV we reluctantly decided that our morning on the golf course had been wasted. So I didn't really, deep down, *believe* in drugs.

Also I was a little drunk.

So I popped it on my tongue, sucked it like a sweet, and swallowed.

"Oh, Juliet!" wailed Juno.

"What?" I said, a little belligerently. I was already starting to get the horrible feeling that I'd done something very silly. Juno had covered her face with her hands and was peeking at me through her fingers.

"You *absolute* idiot," she said in a muffled voice. "Oh God, *what* am I going to tell Paul?"

"I licked a stamp," I said facetiously. "When will it start to work?"

I was rather disappointed the world hadn't been transformed imme-diately, as though a switch had been thrown. I felt exactly the same. Boo.

"Shouldn't notice anything for half an hour. Forty-five minutes.

Something like that. And it lasts for *hours,* what are we going to do with you? Is it too late to get sick?"

"I'm *not* getting sick," I said firmly. I'd done that often enough here as an underage drinker. Reading the fine print of the Armitage Shanks logo at the back of the porcelain bowl. Indeed one of the reasons I'd cut my hair so short back in transition year was to keep my fringe out of Connollys toilets on Friday nights when I'd get sick. Not the main reason, but it had helped tilt the balance at the time. Juno, you will be unsurprised to learn, avoided throwing up on her fringe by avoiding throwing up. Hey, different strokes for different folks.

I snapped back the bolt. "C'mon, let's get ready to rumble. We gotta fight for our right to party. I'm Kool and the Gang, don't worry be happy."

She sighed, but she joined in the game. "Oh lord, please don't let me be misunderstood. Let's stick together, and every little thing's gonna be alright. Idiot."

"*Idiot's* not a song," I objected.

I swung open the cubicle door, and we walked past a cross-legged, bug-eyed girl with carrots in her fringe. I banged open the swing-door with a nonchalant hip, and we were back in the noise and the heat on the dance floor's edge. I gave a little whoop of giddy joy, and we plunged into the wash of hormones, deodorant, and dancers. The air was volatile with cheap perfume and the kind of aftershave that comes free with petrol, and is almost indistinguishable from it. As we emerged on the other side to rejoin Paul and Aengus, it briefly occurred to me that of all places and times to sharpen the senses and throw open the doors of perception, perhaps Connollys the night before Christmas Eve was not entirely the ideal choice, but I immediately put aside the unworthy thought. Why, Connollys was the best Tipperary had to offer, by God, and only the best was good enough for me tonight. I felt fabulously drunk, and the constant checking of my senses for signs of lysergic impact had the effect of making me feel super-alert, super-alive.

Juno was telling them what I'd just done. Paul was horrified, Aengus was amused but pretending to be horrified. I didn't give a damn.

"If you're not in, you can't win," I said.

Paul was really annoyed with me and began to say so. I stood up, walked onto the dance floor, and lost myself.

The night had begun.

32

Suno and Aengus calmed Paul down, but I didn't care about that either. I danced with absentminded fury in the heart of the crowd to half-forgotten songs half-remembered from my brother's ancient record collection.

I'd spent most of my life in Tipperary, locked in my own head, feeling like a visitor to a place where everybody else belonged. It was in Galway that I felt at home and felt it was safe to relax, that no one would come smashing vindictively into my life if I pulled back the bolts and let in a little light and air. It had been so *lonely* in Tipperary, feeling like an observer, living in my mind, feeding it books that showed me a world that felt so much more real than my own. I looked around me at the town I'd been born in, and it seemed so thin, so poor a version of the world. It made me sad in the way that the cheap imitations of good toys almost made me cry when I saw them piled high in the Connollys Super-Store toy department coming up to Christmas every year. I know this sounds pathetic and stupid, but the thought that kids who wanted Sindy or Lego, or World Wrestling Federation figures or Power Rangers, or whatever was popular that year, were going to wake up on Christmas morning and run down to open their presents and find sad, cheap, bad imitations of the present they'd dreamed of for months, that their parents had bought because they couldn't afford the real thing, or because they didn't know the difference, its enormous, heartbreaking *importance*, the absolute perfection of what you truly wanted and the desolation of unwrapping a fake that didn't move right, didn't look right, that was nothing, worse than nothing . . . the thought of these other kids with their wrong presents as useless as the stuff they came wrapped in, hiding their huge, gulping disappointment, or letting it show and tearing at their parents' hearts . . . to be honest I *did* cry, every year.

It began to prey on my mind coming up to Christmas each year of my childhood, those great piles of cheap imitations, bad copies, with their deliberately misleading names. I would cry at night. I even cried in the aisles of the toy department itself a couple of times, feeling like a perfect fool, wiping my eyes on my coat sleeve and trying to pretend I had a cold. But I think, now, that what I was crying for (and this is just amateur psychology at its worst, I have no way of proving this, it just feels to me to be true) wasn't really the toys and the other kids. It was my life, and me. My life was somehow tangled up in those toys, lived in the huge shadow of the special-offer stacks. I'd been given the wrong life, in the wrong town, and there was nothing I could do about it, and every single day of my life I had to hide my disappointment, because it wasn't my parents' fault, they thought I was happy here, they came from here, it was home, wasn't it? But to me my home felt cheap and wrong, and my life felt like an imitation of a real life, and every Christmas I'd dream I was somewhere else, somewhere more real than this, living my real life.

And I would wake up just torn apart, in a thin, poor town that I hated. Cattle roaring from the abattoir. Connollys owning the town. A town without a river through it. Oh Christmas, I hated you.

And as I danced, furiously alone, in Connollys on the night before Christmas Eve, I was back in my head, locked in, sobbing silently about nothing, with no reason for it and no outward sign (because, Christ, you don't let them see that you're wounded). Galway had almost ceased to exist, even as a memory. I felt like I had been here forever and I'd be here forever and I'd die here if I ever died. I felt as if I'd dreamed the rest of the world. That I'd just woken up, and Galway had been a dream. All that existed was this moment in this town. Oh, this fucking town. I was in absolute, frozen despair inside as I danced and danced and danced.

Juno came over and danced with me for a while and asked if I was OK and eventually went away again. The songs were taking forever to turn into other songs. I had no idea how long I'd been dancing. I looked at my watch. The song went on forever. Eventually I looked at my watch again. Less than a minute had passed. The chorus came around again, and I felt a shivery feeling that I'd heard it too often, that it had come around too often, that it should be over, but I'd heard it a million times before, when I was younger, and it had always ended, so it would be OK this time too. But I always heard it again, didn't I? I'd heard it a million times when I was young, and I was hearing it now and it hadn't ended. It wouldn't end.

My mind was exploding with thoughts that were moving too fast, overlapping, entangled, my mind felt shivery, I was thinking too much, it was fine. I looked at my watch again. Oh God, no time was passing. No, the second hand was moving, I could see it moving, but Christ it was slow, how could I ever get *out* of here if time moved so *slowly*, how could this night ever *end*, time had always moved faster than this hadn't it, I'd never noticed time pass so slowly, could it be slower now? It *felt* slower so it was slower, I had to trust what I felt what else have you, you have nothing, what you feel is real or nothing is but if you are mad what you feel isn't real but how can you know because you can't get outside yourself to see if what you feel is really real oh this is a new song oh thank Christ that song is over oh thank Christ I won't look at my watch but if I don't look at my watch how can I know if time is moving fast enough to ever, ever let me out of here but looking at my watch won't *help* oh God this must be the acid it has to be I don't normally feel like this do I no oh Jesus I want to go home

33

I began to try to walk back to the table. Light like liquid flooded heavily amongst the dancers so that several times I had to stop, unsure whether I could walk through the thick, viscous beams of red and orange. When a strobe came on, I had to stop again and wait for it to end. The world looked like the inside of a madman's head. Arms and faces froze and disappeared and reappeared elsewhere, still frozen, but in new positions, with new expressions. Very very fast things were happening very very slowly and I felt a drowning sense that I had quite, quite lost my hold on time, that time had abandoned me and I could never be fixed now, that I had made a mistake that could never be fixed or made right. A big tear slowly crawled down my cheek and touched the corner of my lip and disappeared across my mouth in a burst of salt.

The tear trail left a cool line down my cheek as it evaporated.

The strobe stopped and I walked on.

Eventually I reached the table.

"I want to go home," I said numbly to Juno.

34

Outside, in the car park, Paul decided he wanted chips. He'd left with us to look after us on the walk home, and he'd helped me into my coat when I'd had difficulty finding the armholes, but he was still pissed off with me, and he was damned if I'd rob him of the pleasures of the chip queue. I didn't mind waiting, once I was away from the heat and noise and light. Out here it was cool, quiet, dark. A pleasant, fine drizzle prickled on my face. I'd retreated so far into myself by now that I didn't really feel connected to what I saw and heard at all. I'd been so over-loaded in the chaos of trying to leave the building, by the impossible in-tricacies of answering the questions of Aengus and Juno and Paul, of stripping their voices out of the noise and taking the words out of their voices and squeezing the meaning out of their words and making some sense of the meaning of the words in the voices from the noise . . . and then trying to reply . . . that I had now shut down completely. I just heard and saw, without any attempt at comprehension.

Which was rather a pity, because the camera of my mind was run-ning on quite an interesting scene. If you were an anthropologist. Or a zookeeper. Or a prison governor with some spare beds.

It was by now coming up to chucking-out time; you could tell be-cause people were coming out to chuck up. My distress had cut our evening short, but not by much. Connollys Illegal Chip-Van was already busy serving the first wave of drunken clubbers, the smart ones who'd left early to beat the queue. They were all standing round in the rain feel-ing smug, in a huge queue. Actually, to pick nits for a moment (and you could pick nits all night in the Connollys Chip-Van queue) it wasn't really a queue at all. It was a kind of seething, low-key riot designed to deliver the minimum number of people to the van counter with the max-imum discomfort, inefficiency, and violence. "Queuing" was considered an activity fit only for Brits and homosexuals. And Kilkenny hurlers. And Dubliners in general. (These categories were not rigorously exclusive. All Brits were homosexuals. Most Dubliners were Brits. Kilkenny hurlers weren't Brits, but they might as well be, shaggin' homos. That was never a goal. We was robbed.)

In a peculiar kind of way, standing in the rain in the dark of the car park staring at the queue with my brain in mush was oddly soothing. I'd done this so often before. This was a familiar, reassuring childhood scene of just the sort to calm my acid-drenched mind. There was little Benny Reynolds leaning over casually to puke on the feet of the person beside him, his cousin Jacinta, who was too drunk to notice. Rumour had it that

Benny was the father of Jacinta's child, but then rumour had it that I was a lesbian and that Juno had gone to England for an abortion when she was fifteen. (She'd gone to the Gaelteacht for a fortnight to learn Irish from nuns, along with half her class. But why spoil a good story?)

There was a Toohy picking a fight with a Sheehy over a sachet of tomato sauce. The Sheehy wouldn't give him any of his, or had squirted too much on, one or the other. The Toohy had knocked the Sheehy's chips flying anyhow, and now some older Toohys and Sheehys were intervening with confused shouts.

"We don't want any fucking trouble, now," said Billy Sheehy, smacking Sean Toohy in the face.

"Hold me back, lads, hold me back, I'll feckin' kill him," shrieked the offended Toohy, throwing himself backward into the arms of a couple of his brothers. It was a ritual as old as time, and as soothing as a cool hand on my brow. It *was* a cool hand on my brow. Juno, checking I hadn't overheated while dancing. I had the peculiar sensation of her hand melting into my head, but Juno didn't seem to notice anything strange and took her hand away, satisfied.

"R U O K? Jew, Lee, Et? Are you OK?"

I laboriously deciphered her question and risked a nod in reply. The drizzle was falling sideways, which was worrying me a little, but I had a vague idea which I was trying to pin down than this was somehow due to the triumph of wind rather than the failure of gravity and that I had no need for concern. Then people started to fall sideways, and I moaned in horror before I made the back-connections necessary to interpret what I'd seen, which was a lot of people being knocked over by a small fight sprawling into them.

I closed my eyes again, and got way, way lost in the electric impacts of a billion specks of drizzle on the tight skin of my face.

julian gough

35

The tap on my arm woke me back into my body. I had been some-place very, very far away, almost without ego, spread thin across a great dark space. The violence of sight when I opened my eyes frightened me. Colour and movement and noise (and I was mixing them all up by now, the light seemed to be causing the noises that I'd ceased to notice when I'd closed my eyes).

"C'mon, we're moving," said . . . I deciphered the mass of features which sat without perspective in front of me, moving under light till sound came out . . . Paul. My brother.

We moved.

Information was arriving very late.

My mind was lagging half a footstep behind what was happening; perceptions were coming in, felt early but recognised late, and now cause and effect began to cross over. I felt the pavement suck at and re-ject my feet, again and again. We got to the start of the main street and in a peculiarly distanced, numb despair I stopped to try to count the strands of coloured bulbs that crossed it. If I could only get the right an-swer, the answer that I knew to be right, it would give me a fingertip ledge to cling to, a tiny proof of the existence of an objective world out-side of my collapsing mind, and the knowledge that there was still an ob-jective world out there would mean I had a fragile, impossible hope of returning to it somehow, somewhere. So it became very important to me.

And I couldn't do it. I couldn't add. Nothing would connect and stay connected. My thoughts were a babble to myself. Word and number were blurred, chopped into fragments so small they failed to form units of meaning, so charged they repulsed other fragments or snapped tight to them with no regard for meaning or truth, or with no regard for regard or regard for with or or. Thoughts spiralled out and broke apart or spiralled in tighter and tighter and vanished. The pitch of my terror grew as I tried to count the strands of light but I'd lost the words for the numbers and the words for the words and the lights were finally and forever uncountable and above me forever and I couldn't find that tiny ledge to hold me and I fell up into the light forever.

Johnny Gleeson said, "Is she alright?"

I am to some extent now depending on what Juno told me later, because though I remember every detail of the night very clearly, I remember much of it through the crystal filter of powerful acid, as sound and symbol rather than word and deed.

I stood staring up at the Christmas lights, blurred with the acid and hard, salty tears, as Juno told Johnny that no, I wasn't alright. Johnny asked her what I'd taken, brushing off Paul and Aengus who both seemed in a mood to do him injury on my behalf. Jimmy materialised to back up his brother.

Even in Juno's recollection Jimmy seems to have shimmered into existence rather than walked up to her. The drizzle made everything inconstant and tentative. Juno described the picture on the tab I had taken.

"The red one or the other one?"

The red one.

"Oh, that sheet, I don't know what they did. Half of it did nothing, we had a lot of complaints. It's not even, d'you see, not at all, at all. Very unreliable, we don't deal with them fellows at all anymore. Mad London bastards. It's all Dutch we stock now. The lads in the 'Dam have the quality control."

Johnny talked on as Jimmy reached up to grab my chin and pull my head down to his level. His eyes seemed to have a pulse in them, and the pupils seemed to shudder, to snap small and then expand slowly, and I couldn't tell if that was an effect of the drug I was on or an effect of the drug he was on.

"Oh Juliet, are you hurting?" he crooned.

"The lights," I sobbed. "Make the lights go away," and I pulled my head back up to look at the hurting lights that barred me from the sweet oblivion of the dark and the silence that lay beyond them. They burned me through my tears, as uncountable as stars.

Jimmy followed my gaze, and as he put his hand on my hand I felt *understood* somehow. No less ruined, but comforted by the sure and certain knowledge that Jimmy could see what I saw.

And then he was gone again, grabbing Johnny by the shoulder, shouting "I'll fix it," as they disappeared into the drizzle.

And then they reappeared after a million years of tears, and Aengus and Paul and Juno looked up from their discussion of what the fuck to do with me because I wouldn't bring my eyes down from the lights and I wouldn't stop crying.

Nobody recognised them right away. They were driving an E. S. B. maintenance lorry.

It roared with clashing gears out of Barrack Street and swerved to a halt at the top of O'Connell Street, twenty-three uncountable strands of light away. The engine bellowed again and then calmed to a mutter. Slowly the inspection platform rose above the cab like a great metal cobra's head, on its enormous hydraulic arm. The joint straightened till the platform towered above the street and the lights and the world. I saw it disappear above the foreshortened sheet of lines of light, and I prayed from the heart of my terror for something I couldn't name.

The engine rose to the pitch of my terror and suddenly lurched with a howl towards me and entered the realm of light. And the great metal arm bent the first strand of light into a tight, astonished V that snapped with a noise that felt to me, as the line of light vanished, like a crisp explosion of pure silence in the heart of the great roar of light that still poured on me from the uncountable stars of light that made up the uncountable strands. And the next strand bent to a faster V and was gone, and the next. And the roar of the engine grew closer and greater as it extinguished the roar of the light until the lorry tore through the powerlines that crossed the street fifty yards from us and in a great explosion of light and sound the Gleeson twins ripped every star from the sky. The town went black and the streetlights went out. The last of the strands were torn down in darkness. Tiny sparks flared in the gutter from the severed powerlines, and then even they died.

Sirens began to go off and emergency lights flickered on in a few windows. But the huge sky above me was black and stripped of its great strands of torturing stars.

The E. S. B. lorry braked hard in the darkness behind us. Jimmy and Johnny jumped down from the cab and ran back to join us.

"I fixed it," said Jimmy to all of us, but only I understood what he meant. "You'll be alright now," he said to me, and touched my hand again.

Then they were gone, and I was left staring up into the night as slowly the true, tiny stars emerged here and there in the gaps in the low clouds that moved low and fast over the dark town. The drizzle swirled and cleared, and for a moment I could see the moon racing across a gap in the clouds.

I could go home now. I felt everything ease and soften. I would be alright. Twenty-three, I thought. Twenty-three strands. Jimmy had cut through the knot of my problem. I would never have to count them now. Never have to count them again. Things could be changed. I wasn't doomed to repeat and repeat and repeat till I died.

I was happy as we began to walk home then in the strange, siren-filled dark. My new tears, as I walked with Juno holding my hand and with Paul's arm in mine, weren't for me at all, or not directly. They were for the knowledge that I had gained as I had looked up into the blackness after the veil of light had been torn from the face of the night.

36

I woke up with my head between somebody's legs. On either side, a warm thigh pressed against my cheek. My mouth felt filled with molten metal. Everything was warm and dark, I didn't know which way was up, and I spasmed in fright.

It woke Juno up. "What are you doing down there?" she blurred sleepily. A grey triangle of light appeared far above me. I was in bed. I was in bed with Juno. I was in bed with Juno at home, in my old bedroom, on my side, curled up halfway down the bed, facing Juno, on her side.

Juno peered beneath the duvet at me. "Come up, you'll smother." The ghost of her face floated in the pale cave of moonlight. Shapes and distances reversed and rereversed. She was in a cup of light, I was in an infinite darkness. Now I was in a pool of darkness, she was in an infinite light.

I closed my eyes and pressed my face back between her thighs. "It's nice here," I said, muffled. So to speak.

"I thought you might want company tonight," said Juno.

"Yes," I said. "Stay, stay tonight." I held her closer to me, drew my knees up till they touched her warm feet. She let out a harsh breath.

"Careful . . . I did my ankle carrying you," said Juno. "Turned it."

"Sorry," I said. "Sorry." I couldn't remember. Was that normal?

"Not your fault."

"Sorry." I opened my eyes and moved. Memory. I remembered. "The kerb," I said.

"Sleep," said Juno. The triangle shrank and closed. You've lost it completely Juliet, said a calm voice. Me. My self. I said that, to my self. So my self's back. And my self says I've lost it completely. . . . Well, that's good. If I know I've lost it completely. If I'm here to know I've lost it. Then I can find it in the morning.

Juno's nightdress had ridden up, and I rested my forehead on the tender cushion of what we had once learned in biology to call the mons veneris. The crisp hairs shifted against one another under the weight of my head with a tiny crackling noise that I could hear direct through the bones of my skull, a sound like the world's smallest chips going into the world's smallest deep-fat frier. I swallowed, but my mouth still tasted like licked aluminium. Juno's smell was rich and strange, all warm air, spicy, with a tang of vinegar that made me fill and swell with emotion, that made me love her so much, I don't know why. "Oh, Juno," I said. "Yes?" she said. My heart filled my mouth so I couldn't speak.

"I have to piss," I said.

37

In the bathroom I looked into the mirror.

"Who the fuck is that?" I said. My voice was dry and crackly. My ghost mouthed back at me, and smiled. I smiled back. My ghost's eyes looked huge and exhausted. My eyes swam and lost focus trying to look into hers. I closed one eye, and studied my ghost's huge black pupil and disturbingly complicated iris, and the web of red threads running through the white, like a roadmap drawn with a fine red pen on a boiled egg. My second eyelid slid closed, and I felt muscles relax into rest all over my face. In darkness I slowly touched my forehead to the cold glass. So this is me, I thought.

Later. When I sat on the cold seat, I paused. Closed my eyes again. It was too exquisite. My bladder was so full I was almost afraid to start. It was like a basketball. I had a moment of fear that I was still in bed, opened my eyes, had a moment of fear I was still wearing my clothes, looked down. No, I was naked, it was safe. I relaxed, and the sound of the splashing water and the feeling of utter abandoned bliss, of giving up, the release of tension, was almost mystical. This is what the after-life must be like, I thought. The sound of running water, and perfect peace.

38

"Really?" I said, and supped deep of black tea as our mother rattled on.

"The Allied Irish Bank they were after, of course, they'd stolen a lorry with one of them platforms on it from the E. S. B. yard on the Dublin Road, obviously a well-planned affair, they knew exactly what they were after. . . . Is that too hot for you, love?"

I nodded, added milk, and gulped so much tea half of it ended up on the pillow. I busied myself mopping with Kleenex, face averted. I caught Juno's eye. She buried her face in the other pillow.

"Juno, are you in pain?"

"No, no. Go on," said Juno through the pillow.

"Anyway, Guard Toohy says the plan was obviously to cut the wires to the alarm and break in the upstairs windows because they've no bars on them and get in that way. All very clever, fellas down from Dublin he expects, hardened criminals. Or they might have been from Limerick, but Guard Toohy reckons it had all the hallmarks of a Dublin gang." I tangled my toes delightedly with the toes of Juno's good foot. "They must have had a getaway car parked nearby, because there wasn't a sign of them by the time the guards arrived."

Which was probably half an hour after the lights had gone off. I knew Guard Toohy, and Guard O'Meara, and Guard Gill. Anything more dangerous than double-parking and they'd hide in the station till they were sure it was safely over.

"They seem to have put up the lift, the platform you know, too early though. Knocked all the Christmas lights, I went down to have a look. It's an awful mess, glass everywhere. A child could get hurt." Juno twitched beside me. "The Council sent Sean Hickey down to clear it up with his cart, but sure his back's been out since Halloween, he only got half it cleared before he had to go to casualty to get it set right again. And on Christmas Eve. That man shouldn't touch a brush in his condition, and the size of him, the poor eejit, with that big awkward cart, it's no wonder." I could feel it building up. Juno had begun to shudder. "The shops swept the pavements, most of them, but the gutters are full of bits of lightbulbs. The cars are afraid to park. Thank God they didn't get into the bank, the lorry's still sitting outside it, for forensics, but of course every gurrier in town's been swinging out of it since morning, they'll be arresting every child in the park if they go by the forensics on that. Little Timmy Sheehy was sitting in it banging the horn when I went by, and sure they'd stolen all the police tape by lunchtime and fecked two of the bollards up onto the low roof behind Londis." She frowned at this vision of the darkness in the heart of man. "Right up onto it. Guard O'Meara had to get a ladder."

We exploded.

"Well if you're going to laugh . . ." Our mother picked up the tea tray and teapot and turned to go.

"Sorry . . . sorry," we sobbed helplessly.

"I'm glad you find it so amusing." She disappeared down the stairs, swinging the door shut loudly behind her with her heel.

"Sorry, Mum!"

"And tape *The Simpsons!*"

Juno's hair covered my face as we rolled around the bed, hugging each other and snorting helplessly into each other's ears. We calmed

down. Then Juno gave a little snort, and I roared, and we laughed ourselves out of bed.

"Ow, fff . . . fff . . . feck, my ankle," said Juno as we lay on the floor
wrapped tightly together in duvet.

"Sorry," I said.

"It's OK," said Juno.

"I love you," I said.

"I know . . . I'm sorry," said Juno.

"For what?"

"For not . . . last night, I don't know," she laughed. "I don't know. I
thought you wanted me to say sorry for something. You said you loved me
like you were angry with me."

"No," I said. "Not you. Just . . . angry." It's . . . at the world, I
thought, I'm angry at the world. It was too much, the world was, last
night. I wasn't enough, on my own. I was just me without my defences,
and it wasn't enough. I was crushed. . . .

"Juliet . . . what are you thinking?"

"Nothing."

Juno was shaking her head, making her hair brush against my cheek
and nose. It annoyed me, I turned my head away.

"That's not true, Juju. What were you thinking?"

"Nothing." I was shaking for some reason.

Juno sighed. "I understand, Juju"

"No you don't, everything's perfect, you've got your boyfriend and
your exams, your notes make sense, you have a highlighter. . . ." Juno
started laughing. "You know what I mean!"

"I'll buy you a highlighter."

"You know what I mean."

"I'll give you my highlighter."

"You know what I mean."

We were tied too tightly together by the duvet for me to be able to hit
her properly, but I hit her, and she stared at me.

"You're not joking," she said.

"Of course I'm not joking. You saying you understand me, don't say that, you don't."

"I do. We're the same, Juju."

"Well I don't understand you so we're not the same then are we."

Our faces were up against each other. I could feel her breath, taste it. It tasted of mint. She'd gotten up in the morning and hopped to the bathroom and brushed her teeth.

"It's easy for you," I said. "It's easy."

"This is . . . I don't understand what you're saying," said Juno, wriggling to loosen the duvet, to get further away from me, wincing as her ankle twisted in the tight shroud.

I looked into her face, and it was nothing like a mirror. Was she mocking me? "I always thought you were perfect," I said. "But you're not."

"Juju, that's crazy, of course I'm not perfect. I never said I was."

"But I thought you were. Everything you said, and . . . everything. The soap you bought. The way you could talk to boys."

"Oh, Juju, no . . ."

"You had opinions about everything, these really quiet, confident opinions, and I just had chaos and noise in my head."

"Oh, honey, I had too, I have too. I didn't know."

"And you didn't save me."

"When?"

"Last night. You didn't understand me at all."

"Baby Juju, I never did."

"I thought you did, you just said you did. I thought you understood everything, but you just weren't telling me."

"I don't understand anything. Nobody does. But you don't have to. You get up in the morning and get on with it."

"You get life, and I don't."

"That's not it at all. . . . Maybe I just trust the world a little more, that's all. But that's all. That's all."

I looked into the complicated mirror of her face, and we smiled together.

"Did we just fight?" I said.

"I think we sort of did," said Juno.

"Cool," I said. Life changes. "Cool."

39

We went to midnight mass. Not the modern, McMidnight, convenience mass at eight P.M. on Christmas Eve, but the real one, starting at the stroke of midnight. When we were very young, midnight mass meant being woken up gently and carried to the car, when we still had a car, and driven half-asleep the short distance to the church, and carried inside with our jumpers and coats on over our nightclothes, with Paul trying to make us laugh, fidgeting and giggling and making faces at us as Juno and I held each other's hand and stared solemnly back at him, too in awe of the lateness of the hour and the seriousness of so huge a crowd whispering and shuffling to even smile at our brother. It was so unlike an ordinary mass, more like a great secret meeting of the persecuted early Church. The unaccustomed smell of incense shocked and thrilled me. The great crib with its child-God and animals and kings and straw was such a potent mixture of toyshop and Revelation that it could bring me literally to my knees, dragging Juno down with me. When the mass had ended, I would walk reverently toward the tableau in its side aisle, with its fairy lights illuminating the tiny cardboard houses of Bethlehem in the diorama that stretched out behind the papier-mâché cave, itself lit with a huge bulb that, now that I think about it, must have been an appalling fire risk touching the roof of a paper cave floored with straw. I'd kneel in front of it, tugging down Juno, and stare at the baby in the crib till our father got bored and urged us home.

Walking to church in the rain as a sort-of grownup who didn't even live at home anymore wasn't quite the same, but a little awe tingled the back of my neck as I helped Juno up the broad steps and through the great oak doors, flung wide to embrace us all, through the inner doors and into the huge nave with its crammed, murmurous pews under the distant wooden vault, ribbed like a tremendous longship mysteriously tipped and hoist high above us to provide a Viking roof on a Catholic church. All us fallen sailors, oblivious to the looming hulk above. Only children ever looked up at the roof, I'd noticed that years ago. And me.

My sense of awe and wonder dissipated somewhat, or at least changed direction and fixed on a new source, as we found our seats and I began listening in to the murmured conversations all around me that preceded the priest's appearance.

That the shenanigans of the night before, which had made a shambles of O'Connell Street and left the town without electricity till the middle of the morning, were the consequences of a botched bank raid by Dublin criminals was by now undisputed truth. It was only the surrounding details that still held the status of rumour, and even these were beginning to settle down nicely. There was general agreement on the matter of masks (check) and guns (check). The issue of getaway vehicles had not yet been resolved, though a strong majority favoured two BMWs ("Stolen in Dublin, of course. I'd never take the car to Dublin these days. The train's as handy, and for the Christmas wouldn't you spend the day trying to find a place to park. And isn't it pure gangsters run the car parks, the price of them, and security cameras my arse, begging your pardon, sure it's watching videos they'd be, while some scut of a ten-year-old's fecking your tape machine and maybe going back to break off the aerial if they don't approve of your taste in music. Sure they'd slash your tyres for leaving Daniel O'Donnell on the dashboard, them boys. 'Tis all rap, and the grunge.")

An altar boy emerged from the vestry, swinging the thurible. Clouds of incense mingled with the steam rising from the damp congregation. Outside, rain flogged the saints on the tall, narrow, stained-glass windows that gave onto the dark on our side of the church. You could hear it slap hard against the glass in gusts. I could feel the cold as the glass sucked the heat from the aisle beside me.

("They were seen driving through Birr, you know." *"Really?"* "Oh yes, no regard for the lights, at a terrible speed.")

I developed quite a cough, and sadly missed some of what the couple behind me were saying.

(". . . burnt out in the Curragh. A rogue IRA unit they say." "Really?")

The priest walked to the altar.

"Hrumph . . . ah . . . yes . . . hrmmm," he said, and stilled the secular tongue.

Lulled by the priest's voice and soothed by the richly satisfying blend of candle and electric light softened through incense smoke, I fell asleep against Juno's arm.

40

"Well isn't this fierce Dickensian altogether," said my father, hoisting the knife above the turkey at the head of the table and surveying the family with a sardonic eye. It wasn't exactly a remark you could reply to, so I kept my head down. We'd already had a row about who'd won the contents of the Christmas cracker we'd pulled, and I was pretty sure he was aiming his remarks at me, but I said nothing. A horrible, painful suspicion was growing within me that I'd made a total fool of myself over the cracker incident, and I was too busy avoiding acknowledging that suspicion to myself to risk opening another unwinnable front in our long war. The tiny, malformed purple plastic ape that I had screamed to get sat on my side plate in mute, one-armed reproach. I felt like pulling my pink paper hat down over my eyes and sliding under the table.

"Oh do they know it's Christmas time at all," sang my father as he carved.

Another dig at me that I couldn't respond to without being put in the wrong. He'd give me a hurt look and nudge my mother as if to say, "Look what I have to put up with," and I'd be left storming at nothing. My blood fizzed with fury, and I felt my face go hot. *Bloody* plastic *bloody* gorilla. I'd started fighting for it before I'd even seen what it was, and then I couldn't go back. Oh, God. He'd picked it up from behind his chair, and he must have been so *delighted* to see what a piece of crap it was. I'd felt my heart shrink as I saw it, as he dangled it between finger and thumb by its solitary arm. "Oh, I like monkeys," he'd said, which wasn't even *true*.

I was in danger of flaring again and I couldn't afford to, so I closed my eyes and ground my teeth as he hummed, "Spread a little happiness. . . ." Oh, *Jesus*.

But *I'd* got the big end of the cracker. It wasn't *about* what was in it, it was the principle of the thing, it wasn't *fair*. Just because it jumped out and bounced off his side of the table . . . My blood bubbled and boiled like lemonade in a wok.

"Do you want some more potatoes, love?" said my mother.

"*No,*" I snapped. Oh shit, that wasn't clever. I tried to retreat, but I couldn't make the words come out. And here we go.

"Don't speak to your mother in that tone of voice, young lady."

Oh I couldn't *believe* it. Young fucking *lady*. Who'd he borrow *that* from?

"Well? Are you going to apologise to your mother?"

Oh shit oh shit oh shit totally outmanoeuvred, apologise to my *mother*, as though *that* was what it was all about oh how did he do this?

"What's it to do with you?" Oh fuck what a stupid thing to say, it wasn't even witty, why did I say that, and here he comes.

"I am your *father*, girl, whether you like it or not, and you will not talk to your mother or me in that tone of voice while you are under my roof"—as though he'd built the fucking roof himself—"so I want you to apologise to your mother *now*."

I opened my mouth and I said the first thing that came into my head. And the second. And the third. The first thing that came into my head was an astonishingly awful thing to say to my father. But it wasn't as bad as the second. The third was unforgivable. In fact I managed to go well past unforgivable before I stopped, and what kept me from stopping was knowing that somehow he'd started all this, he'd goaded and provoked all this, but it didn't make me feel any less sick at myself after I'd stopped.

I ran to my room and locked myself in. Cried.

After a while I looked up at Christ on the cross.

"Happy *fucking* birthday."

PART III

Galway

41

Three days later, Juno wanted to get back to Galway to meet Michael, and I went with her.

The country was white with frost right to the edge of the bay. We'd forgotten that there was hardly any fuel for the stove, so we used up everything the first day back and then Juno basically retreated to bed with Michael for a couple of days, leaving me to fend for myself. For some reason (for the masochistic romance of it, because it made me feel like a brave, doomed babushka scrabbling to survive in a besieged Stalingrad), I didn't buy coal and briquettes and have them delivered. Instead, I wandered the streets aimlessly at all hours with a big grubby coal sack and filled it with scraps of wood from the skips, piles of discarded newspapers, and offcuts from the lumberyard further along the docks, and dragged all this back home and up the stairs to create weird, messy fires, with bits of planks I hadn't been able to snap short enough sticking out of the open door of the stove, bringing flames out into the room. I'd stare into the stove for hours, my face roasting, and I'd feed it scraps as though it were a sick animal I was coaxing to health. I never tired of the fire. I sat by it for company, not heat. Copper staples in bits of broken packing case stained the flames green and blue. I'd put on music so I couldn't hear Juno and Michael, but the albums would end, and I wouldn't always bother turning the tape over. A lot of the time they just seemed to be talking quietly, with lots of silences. Friendly silences.

I fed the fire. When I got too hot I would sometimes get up and walk to the window where my face would cool as I watched the winter harbour, and my clothes would leak their heat away till they were comfortable again against my skin.

We didn't do anything special for the new year. Well, that's a little disingenuous. I didn't do anything special for the new year, but I'm pretty sure Juno and Michael did because I could hear them.

42

A couple of days into the new year, Conrad and Dominic clattered up the stairs and burst in, both full of Christmas spirit, each waving a bottle sloshing with more Christmas spirit.

"Oh, hi," said Juno.

"What's that?" I said.

"Jameson," said Conrad, kissing Juno on the cheek.

"Black Bush," said Dominic, leering at my crotch.

"Sit down and I'll make you coffee," said Juno.

"No!" said Conrad in horror. "Never mix your drinks."

"Have you glasses," asked Dominic, "and we'll celebrate."

"Celebrate what?" I said.

Conrad counted on his fingers. "Losing the insurance, losing the Aula, half the cast leaving, so we're cancelling the Coward play. . . ."

"That *fucking stupid* Coward play," Dominic corrected Conrad. They were both quite astonishingly drunk.

"Oh, no," said Juno.

"We're doing *Endgame* instead," said Dominic. "And I want you to play Clov."

Juno didn't know what to say, so I said something. "What's *Endgame*?" I said, and bit my tongue, for my inanity, for showing my ignorance, for everything. Dominic took it in his stride that I hadn't even heard of it, not a flicker. I was relieved and insulted.

"Play by Beckett. Only four people, which is good, and two of them in dustbins."

"A tragedy exploring the meaningless horror of existence," said Conrad.

"Comic classic. Funny as fuck," said Dominic.

"Ah, you'd laugh at Dostoyevsky," said Conrad, disgusted.

"The Russian Spike Milligan," said Dominic.

Juno had been thinking. "I can't do it, Dominic."

It took them nearly half an hour to talk her into it, but they finally did. Relief, delight, celebration. We drank to Juno's health. We drank to the repose of Beckett's soul. We drank to the success of *Endgame*. The conversation drifted on a mellow tide of whiskey till I asked a somewhat insensitive question.

"So what are *your* plays about, Conrad? I've never seen them."

Dominic and Conrad both looked at me like I'd farted "God Save the Queen" at an IRA funeral.

"Love," said Conrad eventually.

"Ah, bollocks," said Dominic.

"Love," said Conrad.

"Sexual repression. In a kitchen," said Dominic.

"Your first play's very good, I've read it," said Juno.

"Really?" said Conrad, with a relief and gratitude that was almost painful to watch. His face opened out and his shoulders rose, like sped-up footage of a desert plant blooming in a sudden shower of rain. "No one reads them. . . . No one performs them. I'm a dead man."

"There's copies in the library."

"Copies in the library . . . yes. But no one takes them out. I've checked."

"I read all of them, in the library. *The Living* is really good."

"You think so? You think so?"

I couldn't bear to look at him, it was too sad. Does everyone feel broken? I looked at Juno, smiling and talking, her voice so kind. Just like a human being. Just like a human being.

So unlike me. I could see what they saw.

"Pity," said Dominic conversationally, "that all your other stuff is shite."

Conrad suddenly seemed on the verge of tears, or anger, his throat working. Juno reached out to touch his hand.

Conrad pushed back his chair and stood up.

"Bathroom," he said thickly, and walked straight into Juno's room, slamming the door behind him. The door handle fell off.

Juno glared at Dominic and went to the shut door. "Conrad, you idiot," she said to the door. There were confused noises inside, then silence. Juno tried to open the door, but the spindle was attached to the far handle, which had come away on the inside in Conrad's hand. "Conrad!" No reply. A muffled banging noise, then silence again.

Dominic came over to help. "Connie," he said. Silence. Dominic half-leaned over, said "Whoa there," and stood back up. "Perhaps you could have a look, Juno," he said.

Juno dropped to her knees and looked. "Handle's gone," she said. "Can't see anything . . . no."

Dominic gave the door another push.

"We could pop the lock," I said. Juno turned and gave me a startled look. Dominic did the same. I laughed. He raised an eyebrow, and I laughed again. The tableau looked so absurd: Juno on her knees in front of Dominic, the two with their mouths open.

"Like in the movies," I explained, "with a credit card."

"We don't have a credit card," said Juno.

"Or a call card," I said.

"I've a credit card," said Dominic. "Well, a half one . . ." He tried to find it, farted suddenly, looked thoughtful, and subsided. There was an expired call card with a Santa Claus on it on the living room table. I got it. Dominic, looking even more thoughtful, walked with tense buttocks to the bathroom. I got to work with the card. It was easy. The tilting, ancient house had gaps between doors and frames nearly big enough to stick a finger in. The call card slid the curved metal latch back into the door, and I swung the door in. Juno and I stepped inside. Conrad wasn't there.

The window was open. Juno walked over to it, looked out, looked down. I joined her, did likewise. There he was, lying facedown on the edge of the flat-roofed extension that jutted out the back of the next building. The roof ridge of the next building, facing the harbour, threw its shadow over him. His back gave a convulsive shudder, and something fell from his mouth in a silver line down into the dark yard of our neighbour.

"Oh, Jesus," I said.

"It's OK," said Juno, and stepped up onto the windowsill. She turned and climbed down the fire-escape ladder to the flat roof. I followed her down.

Conrad turned away from the edge to face us as we arrived. "I didn't want to do this in your room," he said to Juno.

"Why didn't you just get sick out the window?" said Juno.

"I didn't want you to hear me. To hear it. I'm sorry." He turned back to the edge. She shushed him, and laid a hand on his back. He spoke away from her. "I'd write for you if I could, Juno. I would. This isn't me."

He mopped his chin on his jacket sleeve as Juno made soothing noises and circled her palm on his broad back. It shuddered under her hand. "How did I get old?" mumbled Conrad to himself, half crying. "How did I get old?"

43

When Conrad had recovered a little, Dominic joined us on the roof, brought the glasses down full and his bottle of Black Bush open in his pocket, with the careless grace of the happily drunk. Juno and I, unused to spirits in instantly refilled triple measures, grew a trifle tipsy.

The cold, clean air gave us the illusion of sobriety. I found myself lying with my head in Dominic's lap. How did that happen? I adjusted my buttocks and wriggled up a little to avoid an uncomfortable seam in the tarpaper roof. As I rested my head back, I felt Dominic's lap change shape. Wow.

"So where are we going to do it?" said Juno.

"The IMI," said Conrad.

"Better off there," said Dominic. "The Aula's a stone barn. Desperate sound."

"It's a great play," said Conrad.

"We're gonna have you, Beckett!" roared Dominic at the sky. "Hey, Beckett! We're gonna fucking have you!"

Eventually the bottle was empty. "I'm cold," said Juno.

"Mmm," I said, half asleep, warm against Dominic.

"Wear my jacket," said Conrad.

"No, I think I'll go in. I'm meeting Michael later, I want to get ready." She stood and swayed on the edge of the roof, by the long drop to the concrete yard.

"Let me help you," said Conrad, rising, holding her sleeve to get up,

swaying himself. Lonely, lonely, lonely man, I thought. God's lonely
man. I hate that film. Scorsese loves violent men so much. He should
marry one.

Conrad helped Juno up the iron ladder. She, then he, vanished into
the bright block of light at the top. I closed my eyes. Lonely man. Very
sad. Marry him, Juno, I thought. Romantic man. Burn his jackets. . . .
Marry him. "Poor Conrad," I thought. No, I'd murmured it.

"Ah, fuck Conrad," said Dominic.

"Lonely man . . . ," I said.

Dominic snorted violently, and his lap began slowly to change shape
again. "He's free and he's single and he's fairly well off for the first time in
his life, and he fucking hates it. Fuck him. I'd swap anyday. All the drink
he can drink, women throwing themselves at him, and is he happy? Is he
fuck. Oh, get behind me, Satan."

I awoke a while later with a start. My heels drummed on the tarpaper, and I blinked the tears of sleep out of my eyes, trying to see too
fast. My leg. Something on my leg.

Dominic's hand. High on my thigh, my right thigh, inside, stroking
and caressing. My legs wide apart. It's lovely. I don't want this. Should've
asked.

"No," I said, my voice slurred with sleep and Black Bush, and I rolled
my head out of his hard lap and stood shakily.

"Juliet," he said.

"No," I said, and walked across the flat roof to the iron ladder. I felt
him rise behind me.

"Listen . . . Jesus," he said, and I turned to see his right knee buckle,
and he twisted to try and soak the blow with his shoulder as he hit the
tarpaper full length. I almost walked back to him. He groaned. "Dead
leg," he said. I turned back, climbed the ladder into the light, and left
him on the dark roof.

Juno's room was like heaven, so bright and unreal. The smell of her
and the scatter of her things. I walked through into the living room.
Someone had fixed the door handle.

The living room was warm and empty. I threw a broken piece of scrapwood into the stove's glowing ashes to see the sparks swirl and vanish up the flue. A quick flame ran along the rough wood, and all along it splinters flamed in bright orange, then bent slowly into glowing neon red curls, then switched off to black. A real, enduring flame caught it at the bottom and started to haul itself up. I sat back into a chair and watched it like television.

I heard Dominic cursing as he tried to get his dead leg over the windowsill in Juno's room. My pants felt hot and tight against my skin and between my legs, and I couldn't tell if they were hot from the stove or from me.

I turned round in the chair. Dominic was leaning in Juno's doorway.

"Jesus Christ, fucking pins and fucking needles," he said.

"Fuck off home, Dominic," I said, turning back to the fire. I didn't like having my back to him, but I didn't like looking at him either.

"You don't mean that," he said.

"You were groping me in my sleep," I said.

"You're overreacting, I was just . . . You looked lovely and I was just . . . rubbing, you know, stroking your leg, absentmindedly. Like you would with a cat."

I swung round in the chair. "Between their legs?"

"It wasn't between."

"I woke up with my legs spread, Dominic, and they weren't like that when I went to sleep."

"Well, er, Juliet, I mean I hate to say this, but whatever you were dreaming about, it was you that spread your legs, not me." Dominic walked very, very carefully towards me. "And to be honest you hadn't seemed too unhappy with me stroking your leg. How was I to know?"

"Ask me! Ask me! Ask me!"

He came around the table and stood in front of me. He gave me a melting, apologetic, puppy-dog look. Actor, I thought.

"Juliet . . ."

If he touches me . . . , I thought.

He put his hand on my shoulder and dropped into an awkward crouch. His eyes looked into mine. Oh God, I thought.

"Juliet . . . ," he said.

"Yes, Dominic?" I said in a voice remarkably like that of a Victorian headmistress, albeit a rather drunken Victorian headmistress. I felt transported in time, not very far admittedly, back to the school discos of transition year with their ghastly fumbles and stilted conversations. If I squinted he could almost be Harry Brannagan, who had actually got his hand under my T-shirt once in the dark behind the gymnasium, and been so stunned by his success that he had just left it there, entirely unmoving, for ten minutes while we kissed with the Hollywood-influenced Hoover action of the very young and very drunk.

I realized I was squinting, and stopped. He turned back into Dominic. Oh, balls.

His face drifted closer to mine, and I was distracted by the oddest feeling I'd done all this before. Then his lips touched mine and his rather pointed chin crushed its stubble into my chin and I could smell his whiskey, cigaretty breath.

"No," I said into his mouth, and turned my head sideways. He leaned his face against my cheek and stuck his tongue in my ear. He's bloody read that somewhere, I said to myself furiously, he's bloody read that it's erotic and seductive to stick your bloody tongue in her ear, and he's trying it on like a key in a fucking lock.

I stood up, and my shoulder caught him under the chin and snapped his jaw shut.

"Om, fhk, oh Jeshush," he said, clutching his mouth and rolling back onto his behind.

"Oh no, oh God, are you alright?" I said, horrified to see blood on the fingers he held to his mouth.

"I bit my fucking tongue," he mumbled, none too clearly, through his fingers. "Oh fuck, I'm bleeding."

I began to laugh. "Oh dear, I'm terribly sorry," I said. "Oh gosh . . ."

Gosh? His swearing had made me all prim, a nice way of isolating him further as he swore, bled, and winced in pain, sat on his slender rear on the orange rug. I bent towards him, but thought better of it.

"I'll get you something . . . for the bleeding," I said with drunken, owlish dignity and made my way with self-consciously ladylike steps to the bathroom, where I closed the door, sat on the toilet seat, and cried with laughter for a while.

Eventually I summoned up the courage to return to the scene of the crime. Some spirit of mischief possessed me to pick up a couple of Tampax on my way to the bathroom door, and I emerged holding these, for reasons unknown, aloft like the torch of the Statue of Liberty. I tracked Dominic down, with his head in the kitchen sink, spitting pinkened tap water straight down the plug hole with the accuracy of one who had been doing this for some minutes and was now rather good at it. He looked up, and seemed startled to have a couple of tampons thrust in his face.

"For the bleeeeeding," I explained solemnly. He didn't know how to react, and I wasn't in the mood to help him. I stared at him unblinkingly till he, with grave reluctance, took them from my outstretched hand.

"Ah . . . thanks . . . but I'm, ah, it's better now. Almost stopped."

"You'd better take them, just in case."

"Oh, alright so. Yes. Thanks." He held them helplessly.

"Are you sure you'll be alright now, walking home in your condition?" I said solicitously, and he gave a reflexive "Oh, yes, no problem."

Bang! Gotcha! I thought, and he began to look rather thoughtful himself.

"Look, ah . . . actually . . ." But I was already bringing him his coat.

I left him to make his own way downstairs, still clutching his tampons as I closed the door to our flat on his mournful good-bye.

I went to bed in high good spirits, with a hot-water bottle, and a pint glass of water by the bedside for the morning. After switching the light out, I hugged my pillow with glee and wriggled about in the bed like a salmon in a net. When I surfaced for air, I had that giddy pleasurable moment of not knowing which way I was facing, of feeling as though the room had been spun for my entertainment. I blinked, and the dim outline of the curtained window emerged like the picture on a Polaroid—on the opposite side of my vision to the one half-expected—and the room whizzed into place around it, boom. With my head sticking out over the side of my bed, I laughed till I got hiccups.

In my own bed, in my own room. A low-key revelation this time, spreading like the warmth of the Black Bush through me. Galway had become home.

44

A few days later, down by the dockside, dragging my coal sack of debris and offcuts home, I saw David Hennessey. He was stepping off a boat onto the narrow, slippery steps that lead up from the water to road level. He hadn't seen me, and I rushed to make it to the top of the steps before he re-emerged up into view.

When his head did appear, he was still looking down at his feet, fairly vital work when negotiating the quayside steps, so he didn't see me till he was safely at the top, and looked up.

I seemed to startle, almost shock him. For a moment I thought he was going to undo all his good work and take an involuntary step backward, off the edge of the quay.

"Juliet," he said. "Good God." Half-step back. I nearly grabbed him.

"Hello, Mr. Hennessey."

He gave his "Mr. Hennessey?" grimace. "Mister, schmister. What on earth are you doing here?"

"I live here." I pointed. "The tall building. Top floor."

"You live in the *docks*?" He shook his head. "You Capulets. A fine view, though, I'd imagine?"

"Oh yes."

"So were your agents tracking me across the bay with binoculars, or did you just, ah, happen to be standing at the head of these steps this morning?"

"I saw you stepping out of your boat and I, I sort of decided to, to ambush you. I didn't think you'd mind."

"Oh, I don't. Far from it. I was just a bit . . . startled. Sorry if I was abrupt with you. What's in the bag?"

I blushed and explained. I even mentioned my babushka-in-Stalingrad fantasy, to my own horror as I heard myself, but he seemed heartily amused by it and laughed.

"Were you out fishing?" I asked, to change the subject.

"No, not fishing." He looked back down at the boat, a sturdy little launch with a half-cabin and a big bulge of what I assumed to be engine at the back. Not quite a proper working boat, not quite a pottering-about toy. "No, I just came in to do the shopping actually. Horribly mundane explanation. My father's house is a few miles up the coast, right on the water, and you know the Connemara roads. On any kind of decent day like today, it's easier to pop in by boat than take the car." He gave a sort of apologetic smile-and-shrug. "And much more enjoyable, of course."

I was absolutely delighted to learn that he commuted by boat, it appealed to the romantic idiot in me. I couldn't have been more pleased if I'd discovered he came to work in full armour, on horseback, but he seemed terrifically embarrassed by my delight, as though I'd caught him showing off somehow.

"It's very practical," he said helplessly.

"What are you shopping for?" I said, to put him out of his misery.

He cheered up. "Food and . . . um . . . stuff," he said.

I sighed. It was such a hopelessly boyish answer that I felt older than him for a moment. "Do you have a list?" I said.

"Er, no. I sort of wander around. . . . I mean, I know we need light-bulbs. . . ."

I must have given him my mother's Disapproving Look, because he grinned and said, "God, is this what it's like when I'm grilling you all on a book you haven't read? I swear I'll have a list for next week, Miss Taylor."

I grinned back at him. This was just like a Real Conversation. "Would you like a hand? Shopping? I'm quite good at it."

"Oh, would you do me the honour, Miss Taylor?" he said and fell on one knee and kissed the back of my hand mock-reverently.

"Why Mr. Hennessey, the pleasure is entirely mine. And get up, you'll ruin your trousers."

He got up. "What about the, uh, ruins of Stalingrad?" he said, pointing at my coal sack.

"Oh, they're fine here. I'll pick them up later. They're out of the road, and who'd steal them?"

So we left Stalingrad behind us at the head of the quayside steps, and went shopping.

45

"But it's on special offer," said David.

"Great, six hundred and fifty grams for the price of the usual five hundred. It's *still* dearer per gram than Super-Valu's own brand, which is frankly just as good. You're paying for the name."

"Oh God, this isn't shopping, this is mathematics. I just can't do all those calculations in my head."

"Shopping *is* mathematics," I said, in a fair parody of him at his most serious. "And put those down."

"What? But these are the cheapest."

"You're buying air. They wind the rolls loose and puff the pack wrapper full of air to keep it firm. You'll never save money buying the cheapest toilet rolls. They last no time, and it's not worth it for the annoyance of having them run out constantly."

"So what do you recommend?"

"Steal the industrial-sized ones from the lecturers' toilets like I do."

"Jesus, do you?"

"Well, they don't padlock the toilet-roll holders in the lecturers' toilets," I explained, breaking character. "The toilet roll in the student toilets comes out of a thing like a small fallout shelter bolted to the wall. I think they have to cut it open with a welding torch when they want to put in a new roll. Maybe it's different in the boys' toilets."

He shook his head. "No, I know the dispensers you mean."

"Well, I raid the Arts tower. History usually, it's the easiest. They just leave these *enormous* rolls on the cistern. . . . You don't mind, do you?" I said, suddenly anxious.

"Christ, no, fascinated."

"I *never* take the last roll."

"Very Christian of you."

"It's just that we don't have any money, really, or not enough. I can't ask our parents for more."

"We?"

"My sister Juno and I." I'd have said *me and Juno* if it had been anyone else. Now that the conversation was about something real, albeit stupid, I was anxious again. I didn't want him to disapprove of me, but I didn't want to fib either. "My twin."

I was surprised to realise I must never have mentioned her to him before, that to him I was unique. How strange, that he only knew me. How . . . incomplete? No. Misleading. Or was it? My being Juno's twin was such a constant that I couldn't get a clear picture of its importance.

"Cheese," he said. I pretended to take a photograph. "No, I've remembered we need cheese."

"We?" I said in my turn, pleased he hadn't asked about Juno, hadn't said, "And is she just like you?"

"My father and I," he said.

I blushed as though reprimanded.

"Oh, of course," I said.

46

"Don't put the sugar on the fire lighters," I said. "The sugar will taste of fire lighter."

"Good thinking, Batman," said David, and moved the bag of sugar to the other end of the trolley. "That really *is* it. I think."

We'd covered every aisle at least twice as he remembered items we'd already passed. By the end I began to suspect he was doing it deliberately, that he didn't want the game to end.

"Ostrich eggs!" he exclaimed, slapping his forehead. "Nearly forgot." He turned the trolley.

"I don't think Super-Valu do ostrich eggs," I said, turning it back. "Besides, you're better off getting them down the Saturday market. Fresher, and they'll usually throw one in for luck."

"You're right," he said. "We're done, then."

He wheeled the laden trolley toward the shortest checkout queue. I pointed to the second shortest queue.

"Aye, aye, captain," he said, and joined it. "Why, Holmes?" he stage-whispered.

I sighed, and whispered, "This queue is only one person longer, and look at the trolleys. Practically empty. It'll whizz through. That queue has two *gigantic* trolleyfuls, and they're bound to pay by credit card as well, they look the type. Much slower than cash. Lots of form-filling, counterfoil-signing. Probably want them delivered, that's another form."

"By Jove, Holmes," he whispered, "you never cease to amaze."

After we'd got through the checkout and I'd made him take the fire lighters out of the bag with the bread in it and give it a bag of its own and he'd paid for everything, we looked at the huge pile of plastic bags.

"Hmm," he said, "I could probably sneak a trolley out, and dump it in the harbour when I'm finished."

The checkout girl gave him a dirty look. I smothered a laugh.

"I'll help you," I said.

"Oh, no," he said aghast, "I couldn't possibly allow you . . . ," but I just picked up as many bags as I could carry and headed for the exit, which didn't really leave him with a hell of a lot of options.

47

"Have you drink taken?" I asked him as we put our bags down on the quayside at the head of the steps.

"No, God, sorry, do I seem drunk?" he said, concerned. "Oh dear."

"No," I said, "not *drunk,* but . . ." I paused for thought. I was sick of stuttering and sounding incoherent whenever I tried to say anything serious, so I took my time, trying to get it right. Gulls made their alien noises, and a trawler further down the quay throbbed quietly, about to leave.

What I thought was that all of his gravitas had imperceptibly transmuted into levitas in the last hour or so, but I could hardly put it like that.

And pretty soon I'd thought too much about it and couldn't say anything at all. I shrugged, mute and furious with myself. He made urging gestures, raised eyebrows, mimed pulling it out of me with a rope. Made the charades gestures for film, book, play? First syllable? I smiled despite myself. I pointed at him, pointed at my wristwatch, mimed the hands winding back an hour with an anticlockwise forefinger, pulled my mouth-corners down. I pointed at him again, pointed at my watch now, lifted my mouth-corners into a smile. Shrugged. Gave him a questioning look.

I thought for a second he was trying to mime a reply. A shudder shook his upper body and his head swayed for a second, but he pulled himself together at once with a visible effort that tightened the skin across his face, and said, "I can't . . . I don't . . . It's a long time since I had any *fun.*" He said the word with a weird anger. "I'm sorry, Juliet. Because . . . of my home situation . . . because"—he looked at me questioningly—"my father is dying."

I nodded miserably. I hadn't meant to open up whatever I'd just opened up. He was speaking quite calmly now, not angrily, almost as though he was thinking of something else entirely, as though he was giving absentminded directions to a tourist while thinking separately how best he himself should go home.

"I have not had a particularly enjoyable Christmas or New Year, and this morning was very enjoyable indeed. I was very grateful for your company. I allowed myself forget about . . . all of that, and if I embarrassed you or behaved foolishly then I really am truly sorry."

He was so awkward and sad and dignified I wanted to hit him, how could he think that I wanted him to apologise for the last hour of silly, innocent nonsense?

"Don't be *stupid,*" I said violently, nearly crying. I'd thought he understood me. "It was *lovely,* I wouldn't have *gone* shopping with you if I didn't *want* to and I wouldn't have *stayed* if I wasn't enjoying myself, I was *pleased* you got happier, how could you possibly *apologise* to me for it?"

"Oh no, oh no—" He seemed appalled at my distress.

"I had a *lousy* Christmas," I interrupted, "and today has been *great* and for *Christ's* sake don't apologise again."

He seemed lost in thought for a moment, then fumbled in the pocket of his jacket and brought out a battered packet of fruit pastilles.

"Fruit pastille?" he said. "You can have one of the black ones, they're the nicest. Blow off any fluff, they've been in the pocket for weeks."

Miserably I took the first one, orange, and chewed it.

Five minutes later we were both sitting on the ridiculously cold stone of the quay's edge, our legs dangling above the harbour water, happily miserable together. We exchanged the horror stories of our Christmases, just the outlines, nothing too grim, made them sound funny. We talked about films, and the weather, and Christmas television. Eventually a very light drizzle began to fall.

"Why don't you come in, for coffee?" I said, nodding back towards the house.

"Oh, no, I couldn't. I really should be getting back. I mean he won't worry about me or anything like that, but I said I'd be straight back, and we're cooking dinner. . . . Look," he said, and seemed to startle himself with the suggestion, "why don't you come to dinner?"

He didn't startle himself half as much as he startled me.

"Yes, do," he said, pleased, as though seconding someone else's suggestion. I hovered on the brink of saying no for what seemed like a month or a year or some ridiculous length of time entirely unsuited to a conversation, until I realised that absolutely every atom of me was roaring yes.

"Yes," I said, without thinking about it at all, like I was reading the word off a blackboard.

48

I sat in the half-shelter of the half-cabin on a plastic beer crate, feeling grotesquely busty in an oversized bright orange life jacket, attached as tightly as the straps would allow over my grey wool coat.

"If we go fast enough, the drizzle won't get us," said David, gunning the engine as we emerged into open water and headed up the coast into

the wind. Sure enough, the drizzle fizzed against the window at the front
of the cabin, but nothing came in the open rear. I peered out the window.
Windscreen? I wasn't sure what to call bits of boats. The engine was incredibly loud, but the boat smacked through the choppy water surprisingly smoothly. I'd been on buses that bounced more. The view through
the windscreen was tremendous, an endless expanse of grey water,
ridged with low white wave crests pouring toward and under us endlessly, with the mist and drizzle hiding Clare from us on our left so that it
felt like the ocean, not the bay.

"This is *brilliant!*" I yelled. The coast of Galway drifted by, far to our
right. I recognised a building, a hotel, then it was gone behind a sheet of
rain, and the windscreen spattered hard as the rain hit us, but the cabin
stayed dry.

"Glad you like it!" yelled David. "Want a go?" He nodded at the
wheel.

"Oh *yes,*" I said, pleased and scared.

He stood up from his little seat, still holding the wheel, and stooped
under the low roof, legs braced wide for balance, while I left my beer
crate to slip by him into his seat.

"Grab the wheel."

I grabbed it. He let go. I could feel every wave through the palms of
my hands.

"Throttle," he said, and took my right hand from the wheel and put it
on the throttle. "Turn it."

I turned it. The engine roared still louder, and the boat surged under
my hands. "You can swing her around a little if you like. Never hold her
sideways to the waves. She's much more comfortable taking them head
on. Anything makes you nervous—other boats, buoys, rocks—slow right
down, but leave the engine running. Don't point her at the shore. Got
that?"

I nodded.

"Comfortable?"

I nodded.

"Good." He stepped back, out of the half-cabin, and stood up into the rain and wind. I heard the palms of his hands slap the roof above me to brace himself as the wind and water ripped into him. I turned the throttle more, and the engine roared louder than love. Where did I get that from? It was an album Michael played sometimes. *Louder Than Love*. The wind was enough to keep the angled windscreen clear now, water pushed to the edges by the pressure of our speed through the water and the air. Everything louder than everything else.

I swung the wheel, just a little, and the horizon wheeled, and I swung it back, and I shouted silently for joy in the middle of the great noise. Above me I could hear David singing, it was something I knew, words torn ragged by the wind. "Rainy Night in Soho," the Pogues. I joined in, but I'm sure he couldn't hear me up there, outside the cabin, his face in the storm.

Roaring across the grey plane of the water, the wheel and the seat beneath me transmitted the details of the never-ending, complex kiss of the boat and the water, up through my bones.

When eventually David stooped to come back into the tiny cabin, soaking, shaking rain from his hair, and put a hand on the wheel by mine, I was as startled as if I'd been caught kissing by my father.

"We're almost there," he said. "Shall I bring her in?"

I nodded and reluctantly handed over control. Back on my beer crate, I felt as though I was about to start trembling, and put a hand to my face to check if it was hot. It seemed roasting to me, but it was cool under my hand.

He was lost in concentration, bringing her toward the shore and around a great dark bulk under the water, rocks, and then there was a gap in the low grey stone of the shoreline, an inlet with high sides of a darker rock, and the high sides fell away and we were in calm water idling toward a wooden dock, under a low grey sky.

I realized with a shock that it was an ordinary day, quiet, calm, and raining, and that the storm had been private to us, just a creation of our speed, and that for everybody else around the bay it was just raining.

My storm. Juno had missed it. I felt absurdly cheerful about this.

49

"It's got a *tower!*" I said to David as he tied the nose of the boat to a rusting iron ring set into the end of the wooden dock.

He looked over his shoulder towards the house. "Mmm, yes."

I passed up the last of the shopping bags and hopped out of the boat onto the dock. "*Wow. It's brilliant.*"

David was embarrassed again. "Mmm." He finished securing the boat and stood up straight. "Just chuck your life jacket in the cabin, it'll be fine."

I got in a tangle with the straps and he made as though to help, then checked himself. I grinned at him. "Hah. I just missed out on a big pay-day there, didn't I? Report you to the ethics committee and sell my story to the *Sun*. ' "He Took off My Life Jacket," Sobbed Student.' Damn, it's stuck. . . ."

He smiled back. "With your permission, Ms. Taylor?"

"Granted, Mr. Hennessey."

He dealt with the knot I'd made of the straps at the small of my back, and I slipped the life jacket off over my head and threw it down into the cabin.

He'd picked up the shopping bags before I could get to them.

"Spoilt Victorian child," I began singing softly to myself as we started up the path towards the house with the tower.

David laughed. "Your subconscious is showing," he said.

"What?" I said.

"Do you think I'm . . . dreadfully old-fashioned?" He was smiling.

"Oh, no," I said. "Or if you are, it's lovely. I mean, I like it about you. You're old-fashioned in a good way."

"Mmm."

"Every time I say anything nice you clam up and go 'mmm.' I'm going to have to start being horrible to you to keep the conversation going."

He'd said "mmm" again in the middle of that, and now laughed. "Yes, sorry. But aren't we living in rather a neo-Victorian age, Ms. Taylor? One very concerned with correct appearances and with, ah, genteel speech. Always making sure we discuss the unspeakable without offending anybody's delicate sensibilities. An age where . . . we are careful not to touch each other, because altogether elsewhere others rape and murder, and that starts, does it not, with a touch? An age where the privileged try to cure the world by talking." He laughed at himself, made a helpless moue. "If I am old-fashioned . . . am I not a model modern citizen of a most old-fashioned age?"

I smiled at him. I liked him like this, a little embarrassed at his own fire, but still meaning it, not backing down.

We'd got to the house, but he didn't reach for a key immediately. That suited me, I didn't feel quite ready to meet his father, on a drip or in a wheelchair or slack-jawed and dribbling. I took a couple of steps away from the house, toward the sea. The view was bleak, grey, vast, thrilling.

David put down the bags against the big yellow-painted front door, and moved to stand beside me.

"You're lecturing again," I said.

"I'm more comfortable lecturing," he said.

We looked out across the tremendous sweep of the bay where the rain, falling lightly on us still, thickened and blackened as it grew closer to the Clare shore, the small Clare hills buried under black clouds vast as flattened, molten Alps. I put up the collar of my coat and shivered, half from the cold and half from the glory. The power and scale of it. Its indifference to my existence thrilled me, I loved the world when it forgot about me.

As we watched, a bright rod of gold joined the dark sea to the dark sky, far out in the bay.

"That's a bit over the top," I said.

"Gaudy," he said.

"Cliched."

"Sentimental."

"Victorian."

The gap in the clouds widened, and the gold spread like butter in lush, thick smears of light that almost hurt to look at, as countless raindrops fell across the path of the light and spun it through their accidental lenses to our eyes.

It became too beautiful to be flippant about, and we shut up and just looked at it.

After a while David stirred. "My father would like this very much. I think I'll . . ." He turned abruptly back toward the house. I stayed looking. Great spears of gold embedded in the sea, shafts rippling with the pressure of holding up the sky.

Footsteps on gravel, then grass. He stood beside me. It was hardly raining over Galway at all now. The last of the low, heavy clouds were moving out across the bay to Clare. The crack in the clouds tightened, the waterfall of light brightened, twisted, flared as a heavy squall of rain blew through it, then dimmed and narrowed to a thin scratch of silver, flickered, flared, vanished. Black clouds over grey water. No light.

"My God."

I breathed out and turned my head. Not David. David's father.

He turned too. We smiled at each other.

"Gerry Hennessey. David's father." He held out a hand. I was shocked at his accent, far more Irish than David's. Broad West Galway with only some of the edges smoothed off.

"Juliet Taylor," I said, very formal, and shook his hand. God, I practically curtsied.

"Delighted, delighted. David's talked a lot about you." He laughed at the look on my face. "Only good things, don't worry. He showed me an essay you did, on Jane Austen was it? Didn't mean a thing to me, but he seemed very impressed. Oh indeed, I nodded wisely and pretended I'd understood it, ach, a bad mistake. I hadn't read more than a page of it, and he caught me rotten with a couple of questions about God alone knows what. Wasn't that a magnificent display?" he said, sweeping a hand at the horizon.

I nodded.

"Are you hungry?" he said.

I nodded. He looked a little like David but fabulously old and leathery. I looked again. No, not old.

"Good, good. David's preparing dinner. You're not a vegetarian are you?"

I hesitated. I didn't buy meat, or I tried not to, but I wasn't really a vegetarian because I ate it if I was given it, although I sort of *thought* of myself as a vegetarian sometimes, even though I'd buy the lasagne in the UCG canteen when I was really hungry because their vegetarian food came in tiny portions and always contained carrots for some reason. . . .

"No," I said. We walked back to the house. David's father pushed open the front door. I looked up at the tower for a moment before realizing that he was holding the door open for me. "Oh, thank you," I said, and walked into the house.

50

Let me rephrase that.

"Oh, thank you," I said, and walked into a temple of transformations. Look, now.

Down the corridor, paintings blasting colour at me like heat as I pass them, fat with chrome yellow and petrol-bomb orange, bulging out of their frames like the freaked-out spine-damage erections of accident victims.

Maybe I shouldn't have stared at the sea and the sky for so long in such silence, but now as I return to the world of furniture, conversation and dinner, my nerves seem to be sticking out of my skin like tiny sea anemones flowering from the open pores. I'm supersensitised, the damp cotton of my skirt crashes across my thighs as I walk toward the open door at the end of the corridor, my breasts kiss hard against the cups of my bra, kiss, in the dark of my dress, kiss, with every step, kiss, and I'm anointed in adrenaline, I'm fizzing like an aspirin, the folds of my skin are spicy with arousal and social terror. If you licked me, you'd trip.

High on shyness. I'm buzzing.

I take the two steps down into the kitchen.

Kiss, kiss.

He's beautiful. His hair's still wet with rain. Some of it tumbles forward as he leans over the range. He runs his left hand up through it, and his fingers ripple it back into order in one stroke and little droplets of rain are spun out and away by the whip of the hair as the hand passes through it, like the great teeth of a plough through pastureland.

Everything's hyper-enhanced. I'm standing in a Connemara kitchen, thinking in symbol and metaphor. As our cousin Gareth's mother would put it, I'm tired, I'm excited, and I'm beginning to show off. And I'm staring at David, which I only notice when he notices me.

"Hi, Juliet." Oh, God, his eyes. Cue more damp cotton.

51

"Ah, what's for dinner?" I said, and immediately boiled with self-loathing at the inanity of my words.

"I've no idea," said David. "This thing, whatever it is." He pointed at an extraordinarily large, recently deceased oceanic beast that completely hid a merely very large frying pan beneath its bulk of fins and eyes. "Fried

julian gough

sea monster. Dad catches them and expects me to know how to cook them. Creatures previously unknown to science, and he expects me to know if they go well with a butter sauce."

I stood beside him, and we stared at it. It stared back.

"Jesus," I said. Partly an expression of my shock at the odd fish in front of me, partly an expression of my shock at the odd fish beside me, both of whom I felt I was seeing as if for the first time.

I know. I'm a pretty dim bulb. You probably knew I was in love with him halfway through the epigraphs.

But I was a simple, fucked-up country girl. I endured great emotions the way Belgium has traditionally endured great European battles. I mean, they were *painful*, and I was often quite profoundly affected by them, but I didn't really think of them as having much to do with me. I was just where they happened to be taking place. Happy geographical accident. From Waterloo to Ypres. There go those guns again. I wonder what it's all about this time?

So, as wave after wave of nameless emotion swept over me, emitting battlecries of "Name me! Name me!", I rocked from foot to foot, shell-shocked. Here we go again.

I swayed from foot to foot and stared at the sea monster and felt turned on, turned inside out, and on the verge of tears.

Jesus.

He really was ferociously sexy that day, by the way. At the time I was too busy not noticing anything to notice that I'd noticed, but looking through the folders of memory now, oh, yes. Oh, Jesus, he was sexy. It wasn't the clothes, though they were grand, and it certainly wasn't the haircut, which was the subtle, natural look of a man who's been out of prison six months and hasn't gotten around to visiting his stylist yet, but by God he was sexy. And there I was with my hip brushing his as I swayed, and me wondering what on earth was wrong with me.

Believe me, my willful ignorance of the geography of my own heart throughout all this is at least as annoying and frustrating to me as it must be to you. Bear with my youthful self.

His father came in behind us and put a hand on each of our shoulders. It's a wonder he wasn't electrocuted.

"Well, can you cook it, son?"

"I found its guts where its brain should be, and it took me two goes to find its spine, I think it had only just evolved one and wasn't sure where to put it, but yes, it probably won't kill us."

"And how'll the maestro be serving it?"

"With lashings of garlic and a prayer to Saint Anthony."

"There's the boy. And a wine to go with it?"

"I was thinking a Newcastle Brown Ale of recent vintage."

"Ah, you and your beer. I have a cellar to get through, and it's seldom we have guests as radiant as young Juliet here." He patted our shoulders and made for the door. "Makes a change from your bloody fish farmers. I know the very thing." He disappeared up the two steps and out of the kitchen.

"He's a bit unreconstructed," said David apologetically as I blushed all over the place.

"Oh, no, he's lovely," I said, and meant it. "Who are your fish farmers?"

"Ah, Cian and Eamonn. They work in the bay, friends of mine. And his, at this stage, but it's a running joke that the three of us can't tell a glass of Château Zut Alors '61 from Pepsi in a shoe. I'm not very interested in wine, and my sister doesn't drink, so he's drinking his cellar before he goes."

I was almost thick enough to ask, "Goes where?" but remembered in time.

"He looks great," I said.

"Hmm. Yeah, yeah he does," said David, and his father's footsteps came down the corridor and he was back, bearing aloft a dusty bottle.

"The very one!" he said. "Even the shagging dust is probably worth money by now." He turned to me. "Have you e'er an interest in wine at all, Juliet?"

I shook my head, no.

"Well, it's a monstrous world of charlatans, snobbery, and bullshit,

julian gough

but at the heart of it all is some lovely booze. I've three bottles of this fella left, and if my bank manager could see me swinging it about like this, he'd have a shagging heart attack. I *invested* in wine—can you imagine?—in the early eighties, sold most of it on again before everything crashed in the late eighties, made a fortune. No way to treat wine, though. I'm making amends for my sins now by drinking the few crates I have left."

"Was that . . . what you do for a living, selling wine? Trading it." Blush, blush, kick self.

"Ah, no. Sit down there, sit down. No, the fortune I made out of wine was a fairly small fortune, I'd already made my few bob in the oil industry. Working in Scotland a lot of the time, and travelling a bit. Saudi, the emirates, Malaysia, all the usual suspects. Plying my trade. A wandering Irishman with a family to feed, like many another."

"He also invented a deep-water pumping system that's opened up new oil fields all over the Indian Ocean and the North Sea," interrupted David from the range, "which he's too shy to mention. He'll have you thinking he was sweeping the canteen floor of a rig for twenty years if you're not careful."

"Arra, it was a few valves and a cutting head, David. 'Deep-water pumping system,' Jaysus. You make me sound like a fecking engineer." His accent was getting more Galway by the moment.

David continued to address me as his father writhed in embarrassment in his chair. "Dad not only invented 'a few valves and a cutting head,' but he patented them and got some of the most tight-arsed companies on earth to pay him a handsome royalty to use them, including BP, who employed him. What's really funny is that if they'd given him a decent job in research and development to begin with, he'd have had to sign a waiver as a condition of employment, and they'd have owned his ideas. But of course, as he constantly points out, he's an uneducated Galwayman, not a feckin' engineer, so they employed him as a Paddy with muscles. He got his diving cert in his own time, and he figured out

better ways of drilling and pumping as a hobby to pass the hours while
he was decompressing."

"Oh, would you stop, I'm sure Juliet has no interest in all this." The
leather of his face was managing to blush somehow. "And besides, it was
Pat Shanahan did the real work, or I'd have never made a shilling out of
it." His accent had retreated in his embarrassment to the very border-
lands of comprehensibility. I'd thought for a second he was speaking
Irish.

"And did David and . . . David's mother, and sister, did they travel
with you to all these places?" I said quickly, letting him off the hook and
putting him on another one.

"Ah, no, no. Their mother, my wife, she died young." Christ, I
thought, I will never open my stupid mouth again. He waved away my
attempted apology. "We were living in London, for the job. Their mother
was English, well French-English, a Hampstead Huguenot, great woman
altogether, anyway. I thought I could either look after them or make
enough money for them to look after themselves. I probably made the
wrong decision, but this was back a long way. Back then, a father went
out and earned. That's how you were a father. So I left them with the relatives a fair bit, their mother's sister, and their gran, my mother, while
she was alive. And when I'd enough money put away, I retired. Missed a
lot, though. Missed a lot."

"You missed shag all," said David, adding some sort of sauce with a
sizzle to the sea monster. "A lot of puking and crawling. Learning to say
'fuck' from the estate kids. Sarah's Bay City Rollers obsession."

"Oh, Jesus," said David's father, settling back in his chair with a satisfied sigh like a proper father. "I remember. Back from Brunei with a ruptured eardrum from a bad pressure drop, and Sarah in tartan from
bloomers to nightie, screaming along to 'Shang-A-frigging -Lang,' day in,
day out, morning till night. I thought I'd go mad. I thought I'd *gone* mad.
Surely life isn't meant to be like this, Lord, I'd say to myself? Have I committed a grievous sin unbeknownst to meself? Am I being punished?

And sweet Jesus, do you remember Mud? Where did a child that young get the lungs?"

He uncorked the bottle, David served up a melon and a knife and told us to get on with it, and dinner lazily began in a haze of nostalgic stories about David and his older sister, Sarah. David and I took turns to prompt. By the time the first bottle of wine had been polished off, I was contributing amusing childhood stories from Juno and Paul's lives, and by the time a second had been dusted, uncorked, and demolished, I was digging up some of the most embarrassing incidents from my own. So was David. So was his dad. We were roaring with laughter at a story of mine, which I assure you requires a lot of very good wine indeed to be funny, when David's dad fell off his chair. I nearly sobered up, I was so scared he'd died. Then David fell off his chair, quite deliberately, and I realized they were both still laughing, and I was so flushed with relief I deliberately fell off mine too, and we all lay on the kitchen floor like complete idiots, laughing hysterically.

It was David's dad's idea we all go for a walk, and a jolly good idea it was too. In fact, at the time, it seemed like probably the best idea anybody had ever had, ever. I think I said as much. Loudly. I may have sung it.

David's dad disappeared through a small door into a space slightly larger than a closet and slightly smaller than a room, tucked away to the left of the range, and began hurling Wellingtons and oilskins back over his shoulder into the kitchen.

"Hi-ho, hi-ho," he sang, "it's off to work we go," and we all joined in—ba-rum bum bum, baba rum bum bum, hi-ho, hi-ho—and I sat in the middle of the floor and slipped off my shoes and slipped on a Wellington and, after a couple of brave attempts, another Wellington. I frowned at them quizzically. One of them was on the wrong foot. How could only one of them be on the wrong foot? Ah. The green one was on the wrong foot. The black one was fine.

David's head emerged from a bright yellow oilskin. Straight out the neck hole, first time. I admired his savoir-faire.

"Your sea monster," I said carefully, catching his eye, "was *divine*," and I started giggling. "And may I also say how much I admire your *savoir-faire*. And your *sangfroid*. And your . . . *Savoy 'otel*."

"Miss Taylor," said David, taking my heart in his hand; no, my hand in his, "may *I* say how much I admire your certain . . . *je ne sais quoi* . . . your certain . . . *joie de vivre* . . . your certain age . . . your uncertain smile. . . ."

"Your grace under pressure."

"Your face under water."

"Your place or mine?"

"Your . . . fruit of the vine."

"Your hand on your heart."

"My hand on my heart." He put his free hand on his heart. He grinned down at me, I grinned up at him, and he pulled me to my feet by the hand he'd continued to hold as we babbled nonsense at each other. I thought I'd explode. I felt as though I was still rising and rising, even though I was now just standing in the kitchen holding his hand. I swayed, and opened my mouth to say something, and he let go my hand.

His father came out of the boot room backward, zipping up a bright orange ensemble that looked likely to get him through an outbreak of chemical warfare unscathed, let alone a patch of Connemara drizzle.

"Still deciding on an outfit, are we?" he said, looking at my boots.

I blushed.

"Black suits you," he said, and handed me the other of the pair. I leaned over and sorted out my footwear, wishing I had Juno's hair to hide behind. The enormous green left boot came off my right foot with ease. What on earth had I been thinking of? I must be the teeniest bit drunk.

52

We must have been pissed out of our heads. It was *flogging* rain. The inlet with the little wooden dock lay on the sheltered side of the headland, so of course we marched down the other side, onto the beach, into the teeth of the wind. I tried to work out if the wind had changed direction since I'd entered the house, but somehow it seemed to have gotten dark in that time, and I hadn't a clue which way Clare was anymore. I was having enough trouble remembering which way up was. We sang a medley of our favourite Irish Eurovision entries as we stumbled arm-in-arm-in-arm down to the sea.

God, we were drunk. A certain amount of Newcastle Brown Ale had managed to sneak in between the bottles of white, not really adding to the sobriety of the evening. Night. Whatever. As we reached the high-tide mark, and the kelp and the carragheen squelched beneath my Wellingtons, my eyes adjusted to the fractured moonlight coming through the broken clouds that tumbled in perpetual avalanche above us.

A black-and-white landscape with hardly any land in it. Seascape. That's the one. A black ocean. The black sea. Just enough light to frighten you with the colossal amount of darkness it revealed, but only if you were a scaredy-cat. I wasn't frightened. I let go of everybody and ran the last few yards to the sea. The men stopped singing.

"Juliet," said David.

I picked up a rock and threw it out into the dark sea. It made a good splash in the bad moonlight. I picked up another rock. The rain hissed on the sea, and the sea went *shussssh* as it rattled some pebbles in its crawl up the beach to my feet.

Why should I be frightened?

The moon broke free of the clouds, and a silver world froze. I had lifted my arm to throw the second rock, but now I studied the curve of my arm as though it were that of a statue. I was a statue in the moon-light. Diana the hunter. I laughed. Diana in oilskin and Wellingtons, with a rock instead of a bow and a quiver of arrows. A wave made it as far as my Wellingtons, tried to sneak past me, *shusssssh*. . . .

I wasn't frightened. I dropped the rock on it. I made a little bomb noise, *boosh,* as it splashed.

David came up behind me. His father stood higher up the beach, looking back at the steady black of the house against the changing greys of the sky. My eyes were getting better and better. Diana the hunter. I could even see a tiny moon in each of David's eyes. The rain wasn't as strong now. Everything was so changeable here. I swung my arm across my breasts, to press my heart back in.

"Juliet," he said again. I didn't want to hear it, whatever it was. The sea said *shusssh* again. I bent and picked up a rock from the rocky beach. I handed it to him and put a finger on his lips.

"Shush," I said. "Present. Stay." And I turned and walked away from him along the shoreline, my Wellingtons kicking fans of water ahead of me. I could feel him looking after me.

Looking after me. I wasn't frightened.

53

My father was frightened of everything, on my behalf. I'd never needed to be frightened. He'd always done it for me.

"Jesus, you could've been killed."

Walking home alone at three A.M., drinking a bottle of vodka and passing out, getting a lift to Limerick on the back of Jimmy Gleeson's Suzuki with the stupid heavy metal painting of a girl chained to a rock on the petrol tank (Me: "Jimmy, that's sexist." Jimmy: "Yeah, it is, isn't it?" —patting the painting approvingly).

Men and alcohol, mainly, he was frightened of on my behalf. The combination left him stuttering. A pissed Jimmy Gleeson bringing me, also pissed, home at three A.M. on the Suzuki. My father's reaction was a treat worth repeating, so of course I did. Patting Jimmy on the head—"Good night"—and his shiver of pleasure, as he made the bike roar good-bye and was off. Me ringing the doorbell because my father had taken my key off me. (That didn't last long. I cut a copy of my mother's, and nothing was said.)

I think one of the things that I most held against him was his assumption that I was sleeping with the Gleeson twins. He didn't understand (how could he? I never even tried to explain to him) that the Gleeson twins were natural knights. Not in every aspect of their lives, true. Gawain and Galahad didn't deal in drugs and stolen electrical equipment. But to me and Juno, they were chivalrous, worshipful, chaste. They sought our favour, and they beat people up on our behalf, whether we liked it or not, until we eventually managed to persuade them to stop. They beat up Jem Toohy for saying something crude about Juno. (They never told us what. They just blushed and said, "It was fuckin' disgustin'. Cunt deserved it.")

Toohy called around the next day with a black eye, a wrist in a sling, and a small box of Cadbury's Milk Tray.

"For fuck's sake tell them I apologized," said Jem to a bewildered Juno, before he shoved the chocolates at her left-handed and hobbled home.

Next day we found out that they'd told him they'd drop him off the railway bridge if his apology wasn't up to scratch. They'd told him this while holding his ankles, as he swayed in the light breeze twenty feet above the road, so he had little reason to doubt them.

The Gleeson twins liked the railway bridge. It had dinky little fences at its edges instead of the stout walls of stone or concrete the other couple of bridges around the town had, so they didn't have to bring boxes to stand on when they wanted to dangle a miscreant above the abyss. They'd had an accident early on in their career when a beer crate collapsed and they'd dropped Seamus Hickey off the bypass flyover onto a brand-new Mazda parked in Huchinson's forecourt. The insurance battle went on for years. They'd only wanted him to help them with their maths.

Suddenly my feet were very, very wet and cold. I snapped out of my reminiscence and was bemused and pleased to see where I was. A bloody long way from Tipperary. Standing in the sea, which had just swept up to my knees and flooded my Wellingtons. God I was drunk. Drunkety drunk. Drinkety drankety drunk. Drunk as a monk's flunkey, in a bunk with a funky monkey, on skunk . . . blink.

A lighthouse blinked at me from far across the black-and-silver bay. I waved at it—hallo, Clare—and slipped, and fell backward, and didn't hit the water. Hands held me up, under my arms, and only my bottom got wet. Then the hands shifted, and I was lifted right out of the water, with one arm supporting my back and one arm in the curve of my knees.

"David," I said, dreamily thinking, My God, this is the most romantic thing that has ever happened; I could happily die now. "You saved me"

"Christ, you're heavy," he said.

He carried me up the slope of the beach, out of the sea. I looked up at his face in the moonlight and, dizzy with Chateau something, seventy something, lifted my head enough to brush against his cheek. A tiny rasp of stubble on my lips and cheek, and a noise like a sigh, or a kiss. I couldn't tell which it was, or which of us had made it. I was halfway between deliriously happy and delirious.

The lighthouse winked at me over David's shoulder. Moonlight on the wave crests. Great grey, butchered tentacles of cloud boiled above me in the dark, cooking in their own black ink.

He put me down on a rock and collapsed beside me, exhaling hard as he did so, like a mortally wounded zeppelin crumpling to earth. Like Icarus falling.

My mind was away with the fairies, describing metaphorical arabesques. Wheee! I thought, and leaned sideways into David, my head bumping his shoulder and sliding down the Eiger of his oilskin till I lay

comfortably on my back with my head in his lap, looking up at him looking down at me. Rain fell in my eyes. I blinked it away.

"What's a nice girl like you doing on a beach like this?" said David. It
sounded funny, but he looked very sad.

I shut my eyes, and the wind went *wheee*. . . . "Tell me a story," I said.

"I can't tell stories," he said. "I've tried, and I can't. I can only tell you
about stories. That's my job. You tell me a story, and I'll tell you about it."

"Shall I tell you a story?"

"Yes."

"And you'll tell me about it?"

"Yes."

I kept my eyes shut and thought for a while. "There was a girl," I said.

54

And stopped. No. That was the wrong story.

"There was a boy," I said. "A handsome . . . knight. And he was very,
very serious. And he was very, very sad."

I opened my eyes to see that he had closed his. The rain fell down
his face. I closed my eyes.

"The boy lived in the king's castle, by the sea. Every day he would
protect the old king . . . from sea monsters. . . ."

Suddenly I was very tired. I settled my head more comfortably in his
lap. He started to say something, and stopped.

"Mmm?" I said.

"Nothing. Go on."

I yawned, and with my mind quite blank, I said, "And one day a girl
came to the castle. . . ."

"A beautiful princess."

"No, just a girl," I said. "The girl comes to the castle . . . on a quest . . . to rescue the knight."

"The *princess* can't rescue the *knight,*" said David. "It's against the rules of the genre."

"She can try," I said.

"And what's she rescuing him from?"

"Being sad."

After a while I opened my eyes. His eyes were still closed.

"That's the story," I said. "Tell me how it ends."

He opened his eyes and looked down at me and then looked away at the sea. After another while he said, "She doesn't rescue him."

I felt sick. "Why not?"

"Because she's too young."

I felt sicker. "That's not true," I said. "That's so not true."

"I know these stories," he said. "I know them backwards. And she's too young. Another thing I know, she isn't just a girl. She's a beautiful, intelligent princess . . . under a terrible spell . . . that makes her think she's just a girl. But she could rescue anyone in the world. She doesn't want a sad knight. Maybe she feels sorry for him, because he's sad, and that's . . . very lovely of her, but they've both drunk too much Chateau Magic Potion"—I hate him—"and a bucket of Newcastle Brown Elixir and when the magic wears off . . . Juliet, are you all right?"

I'd listened to most of this with my eyes closed, and now I'd opened my eyes, and the rain fell down into them, and the raindrops looked like my tears falling up into the sky, and I was unsure again which way was up. I felt dislodged from the world. I felt about as bad as I ever had. I had drunk enough to have the courage to so nearly say how I felt, and I'd been so misunderstood. He thought I was some silly girl. Too young. Silly. Drunk. I felt older than the moon, and as cold, and as ruined. "It's nothing," I said.

"You seem . . . ," he said "Are you sure you . . . are you feeling OK?"

I felt like I'd been exploring a magnificent palace all day, one famed for the view from the turret of its highest tower, and that I had discovered ever more wonderful things as I moved ever upward until now I'd just stepped through the final door to discover not the rooftop's panorama but a lift shaft. Wheee. "I'm fine," I said. "Really."

Crying in the rain is brilliant. You can just get on with it. No stupid questions. Just keep your face from crinkling, and don't make any noise. I wondered if he was dim enough to really think I just felt sorry for him, or was he trying to give me an out, a way of not feeling rejected. I wondered why he'd rejected me really. My age just wasn't a good enough excuse, certainly not from where I came from. If you made it into your teens in Tipperary without being impregnated by your grandfather, the county council gave you a medal.

I suppose I could have *asked* him.

That didn't really occur to me at the time.

Boy, was I young.

55

He walked me back to the house and called a taxi. I refused the offer of dry clothes, said I was fine, that I'd just have a shower and go to bed when I got home, everything was fine. His father, who had quit the rain before us, made me coffee before shaking my hand with both hands and saying how delighted he was to have met me, delighted, really, it'd been a great auld evening, but he was too pissed to stand, so he thought he'd better go to bed. And he disappeared off into the house, toward a bed from which he said he could see the sea.

David and me, alone in the kitchen. The taxi was late. Rain banging on the windows. A lot of demand for taxis on nights like these.

Tick, tock. Silence, et cetera. David laughed. "I've really fucked up the evening, haven't I?"

"No, no," I said, agreeing with him completely.

"Yes, yes," he mocked. "I suppose I should have just got you pregnant and called the kid Lancelot. Too late now, though."

My insides disagreed, and it showed through on the outside. He lifted a warning eyebrow. "Hoy. Less of it. You don't think I find you madly attractive? Of course I find you madly attractive. Not the way you look, well not just the way you look, but the way you are." He searched for words, raised his eyebrows, made a face. He squirmed, found a word. "Special."

I squirmed.

"You *are*, you idiot. But I'm riddled by scruples, by angst, by all manner of things, I'm brittle as a wafer at present, you don't want to be *near* me, you hear? I'm warning you off. Not because I don't like you, but because I like you too much. If I let myself fall for you, the way I'm feeling now, I'd never stop falling. And that wouldn't do you any good at all. As it is, I absolutely refuse to fall for you. I refuse. I don't want to get hurt, I don't want you to get hurt, I don't want anybody to get hurt. And somebody would be bound to get horribly hurt. And I just couldn't bear it. I'm up to my fucking ears in hurt, and I just couldn't bear any more anywhere near me. I was mad to invite you here, but I'm drunk enough now to see sense. I thought we could . . . talk, and eat, and orbit each other at a safe distance, and go home, and it would be very *nice*. But we can't, Juliet"

And he got up from his chair and walked to my side, and sank to one knee, took my hand, as though it was natural, as though people behaved like that, as though it meant nothing, as though we were having a conversation. "I thought we could keep it light, and pleasant, and fun, and today has been so much fun, but there is too much gravity in the situation, you generate, we generate too much *gravity*, and I don't want to fall Juliet, not now, I can't, I'm needed, it's already so hard to hold everything together, you don't know what it's like, do you understand?" Yes. Yes. "So will you please not think less of me for being such a . . . coward, and sending you off home when I wish I could . . . wish that I could . . ." He lifted my hand, kissed it. "Wish it was all different. But it isn't and I can't. And I'm really, really sorry for fucking up tonight."

I placed an imaginary sword on his left shoulder, on his right. "It's alright," I said. "It's fine." It wasn't, but it wasn't as bad as it had been. "You can arise now."

He arose.

"So you would if you could?"

He nodded.

"But . . . you can't."

He nodded.

I sighed. "I don't really understand. But . . . you still like me? You'll still talk to me? You won't start acting like we've broken up or something?"

He nodded till his head blurred.

"Fair enough, then." Tiredness hit me like a sack of cement. "Life is awfully difficult, isn't it?" I said.

He shrugged. "Yes. But it's the price we pay for its great rewards. It's worth it."

"I don't think I've got to the rewards yet," I said.

He laughed.

When the doorbell rang, we were talking about something as though nothing had happened. And, of course, nothing had.

He poured me into the taxi and paid the driver through my protests.

"Look, I invited you to dinner. I'd be driving you home if I wasn't so pissed, so just shush. There's no question. Here, if there's any change give it to her. Thanks. Just give me the change when you see me. Safe home, sleep well, look after yourself."

The taxi swept away from the house and tower, along the coast road. I turned awkwardly to wave, even though he wouldn't be able to see it. I caught a glimpse of him in the light of the doorway. Waving.

56

When I got home, the light was on in the living room, and the stove was still warm, but there was no other sign of life. I threw some offcuts into the stove and got some change from my room for the shower. Superstitiously, I wouldn't use the taxi change. I left that on my windowsill. For me, coins had histories. They weren't interchangeable.

The shower was just gorgeous. I stayed there forever.

When I came out, wrapped in my big towel, I was surprised to find Michael alone by the stove.

"Hello Michael. Where's Juno?"

"Juliet! Jeesus! Juno's gone out, to the Warwick, with the rest of the ack-tors. I haven't. Didn't." Michael wasn't looking his best. "I'm ossified," he explained. "Langers. We were going to have a row, but I decided to get rat-arsed instead. Good decision. Fine decision. We decided that Juno would go out and I would get pissed. Division of labour. Much better than a row. Have a Carlsberg."

He handed me a can. I sat on the chair beside him.

"Tell me about your day. We haven't had a good talk in . . . since last year. Maybe we never had a good talk. Who knows?"

I rolled the can against my cheek. Lovely and cold. I opened it, and told Michael at length about my day.

"Jesus," he said. "And the fucker wouldn't even sleep with you. The fucker. The sad fucker."

And Michael leaned over and kissed me and without thinking about it particularly I kissed him back. Warm lips, dry, a little chapped. The pleasantly rough surface of his lips moving very gently on mine. And after a few seconds and a very long day, it became less about surfaces, and I melted back into my chair and a little bit of me put my can down on the stovetop, and another little bit of me very deliberately switched off all the little bits of me that were trying to grab my attention, going, Wait. . . .

Click.

And I was melting.

Click.

And for the first time in a long time I wasn't thinking too much.

Click.

And it was very nice.

Reasons aren't really things that make you do other things. Reasons are things that you make up, much later, to reassure everyone that we are all logical and that the world makes sense. We do unreasonable things, because we want to, at the time. No reason. Much later we sit in the wreckage, building reasons out of little bits of wreckage, so we'll have something to show the crash investigators. Look, this is what caused it. So the whole mess at least appears reasonable. So we can convince ourselves that at least there was a reason for the disaster, something we can prevent or avoid, so it'll never happen again. But a lot of the time there's no reason. We just flew it into the ground. Because we felt like it. And we're still dangerous. And it could happen again anytime.

It's easier to live with each other afterwards if we give each other reasons.

Much later a tang of burning paint brought me slowly back to proper thinking. Conscious thought. My mind reluctantly switched back on.

I was lying on my big white towel in front of the stove. Michael's dark head between my parted thighs. He appeared to have fallen asleep. I was unsurprised. No wonder his lips are chapped, I thought, if he does all that every night. I looked up at the stove. The last of my Carlsberg had evaporated, and now the paint was beginning to blister and blacken low on the can. The air was jungly with beer steam. Me, I felt like I was made out of marshmallow. I felt absolutely delicious. I didn't want to move.

The metallic, harsh smell of the hot paint and the can was getting quite strong, though.

Michael said something that sounded very like "Juno . . . ," though it was rather muffled between my legs, and woke up with a start. He looked up along my belly at me.

"Oh, shit," he said. "Oh, fuck."

"I think I'd better go to bed now," I said, pronouncing each word carefully.

"Oh, God," said Michael. "Yes . . . wait! What am I . . . huh. We should talk, about . . . this."

I extracted my legs from under his arms and stood, as he lay there trying to climb up the ladder of a sentence from out of the swamp of sleep.

I picked up my towel, wrapped it back around me, and laughed at myself. Bit late now. My nipples were tender from his teeth and tongue. Absently I brought my left arm across my body so that my forearm lay lightly against my breasts. A mild pain. Not a pain at all. Pleasure, really. And under it some different kind of pain. It's odd how the things felt by our bodies and the things felt by our minds get so mixed up sometimes.

"Goodnight," I said.

"Oh, Christ, Juliet, don't be silly. You can't just *go to bed*."

"Yes, I can," I said very politely, looking down at him.

"We have to talk, you know we do."

"No, we don't," I said. "I'm tired." And I was . . . I was . . . I was going to cry if the conversation lasted another minute. "Night, Michael. Don't burn your fingers taking the can off the stove."

And I went to my bedroom, hunted through my underwear drawer for the key I never used, and locked my room.

And of course I cried, but that didn't mean very much. My tears weren't hard currency in those days. Devalued by overproduction. I wouldn't give too much weight to my tears.

Still . . . But . . .

Still, I'd known Michael loved Juno, even as I was kissing him I'd known it, and I'd always known Juno was different from me in a great bundle of important ways, but I wished Michael hadn't looked at me like that, in the moment after he woke, as he realized I wasn't Juno. I wished I hadn't seen him wake. I wished I hadn't seen him see me, and heard him speak when he was just letting his emotions fall out of his mouth because his consciousness hadn't yet arrived to filter his words. There probably wasn't enough of Michael there at the time to even hear himself say what he said.

As I cried myself to sleep his words felt like a careful description.

Shit.

Fuck.

Slowly they turned from words I heard into things I observed, as I spiralled down the gravity-well into sleep. They gained mass, became batlike, bulky, enemies, part of me. Just before we arrive at the event horizon of sleep and we impact with it at the oblique angle required to smoothly enter dreams, in the moment outside time just before we disappear, the world sometimes suddenly reappears around us, very sharp, very clear, quite transformed. Doesn't it? Sometimes? More real than life. More real than dreams. Just before we disappear. And we can't move, and we can't wake, and we can't dream. We're just there, supersharp, superclear.

I was there, supersharp, superclear. I was transformed. Lying on my back, in my bed, in one of those states so hard to describe because everything has changed its shape and significance and name.

(Beneath my right hand, my belly was still a little sticky, though I'd wiped most of it off.)

(The tracks of the tears that I'd cried earlier, standing up, were cooling and tightening on my cheek as the water evaporated and left faint trails of salt.)

(A new tear was taking the shortcut down to my ear.)

(Never cry on your back. Your ears fill with tears.)

My eyes were closed but they felt open. It was dark but I could see. I could see me, I was the world looking at me instead of the other way around.

And Michael was right.

I was Shit.

I was Fuck.

And then, at last, after a while, I disappeared.

It's so easy to say you cried yourself to sleep. It's so hard to do.

57

It was morning.

"Ouch," I said, and my eyes flicked open.

"Jesus," I said.

58

I walked into the living room. Juno was looking out the window. I walked across the room and stood beside her. The harbour and the bay. Crisp, bright morning. Sky-blue sky. Sea-green sea. Calm harbour below us. Boats as still as sculptures of themselves. All that moved the spark of sun on tiny waves far out to sea. No clouds.

She exhaled a long breath. The window misted, and cleared. Her shoulder touched mine, and I leaned back into it. We watched a sailor walk the length of the deck of the *Aoife*. About a quarter of our navy, she must have come in that morning at high tide when the harbour gate was open. Back from boarding Spanish trawlers far out of sight of land, to check their nets and papers and share jokes in mangled English about the English. There were rumours of a ceasefire in the war over our fish, too. Rumours of peace everywhere, even out of sight of land. Strange days, with the nets being cut and the boy soldiers shot, and everywhere rumours of peace.

The sailor reached the back of the ship and looked around. In the shelter of a tarpaulined gun and high above the quay, with just a lumber-yard to one side and the harbour to the other, he must have thought himself quite unobserved. He lit up a cigarette.

"That's naughty," said Juno. "I bet his mummy doesn't know."

Old joke. When we were tiny we used to say it seriously. At thirteen we revived it, ironically. Later again, at sixteen and mourning our loss of innocence, we'd used it all summer, nostalgically. And now we didn't use it at all. I hadn't heard it in a year. What comes after nostalgia, when you're eighteen?

He leaned forward till his stomach rested against the guardrail at the back of the *Aoife*. Lazily he moved a hand to his flies and, after brief manoeuvring, began to urinate in a high, astonishing arc, out and down into the harbour waters.

"That's very, very naughty," I said. "I bet his mummy *and* his daddy don't know."

"I bet his granny doesn't know."

"I bet Father King doesn't know."

"I bet Father King watches."

We giggled and held each other. He was still doing it. He made the glittering arc go even higher.

"He must have a bladder the size of a beach ball."

Pause.

"He must have hollow legs."

Fascinated pause.

"He must . . . "

"I think I can see it!"

He waggled his hand as I spoke and the pale stream waggled too, like a clothesline when you shake a wave along it. We howled with laughter, and Juno put her lips against my neck and spluttered great rasps of sound off it till it tickled and I ducked.

The flow had begun to slacken by the time we stopped laughing, but it was still pretty impressive, going out horizontally now before falling.

"What a man!"

"He's cheating, he's got a hose in there."

"You looooove him," I said, another very old joke, one we'd often used in childhood to get us through a night of bad Irish television, all cheap English imports and old films and RTÉ sitcoms so terrible they were hypnotic, like the sort of video installation that would later win awards; "Sitcom Without Jokes or Acting," brutally deconstructed critiques of the genre.

"You looooooove him."

Bob Monkhouse. Nicholas Parsons. Mike Read, God help us, on *Top of the Pops*. The man who read the cattle prices on *Mart & Market*. The singer with Norway's inexplicable and doomed heavy-metal entry in the *Eurovision Song Contest*. Everyone in *Leave It to Mrs. O'Brien*. Clint Eastwood, lapels and hair billowing, in *Every Which Way but Loose*. The orangutan in *Every Which Way but Loose*.

"You looooove him." Giggling on the spavined couch with our father scowling at our mother and our mother going "shush."

Juno giggled. "I do not."

"You looooove him, and you're going to maarrrry him!"

"I am not!"

He was still, incredibly, pissing.

If I laughed any more I'd be joining in.

"Maybe he's your pervert," I gurgled. "*Imagine* . . . if he can piss like that . . ."

"Oh, Juliet . . . that's not funnnny. . . ."

We were holding each other up, crippled with laughter.

"*Ju*-no's *per*-vert! *Ju*-no's *per*-vert!"

His superpowers eventually waned.

The arch buckled, and broke.

A last jet, a sprinkle. He tucked it away one-handed. I was vaguely surprised to see that the cigarette he'd started with, on which he'd puffed throughout, was still going. Perhaps he'd lit another while I was blind with tears. Perhaps he'd smoked a pack.

Eventually we stopped laughing. "I'm sorry about last night," I said.

She shrugged, almost a real shrug. "These things happen," she said.

"It was my fault, I was drunk," I said.

She laughed, a real laugh. "He said it was his fault, he was drunk."

"Have I fucked everything up?"

"Mmm. Yes. I'd just decided I wouldn't break up with him, after talking it over for hours with Gemma in the Warwick, and then I come home and he tells me he doesn't know how to tell me this but he's fucked my sister. I mean, Juliet, Jesus . . ."

"But he didn't!"

"Well *he* came, and he couldn't resist telling me *you* came, so you're trying to get off on a bit of a technicality here."

"But he didn't," I said sulkily. "I mean, he . . ." I thought better of it.

Juno sighed. "Jesus, Juliet, you're getting more upset about me getting the *position* wrong than I am about you fucking him . . . *not* fucking him, whatever. About the two of you coming in the same room as each other . . . you did come?"

"Mmm."

"Well, there's a good girl. At least one of us got something out of it. He's surprisingly . . . nice . . . isn't he?"

"Mmm."

"I was surprised . . . I nearly . . . I'll miss him."

I held on to her a little tighter, and she squeezed me back. "Oh, you are a fool, Juliet."

"I'm sorry."

She kissed me on the side of the nose because that was where our faces had ended up.

"I'm sorry, I'm sorry."

You will be unsurprised to hear I cried.

When I could see again, the sailor had gone. Oh, God. Poor Michael. "He loves you," I said miserably. She nodded. "I'm sorry," I said again. She nodded, and held on to me.

59

I hid in my room for a couple of days and read a lot of Beckett. Time passed very slowly, and then changed its mind and passed very fast. Michael's visits to the flat were soon again so frequent that I couldn't really avoid him without becoming homeless. The awkwardness faded slowly. The resumption of college was in many ways a blessed relief. The whole situation seemed in some obscure way to amuse Juno, whose for-giveness ate away at me more than her blame would have done.

Juno and I were sitting snug by the stove one afternoon when Michael stuck his head in.

"I need to buy a book in Boo's, will you run cover for me?"

"Oh no" I said.

"Ah yeah" said Juno. "Let's."

So we did. The walk there was nice. We walked, we talked, we laughed. I watched Juno with Michael, and Michael with Juno, on the sly, out of the corners of my eyes. Watched the air between them, and the way they used the air between them. The way it filled and emptied. What happened when their hands touched. They were again a mystery to me. I brooded.

Apart from the fact that Michael didn't stay the night anymore, hardly anything appeared on the surface to have changed between him and Juno. There were hints and signs that a massive renegotiation of the entire relationship was taking place beneath that surface, but I couldn't tell in what direction, or by whose command. It had seemed obvious to me at first that the balance of power in their relationship must have shifted firmly in favour of Juno, self-evidently, for Michael had put himself so blatantly in the wrong. When Juno said she'd miss him, I had assumed that she had ended everything, regretfully but firmly. As the days and the long nights passed I began to suspect I'd got the whole thing wrong. Sometimes it seemed that Michael, in sleeping with me, had . . . (let's flowery-up the language here, because this is how I secretly thought back then) . . . had shaken off the chains of his love for Juno, and was free.

(And often I still think like that, in great romantic metaphors, unironically. Because sometimes I believe they are more accurate and true than sentences with the words *relationship* and *power* in them. Though I use them too. They can also be accurate, and true.)

. . . That because he had broken the terms of their delicate, failing treaty the initiative was now his, and with it the power to renegotiate their relationship. In yet another tribute to my award-winning naivety, I was shocked at this possibility of vice rewarded.

But, Juno didn't talk to me directly about it and I couldn't ask, I was too guilty and implicated.

Besides, I was too busy worrying about my own Relationships, and their mysterious balances of power.

With David Hennessey. For instance.

Anyway. We were walking to Boo's.

Boo's is A Bookshop of One's Own on Middle Street. Someone had nicked the letter K the week it opened, so A Boo shop of One's Own it remained for a month, in stern brass letters with its many and wonderfully vulval Os. Even after they'd fixed it, everybody called it Boo's. When we were almost there, Michael and Juno bumped into one of Michael's theatre friends.

The friend (I missed it. Aaron? Arnold?) talked straight at Michael while staring straight at Juno's tits. When he decided to give his gaze a rest from Juno's chest by switching it to mine, I drifted a few yards ahead of them. I took a deep breath in Boo's doorway, and teetered. I never felt quite ideologically sound enough, quite female enough, quite brilliant enough to meet with the management's high standards. Boo's practically had a dress code and door policy.

Michael saw me teetering and gave me a little push. "Get in there, woman," he said. It was a joke, but my toe caught on the lintel, failed to clear it, and I stumbled into the shop, falling to one knee. A startled assistant looked up to see an unshaven man in a leather jacket pushing a girl to the ground. I looked at the assistant. I looked up at Michael. I hadn't wanted to come anyway.

"Please, I won't do it again," I said.

Michael looked down at me, mortified. "Sorry," he said, and put down a hand to help me up.

"That's what you said last time," I said, and got up without taking his hand. He looked at me. I looked at him. The assistant looked at both of us, all her suspicions about men entirely confirmed. I turned slightly so she couldn't see my face and smiled sweetly at Michael. He gave me a wryly admiring grin.

"You know you love it, you bitch," he said.

Behind me, the assistant dropped her roll of Sellotape. Over Michael's shoulder, through the doorway, I could see Juno pissing herself with laughter.

Inside the shop, Juno joined in the game. We probably laid it on a bit thick. Michael made me put back the Anne Tyler I'd picked up, gave Juno a Norman Mailer to read, and then made her climb the ladder to get the psychology text he wanted from the top shelf at the back. "But Michael I'm afraid of heights." "Get up there, it'll make a man of ya." We gurlied it up and said "Yes, Michael" submissively every time he loudly recommended another classic of misogyny they didn't stock. I was a bit worried at one point that the manager was going to call the guards. Her disgust at our servility overcame her pity at our plight, however, and she did nothing.

With the book bought, we fled giggling. The three of us had a coffee in Neachtain's. Something was fixed. That night, Michael stayed over. Juno was pleased. Repeatedly. I eventually managed to fall asleep around four.

60

The rocket of my rage accelerated me along the corridor and straight into the lift for Tower 2, which cut in (second-stage booster) to send me soaring up to the English Department. With smoke coming out of my ears, I rounded two corners, more than half an internal orbit of the tower, and crashed to a halt outside David's door, palm first.

"Come in."

I came in. "She doesn't even *bloody* know how to punctuate *Finnegans Wake*," I said.

"Calm yourself, child," said David, pretending great age. "Sit in the seat, gather the thoughts, and tell the tale. It concerns Pamela, no? Or I know nothing of first-year timetables and the human heart."

"Pamela Henderson is a moron," I said loudly. David winced, put down his pen, and walked to the door.

"Careless talk costs lives," he said, shutting it. "And she isn't, really. But continue. Elaborate. Unburden yourself."

"She put an apostrophe in *Finnegans Wake*! She corrected my punctuation! She doesn't even know the title of Joyce's *bloody Finnegans Wake*!"

I waved the essay about my head in an excess of fury almost beyond words. "She gave me a C!"

David looked crestfallen. "Oh, that's hardly a crime. I'd hoped you'd caught her dealing drugs after lectures. Or during. Shooting up at the lectern."

I was so incensed at his not sharing my fury that I actually stuttered an authentic "But . . . but . . . but . . . ," as frequently seen in film and fiction, but not too often in Galway. "Finnegan's?!"

"It's an apostrophe, Juliet," he said, amused.

"It's *Finnegans Wake*!" I said, not amused.

"Well, yes, that's pretty bad," he admitted. "But she probably wasn't thinking. After a couple of hours correcting the illiterate ramblings, begging your pardon, of a shower of first-years, your head is dead. Your brain can't handle the insult. You start to correct e. e. cummings into upper case. I stuck an apostrophe into the middle of Keats once, after four hours of correcting almost identical answers to an already dull question on the Romantics. I was practically hallucinating with boredom. My mind started playing sub-Joycean word games to stay awake. I started reading Shelley as an adjective redolent of the seaside. Their footsteps crunched across the shelley beach. . . . Have you calmed down yet?"

"No."

He sighed. "Give us a look."

I handed him the essay. He read it slowly while I wandered the office, weaving my way around the tall, corallike growths of stacked hardbacks and paperbacks that rose from the floor, often to a height of several feet. I examined the deep, stuffed bookshelves that lined the walls of the room, soundproofing it, practically bombproofing it, and I committed the sin of envy.

"Very good," he said when he'd finished. "B plus, at least. Probably a low A. She does seem to have rather missed the point you were making. But that's partly your own fault, there's leaps in the logic that you haven't really bothered bridging with any planks of evidence, to help your reader follow you. I can, because we've talked about Yeats enough so I know what you're getting at. But you can hardly expect poor Pamela to give you the benefit of her sturdy nonconformist Londonderry doubt when you make it so hard for her. You're attacking her all the way through it, I mean it's obvious . . . well, they're obviously her ideas you're disagreeing with, but you don't bother to rigorously back up your own arguments. And you've definitely mugged poor, defenceless Joyce and dragged him in bleeding to show how tough you are, he's not relevant to your argument at all. I'd bet you had the *Wake* beside you as you were writing this and decided to dip in for a quote just to impress her with your fabulous range."

This was so horribly accurate that I nearly stuttered again. "But . . ." I got the quizzical eyebrow. "But she's so . . . so . . ." I got both eyebrows. "She has the soul of a *mechanic!*" I wailed. "She gets *Finnegans Wake* wrong and she gave me a C and you're on *her* side!"

He put his elbows on his desk, cupped his chin in his hands, and grinned at me. "Don't be silly. I'd bet real cash money you haven't read more than twenty pages of the *Wake*"—more like five—"so it's a bit naughty demanding her head over an apostrophe. And was it not delight-fully human of her to err? Anyway, this essay *is* a C essay, I've changed my mind. You knew exactly who you were writing for, and you didn't even begin to try to persuade her. They're A ideas, but you have to bring your audience with you. C, I'm afraid. And I *am* on your side, you schmoo, but that doesn't mean I have to nod wisely and agree with everything you say. Friends frequently don't."

"Don't want you to be my friend," I sulked. "What's a schmoo?"

"No idea. I read it in a book. Come on, I'll buy you a cup of muck in the old cantina."

David mocked me to the lift till my mood suddenly flipped and I did a mad thing. I kissed him, very quickly, on the cheek, as the lift doors closed on us.

"Didn't mean it," I said, horrified, jumping back. "Just a kiss. Acci-dent. Don't be angry, I really didn't mean it."

David touched his cheek thoughtfully, as though he'd been slapped. "Jesus, Juliet, write out the word *mercurial* one hundred times."

"I mean, I meant it, but I didn't mean to do it, I know you don't want . . . anything. . . ."

"I'm just a boy who can't say yes," he sang sadly, pressing the button to start the descent and then, as the old lift lurched down and the floor stuttered briefly from under us, bringing his hand back up to his cheek again.

Oh God, say something. I opened my mouth. "It was just a because-I-like-you kiss, it wasn't a please-kiss-me-back kiss. . . . How's your father?"

David coughed and hid his mouth with his hand. "Er, yes, he's fine. Still alive and dying," he said, as if it were a quote from somewhere. "Perhaps a little weaker than when you saw him. It isn't affecting him all that much, physically, yet. When it does of course he'll go down rather dramatically and there'll be a couple of, well, ah, desperately unpleasant weeks." We gained weight for a long instant, or a short second, and the doors opened. "Which I'm not looking forward to." He waved me out first, mock-gallantly? No, absentmindedly. The way he was brought up.

"I don't even know what your father . . . has," I said. "I mean, you don't have to tell me."

"Oh, boring old leukemia. I thought you knew. Sorry. He had it before, took the chemo, fought hard, came through."

I was very aware of him as he walked beside me. I could sense the bulk of him, close, shoulder and hip. The left side of my body tingled a bit. "Maybe he'll come through again."

"No. He's refused treatment this time. He doesn't want to do it all again. I think, you see, he sort of came to terms with dying and all that the last time, settled his spiritual accounts. And then he got an extra couple of years, which he considered a bit of a gift from God. I think he feels it would be cheating to duck a second time. Besides which, he has always missed our mother, you know, and his faith is quite strong although unorthodox. The Far East affected him a lot, you know, going there after our mother died. I'm talking too much."

"No, you're not. I like him, I really want to know."

We entered the canteen through the stiff doors, David holding them open for me, and walked towards the smell of coffee. I resisted an urge to put a protective arm around him, and another, more peculiar urge to childishly knock him over and wrestle with him, as Juno and I had done with tall Paul, when we were small.

"Shall we go mad and split a Kit Kat?" he said, examining the austere selection of luxury goods beside the coffee machine. "My treat."

"Oh, yer honour, I couldn't possibly," I said in a thick Tipperary accent. "In dit to a gintlemin. Compromised in th'eyes of the parish."

He laughed at me. "A mere Kat, madam, still less a Kit, hath surely no power to sully so great a Virtue as you possess. Milk?"

"Yes, please."

"Grand. . . . So why don't you speak with an honest Tipp brogue all the time?"

"Because I don't want to sound like a pig talking German with his mouth full," I said succinctly.

David coughed hard up his sleeve. "Sorry. . . . Do your parents speak like that, then?"

"Not really. They're more Tipp than me though."

"More? Oh, more Tipp, yes." He was paying for the coffees, a Kit Kat, and a Snack Bar, the wafery type in the pink packet. The woman at the till smiled at him, put his change on the tray. Looked past me. "No, it's a nice accent."

I snorted.

". . . But it's odd to hear you speak in it. Me, I sound Irish to the English and English to the Irish. And both to the Welsh. . . . You're a harsh judge of your hometown."

"Yes," I said.

"Nothing for you there?"

"No. Really, I'm sort of glad there's nothing for me at home, or I might be tempted to stay, and that'd be . . . awful."

"What were you going to say, there?"

I giggled. "Shite. Or maybe 'fuckin' shite.' " Full-on accent.

"Isn't there *anything* for you in Tipperary? Surely you could build some sort of life there, if you wanted to. I mean, I'm not saying you should, but you could surely."

I snorted again. "Yeah, I'm throwing away a corner table for life in Connollys, and a firm offer of a job in accounts in the abattoir. I'll have to learn to live without the chance to see amateur productions of *I Do Not Like Thee, Doctor Fell* in the town hall, for three quid, with one character missing because some county council clerk has fallen off the wagon again. I'll have to say good-bye forever to a librarian who sucks in air through her teeth every time I take out a book she disapproves of." I looked him in the eye. "Fucking heartbreaking," I said.

"Mmm. Point taken. Points."

We sat and sipped our coffees in easy silence. I stole half his Kit Kat and dunked it. He did a silent-movie scowl of fury and shook his free fist like the mustachioed villain in a Chaplin short. I looked coquettish, batted my eyelids, and pretended to blush, then stole the other half.

After the dinner, and the beach, and my rejection, I'd assumed everything would be ruined between us, or at least damaged and strained. But, even from the start of the first tutorial of the new semester, we had talked and argued quite exactly as before; when we'd met occasionally on the concourse, we had stopped and chatted briefly, quite exactly as before; and now we were having coffee together and nothing had changed, it was precisely as before. We were getting on wonderfully. Everything was great.

It was infuriating. I hated it. How dare something so important and painful have changed things so little.

"God, this coffee is shite," I said.

That was the nicest thing about him callously rejecting me, breaking my young heart, etc. I could snort and swear all I wanted now and it didn't matter a damn. Didn't matter a shite. Didn't matter a fuck. Didn't matter a shiteing, fucking damn.

61

Two days later, rain, rain, rain. Blissful, wasteful, useful rain. I walked along the paths and up the ramp and around the library, on the outside, in the dumb, beautiful rain.

I didn't bother entering the university by the doors of the library foyer, as I hadn't bothered entering by the entrance I'd already passed, the one to the tunnel that ran under the library. They used to call me Tinker Taylor when I was in infants, I suddenly remembered, because I wouldn't wear a dress and I stamped in the puddles and the mud like the boys when it rained. The boys called me Tinker Taylor too.

When did they stop? I couldn't remember.

When we got pretty. I couldn't remember, but I knew it had to be then because that was when everything changed.

Raindrops smashed like quiet glass on the smooth, wet concrete as I walked towards the doors of the concourse. The hiss of the rain was really a symphony on one madly repeated, very quiet note, tremendously staccato. *Hisssssissssssiss.* Pretty lousy symphony. All energy and no talent.

I walked through the doorway into David.

"Hi," I said, and pushed past him.

He stopped me and spun me around to face him, somehow. Long arms. Magnets. I don't know.

"You're crying," he said.

"It's raining," I said.

"Bullshit," he said, and brushed the rain from my cheeks with the curve of his fingers. It was so nothing to do with sex you wouldn't believe it. Even if I hadn't already been crying all the way in to college, I would have started at that warm stroke along each cheekbone, along the sides of my jaw, stopping short of my ears, gone. Like my mother when I'm sick.

"You said *bullshit*," I said, and I could feel a tear fall down each cheek at the same speed.

"Why are you crying?"

"Because it's raining."

"Why are you crying, Juliet?"

"People are looking."

"Fuck them. Why are you crying?"

"You said . . ."

I began to sob. He took my arm. He walked me around the porters' desk where two porters, still sorting the morning mail, didn't even look up.

The corridor behind it, at the Tower 2 lift. Pressed the button. The door opened immediately. "I think I was looking for you," I sobbed. "I didn't think I was, but I was, wasn't I? I thought I was just walking in the rain, but I wasn't, was I?"

When we got to his office he sat me down in his chair, behind his desk. He shoved some books off one corner of the desk and sat. "Tell me."

I closed my eyes. "My sister got a letter," I said, very clearly.

"Juno," he said.

"Yes."

"You live with her. Your twin."

"Yes."

"Go on."

I opened my eyes and looked at all the lovely books. The different coloured spines. Like a rainbow, I thought. Hundreds of bands of colour. Thousands. Like a rainbow for complicated light.

"Your father could have a bone marrow transplant," I said. "Not chemotherapy. Not just. He might live."

"Please, Juliet . . ."

"He might *live*," I said.

"He had one, Juliet, last time. It was my marrow. He won't do it again because he wants to die, he doesn't mind and nor should you. It's not a tragedy, it's not like a child dying, it's a *decision*. You and I, we have no right. . . . Please Juliet, the letter."

I closed my eyes again. "It was very horrible." My detached, precise voice. I admired it for a bit. David said nothing. "I wish he was dead. He made her cry." David said nothing. "You don't know how nice she is, David, you don't know. How dare he. How dare he." Not as precise. Crying again.

"Who wrote the letter, Juliet?"

"Juno's pervert," I sobbed. "The *bastard* who writes to her. The *bastard*. We thought it was *nice,* the first one was *nice*. We thought, I thought he *liked* her. He's a *bastard*. He's a *cunt*ing, *fuck*ing . . ." Not precise at all.

"Anonymous letters?"

Nod.

"How many? When?"

"Third. This is the third."

"When did they start?"

"September . . . when we came . . . we . . . it was, the first one was nice. He knows where we *live*."

"Written or typed?"

"Typed?"

"Printed."

". . . Printed."

"Can I see them?"

"What?"

"Can I see the letters?"

"Juno burnt one, the second one. The first one is in Tipperary. She didn't want it in the house after the second one, but she didn't want to destroy it, in case . . . there was another one . . . and she . . ." Sobbing, and so on.

"Have you gone to the police?"

"No"

"You should go to the police. You should show them the letters."

"No!"

"Why not? They're nothing to do with you, Juliet, they're nothing to do with Juno. They reflect only on the writer. The guilt is the writer's. They're evidence. They're evidence of pathology. That's all. Please don't cry. Please don't cry."

He held my hand.

"He made her cry. Oh, David, he made her cry. . . ." I was talking over him; we said *cry* at the same time, the pitches high and low together, like music, mine a harmony to his, or his to mine.

"She . . ." but the words I have can't carry what I feel, so I reach for more, and the crush of words jam in my mouth. Jams. Ten things. Too much. A crush.

She's good,
How could anyone,
Why,
Oh David,
Is it like this?
The *bastard*
I'm scared,
Please, please, please
If the world is
Christ. Christ. Jesus.

"Oh Jesus. Oh David."

I am holding his hand. He is holding my hand. I feel sick. His hand in my hand in his hand in my hand. I feel dizzy and sick.

"Where is Juno now?"

"We . . . no. God. She's at home, she's fine. She's got friends looking after her. I went to get Michael, she wanted to see Michael, he's, he was, is, her fr . . . boyfriend. Friend. Sorry, sorry, sorry, I'm not doing this very well. She wanted to see Michael, she went out with him, until . . . recently. They . . . I went to get Michael, he wasn't in so I left him a message. And then I kept walking, I . . . went for a walk, I walked here. I felt OK on the walk, sorry I made a scene, I'm fine. It's just, you understand, it's hard, when I can't help her. You understand."

"I understand."

"No, I . . . no. I'm fine now. Oh Jesus, you were going to a lecture—"

"No, it's fine—"

"Oh Jesus David I'm sorry—"

"No no no. *No.* I'm glad you came to me. I . . . wish I could be of more use. Perhaps, I hope I can."

I saw with detached surprise the wet line down his cheek. I touched it with a fingertip. He let go my other hand and brushed his cheek with the back of his right hand.

"You're late for your lecture."

"It doesn't matter."

"Go to your lecture."

"It doesn't matter. This is important. This has to be . . . stopped. This cannot be allowed to go on, because it will go on. . . ."

"Go to your lecture. You can solve the mystery after the lecture. We can stop it next week. It's only words. I shouldn't have got upset. God, I'm more upset than Juno was. It's only words. You're right."

"Are you sure your sister, Juno, that she's alright?"

"She's fine, she's with Connie and Dominic. Honestly David, there's nothing you can do. Go to your lecture."

"But you're still upset."

"I'm not. I'm not, I was, I got upset talking about it there, but I'm grand now really David, go to your lecture. It's only words. There was no harm done. I'm fine. I'm grand. Really." I nearly had to push him out the door in front of me.

"You can stay here, if you like. There's a kettle behind all the . . ."— helpless gesture back at the mesas and plateaux of printed paper—"and coffee and mugs in the drawer of the desk. . . ."

"No, I'll be grand, thanks though. I have an essay to do, there's a book on Aristotle the library's holding for me, I have to pick that up . . . thanks, all the same."

With the closing of the office door behind us we found ourselves, awkward, too suddenly, in the corridor and the public world. A rush of air. A pressure drop, or rise. From intimate to formal. Rooms should have airlocks, for us to adjust our emotions before we re-enter the world.

"I'll leave it open, if you need to . . . I'm finished at three today, if you need to talk, I don't have a lunchtime because I'm meeting Professor O'Neill about the expansion of the department . . . but, if you want to, to talk. To someone."

I'd never seen him struggle so hard with the language. His hands were bunched in fists by his sides. He looked like a boxer giving a speech. I laughed. "You look like you want to hit me."

A small smile. "Not you."

I walked him to the lift. He walked me to the lift. Whichever.

We hardly talked during the brief descent, but that was sort of nice. When it stopped at the concourse, we got out and smiled with awkwardness and turned in our different directions. I looked back, to see him look back over his shoulder at me. He gave me a salute; I waved a hurry-on at him, and he smiled, turned away, and began running down the wide expanse of the concourse, really sprinting, dodging the people coming against him, overtaking a nun, Flannery Ryan, a pack of engineers . . . gone.

I turned away. Went to the library. Locked myself in the toilets on the Arts floor to have a good cry. Couldn't. Realized I felt extraordinarily happy. On the way out I wrote "D. H. is Fab" and "J. T. Roolz" in the steam on the mirror, with my forefinger, and then a couple of badly drawn hearts, with one side bigger than the other, like real hearts. Expressing and mocking my joy with the same gesture, in the modern ironic fashion.

Left the library without remembering to get out the book I'd asked them to keep for me.

Everything would be all right. Juno would be fine. I would be fine. I could feel it. Gut instinct. Just as half an hour earlier I could feel that nothing would ever be right again.

My emotional compass was spinning like a roulette wheel, and my heart felt like the little silver ball.

On impulse, I turned into the Quad as I was passing, hesitated, headed right, toward the College Bar. At the doorway of the College Bar I hesitated again, and on another impulse turned, walked away from the bar and started down the narrow, dark stairs to UCG Art Gallery.

62

I recognised the paintings. This was very peculiar. I wouldn't recognise the paintings if you walked me into the Irish National Gallery, banged my nose off Leech's *Goose Girl,* and wiped away my subsequent tears with Caravaggio's *The Taking of Christ.*

These paintings, though, I knew. Hot, bright, hallucinatory. But, like seeing a familiar face in the wrong place, a taxi driver on the beach, without their context I was stymied. Spotlit, high on white partitions, just themselves. How did I know them?

Then an oldish man appeared from behind one of the partitions, conversing with another man. Weatherbeaten, in comfortable old tweed suits, leaning on stout sticks, the two of them together looked like a bit of Connemara hillside talking to itself, and I remembered.

"Mr. Hennessey!" I said.

"Well if it isn't the bauld Juliet Taylor! D'ye know Jim here, of course you don't, Dr. James Griffin of Spiddal and Paris, a pal of my cradle days and my doctor now at the other end of things, Juliet Taylor, a great friend of my son's . . ." Hallos, pleased-to-meet-yous, and the shaking of hands.

"So these are yours, then?" I said. "I admired them in your house."

"Ah, I've painted a bit for the past few years. You have to pass the days. 'Twas David made me stick a few of them in the exhibition here. He brought a couple in without tellin' me. I said to him one morning last week, where the feck are me paintings on the landing gone, and he says he's put them in for an exhibition of young Galway artists. Hah! Sure you've been an artist no time, he says. You qualify, no bother. But them two you fecked are shite, begging your pardon, said I like an eejit. So by trickery he had me picking six for this thing."

"This one's lovely," I said, which was half true. No, true but insufficient. It was lovely and disturbing. Great angled planes of yellow and blue crumpled suddenly at the heart of the canvas, ruptured and torn. I felt I could put my hand in among the painted shards and pull out . . . something.

"Ah, it's only an auld painting."

"No, it means something, it must. It's not of something, but it has to mean something, to you."

"Well it is 'of' something, in a manner of speaking. It's a painting of a stress fracture in a load-bearing steel support. Not, now, as the eye would see it, mind, but on a crystalline level. It looks a fair bit like that. That's one of the first ones I did."

"It's beautiful." Dr. Griffin had wandered off to where some paintings leaned against a bare wall. The girl who'd been crouched by them, screwing cuphooks into the frames, stood up and turned to talk to him. It was Gemma Mannion. Of course, she painted. A boy with a ponytail, the sides of his head shaved, was standing on a chair at the far end of the gallery, adjusting spotlights. "Am I in the way here?" I asked David's father. "Your friend, Dr. Griffin . . ."

"Oh God, no, child. I only had Jim here to help me with the hanging, and mine're hung. We were only having a look at the other lads' paintings and boring each other with our Theories of Art."

"Bore me with your theory," I said.

"Ah no, you'll suffer enough in this life without that."

I wandered up to my favourite of his. Broad, thick strokes. Flat, abrupt ledges of oil or acrylic, I couldn't tell. Acrylic, I guessed. Vivid, unmixed. Painted with a knife. Painted with a big emotion, though only God knew what. God and Gerry Hennessey and whoever he'd told.

"But this must mean something," I said. "It's not just a picture of, whatever it was, steel crystals. A fracture. The way you painted it, and what you chose to paint . . . it must mean something to you."

"Arra whisht, you sound like David." He leaned on his stick and squinted with gloomy suspicion at the picture, like a farmer pondering a cow with a cough. "He's always going on about them and calling them pictorial metaphors for my emotional condition, when he isn't trying to make me get an agent or comparing me to fellahs I never heard of. They're only shagging paintings."

I laughed. A vivid image of David in the kitchen, embarrassing his father with praise. "How much are they?"

"Oh ask my agent, how much are they . . . sure who'd buy them."

"I would, if I had the money. I'd buy this one."

"Get away, you'll have me blushing."

"No, honest to God I would. I noticed it as soon as I walked into your house, it was in the hall wasn't it? The . . . colours. It's . . . I won't embarrass you. But it's good, honestly. Ah no, I will embarrass you, it's brilliant, I love looking at it, I don't know why but I do. It makes me feel . . ."

"Jesus, you're mortifying me Juliet, will you stop. Have it, have it, only stop."

"What do . . ." I got a couple of words together, but I couldn't make a decent sentence out of them.

"It's yours, take it away when the exhibition's over."

"But, I can't, I mean, what about David—"

"What about him, they're my paintings aren't they, he'll have enough of them soon enough. If you like it you can have it, I'd be delighted and honoured."

"Oh Mr. Hennessey, I couldn't, it's worth money, it's too much . . ."

"And what in God's name would I be doing with money, haven't I money coming out of me arse, would you ever just take it and shush. I'll

put it in the book here, sold to Juliet Taylor. I've sold one, Jim!" This last
shouted across the gallery.

"Oh this world is full of fools," said Dr. Griffin, coming over with
Gemma to inspect my acquisition. David's dad made to introduce us,
"Gemma Mannion . . ."

"Ah, we know each other well," said Gemma.

"But of course," he said, "all ye young people know each other in
Galway. It's like a club."

Dr. Griffin cast a critical eye over the canvas. "Oh, one of your finest,
Gerry, undoubtedly. The modernity of it is only frightening. Sure if it was
any more modern it wouldn't be dry yet. I hope you're making the poor
girl pay in cash, and up front."

"I am of course."

"Good, good. And you'll have it finished, won't you, by the time she
returns with her suitcase of Swiss francs?"

"I will. A good big fishing boat in the middle of it so she'll know
which way up to hang it."

"As long as it's weatherproof. You can't beat the Du-Lux Gloss."

"Oh, you could hang this one outside in the garden, Jim. She'll never
rust."

It was odd hearing men who looked so dignified, so mature, talking
easy nonsense for their own amusement. Gemma grinned at me.

A sudden sweet-and-sour shock, that they'd been young too, once,
and that we would grow old and that we wouldn't really feel we'd
changed at all.

We stand, very still, on the stage, and the sets change and change,
they blur and we are in another play, being treated as a different character, but knowing we're the same.

The true self has no age, or has age the way it has hair colour.

Ah, the old make us philosophical. No wonder we avoid them.

I helped David's father and Dr. Griffin to help Gemma hang her
paintings, dark sketchy oils of gloomy-looking couples that made me
worry about her social life. Both men flirted decorously with us in the re-

laxed and pleasant fashion traditional to the older, much-travelled Irishman. They flirted with a kind of sophisticated innocence that was much nicer than sophistication on its own, and much easier to accept than the raw innocent regard with which I occasionally caught the ponytailed boy looking at me from the far end of the gallery. The older men weighted their flirtation better. You didn't feel you had to respond to it or fight it, or worry about its implications, or their feelings, or your virtue. They meant it, but they didn't want anything in return. Their compliments were not a speculative investment.

Civilized, dignified men. I liked that brief time very much.

When we'd all finished hanging Gemma's paintings, the two men courteously said their good-byes. "You must come for dinner again," said David's father to me. "And you, Gemma, too. Give me enough notice and I'll prepare a proper student dinner for you, baked beans on toast perhaps, and maybe a can of Ambrosia creamed rice for dessert, Deo volente."

We expressed our delight, all shook hands, and the two men departed. Their laughter and conversation echoed down the stairwell behind them as they ascended, sounding like two cheerful boys on the mitch from school. The fire door hissed shut, and with a thunk from the hydraulic cylinder the sound of the old young men was cut off.

Gemma stood back and admired her last painting to be hung, a pool of illuminated gloom high on the white wall. "It's shite," she said, "but it's accurate. He was a miserable bastard, and his chin really was that long. D'you like the way the two of us look as though we're dying of boredom? He was mortally offended."

"Who is he?" I said. He looked half-familiar.

"An ex. You wouldn't know him. He's from Ballina, I broke it off with him Christmas before last, after I went looking for a present for him and I couldn't find anything I wanted to give him. I was tired and annoyed with myself, so I went for a coffee and a fag in Java's, and I realized as I was sitting there that I'd liked the *presents* I'd seen, it was just him I didn't like. So I broke it off and saved myself a tenner."

"How do people ever stay together?" I said.

"They hardly ever do," said Gemma.

She borrowed the chair from the ponytailed boy, and we made final adjustments to the lighting of her paintings.

When the last of the spotlights had been aligned, I returned the chair to the ponytailed boy who, as I said thank you, blinked shyly at me, then blushingly looked at my tits.

"Come on," said Gemma to me. "We're done. Bye, Dan."

The boy said good-bye. So he has the mysterious power of speech, I thought. Good man, Dan. God be praised.

Thunk. We ascended the complicated stairs. "You're a dote for helping," said Gemma.

"Don't be silly," I said. "I did nothing."

"No, it was great," said Gemma. We were at the first landing. She stopped, so I stopped. She moved to face me. "Juliet."

"Yes?" There wasn't a lot of light on the landing, with its single small window high in the thick stone wall. I wasn't quite sure what her face was trying to say. A second of silence as we studied each other's faces in the bad light. A murmur from the College Bar far above.

"Hang on," said Gemma, and reached out to touch the side of my head briefly. "Bit of string in your hair, there." She flicked it free of her fingertip and laughed. "I forget what I was going to say. That distracted me. Something to do with art, the way the light had you then. Reminded me of something. It'll come back to me." She turned, and we continued on our way.

63

Back home, I walked into a modern Irish drama. Juno was violently making tea in the kitchen, while Michael stood scowling with his back to her.

"Hi guys," I said. Juno slammed the kettle up into the pouring tap. Michael's forehead twitched.

"You OK, Juno? Everything OK?"

"Yes." When she flicked the switch of the electric kettle, it brought to mind a Texas Republican fundamentalist personally executing the murderer of her children. I was surprised a spark didn't leap across the room and fry Michael where he stood. The tension was making the fillings in my teeth vibrate.

"Did you get my message at your place? Michael?" No. "Let me guess," I said. *"The Playboy of the Western World?"* They seemed disinclined to cooperate with the joke. I couldn't work it out, so I piled in head-on. "Then did Juno tell you?"

Michael gave a nod as minimal as the flicker back and forth between frames in a video freezeframe. "Mmm."

"About the letter?"

"Mmm." He turned and walked into Juno's room.

"Anything, uh, wrong?" I asked Juno, or the air.

"Apart from Michael being a prick? No," said Juno, un-sotto of voce.

Michael re-emerged with his jacket on and his black bag swinging from his shoulder. "Got to go, I'm late." He went, with a slamming of innumerable doors. The echoes died. The air stilled.

"Fucking hell, Juno."

Juno tinkered with mugs and tea bags and didn't look at me.

"What's up with Mr. Sympathy?"

"I kissed Conrad," said Juno.

"Oh," I said.

"It was just to thank him, for being nice to me. For looking after me. The letter had me, had me really shook. Dominic had to go, so Conrad made me hot whiskeys, and we talked, and he was, you know, *there,* which Michael wasn't. I couldn't reach Michael, we'd tried Druid, they didn't know . . . and Conrad looked after me, so I kissed him, a little kiss."

"Did he kiss you back?" I said

"Jesus, no. He was a bit shocked, I think. I sort of hit his lips by mistake, he was turning his head away. I think he thought I . . . ," she trailed off.

"Wanted to, like, do it, like," I suggested helpfully. "Doggy style."

"Juliet!"

"Wheelbarrow style," I amended.

"What's that?" said Juliet.

"Don't know," I said. "Like a wheelbarrow race? But with him inside you. And not running."

"Who stands?"

"I don't know! I only heard it in the College Bar. And you're trying to change the subject. . . . He'd have to."

She thought. "Yeah. And you'd be facedown. On your hands. Cool."

"Or you could lie on the bed . . . Juno, for fuck's sake. Did Michael catch ye?"

"No, Jesus, there was nothing to catch, seriously. It was just a platonic kiss. But Michael came in a minute after, and Conrad was acting so awkward, Michael said something half-joking about catching us at it, and Conrad like a big innocent gom tried to explain, which made it much, much worse. . . ."

"Shite."

"Yeah, so Michael's convinced I fancy Conrad."

"But you do a bit, you've told me."

Behind her head, steam began to drift out of the kettle. "Yeah, but not to do anything! I didn't do anything! And Michael's acting like I fucked him or something and it's all his fucking ego, his fucking hurt feelings, and I was bloody upset and he's done nothing but sulk." The kettle blasted steam halfway across the kitchen. I adjusted my eye line so the steam appeared to be jetting out of Juno's right ear. "I mean I get a letter where some psycho's threatening to rape me and Michael's *upset* because I *kissed* someone on the *cheek*. He can piss off."

"He does love you," I said, standing up and heading for the kettle. Thermostat stuck.

"Well if that's love he can shove it up his arse," said Juno.

"How many hot whiskeys did you have?" I said, curiously eyeing the half bottle of Jameson on the table as I passed.

"None! Nearly none. Two."

I knocked off the kettle. "Let's have another," I said, digging out two glasses from the washing up, "tea is for guuurls."

"Wish I had fucked Conrad," said Juno.

"You should drink more often," I said.

64

The next day I went with Juno to the guards.

We walked into a small foyer and looked about us. Four plastic chairs bolted up against the right-hand wall. The chairs faced, across the foyer, a wire-reinforced glass window, with a standard doorbell button mounted on the wall beside it. A stout traveller woman stood in front of the window, resting her thumb on the button. Occasionally she would pump the button with her thumb. Behind the glass, uniformed guards could be seen, working at paper-piled desks or walking about a large room. Now and again a guard would look over at the window.

We sat on the middle two plastic chairs, and waited. The sound of phones and voices leaked through the three-inch gap between the bottom of the reinforced glass and the counter. The drill of the bell. Bursts of laughter. The drill of the bell.

The woman slammed her free palm against the glass. "Bastards!" Slam. "What about my son ye bastards." Slam. "Are ye men at all ye bastards." Slam.

It went on.

Eventually a guard came to the window. "Go away or we'll have to remove you from the premises."

"I know my rights."

"You've no right to make a nuisance of yourself in a garda station. Go away and calm down. We've done all we can. We can do no more."

She slapped the glass in front of his face and spat at it. He didn't flinch. A younger guard emerged through the security doors and spoke to her with a gentle urgency. She brushed his hand away as he tried to touch her arm reassuringly.

"There's no justice for us, there's no justice for us," she muttered as he escorted her outside. The spit, high in the centre of the window where the older guard's forehead had been, crawled slowly down the window, a bulk of bubbles leaving a shining trail.

I found I had been holding trembling hands with Juno. "I can't do this," Juno said to me, as we were left alone. The guard at the hatch had gone. The window was empty.

We stood, to go or to approach the window, no way of knowing. The older guard now entered the foyer through the security door, with a big blue sponge bursting out of one huge hand and a tiny yellow plastic squeezy bottle almost hidden in the other. He looked from Juno to me and back, and turned. With a casual swing of his right hand he squirted a line of thick yellow liquid diagonally down the window, from top left to bottom right, slicing across the vertical axis of the dribbled spit. "Yeah?" he said, his back to us.

Juno tried to speak, couldn't, moved forward so as to see his face, be seen. He wiped the glass carefully with the blue sponge, folded it over like a sandwich, wiped again, both times down along the diagonal of the

yellow fluid, then down the vertical of the spit. I could smell the industrial lemon smell of cleaning products. It's nothing like lemon, I thought
suddenly.

"Yeah?" he said impatiently, turning to look at Juno.

"I wanted to report something," she said.

"Fire away," he said, folding the sponge over again, into a tight little
pad, running it back and forth across the window.

"Someone's been sending me letters."

The guard turned and threw the sponge past Juno at a tin wastebin
in the far corner. The sponge unfolded and expanded as it left his hand,
losing all its momentum as it turned from a dense projectile into a handful of air. It landed softly halfway between him and the bin. He ignored
it. "Students, are you?" he said.

"Yes," said Juno, puzzled, "in UCG."

"Anonymous letters, is it?"

"Yes."

"Some fella that fancies you?"

"It's, they, the letters are, they're sexual. . . ."

"Do you know who it is, or has anyone followed you or threatened you?"

"No, well, he may, he must have followed me, or seen me, he knows
what I wear. . . ."

"But you've never been threatened, or attacked, or followed at night
or anything?"

"Not, well, the letters are very . . ."

"It's just letters, though?"

"Yes." She'd given up.

"There's always a bit of this goes on with the students. I suppose they
think it's funny."

"You don't know it's a student, you haven't seen . . . it could be
anyone."

He ignored her. "You can report it if you want, and we'll put it on file,
but I should warn you we have higher priorities. There's murders and

drugs and rapes and assaults out there. They burnt out three cars in Rahoon last night, and we don't have the resources to chase students with dirty minds. They keep telling us this is the fastest growing city in Europe, but we have less guards than we had two years ago."

Juno just wanted to get away.

"So you won't take this down?" I said, boiling.

He turned to me. "I didn't say that. I'll take a statement. I'll take copies of any letters, I'll place it all on the record, but I'm trying to be straight with you here, a lot of people get letters. There's a lot of crazy people out there. There's religious lunatics and queers and lonely auld fellas and madwomen and they bother other people and they get notions in their heads and they phone some poor fecker at all hours and they write them, and they follow them around. But if that's it, then there's feck all we can do. We can talk to them, but if you don't even know who it is, what can we do? Stake out your house? Have you handwriting, is it—"

"No," said Juno. "Come on, let's go."

The big guard shrugged. "Off the record, the best thing you could do is find out yourself who's sending you these Valentines, if they're distressing you, and get some friends of yours to go round and sort him out."

Juno nodded. "Let's go," she said again, tugging my arm. I was staring at him in amazement.

"Are you . . . ," I started.

"Come on." Juno jerked me out the door into the drizzle.

At the gate to the garda station car park I tried to turn back. "I should have spat on his window, I should have spat on his fucking window. . . ."

The young guard was standing on the pavement talking to the traveller woman. "They're bastards," she said to me over his shoulder.

"They are," I replied.

65

I started the next day in college by skipping my morning lectures to chase notes for the lectures I'd missed the previous day. By lunchtime I'd tracked down and photocopied everything, so I celebrated by skipping my two o'clock history lecture. An in-depth look at the Irish Famine, it wasn't my favourite hour of the week.

I figured I'd loop through town and check out Timmy O'Dea's Bookshop for a P. G. Wodehouse.

On my way across the Salmon Weir Bridge, I considered whether or not I should ask for a weekend job in Timmy's, or maybe in Boo's across the road. The money would help. A lot. And I'd far rather a bookshop than waitressing for three quid an hour. I'd tried that in Tipp and only lasted six quid. Had my arse felt or my breasts brushed up against every fifty pence. Dropped two black coffees into the lap of the twelfth feeler, ran home and locked myself in my room, and cried for a pound-fifty. As, no doubt, did he.

Boo's first. Boo's stood stiffly in Middle Street on the side that didn't get the sun. I arrived and stood outside it for a moment. I composed myself, gathered my breath. And crossed the road.

I went into Timmy O'Dea's and asked them for a job, and they didn't have one.

So I crossed the road again and went into A Boo shop of One's Own and walked up to the counter and the two women behind the counter stopped talking and saw it was me and one of them said, "Yes?" And I said, "I was just . . . ah yes" and I picked up a flyer from the counter advertising a poetry reading in the Atlanta Hotel by somebody I'd never heard of and studied it intently till they returned to their conversation.

I waited another minute to be sure they'd forgotten me before I tiptoed away into the gloom of the sexual-politics section.

Bloody bloody bloody bloody bloody bloody bloody fool, Juliet. Why on earth had I done that? All I was asking for was a job. At worst, all they could do was say no, and possibly make me sign a petition about Bosnia. How on earth could I ask them now? Oh Juliet, you must. But I can't. You must. I can't. Must. Can't. Must. Can't. Mustcan't, mustcan't mustcan'tmustcan't . . . My internal debate wasn't very complex. Reason and instinct just ended up making faces at each other. By a gigantic effort of will, I managed to lurch a couple of feet closer to the counter, into the alphabetical fag-end of the modern fiction section. Both women looked over at me. Panicking, I picked up a book as camouflage and smiled at them inanely with an oh-that's-where-it-was smile. They looked down at the book. They glared at me. Does your treachery know no bounds? their eyes seemed to say. I looked at what I was holding. Omigod, the new John Updike. *In Urbane Praise of the Killing of Women* or whatever it was called. It fell from my suddenly nerveless hands. I scrambled to pick it up. The dust jacket fell off.

I am in hell, I thought calmly. The conversation behind the counter had by now stopped so thoroughly that it was probably going to take intensive posttraumatic-stress counselling of both parties to restart it.

I had almost got the dust jacket back on, with fingers that felt like they were wearing rubber gloves, when it tore. Not much. An inch or so, along the fold between backflap and back cover. Loud, though, the tearing noise. I didn't think paper could make such a loud noise, just tearing like that. Gosh, it was loud. In the quiet shop.

I decided I wouldn't ask for that job after all.

One of them opened her mouth, perhaps in preparation for speech. Or possibly in search of oxygen. I took a step backwards, into the children's section. She froze. I froze. Her colleague began to open her mouth. I took two steps backwards, and stepped on a child.

"For fuck's sake," came a familiar voice.

I turned around, looked down, and with enormous relief and pleasure said, "Juh! J . . ."

"Jimmy," said Jimmy Gleeson. "Jesus, Juliet, you look like a million fucking ECUs in that yoke." This of course is back before ECUs became euros, and euros became real. Both Gleeson twins were passionate, instinctive Europeans, big, big fans of a single currency and an end to internal border controls. They would quiz me and Juno on arcane points of European trade law as though we were experts, because we read the *Irish Times* every day in transition year. Jimmy had once even shoplifted a copy of *The Economist* from Healy's for its cover story on European customs union so I could read it for him and explain the implications, back when they were starting to distribute smuggled rolling tobacco, cartons of Marlboro, and lighters. They supported European Union the same way they supported Liverpool Football Club and Metallica. Their Europeanism had become another of our private jokes.

That's a ridiculous amount of explanation for the presence of one word, not even a word, an acronym. European Currency Unit. One tiny unit of currency in our peculiar love. A shell on that small beach. I did half-think of changing it to "a million fucking dollars" and saving myself the explanation, but once you start that, you're lost. And they're lost. Everything takes an easier shape, but it's the wrong shape.

Also, digressing like this gets me out of describing what happened next.

I suppose I should just grit my teeth and go for it.

On with the story.

The women behind the counter had closed their mouths, the better to purse their lips.

"Oh Jimmy, it's great to see you," I said. Jimmy looked pleased but embarrassed and tried nonchalantly to slide a Famous Five back into the Secret Seven section, spine inward. I pretended I'd seen nothing. "So what are you doing here?" I said, meaning Galway.

"Looking for a book," he said, choosing to interpret the question more narrowly.

"Anything in particular?" I said, resisting an urge to rub his suede head with gratitude.

His genie-like ability to pop up when I was in trouble had seldom been so appreciated by me. From scrabbling on the ground, reassembling an ideologically unsound hardback under the baleful glare of the guardians of ideology, to having a civilized conversation about books with an old friend . . . it was a reversal of fortune worthy of a Shakespearean happy ending. The two behind the counter were thinking of unpursing their lips. They turned to each other. They seemed to be on the very brink of restarting their conversation. Of forgetting about me. I was going to survive.

"Frogspawn" said Jimmy.

"Pardon?" I said.

"Frogspawn."

"You're looking for a book on *frogspawn?*"

"Fuck no," laughed Jimmy heartily. "Tadpoles 'n' shit? No." He shook his head. *"Frog,"* he said loudly and carefully. *"Porn."*

This regained the attention of our tiny audience. I didn't particularly need to check to see if they'd suddenly glanced our way. It was like being hit in the back of the neck by military lasers.

"Porn by Frogs," Jimmy explained even more loudly and carefully. "I read some shit by this French cunt last time I was in the 'Dam, classy stuff, none of your *Asian Babes, Readers' Wives, Juggs* bollocks, a proper book, now, no pictures." He blushed with pride. "And it was fucking good, I got to the end and everything." The clarity of Jimmy's diction was startling. Perhaps he was making an extra effort after the Frog-porn misunderstanding. And had he been taking voice-projection lessons lately? My, the shop was quiet today. I'd seldom heard it so quiet. Not a kook from the women behind the counter, the two or three other customers, the leading minor local poet who stood now frozen in the doorway, unsure if he was interrupting a theatrical event of some kind as everybody stared at Jimmy. And me.

Entirely oblivious, Jimmy continued his book report. "Brilliant, it was. So I asked Karl, my mate, you've never met him, does a bit of import-export, if he'd any more. And he said I should get this other book by some tart, sorry, but I can't fucking pronounce it, named after a perfume.

He wrote it down. French, wrote books." He looked at me appealingly. "And I can't fucking find it."

"The book, or the piece of paper with the name?"

"Neither," he said gloomily. "I went into Eason's, and they said they didn't think they had it. I think they thought I was thick because I didn't know the name. I asked for the manager. Bloke was alright for a Man U fan. Said I should come here, they'd all that kinky Frog shit. But I can't find it."

"I think you're in the wrong section," I said.

"Oh, yeah." Jimmy blushed again. "I got bored. Saw, you know. Paddington and stuff. Going to get something for the kid." His little brother Anthony. "He reads. You know. This shit."

I nodded. We shared a smile. Books with pictures. Kids' books. Huh.

"So this book you want's named after a perfume," I said.

"No, *she's* named after it. Your one who wrote it. Begins with an *A*."

A, A, A . . . "Anaïs Anaïs!" I said. "Anaïs Nin!"

His worried little face opened out like a sunflower with delight. "You're a fucking genius," he said. "The very one. Annay Annay Nin."

I felt so pleased with myself, I nearly bowed to our little audience.

More used to the layout of bookshops than Jimmy, I led him to the kinky Frog shit section, and we found *Little Birds*. He flipped it open, slowly read half a page, and pronounced himself satisfied. "Class," he said. "The Frogs for the porn." He tucked it under one tiny arm and reached up with the other to take the Updike, the existence of which I had entirely forgotten, from my hands. "And what are you having yourself?" he said, turning it to see the front. "Tits on that," he said admiringly. Completely disregarding my feeble protests and explanations, he marched straight to the counter with both of them.

He reached up and, on tippy-toe, slid them onto the countertop. The guardians of ideology leaned over the counter to look down at him. "How're ya," said Jimmy. He took a roll of notes out of his back pocket, removed the elastic band from around them, ruffled their edges to loosen the tight cylinder of paper, and peeled off a couple. "Oh, and a Famous

Five. I'll pick one up on me way out. You don't do Coke, no? The drink?
Pity. Or fags? Ah well. It's funny the way bookshops only ever sell books,
and newspaper shops sell everything, isn't it. Funny that. Ye should sell
fags, every fucker smokes when they read, it's nearly a law of nature. I'd
say you'd shift a packet of fags for every book. More. And yere porn's in
the wrong place, I nearly didn't find it. You'd sell a lot more if people
could find it, y'know, because it's bloody hard to get in Ireland. Ah that's
grand, keep the small stuff." He waved away his nonpaper change,
hauled the recycled paper carrier bag containing his purchases off
the counter, and I practically pushed him out the door, knocking aside
a paralysed poet in my haste. Outside at last. The pure, clean air of
freedom.

"Hey, the kid's Famous Five, Juliet, for fuck's sake. Hold this," said
Jimmy, breaking free of my grip and dashing back into the bowels of the
shop, leaving me with the carrier bag and my thoughts.

I mentally surveyed the wreckage Jimmy had made of my promising
career in bookselling, undecided as to whether to laugh or cry.

"What the fuck are you laughing at?" inquired Jimmy, genuinely interested, when he emerged a minute later clutching *Five Go to Billycock
Hill* in a tiny hand.

66

"So what are you really doing in Galway?" I said. We
were walking down Quay Street towards the Spanish Arch where Jimmy
had left his bike.

"Ah, expanding the business. You know yourself. You can't stand in
the one place."

"And which business is this now, Jimmy?"

"Ah, you know. The E, like. And the auld acid. Bit of hash. But it's the E really, with all the clubs. Galway's crying out for it. Salthill's worse. The distribution in the west is a shambles," he said disapprovingly. "A fucking joke, it is. Bloody students and amateurs. My fellas had to do something, or the Dublin lads would be in, and we couldn't have that. Dub scuts doing the business this side of the country." He looked at me for confirmation that this would indeed be a thing that we couldn't have. "D'ya see what I'm saying?" I did. "I'm up and down since the New Year, sorting the west. Galway, Ballinasloe. Sligo. Tuam's already sorted. But Galway's the big one, with the students and the clubs. I was testing the water myself out Salthill New Year's Eve, Jesus Christ. I'll tell you the story, you'll laugh. Drugs squad caught me going into the Castle, three fuckin' plainers, looked more like they were training for the priesthood than raving, real Templemore bogmen on their first day out. Caught me fucking bang on, though, I'd fucking no chance, with fifty fucking E in me jocks. I'd brought a good stash of new stuff from Edinburgh, supposed to be well clean, a harmless cut, none of your poxy speed in there for the flash, or your strick. I thought I'd see how they'd shift in Galway, test the water for the expansion. I don't like flogging a new line too close to home in any case, so it was the two birds, you know? So I'd fifty of the fuckers in a wee bottle tucked in me kecks when suddenly I'm up against the wall, slam. Nearly broke me fucking bottle." He chuckled nostalgically. "They were into my pants like Christian Brothers. Found the bottle. Well now I'm fucked, I thought, 'cause I was on bail already. They knew me name. Down to the station. Grand. Charged, no bail, I'm fucked. And here's the laugh. They rushed it away to forensics for analysis, and they analyze it, fifty fucking tablets, and get this: no strick, no speed, no brick-dust, alright . . . and no fucking E. The cunts in Edinburgh did me. Chalk, aspirin, and vanilla fucking essence. Isn't that a gas one? So I walked. Even my solicitor thought that was a good one. I told them they could keep the tablets in case they got a bad head on them some morning." He shook his own little head. "Gas."

We got as far as the Spanish Arch and walked under it in companionable silence. His bike was just the other side of it, the familiar old one with the incredibly low-slung seat designed to push the normal rider's knees up past his ears, but on which Jimmy could ride as straight and erect in the saddle as Archduke Franz Ferdinand leading a parade on horseback. "Oh you still have her," I said, pleased.

"*Jesus*. Look what some of your Galway gurriers just fucking did to my bike," said Jimmy, pointing at the painting on the fuel tank.

"Oh, Jimmy." I laughed, and put a hand over my mouth. Someone had crudely Tipp-Ex'd a bra and panties onto his beloved naked lady.

"Dirty little fuckers," said Jimmy, disgusted. "I'll have to get some of the kid's Tipp-Ex thinners to get that off." He scratched at the disfiguring knickers with a thumbnail. "Little bastards shouldn't be let near Tipp-Ex. Or the toxic markers. They make a right fuck of everything." He continued to scratch the tank with his thumbnail. "They had Juno's name up in the phonebox in the square. The square back home now, not the one here"

"I know," I said.

"I got rid of it," he said. "Went over it with a marker and a lighter."

"Thanks," I said.

He looked up and smiled his worried smile at me. "Made shit of the plastic," he said. "But you can't read it anymore."

"You were always very good to us," I said. I could feel something was wrong. I'd felt it under all his talk. "How's Johnny?" I said. He went back to his scratching. Some of the white panties had flaked off to reveal the dark, airbrushed hair.

"He's in the 'Joy," said Jimmy, and looked up at me again, not smiling. "He's doing my time. I couldn't go in. The thing I was on bail for. He said he'd done it. I didn't want to be inside when, you know. Ah you don't know. I never told you. Nuala Driscoll, I've been seeing her a while, and she's going to have a baby in July."

I didn't know what to say. He'd admitted it like an infidelity, which was ridiculous. We'd never even kissed.

What was more ridiculous still was that I felt an almost overwhelming desire to pound him with the useless fists that he and Johnny had always gently mocked because I always had my thumb in the wrong place, inside or outside the fist, I could never remember which was wrong.

How could you how could you how could you when you were always meant to be there to protect me?

"That's great," I said. "That's great. Congratulations."

He shrugged it off. "Nothing to fucking congratulate, it was an accident." We looked at each other, and I could find nothing in me to say. Jimmy shrugged again and began to undo the lock that attached his bike to his helmet. "How's Juno?" he said.

"She's great," I said. "She's in a play, acting."

Jimmy slid the helmet down over his face and flipped the visor up. He smiled out at me, a kind of relieved smile, because he'd told me and I hadn't made a scene. "There's no harm in a little playacting," he said, and smiled even more in pleasure at his wordplay, his joke. I couldn't stop myself smiling back, I didn't want to stop myself.

"She'll be giving them some of your trips," I said. "They're having a party when the play ends, an all-nighter. A trip party."

"Oh. They were meant for ye," said Jimmy, a little hurt, and I bit my tongue.

"They're friends of ours Jimmy, nice people, honestly. And we never . . . we'd never get through all that acid on our own. It was very good of you."

Jimmy nodded. "We wanted to get ye books, but we didn't know what ye'd like. At least I could get you the one you wanted today." He dug the Updike out of the carrier bag and gave it to me.

"Oh thank you Jimmy. You know you shouldn't have."

He shrugged and smiled. "Sure it's nothing. A *mere bagatelle*." He said it like it was in French. I'd taught them that. A mere bagatelle. And "Come, we sit too long on trifles." My favourite line of Shakespeare. I'd taught them that. My eyes filled with tears as he tucked the carrier bag under the elastic straps on the pillion and swung himself onto the bike.

"Tell her I said hello," Jimmy said, rocking his machine back down off the stand.

I nodded. "Tell Johnny . . . ," I said, and faded out. "Tell him thanks. For the Christmas present. We didn't get a proper chance to say thanks."

Jimmy nodded and started the engine. "Do you want a lift anywhere?" he said.

I couldn't hold this together much longer. "No," I said. "I'm grand here. Thanks." Jimmy gunned the engine, opened his mouth, closed it. "Come, we sit too long on trifles," I said, and closed the smoky visor on his subdued face.

He revved her up and was gone in a smooth surge out through the Spanish Arch. I walked under the arch and watched as he mounted the pavement, crossed into the traffic, and vanished over Wolfe Tone Bridge toward Salthill.

I stood under the arch for a while before I went home.

67

I descended rapidly from the stairhead of the flat, swinging my sturdy Timmy O'Dea's carrier bag, its clean lines distorted into a polythene polygon by the trapped corners of the books, notebooks, and pens I'd hurled into it at random in transit on my sprint from the bedroom.

"That's *cheating*," wailed Juno behind me, "I wasn't *ready*"

"Save it for the Second Coming," I shouted up, "and it'll be no excuse then, either."

While I waited for her, I had a halfhearted rummage through the slurry of junkmail slopping over the edges of the hall table. I noticed it just as Juno was slamming the door on the top landing. It was impossible to tell how long it had been there. I felt sick.

Oh no, I thought. That's not fair. It's her first night tomorrow night.

I grabbed the familiar envelope in the dark hall and slid it into my carrier bag as Juno clattered down the last few stairs.

"What?" she said.

"Fairy Liquid vouchers," I said. "Might use them."

"Miracle the mouse-people didn't grab them," said Juno as we stepped out of the gloom of the hall into the gloom of the day.

We were both quiet on the walk into college. She was trying out line readings under her breath, I was sick wondering what to do. I couldn't show it to her, not today, it would wreck her head. But she'd want to know, needed to know. And when I did tell her, I'd have to tell her I hadn't told her. Beside me, Juno mumbled the word *hopeless* with different intonations. Hopeless. Hopeless . . . Hopeless? Hopeless!

Fucking great help you are, I thought.

Juno actually took notes during the lecture. Unbelievable. What in God's name was she doing at a lecture the day before a first night anyway? Jesus Christ. An actress at a lecture. It was unnatural. I knew nonspeaking extras in lunchtime pantomime who'd repeated the year on the back of it. I invested the fifty minutes in circular argument with myself. As we left the lecture hall, I didn't even know what subject it had been in. Our fellow scholars dispersed in a cloud of complaint. I caught the word *potato*. Ah, history, I thought.

"I'd better go to rehearsal," said Juno.

"Grand," I said. "Good luck."

"See you back at the flat," she said.

She walked away, looking so heartbreakingly vulnerable and delicate and innocent, I felt fear rise again like sick in my throat. I went straight round the back of the porters' desk to the lift and up to the second floor.

In the English Department toilet I sat on the closed lid. I rested my forehead against the cubicle door till the tide of nausea went out. Then I rooted in my bag for the envelope, found it between the pages of *Catch-22*, and took it out to look at properly. Same small, white, nondescript envelope as before. Typed, same as before. No stamp this time, to let you know he'd physically been at your door. It was odd how I knew without even opening it. It was odd how we could tell so much from so little. From absences.

Then I read the front of the envelope again. No. No, I didn't know. In neat type, it said:

Juliet Taylor
14 McDonagh Quay
Galway

68

It said everything you would expect. About me, about what he wanted to do to me. About what he would do to me.

He described clothes I had worn, things I'd done, to let me know how close he'd been. It was very clever. I would have preferred the ravings of a madman. He described only my actions in crowded places, things I'd done often where anyone could have seen me, where hundreds were, that narrowed down nothing. A walk on the prom. Shop Street, watching buskers. And the language was deliberately flattened, dead. No adjectives. No floweriness. No style. Cold descriptions of actions. What he could have done to me. What he had done to others. What he would do to me.

What he was going to do to me.

69

By the time I got to David's office I could hardly see. The door was unlocked, I pushed through and inside. The opening door smacked into a small heap of paperbacks, they tilted and slid, pushing the door back, half-closing it, half-blocking it.

The room was dark. The blinds were drawn against the heavy overcast. Some sort of under-floor heating had come on automatically, and the air was stifling. There were no controls visible to turn it off. David's chair seemed empty in the gloom.

I closed the door behind me and started to pick up the paperbacks and stack them, all the same cover, familiar. *Heart of Darkness*.
Heart of Darkness.
Heart of Darkness.
Heart of Darkness.

When I'd finished I sat on the grey nylon carpet tiles in the grey half-light. Then I lay down, bunching my fists under my cheek to keep my face away from the dead, dusty smell of the floor. With the dead air rising forever from the warm floor past my knuckles and my face, I waited for him.

When I woke up my jaw was stiff and my mouth was half-open, harsh and dry. I lifted myself out of a dream like a swimmer out of a river, and forgot the dream at once, a place, a face, and gone. My fingers tingled as the blood returned, my knees cracked as I stood. I walked to his chair and sat down in it. I swiveled it till my right knee hit something under the desk, then I swiveled back till my left knee hit something. The action of the chair was totally smooth, no squeak. I reached out and picked up a plain blue mug, brought it to my nose. Coffee. Cold. I touched the lip of the mug to the hollow under my nose, brought it down to my lips. Cold. I tilted it and sipped some of his cold black coffee. My

dry mouth moistened. I held the mug to my lips, rolled it slightly against
my teeth in a cold kiss.

I wrote him a note, and left.

70

The first night was very well attended, by Dramsoc's appalling standards. More than forty people were milling around the drafty
shed of the IMI by the time I arrived. With the crowds Dramsoc traditionally got, milling wasn't an available option. It was not unknown for
Dramsoc productions to pull in audiences insufficient in number not
merely for milling, but for the playing of a decent game of snap, or, by
premature close of run, solitaire.

This crowd milled, though. I brushed the rain out of my hair, thought
of fixing it up a bit, didn't bother. I hadn't seen Juno all day, as the entire
cast and crew had been busy making nine or ten hours' worth of last-
minute changes. I stood in the doorway and looked around.

The IMI was a disastrously bad theatrical space, smack bang in the
grand old tradition of bizarre and inappropriate Galway venues. They've
Galway ruined now of course with their modern theatrical spaces, but in
my day it was all sheds, pubs, and garages, oh beautiful it was.

Strictly speaking, the IMI wasn't a shed; it was three sheds, all enormously long, enormously high, enormously narrow, and parallel. Ideal
for, say, the mass production of railway trains complete with carriages, it
made for a tricky theatre. Only used for drama when the Aula was unavailable, and entirely empty but for pigeons the rest of the time, it was,
as one might say, a Challenging Space. Juno had told me of the problems
the venue posed, and I could see what she meant. The speed of sound
being as slow as it was, you couldn't really use the full length of the
place. By the time a line of dialogue had made its lonely way from the

front of the shed to the back, there was always the danger that the language would have evolved and the audience's descendants wouldn't understand it. Of course you could always bunch everybody up one end, with the audience huddled round the footlights for warmth, but the enormous ache of space behind them made them nervous. It was like watching a play with your back to the steppes of central Asia. People kept looking around into the darkness to their rear, thinking they'd heard a wolf.

So a smaller space had been compromised into being, with a flimsy partition closing off the far end of the first shed, and behind it, even flimsier, jerry-built raked seating that left splinters in you, and a small stage. A cosy space. Apart from the odd pigeon flying over the partition and into the lights, it seemed to work.

As I stood in the IMI doorway then, what I looked into was a kind of giant, fluorescent-lit reception area, with the actual "theatre" down the far end behind its partition. Along the left wall were scattered, at large intervals, huge closed doors behind which lay the next enormous shed, behind which again lay the third of these absurd empty cathedrals dedicated to some industrial god in which the people had long ceased to believe. I felt somewhat dizzy on the brink of even this one vast room and was glad the doors weren't open into the others.

Forty people, no matter how hard they milled, weren't going to fill all this space, so they'd sensibly decided to concentrate on the area just inside the door. Gemma was helping out by selling coffees. I greeted her with relief.

"Hiya Gemma, is Juno around?"

"Juliet, how're you, she's not. It's nearly starting, I'd say they'd be backstage, pissing themselves. Do you want a coffee, for nothing?"

I took it. The thin plastic beaker was impossible to hold without burning your hand. I quickly put it back down on the black Formica tabletop, without spilling much. "Thanks," I said. "Good crowd."

"All the blaggards who dropped out of *Cavalcade*," said Gemma. "Coming to bury it, but they'll stay to praise. I've seen the dress rehearsal. It works. They know their lines. Even the long ones. All the way to the end. You wouldn't believe how fucking rare that is, they all smoke too much dope in Dramsoc to be memorising anything."

A woman by the left wall cleared her throat in that I've-an-announcement way. We all looked over. "The play is about to begin, so if you'll take your seats . . ." People began moving obediently toward the partition at the far end. "Ah, excuse me, sorry. Tonight's performance is taking place in the *middle* unit, not, ah, in this unit as is usually the case. Just use this door here, and you may sit where you like. You may move the chairs if you wish, and of course there's no smoking anywhere in the building, is there Joe?"

She looked over at the UCG security man standing by the front door. Several people laughed, and he cheerfully put his hands up, palms out. "Nothing to do with me," he called back, and people laughed again.

The big door was swung open from the inside by two people, one of whom I recognised as the play's lighting technician, from Juno's pointing him out to me the week before. The two scurried back into the dark, to their positions I supposed. I felt a little tingle of excitement. And then I felt a hand on my shoulder, heard a pleased voice. "Juliet!"

I turned. "Michael! I was wondering if you'd come."

"Ah, had to see her first night, fuck Druid."

"She'll be delighted," I said.

"Coffee, Michael?" said Gemma.

"Bless your bones, Gemma, no. I've had a gallon of it today."

A familiar figure passed behind Michael, heading for the queue. Shite. Dominic. I'd been dodging the Tampon Kid for weeks. I was suddenly mortified by memories.

Michael was saying good-bye to Gemma. We began to drift towards the doorway. In the queue ahead of us, Dominic could be seen glad-handing the faithful and soaking up the good-lucks and best-wishes. The last back slapped, he turned and began walking towards us. I grabbed Michael's hand and as Michael gave me a startled look I whispered, "So tell me all about Arsenal," and stared adoringly into his eyes.

"What the fuck are you on about, woman," said Michael, baffled, as Dominic tried to catch my eye, failed, and turned back. I kept up the adoring gaze a moment longer just in case.

"Oh, nothing," I said, dropping Michael's hand. "Got a sudden craving to learn about football. It's gone now."

Dominic disappeared through the dark portal. Horrified at my cowardice, I felt terrible, but not half as terrible as I would have felt trying to hold a conversation with Dominic.

As we handed our tickets to the woman who'd made the announcement, I remembered I'd left my coffee on the Formica table. Oh well. It'd probably be cool enough to pick up by the time the play was over.

We walked through the doorway. A dim light came from our right, away down the far end, where I could just about make out traces of a human settlement. We walked towards the light.

As we approached it we came across the occasional chair, then couples of chairs, and finally clumps of chairs clustered close to what had to be the playing area because it was up against the back wall. We picked seats and sat next to each other. The rest of the audience lay shipwrecked all about us, sat scattered among groves of black plastic chairs that rose from a Ukraine of concrete floor. Dominic had obviously decided to go for the steppes of central Asia option.

I looked nervously into the darkness behind me for wolves.

71

It worked. The great void at our backs had pushed us up timidly into the tiny and only oasis of light, and what went on in that light over the next hour worked very well indeed.

Dominic had casually turned the play on its head, and with Juno as Clov and himself as Hamm he had made the play a giddy hybrid, both cold and warm, desolate and erotic. I had read Juno's copy in an hour the day before, and thought it harsh and sad, the humour funny but freezing. It was without hope, without sex, without love. It was a wry essay on aloneness and death.

Changing Clov from male to female gave a bizarre, sexy sitcom spin to the play, lines were played for a warmth that simply wasn't there. It was very unsettling. A ghost of sensuality simply shook the play apart. They were talking about death and acting about life. I couldn't tell if Dominic was a directorial genius or simply didn't understand the play.

Juno made my heart hurt. I had no idea if what she was doing was acting, or if she was any good. I just watched her with helpless, hopeless love. She seemed to me to be simply herself, but somehow, under the lights, speaking those words that weren't hers, she hurt my heart. I became so painfully aware that she wasn't me that I almost rose from my seat in a panic the first time she left the stage, for fear she would never reappear, because she had become completely unpredictable to me under those lights. So utterly herself, so utterly alien. If you don't understand, that's alright. I hardly understood.

Dominic was very, very good.

What the bare words were saying and what the actors were saying without the words were totally different things, and yet it held somehow together, and that could be put down to Dominic. He was simply a tremendous actor. The actors playing Nell and Nagg were weak, but it didn't matter. They were irrelevant. Dominic and Juno burned.

It wasn't perfect, it wasn't a revolution in theatre, I've probably enthused too much and I've skipped over the flaws. But it was so much better than I think anyone in the audience had really expected, and it really had something good at the heart of it so that when it was over we rose without thinking to our feet and applauded until several pigeons, awoken and distressed by the noise echoing and re-echoing through the sombre shed, flew the length of it and passed low over our heads with a whoop of wings into the lights of the stage, which lit them serene for an instant before they flurried and panicked their way back into the darkness of the

girders overhead. Their sudden appearance out of the light made the
actors duck in the middle of their third curtain call so that they and the
audience laughed, and the tension and the applause and the crowd
slowly dispersed, everyone talking excitedly like they'd just come out of
an adrenaline-pumping action movie, not a Beckett play. Or were all
his plays always like this? My God, was it the play? Who'd hidden this
from me?

Michael went to congratulate Juno, but I was too moved and confused. I walked out into the reception area, where Gemma was packing
away the coffee machine. "Isn't it great?" she said when she saw me.

"Oh yes," I said. "I'm all . . . I don't know how I feel."

"It's doing two things at once, isn't it?" Gemma said. "They don't let
you settle. I loved it, I snuck in down the back. Better than the dress rehearsal, the crowd makes it."

"It wasn't at all what I expected," I said. "It was . . . oh, it was lovely.
Michael's gone to tell Juno she was great."

Nonsense phrases were going through my head—she isn't me; I'm all
alone—I felt exhilarated and sick. Little groups and couples stood about
talking.

"Have you seen David?" I said.

"David who?"

"Hennessey."

"No. Why?"

"Nothing. I just thought he might be here." I looked around. "Did
Conrad not come?"

"Back on the bottle."

"Oh no."

"It's not unusual."

"Juno likes him."

"I know, it's her has him back on the booze. Upset he made a mess of
things between her and Michael."

"Oh that's terrible, it wasn't his fault."

"Ah, nothing's ever anybody's fault. Don't we all mean well?"

I didn't know what to say. The play had unsettled me, my mind was all over the place.

"I think your coffee's cool enough," said Gemma.

A shock wave of nervous energy arrived, immediately followed by Dominic.

"Didyoulikeit? Didyoulikeit?" One each for Gemma and me. Juno and Michael washed up in his slipstream as we assured him we did. They looked good together but they didn't look right. It wasn't fixed. The trust thing. "Wasn't it great? Wasn't it great?" Dominic cackled, the stereo effect still on. "I want to marry Juno, I'll have my bed extended." His glee erased my unease. We'd forgiven each other without talking about it. If he was over it, so was I. A sigh of rich relief.

"What . . . did you *do* to it?" I asked, and he understood immediately.

"We betrayed the text," he said, hopping with glee. "We did the dirty on Beckett. We flooded the whole fucking play with affection and love. Oh he'll be rotating like a chicken on a spit tonight. We didn't change a bitter word of it, but did you see, did you get it, didn't we fill it with life, fill it with love? Because he was wrong, he was wrong, he was wrong about *the whole thing*. I love him, a genius, but wrong. Life is wonderful, he was talking beautifully out of his terse, eloquent arse. Come on, College Bar for a pint, fuck the Student's Union coffee machine Gemma, leave it, they're just being pricks wanting it back every night, fuck 'em, Jesus, forty-six paying fucking customers, it's the *Batman* of Dramsoc openings, it's *Gone With the* fucking *Wind,* to the Batmobile, come on, before they stop serving, come *on*."

72

I was standing outside his office when he arrived after his last lecture of the day. "You didn't come to the opening night . . . ," I said as he said, "Juliet, I only just got your note. . . ."

We stopped. "Go on," I said.

"I wasn't in my office till this afternoon, Dad had a bad night, he's fine, but I took yesterday off. . . . You said you wanted to talk, was it urgent?"

I felt a peculiar reluctance to speak. I didn't have the energy to start this conversation. If I didn't mention the letter to anyone, then it wasn't yet real. It had no consequences. The pain didn't have to start. Please God put this off a little longer. "No," I said. "No." And suddenly, "Do you want to buy me a coffee?"

"God yes, love to, but I can't," said David. "I'm a man on a mission, I'm just collecting some discs and I'm gone."

My face fell. Well, OK, I could have hidden my disappointment if I'd wanted to, so strictly speaking it didn't fall, it was pushed. Even David, noted insensitive oaf, callous swine, and casual breaker of my young heart, noticed. I'd pushed it pretty hard. "That was the wrong answer, wasn't it?" he said.

I nodded glumly.

"Give me another go," he said.

"Want to buy me dinner somewhere expensive?" I said vindictively. He laughed. I stuck my tongue out at him. Flannery Ryan came round the corner and walked past, pretending not to see us. I left my tongue out and rolled my eyes. David snorted with amusement and turned to stand beside me, sticking his tongue out at Flannery Ryan's retreating back till Ryan disappeared round the next bend.

We turned back to each other, still sticking our tongues out. I crossed and uncrossed my eyes at him in a fashion meant to be comic. The English Department secretary came round the bend around which Flannery Ryan had just disappeared, and gave us a very startled look. David, to his eternal credit, continued to hold the pose. "Weh dust stigging ow tongues oud ad ead udda," he explained in a casual aside as she passed.

"H'llu," I said politely.

"Good work, keep it up," she said, and continued on and around the corner.

We went back to normal. "No time for coffee or an expensive dinner right now," he said, "but you're an idle student with nothing to do for the next hour or two, aren't you?"

I looked at my watch, checked the position of the sun, and consulted my folder of notes. "Yes," I said. "Why?"

"You can join me on my mission if you like, it's a boring one."

"Gee, thanks."

"Well, it won't be as boring if you come along. I can drop you back in town in an hour or so."

"Fine. What's the mission?"

"A friend of mine's gone to a wedding in Sligo, and I have to feed his fish."

"You turned down coffee with *me* to feed somebody's *fish*?"

He grinned. I didn't. Gah!

"If I don't feed his fish before five o'clock he might lose his job. Come on, got to run."

He grabbed his discs out of the office, and we ran.

73

The bay was like glass as I lay on my back in the moving boat, and in the chill blue sky white flecks of gulls circled high.

"*How* many fish?" I said again.

From the wheel David looked back at me. He groaned. "Between twenty-five and thirty thousand. *Must* you do that?"

"I want to get a tan," I said.

"We are, you realize, some few months away from summer."

"I don't mind. The sun's out. I'm hardy."

"Indeed."

In fact it was quite cold, but the warm glow of pleasure from winding up David more than compensated for that.

"Are *you* hardy, David?" I said in my best Lauren Bacall. The back of his neck slowly went red.

"Almost at the cages," he said after a while. I sat up on the bags of pellets I'd been lying on and looked. It was very unspectacular; a large, dull, floating, metal walkway with a safety rail, forming a big rectangle, maybe thirty yards by twenty. Black-and-orange plastic floats seemed to be keeping it all just above the water, and there was an impression of bulk beneath it, of suspended structures. The entire thing rose no more than three feet above the calm surface of the bay.

"They call this a farm?" I said, disappointed. I think I'd expected acres and acres of . . . something. Fences, sticking out above the water. Floating barns of indeterminate purpose. A windmill on a raft to power . . . whatever. Electric fences for electric eels.

"Fish farms are as dull as it gets," said David apologetically. "Some metal cages and a couple of anchor lines. I told you it was a boring mission."

"Who's getting married?" I asked.

"Hey? Oh. An old girlfriend of Eamonn's. They're good friends. This is one of his more reasonable excuses for skiving off, sometimes I get a phone call from Donegal at four in the morning, and it's Eamonn saying, 'Can you feed the fish before ten A.M.? I'm stuck in the middle of a poker session.'"

"And you do it?" I said.

A shrug. "He's a friend. His boss is a very decent man, an old friend of my father's actually, but he's very intense, very uptight."

"So unlike you," I interjected.

"Ouch. . . . He expects Eamonn to do everything by the book, but Eamonn . . . is not a big fan of the books."

"So he's your bit of rough," I said helpfully, "a horny-handed son of the sea-soil. An honest working man. The two of you have a couple of jars and talk about greyhounds and hurling, and none of your booktalk." I felt skittish, my mood was light but fragile.

"Mmm," said David as he concentrated on bringing the boat in to the floating walkway. He looked lovely in the watercolour light of a sunny spring afternoon, silver ripples of light racing across his face and neck, under his chin, from the sun on the rippled water. I wanted to kiss him and I wanted to kick him overboard. His idiotic scruples and his dumb idea that he was somehow protecting me, and protecting himself. From *what* for God's sake? Nobody move, nobody get hurt.

The boat touched the metal frame, softly, and the whole structure rang deep like a low bell. The water shivered inside the frame.

David tied the boat loosely to the handrail, nose and stern. "Shift, you," he said, not looking at me, and began to heft the big bags of fish-food pellets over the gunwale and the handrail and onto the walkway's metal mesh floor.

I stood behind him, doing up my buttons. When I'd done up the last one, I swung back my right foot till the sole touched the side of the boat. I thought for a second. Looked at him, heaving another bag over the gunwale. The gold of the sun in his hair. The tight curve of the sober black jeans over his almost perfect behind as he bent to lift the last sack of food. Better than almost perfect. Perfect.

I kicked him as hard as I could.

He gave a little dance of wordless pain, which lasted for some while.

"*What* the . . . *giddy* . . . *blazing* . . . *hell* was that about?" he came up with eventually, leaving the realm of wordless pain rather slowly, a painful word at a time.

"It's alright," I said consolingly, "I feel much better now."

"*Jesus.*"

"Your face has gone very red," I said, interested. I looked closer. "Oh wow," I said, excited, "tears of pain! I thought that was just a book thing."

"That," he said, and breathed deeply for a moment, then another moment, "*hurt.*"

"Well, it was either that or kiss you," I said, "and I knew you didn't want me to kiss you. So I *had* to do it. For your sake. Don't worry, I've got it out of my system now."

"Good . . . to hear."

"Actually, I didn't think it was going to be quite that dramatic."

"You got me . . . right on the tailbone. . . ."

"*Cool,* it felt like I'd hit something solid alright. Hey, if you break your coccyx, can you end up with a paralysed, you know, arse? I mean, medically, could you walk around and everything but not feel anything in your bottom ever again?"

"Interesting . . . question, Dr. Taylor . . . I'll get back to you . . . on that one."

I skipped nimbly over the gunwale and rail, and onto the walkway beside the pile of sacks. Their weight tilted the structure almost imperceptibly in the water.

"What's keeping you, come on, I wanna feed the *fish*." I did a childish impatience dance.

David wincingly joined me. I was glad he wasn't mad at me. I'd have been furious. "Glad you're not mad," I said.

He waved a pained, dismissive hand. "Useful research," he said, "for my thing on pain in fiction." His breathing was almost back to normal now, and a healthy paleness was returning to his cheeks.

"How's that going?" I said. "I loved the bit you showed me."

He began lifting a sack, winced. "It's going quite well." He turned and very, very gingerly sat on the sacks, then lay back across them, shielding his eyes from the sun. "Excuse me a moment, I think I'll rest for a minute or two before I try that again."

I leaned on the handrail and looked out across the vast sea at the vast sky. I covered one eye with my hand until my perspective went and the sky looked like a distant cliff of infinite height rising straight up from the flat ocean.

"Tell me more about pain," I said.

"Pain in fiction?"

"Whatever. You're the expert."

"The surprising thing," he said in a dreamy voice from behind me, "about pain in fiction . . . is that there is so little of it. Physical pain hardly exists. Writers are by and large only interested in psychological pain, distress, and trauma. Physical damage and the feeling of it, the sensation of actual pain . . . is seldom described, analyzed, or discussed. Psychological pain is described, analyzed, and discussed exhaustively, across the entire range of literature, across almost all genre boundaries. Psychological pain is at the heart of the novel, physical pain is absent."

I noiselessly lowered myself to the metal mesh and lay along the walkway full length, my head on my arms. The motion of the platform seemed exaggerated by my closeness to the surface of the sea, and the great blue desert of bitter salt water tipped and tilted gently around me. The suck and plash of the water beneath me was intimate, very close and quiet. Lazy. Overheard, not heard. Behind and above me, David sounded like he was talking to himself now as he lay on his back, facing the sky, arms across his eyes. He had adopted a pompous, self-mocking tone as though he were reading aloud something he didn't wish to be associated with. "Is it that writers, then, have no interest in physical pain, or is it that they know nothing of it, or nothing special of it, and everything of psychological pain? Writers are not, by and large, of the warrior class."

The sun flashed on something, and again, very bright. I squinted. A Coke can high in the water, not far away, rising and falling with us in the middle of the bay. It swung lazily around as a light breeze, gliding across the smooth rolling plain of the sea, caught on its aerodynamic snag. The bottom of the can swung to catch the sun in its silver dish, a silent bang of light out on the ocean. Dazzled me. The high-floating can and the sea and the light were effortlessly, elegantly beautiful. A sculpture by God. Just a little something he dashed off, blush-blush.

And a thought spoke quietly from under that thought, there is no God. God is a pattern we impose on the chaos. Just like beauty. Saying, there, look at that, there he is, in this moment. No, not that one. Don't look at that one. God's not there. Nor beauty. He's over here, look. The red can cupping the silver coin of light. God's beauty. In the desert of salt that we can't see at all, that surrounds us.

"If writers knew pain, physical suffering . . . would they give it more weight, pay it more attention? It seems so. Dennis Potter, with his skin in foul revolt against him; Dick Francis, with his shattered and mended and rebroken bones—they write of worlds where disfigurement is not simply a symbol, and pain not just a metaphor, but also things in themselves, very real, very hard to bear. When they write of skin and bone, we worry about, we care about the skin and the bone, not just the soul within. Because the soul is also in the skin, not merely under it. And the soul is not merely supported on a crutch of bone, the soul is also in the bone. . . ."

"Why are you writing a book about pain?" I said, out to sea.

No answer from the sea. No answer from behind me. I held my breath. Released it. "Does your father . . ."

"Nothing to do with it. My father has absolutely nothing to do with it." I heard him sit up. I didn't look around. "If you think I'm writing this because my father is dying, or because he was saved once and now won't save himself, you're quite wrong. It's not a . . . displacement activity. My father has had a long, extraordinarily happy remission period, and he has been hardly affected by the return of the cancer. He is certainly not in pain. When the collapse of his white cell count goes far enough he will . . . it will all be relatively quick, a week or two, and there's morphine and so on. He should have died months ago, who knows, perhaps, it's quite possible, he won't die at all. Of leukemia. The body is a mystery, the cancer may have stopped, gone, come to terms with the body. He won't let us test him anymore. We don't know what's going on in there. Perhaps nothing. Perhaps miracles."

I turned to face him. "The soul is in the bone," I said.

He smiled. "Maybe it's on my mind a little as I write. But it's not . . . the reason."

We looked at each other. I don't know why I felt the right to ask this, but I did. I don't know why I wanted to push him so hard, but I did. I knew it was a question that he didn't want to hear. I knew he'd forgive me. The question, anything.

"What happened to your mother?" I said.

He said nothing. I looked away after a while. The Coke can had drifted further away. Beyond it, above it, out in the mouth of the bay, the hard smudge of a cargo ship was still smaller than the can to me. I waited till the can flashed again. Waited.

I sat up, crossed my legs under me. "Sorry," I said.

"No," he said. "No need."

There was another silence. Suck, plash. A gull's high skree.

He started slowly. "We aren't explained, you know, by a bad thing. Something terrible, when we're young, it can change us—of course it can—change the whole shape of our life, but it's still our life. Under our control. The bad thing that happened, it doesn't explain us. You know what I mean, don't you?" Yes, I knew. "And that bad thing, it is not an excuse for our life being all wrong, we can't just say, 'Well of course I'm unhappy, a terrible thing happened long ago.' We have a duty, to ourselves and those around us, to deal with it and move on. Both are important. We have to deal with it, and we have to move on. If it is difficult, and if it takes time, well what else is a life for?"

"That's very lonely," I said.

He shrugged. Shook his head. "No. But to make room for the other things in life, that task, perhaps in itself a lonely one, has to be performed. Do you understand me?"

I nodded. I understood him.

"So if I say that I don't want to talk about something, that doesn't mean it's not important, but it doesn't mean it's the secret key to my life either. It just really might be that I don't want to talk about it. That it's bad, but it's not that bad. Not that I'm afraid to tell you, or unable to tell you . . . but that I'd just prefer not to. That it's just something I'd rather . . . you know."

I nodded. He looked at me for a moment. He half-smiled. I half-smiled. "Yes, I'm sure you do," he said. "I'm sorry for preaching again."

"Didn't mean . . . ," I trailed off.

"No, thanks for . . . let's change the subject before we both die of embarrassment."

"Let's feed the fish before they all die of hunger."

"Oh my God, the bloody fish." He stood up.

"How's your rump, Yugoslavia?" I said. A topical joke, from the headline in that morning's *Irish Times*.

"A peaceful settlement is hoped for shortly," he said. "There's a knife in the toolbox in the boat, will you get it?"

I got it.

He hefted a sack and cut a corner off it with the knife. He began tipping the musty brown pellets over the inside edge of the walkway, through the unobtrusive wire tops of the cages. He swung the bag gently and the stream of food arced from side to side.

The water frothed and stormed with instant life, a thousand mouths and bodies battling to get to the surface and the food first, whipping the water to foam in seconds, and as David began to move along the walkway, pouring great swathes of food across the wire tops of the cages, the frenzy spread and followed him, cage by cage. The flat yards of water churned and bulged. By the time he reached the near corner of the walkway, the sack was empty and all the sea between us spat and danced with life as the salmon broke the surface of the sea to feed, their bodies thick and supple with life.

74

I got to pour the second bag, and the fourth. They were heavy, and it was satisfying and right the way they lightened as you walked from cage to cage till their weight had disappeared.

When we had poured the last of the pellets into the hungry sea, we stood for a minute by the boat, unwilling to leave immediately. The surface of the sea grew calm under us as the last of the food sank, was eaten, vanished, and the salmon calmed and allowed themselves drift lower in their cages until all that was left of them for us was that sense of bulk and suspended mass beneath us.

"Beautiful," said David. I nodded.

We faced the mouth of the bay. Nothing between us and America. To our left the water, to our right and behind us the low coast of Galway.

The cargo ship was closer now and beginning to swing about to make its approach to Galway harbour. We watched it, didn't bother talking. It was nice.

I got into the boat first, put the knife back in the toolbox. David started the engine, cast off. It was a quiet journey.

When we were almost halfway home, "Look," I pointed. "A seal."

David throttled back the engine. The seal rose and fell with the roll of the ocean as she looked at us, sixty or seventy yards away. David cut the engine completely and we drifted closer in silence.

The seal gave a hoarse bark and disappeared, to reappear ten yards away, the slick head and big eyes slipping up out of the water without the water seeming to notice. Not a ripple.

"Ah, too much beauty," said David. "It hurts."

I looked at the seal and she looked at me. To be so easy in the world that there was no barrier for you between the elements of air and water. To glide through life. For a stupid second I envied her. "She has Juno's eyelashes," I said facetiously.

"What a coincidence," said David, "so have you" and I was startled to realize that I'd actually forgotten that. I'd managed somehow to see the resemblance and make the remark without remembering that I too was inextricably involved in the equation.

The seal looked from me to David and back, barked again, and dived. When it reappeared briefly it was a hundred yards away and it didn't look back at us before vanishing again.

David restarted the engine. He offered me the wheel with a nod of his head. I took it and steered for the harbour.

We crossed the exhausted wake of the cargo ship close to the open harbour gates and entered the harbour as the ship was still tying up at the far side of the docks.

I gave David the wheel and he brought us in to the stone steps close to Juno's and my building. He held on to a rusted chain that looped along the stone face of the quay as I clambered out onto the steps.

"Do you want to come to see Juno's play tomorrow night?" I said. "It's the last night, there's a party afterwards if you want . . . I mean, you don't have to go to the party . . . or . . ." I could see it in his face, in his shoulders. "Oh David."

"I'd love to. But I just can't."

"Why, what are you doing?"

He couldn't even lie. "I just can't."

"Nobody move, nobody get hurt," I said. He breathed out but he didn't say anything. "Go home," I said eventually and turned and started walking up the steps. When I looked back down he hadn't moved. He swallowed and his mouth moved. I was afraid. I didn't want to hear almost anything he was likely to say.

". . . Thanks for thinking of me," he said.

I do little else, I nearly said but was afraid he wouldn't take it as a joke. I turned back and kept going.

When I reached the top step I turned and gave a dramatic, *Gone With the Wind,* Cinemascope wave. He pushed the boat off, engine idling, and waved back. I could see the line of orange rust across his palm from where he'd held the chain.

"Safe home, Ulysses!" I shouted down as he let the throttle out.

"We'll always have Paris!" he shouted back sadly, and turned the boat toward the gates and open water.

"We don't even have Galway," I mumbled to myself as I turned and walked toward my front door.

75

As Juno got ready to leave the flat for the IMI and the preparations for her final performance, I felt like our mum.

"Have you got everything? Are you sure now? Have you the acid somewhere safe? And the tapes for the party?"

Well, maybe not exactly like our mum.

"Juliet, stop worrying. Everything's grand. I'll see you after the play. If you decide to head in early, give us a shout, we're only running through the lighting cues with Eddie's replacement."

"OK, I might. Good luck." I gave her an awkward kiss. I was aware that there were other types of kiss on the market, which were supposed to be just as good or, theoretically, even better, but I didn't hold with them, not even with Juno.

The bell rang. "That'll be Conrad," said Juno.

"Conrad?"

"He's only walking me there, we're going over some lines on the way in. He offered to help me. That's all."

"I didn't say anything."

"Yes you did."

"God bless your hearing."

She went.

I flicked on the radio, flicked it off again before I'd even recognised the song, a *Da-* of voice and drums immediately cut off by the little *whump* noise the machine made when you turned it off.

I picked up one of Juno's books from the table, looked at the back of it blankly, might as well be in another, oh, it was in French, that explained it. I put it down.

Small pile of dusty tapes beside it, obviously not Michael's or there wouldn't be dust on them. *Hounds of Love!* That's mine. Can't believe I haven't played it in so long.

I put on Kate Bush very loud, thought about my brother, thought about how big the world was, thought about nothing, danced around the room.

76

Was that the doorbell?

I banged the machine's stop button with my petite fist in the way that always made Michael cover his eyes with horror. The room was suddenly silent. It was like a huge pressure drop. I imagined I could feel my eardrums bend suddenly out like tiny sheets of rubber. A tiny avalanche in the stove. A click, a creak of the building settling.

The doorbell rang, loud as gunfire. I opened our door and ran downstairs, opened the front door.

"David."

"Juliet." He produced something from behind his back. A rose.

"It's white," I said, disappointed.

He rolled his eyes in probably only half-feigned despair. "What's wrong with white?" he said.

"You can't lecture me for ten million years on the importance of symbols," I said, "and then expect me to faint with delight over a white rose."

"But, God damn it, it's a symbol of . . . *friendship, affection*."

"It's a symbol of *grannies* and *nuns*," I said. "It's about as sexy as . . . as . . ." I couldn't think of anything. "You might as well have given me a bunch of lilies for my lonely grave, because I'm obviously beyond *passion* and *sex* and being remotely *attractive*."

"Er, I wouldn't go quite that far," said David, blushing infuriatingly attractively. "I mean, you're a red-rose sort of girl." He bowed at me and I bowed back to acknowledge his concession of this important point. "But if I'd given you a red rose, well, you might have interpreted it, ah, as . . ."

"Yup," I said, nodding vigorously.

"Hmm," he said. "Yes. Well I would . . . if it's not too late . . . I would like to accept your invitation to the play. After all. If you haven't . . ."

"Come in, I'll cancel the gigolo."

"Will you get a refund?"

"Oh I get freebies, I'm special. Come in, come in, it's freezing, I'll dress."

He stood awkwardly by the stove the whole time I was dressing. I left my door open a crack as I dressed, but didn't hear any of the giveaway floorboards creak. When I came out he was exactly where I'd left him, he hadn't moved to sneak a peek. What did I have to do? At least he swallowed hard when he saw me.

"You like?"

"I like. Well, come on, Granny, or we'll be late."

Our conversation on the walk to the IMI was, disappointingly, as relaxed, enjoyable and friendly as it had ever been. It was agony. The backs of our hands brushed against each other once, as we turned into the college grounds, and we both jerked our hands away as though from a glowing hot plate, apologising profusely.

I made one last attempt. "David . . ."

"I want to be friends," he said immediately, cutting me off. "It has to be possible."

"Some friendships shouldn't be, can't be, platonic," I said. "It's in the fucking stars David, look up."

He looked up. I looked up. The clouds looked like they started ten feet above our heads and kept going till they ran out of atmosphere. I nearly laughed. Nearly.

There was an extraordinary turnout, by Dramsoc standards. "We're packing them in tonight!" gloated Dominic, buzzing past us as we queued to get in. "We're within fifteen of the fire regulations!"

"Packing them in" was a relative term in the context of the IMI. Well, no, it was a lie. Or metaphor. We got good seats up near the front, as did everybody else.

The play was wonderful. Dominic was wonderful. Juno was wonderful. The new lighting man only missed his cues twice and I wouldn't even have noticed that if I hadn't seen the play already. The two in the bins had improved alarmingly.

I cried at the end, but then again, when don't I.

I went up afterwards with David to congratulate the cast. They were completely hyper. Dominic shook my hand for about a minute and said, "Jesus Juliet I'm fucking tripping already and I haven't touched a tab I've an ounce of Moroccan are you on for the party" in one explosive un-punctuated breath, and did not stay for an answer. We couldn't even get to Juno, who was buried in blushing admirers.

Dominic now wandered back from out of the darkness with a large dustbin over his head and most of his body while the thin, habitually un-happy boy who'd done the costumes followed him, grinning like a ma-niac and loudly slapping the dustbin with a very baggy old hurling or football sock in the county Galway colours of maroon and white, which lent it the look of a senior ecclesiastic's surgical stocking. Occasionally the words "I'm a fucking genius!" boomed from beneath the dustbin. The stand-in lighting boy was hanging upside-down by his knees from the lighting rig, kissing the tiny girl who'd played Nell, who was standing on her upturned dustbin to reach him. To my innocent eyes it already resembled a drug-debauched party, and the audience hadn't even finished leaving the theatre. Dear God, what would the introduction of actual drugs and the commencement of the actual party entail?

Juno finally broke free, came over, hugged me. David stood respectfully back as some serious sisterly bonding went on. I cried in her ear, told her how impressed I was. God, I nearly gave her another awkward kiss. Emotions, yuck.

"How's the Big Date?" whispered Juno giddily, nodding at David, when we'd both run out of ways of saying how much we liked each other without actually *saying* it.

"Oh shush," I whispered, squirming.

She squeezed me. "No, really."

"Terrible," I said, "I took him to this play about dustbins. . . ." She pinched me. "Fine," I said, "we're still . . . the best of friends." Perhaps it came out a smidgen bitter.

"Oh Juju, you probably—"

"I don't want any words of wisdom or consolation," I interrupted, "I'm fine, it's fine, it's wonderful, it's perfect, I don't even have to worry about getting pregnant. Mum would be delighted with me."

Juno squeezed again. "Well you're doing better than me, none of my harem have turned up." A handsome, gangly boy, no doubt a friend of one of the company just arriving for the party, gave us a curious stare as he passed. Hugging each other and whispering, heads together, shielded by Juno's long hair, we must have seemed to present a curiously narcissistic, Sapphic spectacle, impossible to see as innocent in the context of the increasing debauchery all about us. I kissed Juno's ear and he looked hurriedly away.

"I'd say you could assemble a new harem in no time tonight," I said. Beyond Juno's shoulder, David seemed to be talking to Dominic about Beckett. Dominic was still wearing his dustbin, which made conversation more difficult, but he had also just walked into a pillar and fallen over, which made conversation easier. David had merely to bend and talk into the open mouth of the dustbin, from which Dominic's voice and feet emerged. For Dominic, the party had definitely begun.

"I don't want a new harem," said Juno. "The harem I've got's difficult enough. I've got to go now and find Connie and drag him back to the party. He wouldn't sit through the play because of some stupid row with Dominic. He's probably sulking in his office, thinking the world doesn't love him. Unless he's sulking in the College Bar thinking the world doesn't love him."

I thought about Conrad and his air of being stranded in a time he was afraid of and didn't understand. "I don't think the world does love him," I said.

"True enough," said Juno sadly.

"Are you kissing him?" I said.

"No . . . it's not really like that," said Juno. "It sounds silly . . . he's desperately sad, and I want to . . . save him, or something."

"I know exactly the feeling," I said drily, looking at David leaning over, happily discussing Beckett with a drunken, talking dustbin.

Juno gave me a last kiss and swirled away in a cloud of happy blondness. Twins my eye. I lugged my raincloud over to David. Maybe I should dye my hair black.

"Juliet's legs, by all that's holy," boomed Dominic from his cave. "Did you bring Juliet with you by any chance?"

I kicked his ankle. "No," I said, "she's at home practising dress-making and subservience."

"Ouch. Good to hear. She'll make some happy man very lucky. If you see her tits, give them my warmest regards."

I sighed and walked round to the bottom end of the bin. Kicked it a few times and came back.

David applauded ironically. "Well put."

"I thought it rather witty myself," I said modestly, in a refined accent not native to my tongue.

Dominic wriggled out of the bin clutching his head. "You are a bounder and a cad, Flashman," he said, "and there is no place for you in this school."

The general theatrical air was having its usual effect on all our human voices. Irony, accents and references. I felt a mild welling of panic but fought it down. We do not have to be ourselves all the time, I reminded myself. It's not like I enjoy being me lately. And I remembered the letter, tang of sick suddenly in my throat. Nothing is real. I shook my head to shake the memory. Crushed it back into the attic. Forget it. Forgot it. Nothing is real until I say so. Nobody can impose their reality on me. Enjoy the party.

77

I enjoyed the party very much. The crowd swelled. Alcohol and those small foodstuffs unique to parties appeared in great profusion. "Eat the profits!" cried Dominic, standing now on Nell's dustbin, Little Nell having left it for a Better Place. "Drink the surplus! They'll only spend it on Brecht! For God's sake eat up!"

Everyone (bar the Dramsoc treasurer, a couple of the more responsible committee members and the unfortunate youth who'd directed the previous year's Brecht disaster) cheered. Trestle tables were improvised from chairs and the flats of the set. Somebody made a raid on Dramsoc's props, stored in the third unit, and these began to flavour the party. Nagg mounted an old black bicycle and cycled away from the party into the dark of the epic shed, ringing his bell.

The hugeness of the space began to be used. Life spread out from the light of the stage and the twilight immediately around it, and the party colonised the darkness. High above us, the ramshackle lighting box, strapped to the girders with a web of nylon ropes, had pulled up its rope ladder. It swayed in its cat's-cradle (and elsewhere a spotlight above the stage blinked on and off in mysterious rhythmic sympathy) as the stand-in lighting boy and Little Nell got to know each other better.

"Is it a full moon or what?" I said in bemusement to David.

"Thank God," he said. "I thought you were taking all this in your stride."

We walked further into the dark to avoid standing under the shuddering lighting box. A distant tinkling sound grew louder and Nagg sailed back past us out of the darkness on his bicycle, ringing his bell. Swerving to avoid a group of revellers, he ran straight into a clump of chairs and lay among the ruins, still ringing his bell in the wreckage, till the revellers pulled him out, lifted him onto their shoulders and ran roaring toward the stage. Nobody they passed paid them a blind bit of attention.

Dominic wandered up wearing a minotaur's head. "Where's that sister of yours?" he said, offering us plastic cups of punch to supplement the plastic cups of punch we already had. We declined the offer gracefully.

"She's gone to collect a friend from the College Bar," I said, naming no names. I strongly suspected David wouldn't approve.

Dominic nodded the great bull mask and poured punch from his cups into our cups till our cups overflowed.

"What play do you plan to do next?" asked David, "I'll definitely go to it."

"Fillum," said the Minotaur. "Fillum's the business. I want to make a filllllum." He swayed and nodded. "Or maybe an advert," he said. The party roared behind him. Someone had done something funny. The Minotaur with Dominic's body continued to nod. "That's where Orson Welles went wrong," he said, nodding. "He should have *started* with the sherry ads and *finished* with *Citizen Kane*. Then you'd have none of this poor-Orson-what-a-wasted-talent bollocks. Poor eejit did it the wrong way round, that's all. You should save your triumph for the end. Only an eejit starts with it." He abruptly stopped nodding. "I'm drunk," he said. "And I've a bull's head on me." He dropped the empty cups he held, and carefully pulled the head off. He handed it over to me and stood rubbing his ears. "That's a secret now, mind," he said. "You won't tell?" We said we would not. He nodded again, pleased. "I want to live Orson Welles's life!" he roared into the darkness. "Backwards!" Then he looked at us, frowned, grabbed us both and pushed us together. "That's better," he mumbled and, putting a finger to his lips, looked from one of us to the other. "Shush now. Secret," he said, and turned and walked back into the crowd and the light.

I snuggled closer to David before he could pull away, and he said, "Christ," and dropped his cup.

I gave up.

78

I've probably talked enough about the party, haven't I? I should just take another deep breath and plough on.

We socialised, we mingled, we talked to other people, we talked to each other. We kept ending up on the edge of the party. When we'd washed up in the darkness at the edge of things for the third or fourth time, I said, "We're just not party people, are we?"

David had somehow acquired two tennis racquets and a ball. "Tennis?" he said.

We walked further into the dark away from the noise, past couples writhing in the gloom, a drunken smiling boy trying to catch pigeons with a ladder and a butterfly net, and a fire-eater, till we were in a limbo barely illuminated by the distant stage lights and the occasional gout of blazing petroleum. The money Dominic had paid security to patrol elsewhere had been wisely spent. Already not a fire regulation remained unbroken, there was serious talk of toasting marshmallows on a bonfire on the concrete floor, and the night was yet young.

"Something's up," said David. "Something's up and it's not just me. That note, where you wanted to talk. It was something important, wasn't it? It wasn't just us."

I was silent. David served. The ghostly ball floated gently down, bounced startlingly close. I lobbed it back. The pock . . . pock of our shots was very soothing against the ambient noise of the far-off party. I didn't want to answer.

I didn't want to make it real. Nothing is real until I say so. But that's not true.

Pock . . . pock. Zen tennis, with no scoring system and no attempt to beat each other, because if we lost track of the ball we'd never find it again.

OK, deep breath. Gemma appeared out of the gloom. "Where's Juno?" she said. I lowered my racquet, and the returning ball bounced past me and away into the dark.

"She's not back yet?" I said. I'd assumed she was around and I'd missed her in the crowd.

"Well, I've not seen her and I've been looking," said Gemma. "Some people were thinking of maybe taking it now, so if you see her give me a shout. I'm over at the punch table."

"Right oh," I said. Gemma winked and left.

"David," I said, "I might have a look for Juno in the College Bar, she's probably stayed on for a pint. She has some stuff Gemma needs."

"Want a handsome gigolo escort?" said David, striking a pose with his racquet.

"No, you'll do," I said. We got our coats.

We found the door from unit two into unit one.

We found the door from unit one into the world outside.

It was raining. We found Juno.

79

Deep breath.

"Juno," I said.

"Oh Juliet," she said and collapsed into my arms. I held her weight as she cried. Her hair was soaking and it stuck to my face. My arms felt numb around her. My body felt numb. Everything felt numb except my face. I leaned back against the concrete wall of the IMI, holding up her dead weight as the rain patted the tarmac. David stood, pale eyes widening and then he blurred on me and I couldn't read his expression at all. My eyes were very hot, hot strokes on my cheeks from abrupt tears, and the cold wet weight of her hair.

"Oh Juno, oh please, oh Juno"

"He wrote the letters, oh Juliet, he wrote them all, he wrote the *letters* and I told him, I'd told him, and he, and he never said"

"Who wrote the letters? Who wrote them, Juno?" David's voice didn't sound right, the words jerked out through a tight throat.

"Conrad Hayes, Conrad Hayes," her sobbing was shaking my body.

"Oh sweet Jesus," said David and took a stride away from us.

"David don't *leave* me," I sobbed.

He froze, stuttered forward, came back to me. Us. His face was clenching and unclenching like a fist, his jaw and his mouth and his forehead.

"Oh Juliet," said Juno, sobbed Juno, oh God, "It felt all wrong, I knew, I knew it was all wrong, I should have known, it wasn't *nice* Juju it wasn't *nice* and when he'd finished it was all wrong he was drunk but that wasn't it that wasn't it at all, it was, I could tell, there was something wrong, oh God he wrote the *letters* how could he do that Juju?"

I couldn't say anything. I felt like I'd been in a car crash and airbags had bloomed in an instant inside me as well as around me and now I was all protected and empty as the crash continued all about me.

80

David talked to her as I held her in my useless arms and my shoulder blades ground through my thin wool coat against the concrete wall behind me.

She talked into my shoulder to David and she calmed against me, growing lighter in my arms as the words came out of her and she could take back the weight of herself from me.

As David coaxed the words from Juno he placed a hand on my hands where they joined on Juno's back and my mouth opened in an *O* sucking in little shudders of breath, *o, o, o, o, o.*

When her tears were fully words again David grew silent but his hand on my hands meant I didn't have to open my eyes. I didn't want to open my eyes.

"We hadn't even really kissed, I never thought that was what he, we talked about plays, his play, the other times, but he was drunk and he wouldn't talk, he wanted, I said, well he wouldn't stop and I knew it was safe I said yes, so it wasn't . . . I could have said no, I'm sure I could've, and he wouldn't have, would he? But it felt all wrong, because it, he wasn't, I didn't like it but it was too late to say no, I thought it was in my head, I was imagining, I don't know, but the way he, and he didn't speak to me, I felt like I was someone else, and when it hurt he didn't, he didn't, oh Juju it wasn't like"

I couldn't bear it and my mind filled with visions to distract itself, to stop any more of this coming into me. I felt the ache of my shoulder blades against the concrete wall and my mind in one sharp moment transformed them into the stumps of severed wings, so that all the muscles of my back bunched and tensed at the vivid illusion.

David's hand clenched around both mine.

". . . and when he'd finished, it was the place he sleeps in there, it's a terrible kip Juju" she laughed, which hurt me worse of course because it was her laugh in the middle of this, which made it real and I didn't want it to be real "there's no bathroom even, he just walked out, he left me there and the smell of the pillows oh God I got up and I was, I don't know, I was restless or maybe, I don't know what you'd call it but I felt awful, it had all been wrong Juju, I mean he hadn't asked, you know, checked, it was like he didn't like me or that he didn't care and we'd been talking about, about the *weather* and *books* and everything yesterday and it was *grand* then, I couldn't think if I'd said anything wrong or what so I was, I wasn't happy and I sat in his chair at his desk and I rooted around in all the papers there, I'd never do that Juliet would I you know that but I felt all wrong and I wanted to know, I knew, I think I knew already does that make any sense to you" and I nodded yes and held her, so strange for me to be holding her, it wasn't meant to be like this, who would hold me up now if I took the full weight of her sorrow and what if I fell under it I'm so lonely can't bear this oh Juno "Oh Juliet at the back it was all big envelopes with names and my name was on the top one and I pulled out these pages and the top one was the first note to me, with all these changes, the changes were the note I got, he'd written me a letter and taken out the long words and made it like the others and I thought, maybe it's only the first note, he just wrote the nice one it's a coincidence, the others, he couldn't, because I *knew* him for the last one how could anyone . . ." Oh Juno, how could anyone and all the muscles of my back tried to lift me free of it with my sister in my arms and her breath on my cheek was like the wind going past I had to open my eyes to check.

"And I read the other pages and he'd written all of them."

She lifted her head beside mine so that she must have been looking at the concrete wall in front of her, or at nothing at all, or maybe she hadn't opened her eyes, I didn't want to turn my head to see. David was looking at me and his face was almost calm and I was glad because I'd been afraid when he'd begun to move away that he might do something terrible. Juno was calmer now. Everything would be fine.

"He had copies of the other letters he'd sent me and he'd copies of forms I'd filled in to sit exams and copies of exam rosters and some of my essays, things in different subjects, like a file on me. And more stuff like in the letters, for himself. There were other envelopes like that, for other girls. And . . . oh Juju, he's started an envelope for you."

"Oh dear God," said David and took his hand from mine.

81

Juno laughed, an oddly little-girl laugh, as though she had been naughty and knew she shouldn't be laughing but couldn't help it. "Shall I tell you what I did then?" she said. "Oh, maybe, no I shouldn't have done this. . . . I took his bottle of Jameson from the desk and I took all the acid tabs I had for the party and I put them in the bottle and shook it. And I crushed the little microdots with a biro and I put them all in too, folded a piece of paper and poured them in. Was I terrible? I wanted to hurt him or, I don't know. Was I wrong? It seemed . . . I got all the bits of paper out with the biro they were floating on top. And I left . . . I left the envelope with all the things about me, I left it on his desk, so he would know, I wanted him to know. . . . It won't hurt him though will it? The acid I mean, all the acid in the whiskey I mean you can't overdose so, I mean . . . but," she said with sudden anxiety "It just seemed, I thought, I wanted to get him back. It was stupid wasn't it. I shouldn't have done that," she was upsetting herself oh don't please don't "But I'd said yes and I wouldn't have if I'd known so it was like, it was like he'd" oh don't Juno don't "and if only he'd liked me, why did he have to do that when I liked him anyway there was no need to do that"

"I could have stopped him," said David calmly, oh Jesus Christ, don't be part of this I love you "This is all my fault. When Juliet told me you'd got these letters I thought it might be Conrad, because of things I'd heard about his time in Austin, rumours I'd heard here. But I didn't want to damn a man on hearsay, I talked to him, he swore on his honour, he was upset, I believed him. I had to apologise. I had to apologise. Oh Jesus Christ. I could have stopped this. I could have warned you. I could have done more. I could have checked, told the guards. This is all my fault."

"Oh, David . . ."

"How could you know? It's not . . ."

But he turned and walked away from us and as I followed he began to run.

82

Juno came and took my hand and I looked in panic from her to where David had gone, and back to her. "He'll do something stupid," I said, but I couldn't leave her.

"Come on," said Juno and pushed her wet hair back off her face and together we ran, her hand in my hand, my hand in her hand.

83

It wasn't far from the IMI to the Quad.

We came through the Quad gate close behind David. He'd stopped running, we hadn't. The rain faded out as we ran, the fickle weather of Galway. The few people we'd passed had paid no more attention than usual to two girls running, hand in hand. As they'd paid no attention to Juno as she'd stood outside the IMI in the rain, afraid to go in, afraid to start crying, waiting for me to come looking and find her. The things she'd said, do you think I've told you everything? I had a sick, exultant sense of just how dark the world would be if we could see into the lives of all the strangers passing by us.

We caught up with him by the door at the foot of the tower, in the corner of the Quad. Light came from Conrad Hayes's window high above, as it almost always did. From the College Bar behind us came the muffled chorus of a Pogues song was it, yes, "The Sick Bed of Cúchulaínn." I remembered the foggy morning I first heard Conrad Hayes, singing unseen from a window high above. And if that fog had lifted and he'd seen me then, would I have found myself befriended, would he have supervised my fraught exams, a pleasant and a helpful man?

"David," I said, "don't."

"I have to talk to him."

The door wasn't even closed, after Juno's flight. He pushed it wide. A dark space, dim stairwell rising.

"Please David, leave it, we'll call the guards, tell the department, they'll deal with it. . . ." But we could see it in each other's eyes. He touched the tip of my nose sadly with a fingertip. Juno said nothing.

What charge, when it became a kind of rape only in retrospect? How subtle a law is required, for a violation where only the evildoer knows at the time the truth and the depth of the evil? Letters, bad sex. Nothing.

I held Juno's hand and made no move to stop him as he walked through into the hall.

He took the stairs two at a time. I felt a tremble in my hand and couldn't tell if my hand was shaking in hers or hers in mine. I looked at Juno and brushed her hair back off her face again with my free hand. We followed David up the stairs into the dark. Through my head like an irritating jingle ran the title of a Browning poem I hadn't even read though I'd always meant to because I'd liked the title, "Childe Roland to the Dark Tower Came," "Childe Roland to the Dark Tower Came," "Childe Roland to . . ."

We followed David up the stairs into the dark.

How rich and dark the world would be if we could see into the lives of all the wives and daughters we call strangers passing by us.

84

A sense that we were now in a realm of sorrow and darkness shook me somewhat as we approached the final landing. My mind was, I think, a little loose in its moorings by now. Tears and adrenaline and high emotion had lifted me to an unstable peak from which the world seemed transformed. I think some sort of gap had opened up between all of us and the ground of the ordinary world.

But Conrad's actions had transformed the ordinary world, we couldn't fight him on the old ground, he didn't truly live there. Up here in the sorrow and the dark, we were perhaps right to allow the transformation of ourselves into these unstable things that came running up the winding stairs, somehow laughing. At what? God knows. God knew. I kissed Juno, and she me.

A crashing sound as we came up the last steps to the final landing. It was only David's knuckles on a wooden office door. We ran up behind him, snorting back our laughter because it was too loud on the tight landing with its thick, still air.

No answer. Another clatter of knocks, incredibly loud on the landing. No answer.

David turned the handle and the door swung open. A thin crack of grey fluorescent light widened and a wave of light gushed over us, flooding the small landing, light pouring down the stairwell into the dark. I watched David's eyes narrow and blink, before he took a step into the room. We followed.

85

Conrad Hayes sat in a leather armchair behind his desk. He faced us, with the window behind him framing chair and man against the black of the night sky. He clutched the arms of his chair with hands that were long-fingered and strangely beautiful. His head was thrown a little back, the neck supported by the back of the chair. The resemblance to one of Francis Bacon's paintings of a screaming pope was at once hilarious and frightening.

His stare was so fixed that I thought he was dead until Juno moved uncomfortably beside me and his eyes followed her. Neither David nor I seemed to exist for him at all. His throat convulsed and we waited for him to speak.

"What have you done to me?"

A stale smell rose from the crumpled sheets of the camp bed along the right-hand wall and my mind mixed it up with the terror in his voice, so that I thought for an eerie second that I could smell his terror. Juno couldn't look at him, buried her face in the hollow of my neck and shoulder.

"What have you done to me?" And now he was looking into my eyes and I knew with absolute certainty that in his mind he was seeing Juno as he looked on my face.

"What have you done to her?" said David quietly and Conrad's head jerked so abruptly round that a droplet of spittle at his mouth corner was left to drag across his cheek by the movement.

David had walked around the desk to stand by Conrad. The two now looked into each other's eyes along a line of sight as taut with tension as a yard of bridge suspension cable. Juno turned her face from my shoulder at David's question and looked at the tableau. Her hand tightened. Her hand in my hand. My hand in her hand. I was suddenly embarrassed, as though somebody would see us, frightened, holding hands at eighteen, and mock us. But David was looking into Conrad's eyes and Conrad was looking into the abyss. And I had a moment of, what would you call it? Secular clarity. An agnostic vision. I saw not the light, nor the opposite of the light, but . . . the back of the light, the light going elsewhere. I saw in this room, very clear, not the face of God but the enormous and distant back of His head. God was altogether elsewhere, vast, supervising the suffering in Africa and Asia, suffering the children to come unto him. Working industrial miracles of suffering. Upping production. Making his quota. We, here, in this room, were too small-scale for the personal supervision of God. And, also, overqualified. We were grown-up, educated, European. We knew all about suffering, theory and practice. We'd read books on it. We could suffer without benefit of plague or hunger. We could suffer while wealthy and healthy. We had a genius for suffering. God trusted us to get on with it. He knew we'd see it through.

David sat on the corner of the crowded, messy desk and leaned down a little to bring his eyes level with Conrad's. Conrad looked back and from his acid-drenched and melting, drowning world whimpered, "Who are you?"

And David said in a calm and even voice with no trace of the bunched fury that had shuddered through him outside the IMI, "Your conscience. A mirror. Nothing."

And Conrad whimpered in genuine and frightening horror.

I couldn't look. My eyes dropped from his face, and my gaze snagged in passing on a word on a page upon his desk, in the centre of the mess. The loose page was the top page of a small stack, on an envelope. I reached my hand out cautiously into the electric field that overspilled the space between the two men, and picked up the top few pages. Behind me Juno started to speak, stopped. Handwritten. The ink was black and the writing very even, a good strong hand, well-formed letters, almost copperplate. I turned it round, and reread the first line, that had caught my eye.

My dear Juno.

My was crossed out, replaced with another *dear*.

I know that you don't know me, and I make no claim to know you.

He had replaced the *don't* with *do not*, simplified the *make no claim to* as *do not*. I read the original, in his beautiful old-fashioned handwriting, beneath the bleached and dead replacement words.

My dear Juno,

*   I know that you don't know me, and I make no claim to know you. You will think this letter foolish, perhaps. So be it. All I wish to say is that on a recent day when my life had darkened to the point where I was contemplating quitting it, I saw you pass, you shone: I followed you. I know it is inexcusable, and had courage been equal to desire I would have thanked you then, but please accept even these coward's thanks. In contemplating you, I cured myself somehow. Your beauty pulled me through. That's all. And I thank you.*

A love letter. Oh this will end in tears Conrad. I read the next sheet, the second letter, in the original, so beautiful, darkening, vicious, black with blood and hate. "*. . . I will have you like a whore. You will whimper on all fours. . . .*" This will end in tears.

I looked at Conrad, my eyes dry. He had ceased whimpering, and was silent. He was listening now. David was speaking.

"I'm not here to punish you," said David soothingly. "I'm not here to hurt you. I'm just here to show you exactly what you've done. To explain it to you so you understand. Because you've done a very terrible thing, Conrad. You've hurt a girl very terribly, you've made her afraid and you've made her cry, Conrad, you've made her cry. You've treated her as though she wasn't real, as though the hurt you caused her wasn't important, hardly mattered, didn't really exist." Conrad's head jerked round like a damaged toy to stare blankly at Juno, at me, his eyes flicking, helplessly, and Juno couldn't bear to look at him and turned to me again, buried her face again in my shoulder, so that now Conrad looked straight at me with my short hair and my sister's face. He saw Juno in me and I felt curiously relaxed, as though that were entirely correct under the circumstances. As Conrad looked on me and saw Juno, David spoke of Juno and I knew (I could see it, as clear as a photograph) that the picture in his mind was of me.

"This girl is real," said David. "The hurt you have caused her *exists,* just as much as this book exists." He picked up and slammed down the *Concise Oxford English Dictionary* on Conrad Hayes's desk so that the empty Jameson bottle shivered on a swaying stack of paperbacks, and Conrad's frightened eyes snapped free of mine to lock back into David's steady gaze. "The hurt you have caused her stains this universe in which we all must live. You have caused real damage in the real world, Conrad. A damage you would never dream of doing to yourself. How could you conceivably have had any right to damage her, Conrad?"

"I'm sorry I'm sorry I'm sorry," said Conrad Hayes.

"Put that in writing, Conrad."

Conrad groped for a pen on the crowded table without taking his eyes from David's eyes. The pile of books and the bottle fell to the carpet. A mug fell, and papers in a long, fanning slide that took them yards across the carpet. When he found a pen in the wreckage he brought it up to his face, into line with their eyes.

David nodded. "Write a letter to all of them, Conrad. To Juno. To Juliet. A letter to all the girls. One you can sign your name to. Are you sorry you hurt them?" Conrad nodded and whimpered like a beaten dog. "It's a terrible thing, isn't it, to deliberately add to the hurt in the world."

Conrad nodded, "I'm sorry I'm sorry"

"Write it down. Tell them you're sorry."

"I'm sorry I'm sorry. . . ."

Juno let go my hand and turned and walked to the desk. My heart slapped into my ribs but I didn't try to stop her. I felt like a ghost, invisible. Conrad turned from David to face her. Only the desk between them now. His face rippled with fear, a thing I had never seen, the muscles in spasm from his neck and the jaw under the trim beard to his forehead and temples. It was as though a stone had been thrown into liquid flesh.

The spasms passed, to leave a tiny muscle twitching under his right eye and another on his right temple.

I drifted closer, like a ghost. I leaned on Juno's shoulder, looking over, like a ghost in a waxwork museum, among the exhibits. Juno looked at Conrad, and I couldn't tell what was in her mind. Conrad looked at Juno, and I didn't want to know.

The tableau unfroze. Conrad pawed a page from a pile of pages. It had a few lines of print on it, upside-down to him, but he treated it as though it were blank. In a drug-shattered hand, a debased, collapsing form of the perfect calligraphy of the original of his first and charming note, he convulsively wrote, "I'm sorry I'm sorry I'm sorry I'm sorry," until the words ran out onto the desk and he lurched his hand back for another line. "I'm sorry I'm sorry I'm sorry."

"You shouldn't have hurt them, Conrad," said David sadly, almost to himself.

"I'm sorry I hurt you I'm sorry I hurt you I'm sorry I hurt you" wrote Conrad, line after line, until the writing reached the typed lines and ran over them. They were the last lines of a poem I half-knew, by Yeats. Juno reached behind her to find my hand as Conrad wrote, "I'm sorry I hurt you" again and again in a broken hand across the scrap of Yeats turned upside-down to him.

> *Transparent like the wind*
> *I think that I may find*
> *A faithful love, a faithful love.*

It was perhaps the most savage thing I had ever seen, but I could not make myself intervene, to stop it. Because I did not want to stop it. Because I believed it was just.

86

"Now sign it," said David. Conrad's hand fluttered over the packed page before finding a space where two scribbled lines of his apology had diverged to form a long blank island of white. He wrote his name on the island. David picked up the sheet and looked at it. He nodded. "Very good, Conrad. Now give me the envelopes, and we can leave you in peace." Conrad looked up at David, and his mouth moved. David leaned down again to his level. "Yes, Conrad?"

And Conrad said quietly, in a child's voice, "Am I in hell?"

David shrugged sadly. For the first time tears appeared in Conrad's eyes, welling on the lower lids and spilling down his cheeks into his beard. David stood up, holding the apology, and walked around the desk to us.

"Here you are," he said to Juno, and handed her the page. She let go my hand to take it from him in both her hands. "Thank you," she said.

"Am I being judged?" said Conrad from the far side of the desk. His voice had grown even smaller. He was collapsing into himself like a dying star, the words were barely able to escape him now.

We looked at him. I felt something like pity, or compassion, at the last. Very late. I am not as kind as I would like to be.

"Is this judgement?" he asked again.

"No," said David, "we have no right to judge you. Only you can judge yourself."

Conrad closed his eyes. He nodded, and tears fell to the cluttered desk. Opening his eyes again, he pulled out the top drawer almost all the way, pulled out the envelopes and piled them on his desk. He looked up at Juno. At me. At Juno. "I'm sorry I hurt you," he said. "I'm sorry I'm sorry I'm sorry"

David gathered Juno's pages, I gave him those I held. David reached for the pile of envelopes, and Conrad shrank back in his chair, so small a man now, so broken. David picked up the envelopes, turned to go, saw the name on the top envelope now. My name. He hesitated, looked from it to me. "And you've received a letter, haven't you?"

". . . Yes."

"That was what you wished to tell me, why you wished to meet me."

". . . Yes." His face asked me a question. I didn't know the answer. "I was afraid . . . ? Of . . . what you would do."

He nodded and slipped the slim single page out of the envelope, still looking at me.

"Childe Roland to the Dark Tower Came," I thought, in lieu of thinking.

David read the letter.

"You two go on, I shall join you," he said when he had finished, and handed me the letter, the letters, the full envelopes. There was something so certain in his voice that we did, without thinking. Juno held my arm as we walked out the door, leaving it open behind us to spill light down the stairwell as we walked down the shadowed stairs. Behind us we heard the murmur of a voice, David's voice, conversational. A moment of silence. A murmur of reply.

And then David's voice was like a thundercrack, an avenging angel's roar, a weapon of execution. We were afraid and we ran, pursued by the crash and echo of our footfalls through all the long spiral down.

Outside in the rain we held each other. Then David came quietly out through the great doorway and put his arms around us like a brother or a father. "It will be alright," he said, and we walked toward the archway in the rain.

At the archway I stopped. We stopped. "What did you do to him?" I said.

Drunks passed us, going to and from the College Bar. "Babe alert!" shouted one. "Babe alert!"

"I helped him come to his judgement," said David.

I looked up at the high window of the dark tower, to see Conrad in silhouette against the light. Where first I heard him sing. Conrad seemed to be staring up at . . . I looked up. Nothing. The bellies of clouds. Darkness. David, looking too where Conrad looked, spoke. Not his own words, a quote, his voice heavy, saturated with sorrow. " 'Two things fill the mind with ever new and increasing admiration and awe, the oftener and more steadily we reflect on them: the starry heavens above and the moral law within.' "

The featureless night poured past us. The mercury-vapour lights that illuminated the Quad denied us the sky. I didn't mind. My neck stiff, I moved my head a little, to look again at Conrad, framed in the window.

I wanted to leave but couldn't, the night was unfinished.

"What is he doing?" asked Juno.

"Coming to judgement," said David. "It's probably best if we leave." But we didn't leave. Another drunken boy wolf-whistled as he passed us.

A girl and two boys entered the Quad behind us, swaying, joined us, looked up.

High above, Conrad, swaying, dark against the light, hands raised, looking up into the night.

"Too late," said David sadly, beside me.

As Conrad swayed behind the glass, he looked like someone underwater, in a flooded room, a drowning man.

"I'm so sorry," I said suddenly. To whom? I still don't know.

Conrad came towards us, then, and the window turned white and vanished and he was through it now and falling and all the shards and fragments of the shattered glass about him spun in the harsh light in a gush of diamonds.

His dark bulk with arms outstretched outpaced the glass and light, and even as he fell I thought quite calmly, Oh, that is the air slowing down the smaller bits of glass, as the wheat is sorted from the chaff.

His dark arms outstretched he began to turn slowly in the air and then with the most astonishing shock, for I had forgotten the inevitability of this, he ran out of air, and the sound as he hit the ground was strangely wet and muffled, with drier sounds inside it, breaking sounds like plastic forks snapping in the canteen. He lay there, astonishing, and then the glass began to fall on him like diamond snow.

In the silence that followed the last of the glass the sky broke and it began to rain.

87

David rang the police from the porters' office inside the archway of the Quad. He re-emerged to find us standing in the bright electric light of the archway, out of the rain. In the Quad, under the rain and the mercury-vapour light of the high lamps, people moved in ones and twos toward the body, and away. Others drifted out of the College Bar to see. Joe from security, who should have been at the IMI, quietly kept them back from the body with words I couldn't hear from where we were.

We stood there in the archway, silent. Thinking, I suppose. No, not thinking. Adjusting. A lot to adjust to.

"I'm glad," I said. Juno leaned on me, nodded. I brushed her hair back from her face again and smiled at her. She closed her eyes and rested her head on my shoulder again.

David glanced over at the body in the rain. "They're coming. Five minutes." He looked exhausted and depressed. "I failed at everything," he said, "I couldn't save you, I couldn't save Conrad. . . . I've misjudged and I've messed up everything, God . . ."

"No you didn't," said Juno.

"David, you haven't," I said. His hands were fists. We put our hands on his hands. "How could you have known?" I said. "What more could you have done?"

"I've practically killed a man." His fist jumped in my hands.

"*No*. Don't be stupid. Shut up," I said, furious. "*He* did it. *He* lied and he deceived and he hurt Juno and now he's done this awful thing to *himself. He* did it. Not you."

"He was obviously out of his mind with guilt and fear and I goaded him, I pushed him . . ."

"If he felt guilt it was because he was guilty, and he felt fear because he was right to be afraid. Don't be so *stupid*, David. Everyone can't be a victim. He was a *bad man*, David. So you told him to judge himself. Well, he judged himself. And I'm *glad*."

David shrugged, and rubbed a hand over his face. "When the police come," he said to Juno, "don't tell them you put the acid in his whiskey. It's a class A drug, and the coroner is likely to judge that it contributed to his death. You can't be associated with it. If he took it himself it's straightforward guilt-induced suicide by a depressed man about to lose his reputation, made all the more likely to do something foolish by drink and drugs. There's no need for you to mention the acid." Juno nodded. "Everything else, if they ask, we tell the truth." We nodded. "We came to confront him, took the envelopes, left, and he killed himself. We've what's practically a drunken suicide note, a thick file full of reasons, and a Quad full of witnesses. I can't see them investigating this too thoroughly. But if you've any more acid, I would strongly advise you to get rid of it."

"No, I've none. I used it all."

"What did you do with the paper tabs once you'd fished them out?"

"I wrapped them in a tissue in my purse."

"Jesus. Well, flush them down the toilet or something when you get home. And don't blow your nose while the police are questioning you."

88

In the event, the police were a huge disappointment. Two of them eventually arrived, on foot. One was the young guard I had seen at the station, who had been talking to the traveller woman. He didn't recognise me, and I said nothing. They seemed bored and depressed by the body and the circumstances, and hardly asked us any questions at all. The note and the envelopes and our story seemed to explain everything to their satisfaction. The position of the body met with their bored, sad approval. The several drunken witnesses, now much sobered, who had also seen the fall told their confirming stories. The guards didn't even bother to separate us all, to get our stories independently. I was astonished to realize, very, very late, that this wasn't a murder investigation. Despite all my words of reassurance to David, I quite firmly believed he had essentially killed Conrad Hayes, that he had quite deliberately magnified and reflected Conrad's fear and hatred back against Conrad's disintegrating self. David knew he had carried out an execution. He had acted as a mirror, and a conscience. As he had promised.

But as the two guards put away their notebooks and an ambulance arrived quietly, with no sirens, I realized that even if the police had been in the room and witnessed everything, they would have seen only a suicide.

I walked out of the arch toward the body on the slick black tarmac, just short of the soft blue grass. Past the solemn couples, to the broken man.

His head looked half sunk into the ground, his skull and cheekbone shattered inside the skin. Diamonds flecked his clothes, his face. The blood pooled in his open mouth, a trickle ran from the corner. Something shifted inside him and a trickle of blood ran from the nostrils. Blood welled and filled his ear, flooded its curves, filled its pool to the rim and ran, and was slowly thinned from his face by the rain. I knelt. His face lay in a pool of blood and water. I looked into the dark pool. I studied Juno's face, my face, in the black mirror of his blood under the mercury-vapour light. I could smell iron and urine.

"Ah, miss," said the older of the two gardaí from behind me. "Miss."

I could hear the clink as the closed half of the big gate swung open in the archway. Joe, letting the ambulance in. I stood and turned. Its blue lights pulsed out through the archway ahead of its coming.

"Miss, if you could just move back a little," said the older officer in a kindly tone. Escorted by the two guards, I walked back and joined Juno and David. We moved aside as the pulsing ambulance passed us almost silently. It stopped by the body. Its blue light flashed around slowly, casting a tint all along the high walls of the Quad.

As I stood beside Juno she gave a mischievous little sneeze. I giggled and David glared at us, which made me giggle more. The younger officer looked at me sympathetically. Obviously delayed shock. "Are you all right, love?" he said, trying to sound reassuringly world-weary and experienced, but his voice went squeaky for no reason at the end. I saw the older guard give an amused glance across and I clenched my jaws shut to stop myself laughing. I gave a serious nod, bowed my head. I was alright, love.

89

The three of us walked out through the archway. I was almost shocked, no, I *was* shocked at how normal the world felt. How unchanged.

"So back to the party then," I said. Juno and David looked at me. "Joke," I mumbled.

"I should talk to Michael," said Juno, and then to me, "Will you walk me there?"

"Of course," I said. "Oh, God. Conrad split you up deliberately."

"I've judged Michael too harshly," said Juno, and I winced.

"Am I in the way?" said David awkwardly, "If you want to talk or . . ."

"God, David, I'm going to hit you if you don't shut up apologising and being all soggy," I said, not as harshly as it sounds. I hope. "You've just slain the Dark Knight in his tower for God's sake, don't be so modern and angsty about it." I grabbed him by the hand as we walked so the three of us were linked—Juno, me, him. "You were brilliant, he deserved it, you did no wrong. Shush. Help me walk Juno to Druid. There might be dragons."

"Dragons are extra," he said, smiling. "Childe Roland to the Dark Tower Came," I sang to myself, "Childe Roland to the Dark Tower Came." Everything's going to be all right. Anything can happen now. Everything can change.

90

When we got to Druid, Juno took both David's hands and kissed his cheek in the warm foyer. "Thank you for everything, for what you did," she said as he blushed. "You were kind and brave for me, and anything bad that happened wasn't your fault. Juliet's right."

"Nothing bad happened," I piped up, "I'm glad the *bastard* is dead," which wasn't very Christian of me but had the slender virtue of truth. A woman in paint-spattered overalls, emerging from the box office just in time to hear me, gave me a strange look, and I gave her a strange look back. She smiled and put up her hands in a *sorry!* gesture as she left the building. I'd probably supercharged my look a little. Everything I did now felt a little supercharged. David let go Juno's hands.

"I'm terribly sorry about the whole mess . . . ," he began.

"*David,*" I said threateningly, and he smiled.

"Good luck," he said. Juno kissed his cheek, kissed me.

"We'll wait," I said. I pulled a couple of chairs together, and we sat down as she bounded up the three steps and through the soundproofed door into the theatre. When the door had swung shut, I said, "You did it for me."

He shrugged. "What do you mean?"

"You did it because it could have been me."

"Did what?"

I frowned at him, and he sighed and rubbed his jaw and cheek. "Perhaps. Look, you can't expect me to feel good about this. I set out to destroy a man, and I probably did. Christ, what right had I? How can I be happy discovering that's in me?"

It sounded fine to me. I tried to hide my surge of primitive pleasure, and didn't quite succeed.

"You bloodthirsty creature," he smiled.

"You think too much," I said. "You worry too much. We're only responsible for our own lives, really, in the end. His life and his death were his own decisions. Can we shut up about him now?"

"Absolutely."

So we talked about ordinary things, and I told him about the Gleeson twins, just stories, not what they'd meant to me, and made him laugh. And he told me about his childhood friends and their tiny crimes, funny stories, charming, far more innocent than the amusing thefts and the comedy beatings I'd regaled him with. And I realized how innocent he was, compared to me. He thought the world was honourable and decent in a way that I only fantasized it was to cheer myself up. In his innocence, he had destroyed Conrad Hayes. A less innocent man couldn't have done it. Not like that. So pure and cold.

When Juno came back out to rejoin us we were chattering away like children, and he sat up straight, guilty at his happiness, as she came down the three steps. I sighed. Lot of work to be done. Ah no, he was lovely the way he was. Madly annoying, but lovely.

"I'm staying with Michael," said Juno. She looked radiant. "His sorrow and remorse are only brilliant. Will you be alright?"

"God, yes," I said. Ouch. A little pang that she hadn't chosen me as her harbour in time of trouble. A little relief that she hadn't. I made a pretty turbulent harbour. And I was glad, I think (I hope) unselfishly, that she had someone who liked her or loved her so much for herself. Bleuch, I'm making myself sick. But you know what I mean. The feelings he had were actually for her, as she was. They meant something.

"I won't be back home tonight," said Juno. "Is that OK?" She was acting like I was the one who needed tender concern and delicate handling after the traumas of the day. I felt a fizz of unsisterly, well no, incredibly sisterly irritation.

"Of course it is, nitwit. You'll be alright?"

She nodded. Smiled. More than one great weight seemed to have been lifted from her. She was radiant, and I'd been so scared she'd fall to pieces. What the *fuck* had Michael said to her? Or done.

Whatever. All couples are mysteries. "Walk me home?" I said to David.

"Honoured."

We good-byed Juno and set off on the brief journey to the harbour. As we walked away from the theatre down Druid Lane, I said, "David, who was Childe Roland?"

"Childe Roland who came to the dark tower? Browning invented him. He dreamt the story of the poem, it's all made up. It's just a dream, I'm afraid."

"Hmm. How old was Childe Roland?"

"No age, he didn't exist. . . ." David saw how dangerous this style of answering was, and switched off the teasing before I started to cry. "Well he wasn't actually a child. He was a Childe, with an *E*. It was a sort of rank in medieval society. A young man who could still become a knight."

"Hah!"

"Pardon?"

"Nothing."

I felt great. I felt like air after a thunderstorm. I absolutely knew that Juno would be fine. I knew it like I knew my name, I felt it like I felt happy, it was just a fact that was true that I knew. You can choose not to be a victim. No, we were never victims. If you let them fuck your life up, they've won. And I knew that Michael would be good for her, and she wouldn't do him any harm either, and they'd work it out, for at least a while, and that I hadn't wrecked it, that the dumb thing that I'd done with Michael didn't matter. And Jimmy Gleeson's having a baby, I thought. Jesus, poor Nuala. Childe Gleeson to the Dark Town Comes. Slouching towards Tipperary to be born, with a fag in his mouth and fifty E down his Pampers. Childe Gleeson with an E. Good-bye, Jimmy. Good-bye, Johnny. Good luck, Jimmy Jr. I'll visit.

I'd always felt I was the wrong shape for the town I was born into, scuffing my cramped and awkward way through childhood, catching myself on the snags of the town as I tried desperately to grow up without damaging myself too badly, choking on claustrophobia and ducking low expectations in a town with a trip wire for a horizon. As I walked and talked with David, as we rounded the corner onto the docks and walked to the quay steps in front of my house with his boat at the bottom of the steps, my life at last felt big enough to stand up and move around in. Stretch out. Swing my arms. My life would never fit back into Tipperary now, and that was fine.

We stood at the top of the steps. In the cheap sepia of the quayside's sodium light he looked monochrome, tired, Bogart-beautiful. Very lovely. Very lonely. I almost reached out to touch him, didn't. He stirred, as if to, I don't know, say something, do something. I made a wish in my head. Say something. Do something.

We stood there, in the sodium light. A great roar from Brennan's Bar, further down the docks. The slap of the water against the quayside wall. Nothing. A gull wheeling into the light and then gone and very far off another gull's cry. A heart-piercing sound. Harsh and high. A sound made to carry far, across wide ocean water. A cold scream of loneliness without a trace of self-pity or any pity. A sound that reminds you that birds are reptiles that took to the sky. Maybe the least intimate sound in the world. Nonsense words. Why do you fly? The better to be alone, my dear, the better to be alone. I trembled.

"I'd better get back," David said abruptly. "You'll be OK?" He pointed across, without looking, toward the building.

I nodded, my happiness cooling and freezing in the chill of another gull's scream, miles away, distant, high. Could he feel that?

He nodded as though in answer, but he turned, and walked down the steps, away from me. Oh Jesus. Into that dark night. No. Over that cold deep water, alone. Leaving me here on the cold stone steps, under the frozen single frequency of this monochrome light, alone, why, for Christ's sake? I ran down the steps, slipped, grabbed on to his jacket and he turned, held me up, startled.

Deep breath, turned off my mind, opened my mouth.

"You said you didn't want to get involved with me, that one of us would get hurt and how you couldn't bear that. Well that just isn't good enough. Look what happened to Juno, and she didn't want to get hurt. Look what happens to people just living their lives. They get *hurt*, it's not *fair* they get hurt but they *do*, all the *time*, no matter how careful they are. Somebody can just come along and hurt them, for a stupid reason or no reason, and I *like* you David, I *like* you an awful lot, way more than you imagine, and if you still like me as much as you said you did when we went shopping and you invited me to dinner, and if all that's stopping you from . . . from *getting involved*, is that you just don't want anybody to get *hurt*, then . . . I don't *care* if I get hurt, and you shouldn't care either, because we like each other." I was crying now. "And we're going to get hurt anyway, so what." I felt utterly miserable. I didn't think I'd said it right at all. I looked up and blinked the tears clear. "Do I sound like an American?" I said, and he laughed and put his arm around me and as his face moved towards mine I saw just before I closed my eyes that a tear had squeezed awkwardly out of his right eye and hung from an eyelash, heavy and clear. Our lips touched and I felt his tear fall on my cheek. He must have closed his eyes. I opened mine as he opened his. So close. We closed our eyes again. Love, I thought to myself abstractedly. Not "This is love" or "Is this love?" Not a sentence, not a certainty, not a thought with moving parts or direction. Just love, all of it, as it is. Whether it's enough or not. Whether it's real or we're making it up. However shoddy it gets, or bent out of shape. It's still extraordinary. However foolish, however vain. However badly it ends. Love.

We kissed, and I contemplated, static, accidentally transcendent, love.

Time passed. The world turned beneath us. Later, it spun.

Eventually the kiss ended. I was warmer than the sun. David held me while we practised breathing, got the hang of it again. I took it as a sign of God's special favour that we'd managed not to fall off the steps into the harbour. We kissed again. We were getting very good at it. Practice makes perfect. Like anything, you have to put in the hours.

Time passed pleasantly.

"You've convinced me," said David. "I was completely wrong. Get in the boat."

91

𝓘 set out to tell you Juno's story, Juno's and Michael's, and Conrad's. Looking back, I seem to have ended up telling you mine, and David's. Perhaps that was the story I wanted to tell all along, and I had to trick myself into telling it. Who knows. I've given up thinking I'll ever understand myself, or anybody else. It's a great relief.

Certainly we're too complex to judge ourselves. Conrad Hayes was almost certainly far too harsh in his judgement of his poor, whimpering self. But then again

Seldom went such grotesqueness with such woe;
I never saw a brute I hated so;
He must be wicked to deserve such pain.

I've read "Childe Roland to the Dark Tower Came" since, as you can see. It's very silly, but it ends well.

I've read a lot since, done a lot. Where a story ends is a choice you have to make when you're telling the story. Choosing to end it here makes it a happy ending, almost a Shakespearean comic ending, with happy couples all over the shop, Juno & Michael, David & me. Almost a Hollywood ending. The starcrossed lovers kiss under the, well OK it's not moonlight but it's close, they've made it through somehow, audience dabs eyes and files out happy. Happy ending.

And some people are suspicious of that, because lives *don't* stop with a kiss and stay happy forever. They think, and I appreciate their point, that a happy ending is cheating, because if I'd chosen to end it a day earlier it would be an ambiguous ending, an hour earlier and it would be a sad ending.

So I think it's only fair to say that I really have thought about this, and both the story I've tried to tell and the story I've ended up telling really do have happy endings. I'm not saying we all lived happily ever after. Christ, not only would that be ridiculous but it wouldn't even be half as much *fun* as the more complicated truth. I'm not even saying that Juno and Michael stayed together and prospered, or that David and I did likewise. That's not the point. That would just be me, now, putting another arbitrary end on the story. I mean, ultimately we all *die*, all stories end in death and all endings short of that are a bit dodgy, they all rock a bit in the wind. So if you're very, very uptight about happy endings and a stickler for not being manipulated, well there's an honest answer for you, we're all going to end up dead.

But it's truthful to give this story a happy ending. Because we were all happier afterwards than we were before. And if all that extra happiness eventually led to a little extra hurt because we'd all more to lose, well so what. Hurt is part of life. To be honest, I think hurt is part of happiness, that our definition of happiness has gotten very narrow lately, very nervous, a little afraid of the brawling, fabulous, unpredictable world.

But what harm. If we won't come to life, well, life will come to us. You can't avoid it.

So I'll end the story now. No. Not on the dock. I think I'll end it the next day, and you can take these kisses as shorthand for a million kisses.

The next day, in David's father's house, well not exactly *in*, I was standing on the roof of the tower, leaning my hips against the low stone wall and feeling like God had polished and serviced me. The sun on Galway Bay, not up long. Mist burning off Connemara behind me. The pale blue empty sky above. Love, love, love. A gull swooped in front of me, a few hundred yards away, level with the tower. I stuck my tongue out at it, pressed my hips against the wall, and shivered with a kind of happiness I'd never known before.

Up the stairs behind me came footsteps. "Breakfast," said David, his head appearing through the trap. "Another of Dad's bloody dinosaurs, with fried eggs, fried tomatoes, fried mushrooms and coffee. Or would madam like to see one of the specialist menus?"

"Look," I said.

He came all the way up, stood beside me. Looked. "It's going to be a lovely day," he said. "Yes," I said. I turned, and kissed him, a little kiss, a lovely kiss.

We stood on the tower, in the sun. Breakfast noises came from the kitchen far below. A clatter of cutlery. Pan on the stove. Kiss, break. Kiss, break.

David's father's voice, faint, from down in the heart of the house. "Breakfast, Juliet! Breakfast, Romeo, you big eejit!"

We managed to squeeze in a last quick kiss before breakfast.

No, I was wrong earlier, I gave in to the modern fear of the happy ending. The devil take our fashion for irony, misery and ambiguity.

Here's what really happened.

       We all

            lived

                  happily

                        ever

                             after.

THE END

“Don’t ever expect me to tr… and seduce … said, yanki… stall door

Ken stood frozen, … down his perfect … learn how to knock?” he asked, his voice a low, husky drawl.

Pamela’s tirade ended as her breath exited her lungs. “Oh, my,” she whispered, unable to look away. She had already seen his beautiful bare torso and flat stomach so rippled with muscles, but now she saw the rest of him—the lean hips, the long legs and, oh, the *rest* of him.

Pam began to shiver. “I want you, Ken McBain,” she said, tugging off her T-shirt and tossing it to the floor. “But your nobility is killing me. So take me or leave me.”

He’d been able to hold firm before. But there was no way he could resist her now, the burning look in her eyes, the anguished need in her voice.

He nodded toward a basketful of condoms on the bathroom counter. “Grab a handful of those, would you?”

Dear Reader,

What could be more irresistible to a woman than coming across a gorgeous single man whose eyes tell her how much he wants her? That's the dilemma facing Pamela Bradford on what should have been the worst night of her life. A bride without a groom, a woman who's spent her entire life denying her sensual nature, she's now ready to indulge in her wildest fantasies. And sexy Ken McBain is just the man with whom she'd like to indulge.

Ken, however, just wants to look after Pamela. Sure, his libido kicks into high gear every time he's around her, but as far as he's concerned, there's going to be *no sex!*

It's going to take some serious convincing—in a resort that promises to "wash away every inhibition"—for Pamela to change his mind. Let's just say she's *relentless* in her pursuit.

This is my first Temptation HEAT novel, and I've had a lot of fun writing it. Where else could I have come up with a setting like The Little Love Nest—a resort with round beds, mirrored ceilings, suggestive statuary and a hostess named Madame Mona. I think I like pushing the envelope. I might just have to try it again.

I'd love to hear what you think of Pamela and Ken's amorous adventures. You can write to me at P.O. Box 410787, Melbourne, FL 32941-0787, or e-mail me through my Web site—www.lesliekelly.com.

Enjoy,

Leslie Kelly

Books by Leslie Kelly

HARLEQUIN TEMPTATION
747—NIGHT WHISPERS
810—SUITE SEDUCTION

RELENTLESS
Leslie Kelly

ISBN 0-373-XXXXX-X

RELENTLESS

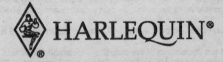

HARLEQUIN®

TORONTO • NEW YORK • LONDON
AMSTERDAM • PARIS • SYDNEY • HAMBURG
STOCKHOLM • ATHENS • TOKYO • MILAN • MADRID
PRAGUE • WARSAW • BUDAPEST • AUCKLAND

Dedicated with love to Ray Smith....
Dad, thanks from the bottom of my heart
for always encouraging me to be a dreamer.

ISBN 0-373-25941-7

RELENTLESS

Copyright © 2001 by Leslie Kelly.

All rights reserved. Except for use in any review, the reproduction or
utilization of this work in whole or in part in any form by any electronic,
mechanical or other means, now known or hereafter invented, including
xerography, photocopying and recording, or in any information storage
or retrieval system, is forbidden without the written permission of the
publisher, Harlequin Enterprises Limited, 225 Duncan Mill Road,
Don Mills, Ontario, Canada M3B 3K9.

All characters in this book have no existence outside the imagination of
the author and have no relation whatsoever to anyone bearing the same
name or names. They are not even distantly inspired by any individual
known or unknown to the author, and all incidents are pure invention.

This edition published by arrangement with Harlequin Books S.A.

® and TM are trademarks of the publisher. Trademarks indicated with
® are registered in the United States Patent and Trademark Office, the
Canadian Trade Marks Office and in other countries.

Visit us at www.eHarlequin.com

Printed in U.S.A.

SUFFOCATING BENEATH ten pounds of buttercream icing in a paper, cardboard and wood-framed tomb, Pamela Bradford noticed immediately when her whiskey sour buzz wore off. Her mind suddenly cleared, her stomach began rolling around and her hands started to shake.

"Get me the heck out of here," she ordered in a loud whisper, not even knowing if any of her bridesmaids were still nearby. A giggle and a muttered "hush" told her they were. "Sue? Sue, I've changed my mind. I can't do it."

"Yes, you can," someone replied.

That wasn't the voice of Sue, her sweet-natured maid of honor, who was timid as a rabbit about everything except her passion for romance novels. No, the voice sounded cynical but amused, gravely and authoritative, as only the voice of a strong, confident, two-hundred pound African American woman could.

"LaVyrle, please, this was a bad idea. Peter's not going to be very happy about this."

"Not happy? Girlfriend, puh-lease! That man's going to bust into a raging ball of male heat when he sees you come outta this cake. And if he doesn't, well, at least you'll know tonight, rather than tomorrow after you

marry the pansy. Now be quiet, we're still working on our evacuation plan."

Pamela sighed, knowing LaVyrle would not take pity on her. Sue, yes. Pamela's best friend Sue, who'd been a perfect little angel as a child—except, of course, when Pamela was around—would have let her out in a heartbeat. But not with LaVyrle and Wanda in the room. She'd be no match for Pamela's two friends and co-workers from the teen center in downtown Miami.

Since Pamela had once seen LaVyrle physically tackle and take down a street dealer who'd approached some of their boys leaving basketball practice, she didn't think she *wanted* Sue to try standing up to her.

She could burst out of the cake now, she supposed, avoiding the bachelor party altogether. But since her friends had pushed her into a hallway of the Fort Lauderdale hotel, she figured that wasn't such a great idea. With her luck, she'd run smack dab into the local gossip columnist or a vacationing family with six young kids, complete with Mickey Mouse caps, big eyes and a camera!

"Good grief," Pamela muttered, knowing she was stuck, in more ways than one.

Folded in half, with her knees tucked under her chin, she couldn't move an arm to scratch an itch without risking a heaping headful of icing. She glanced up, seeing that the top of the paper cake, just inches above her eyes, was lower than before. The wooden frame wasn't dealing well with the weight of the gooey icing. "I didn't think they put real icing on these stupid things,"

Pamela said and glared at the frame, hoping like hell it would hold up a few minutes longer.

"They don't, usually," LaVyrle said. "The best man, or whoever the dude was who hired my friend Nona to strip tonight, paid extra for the icing. Some guys do that, you know. Then the birthday boy—or the groom—has to lick the stuff off the dancer."

Pamela swallowed hard.

"Of course, we all know Peter wouldn't do that," Sue chimed in. Thank heaven for sweetly optimistic Sue.

"Well, he'd sure better now," Wanda retorted. "Pamela, I bet Peter's gonna want to lick off every speck. Unless he don't like girls...uh...I mean, sweets!"

Pamela's stomach rolled again. "Please let me out."

"You just have cold feet. Quit whining!" LaVyrle ordered.

"I have a cold butt is what I have," Pamela muttered. Her friend's low chuckle told her she'd heard. Pamela shifted a little and wondered how she'd gotten into this mess.

Though she couldn't move her head too well, she did cast a quick glance down at herself, and shuddered. Yes, she still wore the ruby-red, glittery pasties and matching thong, plus the spiked high heels LaVyrle called "do-me shoes."

Okay, so she had a top on over the getup. But the filmy, nearly sheer shirt fell only to her thighs. It was also so thin it offered no protection for her nearly naked backside seated directly on the cold metal shelf of the pushcart.

This was one heck of a way to spend the night before

her wedding. She still couldn't believe she'd agreed to it. What had she been thinking?

Well, actually, she knew what she'd been thinking. She'd been listening to that teeny tiny voice in her brain that had been nagging at her lately, asking why Peter hadn't tried to move their relationship from emotionally intimate to physically intimate.

Her fiancé hadn't so much as attempted a single grope in the entire six months of their relationship! He'd kissed her, yes, sweetly gentle kisses that hinted at a restrained passion. But nothing more.

So why are you marrying him? she asked herself in a rare moment of pessimism brought on by whiskey sours and itchy spangled underclothes.

She didn't have to search for an answer; she knew why. Peter might not have seduced her physically, but he had bowled her over emotionally. She'd never met another man with whom she was so perfectly in sync. They shared the same tastes in everything—from sports teams and ice cream to rock groups and political affiliations. They'd never had a single argument, never exchanged a cross word. Given Pamela's battles with her parents, she found Peter to be a soothing presence in her world.

It went even deeper than that. Peter was also the first man she'd dated who completely and without reservation supported and applauded her career decisions. He encouraged her to keep fighting for the underprivileged teens she felt so passionately about. He consoled her when she cried in frustration at her parents' continuing refusal to accept the choices she'd made in her

life—choices that didn't include their country clubs, golf dates or yachting trips.

In their minds, she was merely going through a stage, or intentionally being difficult as she had been when she was a child. Okay, so she'd been a tough little cookie as a kid. She'd performed operations on her stuffed animals on the kitchen table, and used green and brown markers to draw camouflage outfits on all her Barbie dolls. She'd dreamed of making the basketball team rather than being a cheerleader. Not out of a desire to be difficult, but because she'd been born with a need to be true to herself—which meant being different from those who loved her!

Peter had supported that. He'd appealed to her brain, seducing her completely with his unwavering support.

But as for her body…. Had there been touches? Heated caresses? Seductive whispers or downright horny grins? Nothing. Nada. Zip. Zero. Zilch.

Pamela wasn't a sexual connoisseur—far, *far* from it!—but she had enough experience to know that people who were supposed to be in love enough to marry one another usually had some physical desire going on, too. Yet Peter had never made one serious effort to make love to her, even though she'd hinted that she wanted him to.

She'd heard about his reputation as a ladies' man. She'd been around her father's offices enough to know that Peter had had more than his share of female companionship—though, of course, that was all in the past. That fact made his disinterest in pursuing a physical relationship with her even more disturbing.

She'd gone so far as to plan the most romantic, enticing honeymoon she could think of! Egged on by one of those seductive ads in the back of a bridal magazine, she'd paid a small fortune to book them a room at a new honeymoon resort at Lake Tahoe. Peter thought they were going to a friend's lakefront cabin, and Pamela wasn't too sure how he might react to her surprise when they arrived at the luxury resort that promised to "wash away the outside world...and every inhibition." What if he hated it? What if he wanted to leave?

She shouldn't be having these fears about the man she was going to marry. They bothered her. More than bothered, they concerned, even *angered* her. So much so that, tonight, at her own bachelorette party, she'd allowed too much alcohol to loosen her tongue and had spilled her secret to her bridesmaids.

Sue's eyes had widened. Wanda had given her a look of outright skepticism. And LaVyrle had shrieked, "He's gay! I'm tellin' you, girl, you're about to marry a man who hangs out in steam rooms and goes to Bette Midler concerts!"

"He's not gay," Pamela muttered inside the cake. She knew Peter was straight, particularly given his love 'em and leave 'em history, yet she was unable to come up with a more logical explanation for her fiancé's physical disinterest in her.

One thing was sure. She could not be married to a man who had no interest in sex. Love was wonderful and she felt sure...pretty doggone sure, anyway...that she loved Peter. What wasn't to love? What woman wouldn't want to be married to a handsome, successful

man who anticipated her every need, agreed with her every thought?

"Maybe a woman who needed some passion in her life," she muttered. Pamela simply could not imagine a marriage without desire. Not after seeing the passionate love her parents had for each other, still, after thirty years of marriage.

"My parents," she said with a grimace. If they could see their little princess/pumpkin/pookie-face Pamela now, they'd both be clutching their hearts, leaning against their matching red Beamers in horror.

"Okay, honey, we've got us a plan," LaVyrle said from somewhere above and to the right of Pamela's cakey coffin. "Sue's going to go in and tell Peter she has to talk to him about a last-minute wedding problem. While they're talking, Wanda and I are gonna bust in and say there's a bomb and everybody has to get outside. Only Sue'll hold Peter back."

"That's the stupidest idea I have ever heard," Pamela yelled. "Don't you think Peter's going to wonder why Sue wants him to stay and risk blowing up if there's a bomb?"

"She'll tell him you're the bomb, sweet cheeks! Besides, you got any better ideas?"

Pamela blew at a wisp of brown hair that had slipped from the loose mass of curls at her nape to fall over one eye. "Why not just tell the groomsmen there's a wet T-shirt contest in the bar?" Beneath her breath, she added, "Peter probably wouldn't be interested anyway."

"Yeah, Peter probably wouldn't be interested in that, anyway," LaVyrle said with a snorty chuckle.

Pamela muttered an obscenity.

"I guess it'll do. You just sit tight—don't you go anywhere now." The other woman snickered again. "We'll go find out where the bar is and then come up to the suite to get the other men out. Back in ten or fifteen minutes to getcha."

"Please, LaVyrle," Pamela pleaded, "make sure you get every other man out of there. This is humiliating enough—the possibility that anyone other than Peter could be there to see me come out of this cake is too horrible to think about."

Particularly since most of the men at the party were Peter's coworkers—which meant they also worked for Pamela's father! The image of all of her father's navy-blue-suit-and-tie-wearing middle managers seeing her in the pasties and thong was beyond bearable.

"Back soon, Pammy," she heard Sue whisper. "It'll be okay." She listened as the three women walked away, their giggles lingering after them. That left Pamela alone in the small alcove near the hotel suite where the bachelor party was taking place. They'd moved her here after helping her get into the giant cake, which had been prepared for LaVyrle's stripper friend, Nona.

What an oddly bad coincidence that LaVyrle had happened to know the woman who was performing at Peter's bachelor party tonight. What a worse one that Pamela had chosen tonight to overdo it with the spiked punch. She'd been tipsy enough to spill her guts about her concerns regarding her potential sex life with her future husband. Her three friends hadn't let up once

LaVyrle had gotten the idea for Pamela to switch places with the stripper.

And now look where she found herself. Mostly naked. Inside a paper cake covered in icing so sweet the smell was making her nauseous. Curled so tight her legs were probably going to fall asleep and give out before she could pop out of the cake like a deranged, spangled jack-in-the-box. Unable to stop shaking as she waited to see either a wonderful look of lust or a horrible grimace of disdain on the face of her groom.

Why, oh, why had she agreed to do this?

As she had explained the time she'd broken her arm trying to see if she could fly by leaping off the roof of her parents' garage, Pamela muttered, "I guess it just seemed like a good idea at the time."

KEN MCBAIN sat in a back corner of the opulent hotel suite, alone, nursing a beer and asking himself for the tenth time why on earth he'd ever bothered coming to this bachelor party. He didn't know the groomsmen. He barely knew any of the men attending the party, their conservative, clean-shaven faces wearing similar goofy expressions that said, "Let's do something real dangerous like watch a dirty movie on the Playboy Channel." And to top it all off, he didn't even like the groom!

All in all, it was proving to be a wasted Friday night. Though he'd only been at the suite for about an hour, Ken was more than ready to leave.

"Pete, you remember these ladies, I'm sure," a man Ken recognized from the personnel department of Bradford Investments said as he entered the room. Be-

hind him were two women—two very blond, very
stacked, very professional-looking women, their pro-
fession being the world's oldest, that is.

The partying junior executives exchanged nervous
glances and more nervous grins. Their eyes widened as
Ken's rolled in amused disgust.

"Now this party's gonna roll," the groom said, lifting
a beer—imported, of course—to his lips and chugging
it. Well, he tried to chug it. He drained about half of the
green bottle before pulling it from his lips and sucking
in a deep breath.

The entrance of the party girls was Ken's cue to cut
the hell out. He'd never had to pay for sex in his life and
had absolutely no interest in being around guys who
did.

He stood, preparing to do just that. Two of the other
men—ones Ken had dealt well with in the few weeks
he'd been working on the Bradford project—did the
same thing. His respect for them went up a notch. As
the groom grabbed the hip of one of the passing
blondes, Ken's respect for him—already pretty damn
low—dropped to toilet bowl range.

He couldn't believe Pamela Bradford—the Pamela
Bradford whose smiling face had captivated him from
the moment he'd seen her photo on her father's desk at
their first meeting—was going to marry this womanizing loser.

Peter Weiss must have one amazing acting ability to
go along with the *GQ* looks and oozy charm. Because,
as far as Ken could tell from his single encounter with
Ms. Bradford, she could have just about any man she

wanted with the crook of a finger. Ken grudgingly conceded he had to include himself in that estimation.

And she'd chosen Peter. So either she was stupid and gullible, which he doubted, or Peter had snowed her about what he was really like. That seemed almost inconceivable, too. Ken had only been working in the Bradford office building two weeks, and he already knew Peter had had affairs with three secretaries and had been caught nailing one of the bookkeepers in a stall in the men's bathroom last year. Could she really not know?

Of course, it was possible Peter had been on the straight and narrow since meeting his fiancée. What man would want anyone else with Pamela Bradford in his life?

"Horse's ass," he muttered under his breath as Peter began untying the prostitute's halter top with his teeth. "She could do *so* much better than you."

Ken wondered why he thought so much about a woman he'd never formally met. But he did. He thought about her quite a lot, particularly when sitting in meetings in her father's office, glancing at her photo and catching glimpses of a hint of wicked humor in her wide eyes.

Pamela Bradford had sparked something in him. He'd like to call himself a gentleman and say it was his chivalrous side, rearing up in protest of the colossal mistake she was about to make. But he had to concede it was more than that. His libido definitely had something to do with it, too.

He had a serious case of the hots for his client's

daughter...and they'd never exchanged as much as a nod of hello. In the two weeks he'd been in Miami, working on a major software project for her father, he'd seen Pamela Bradford's picture on a daily basis, heard her name on her father's proud yet frustrated lips dozens of times, and seen her in the flesh once. Just once. But what an impression she'd made.

She'd just emerged from her father's office where, he'd learned later, she and Jared Bradford had argued again over Pamela's job. Jared had often moaned to Ken that his daughter, who'd been offered every advantage two doting, wealthy parents could provide, had never willingly accepted a thing from them.

Her father was afraid for her, plain and simple. She worked with inner-city kids at a teen center in Miami. The distance from her family's pricey estate in Fort Lauderdale went way beyond the mileage on I-95. It was like a different world. Pamela had chosen that world—which was completely foreign to her father.

That day, Ken had leaned against the doorjamb of his temporary office, which had been provided by the company for the duration of the three-month-long project. Arms crossed, he'd unabashedly listened to the raised voices from the next room. He'd watched as Pamela literally burst out of the heavy, oak-paneled door to her father's private sanctum, giving it a solid kick with the heel of her sneaker for good measure, before she stalked away toward the elevators.

She'd been magnificent, from the curves in her tall, lean body, to the flash of fire in her huge brown eyes. A sheen of light from the overhead fixtures cast highlights

of red and gold on her chestnut-colored hair. Ken had simply stood silently, watching. She hadn't even seen him, but he'd paid close attention to her. Her chin was as proud and firm as her father's, and her shoulders were stiff under her simple green shirt. She also had a gorgeous, wide mouth made for smiling. And kissing. And...more.

It wasn't just the Pamela he saw with his own eyes that so attracted Ken. It was also the Pamela he saw through her father's eyes—through his stories, his commiserations and his fond remembrances—a woman who was stubborn, yet full of heart. That Pamela sounded like someone he'd very much like to get to know.

Unfortunately, she was about to become the wife of an oversexed moron.

"Go, go, go, go," the men around him chanted, drawing Ken's attention back to the party. Peter was chugging again, cheered on by the crowd. After the groom drained the bottle, he threw his arms up in the air like a college jock and howled.

And Pamela was marrying *him?*

Ken walked through the living area, dodging puddles of spilled beer, looking for his suit jacket. He'd taken it off when he arrived, and knew he'd left it on the back of a chair near the door. It wasn't there now. Several more guests had come in and someone had obviously done some jacket rearranging.

Frustrated, Ken looked around and saw the door to the suite open yet again. Another of the groomsmen,

who'd left earlier to find cigarettes, yelled from the hallway, "Look what I found waiting around the corner."

The man turned away, pulling at something, his already alcohol-reddened face beading with sweat. Interested in spite of himself, Ken watched as the man pulled a cart into the room.

The cart, it appeared, had other ideas. It was pulling back. From where he stood, Ken was able to see one high-heeled red shoe sticking out from beneath what appeared to be a large white-iced paper cake. The shoe tried to stop the cart by digging into the floor. The spiked heel, however, slid through the plush weave of the ivory carpeting like a knife through soft butter.

Whoever the lady was, she didn't seem quite ready for her performance. Ken could even hear her hissing at the man to put her back where he'd found her. No one else seemed to notice.

"The entertainment has arrived," the man said as he finally managed to pull the large cart and cake into the room.

The two blondes exchanged amused looks. "You're gonna like Nona, sweetheart," one of them said to the groom, who responded by pulling her onto his lap.

Ken, still closest to the cake, heard the person inside say, "I need to get out of here. There's been a mistake!"

The man who'd pushed the cart in—Ken thought he was Dan from Billing—leaned close to the *P* in the word "Peter" written in red icing. "Don't be shy, sweetie!"

She wouldn't come out.

"Maybe she needs music," someone said doubtfully. Considering the stereo was blasting loud enough to

shake the walls, Ken wondered what *that* guy was smoking!

Dan from Billing tried again. "Hello in there," he said. This time he poked two fingers into the side of the top tier of the paper cake, probably about level with where the dancer's face was. Ken hoped she hadn't lost an eye.

Dan nearly lost a finger. "Ouch!" he yelped as he yanked his hand free. "I think she bit me!"

Biting? Strippers? Prostitutes? Okay, Ken had seen enough. It was time to leave before they started bringing in the livestock.

But he still hadn't found his jacket. Since his car keys and phone were in the pocket, he didn't think he was going to be able to just ditch it. Walking into the kitchen area of the suite, he glanced around and began digging through a pile of coats someone had dumped on the counter.

He kept an eye on the party. Dan and another guest pulled the reluctant cart farther into the room, so it was practically right in front of the groom. Though the men tried to coax the dancer out, Peter didn't seem too concerned about his entertainer's reluctance. "We've got all night," he said with a chuckle. The blonde on his lap curled tighter against him.

"Better make it worthwhile, Pete, since it's your last night of freedom," one of the men said. Ken, who'd just about given up finding his coat, grabbed a canned soda from a cooler and rolled up his shirt sleeves. The room was getting hot and he imagined whoever the woman

in the cake was, she was going to be wilted and steamy if she hid in there much longer.

"I don't think I'm going to miss my freedom much once I get my hands on my new wife. Holding her off has been killing me!"

That got Ken's attention like nothing else this evening had. It almost sounded like Peter was saying he and his bride hadn't anticipated their wedding night, which would be a shock given the groom's notorious sexual escapades.

The blonde giggled. "You mean you haven't..."

"No. Princess has to be a virgin on her wedding night or Daddy won't be happy, and that's all that counts. After waiting this long, she better make tomorrow night worthwhile."

Though Pamela wasn't here, couldn't know what was being said, Ken felt a sharp pang of embarrassment for her. This jerk was spouting off locker-room talk about the woman he was going to marry! Not only that, he was talking to a roomful of men who got their paychecks every week from that woman's father.

"Whaddya mean keeping Daddy happy?" one of the less intoxicated guys asked.

Peter's beer consumption must have been pretty high, because he answered the question, not noticing or not caring how much of an insensitive ass his answer made him appear. "She comes with the keys to the kingdom. As long as I keep her pregnant, at home and away from those dregs from the inner city she's so devoted to, I write my own ticket with dear old Dad-in-

law. He and I have something of a 'gentleman's agreement.'''

Ken felt sick on Pamela's behalf. Because it sounded, from what Peter was saying, like Pamela's own father had conspired with her fiancé to get her to give up her career and be the good little socialite wife. As much as he liked Jared Bradford, Ken had to concede that as far as Pamela went, the man probably wouldn't be above such meddling.

"You can't imagine the hell I've gone through—my wife's gonna be a wild one in bed, I can tell. Practically every time I've dropped her off lately she's given me this pouty look with those lips of hers, and I've had to go cruising for some female company before I could go home!"

Ken shook his head in disgust. Of course Peter hadn't curbed his appetites in the months since his engagement. He was an oversexed *cheating* moron.

As far as Ken was concerned, once you put a ring on a woman's finger, you've promised her you'll be faithful. It was like shaking a man's hand over a business deal. You don't welch, you don't whine. You give your word to a colleague that you'll accept his offer? You stick to it. You're engaged to a woman but can't have sex till the wedding night? You start enjoying cold showers and get damned friendly with your hand. You *don't* cheat.

Shaking his head, he gave one more quick glance around the room, again looking for his coat. Then he noticed something funny. The cake was shaking. It had started to tilt a bit, and now, from here behind the cart,

Ken could see the back jerking as if the person inside was pounding on it. Slowly. Rhythmically.

"If I'd known old man Bradford was that hot for someone to take the girl off his hands, I'da tried a lot harder to get her to go out with me," someone said.

"As if you didn't already try enough—to the point that you made a complete idiot of yourself every time she walked by your cubicle," another man replied. "Not that I blame you. She's not hard on the eyes— she's got legs that'd make a man weep."

"Not to mention her sweet..."

Ken didn't hear the last word because, suddenly, the cake erupted. Two fists punched through the paper and icing on the flat top, putting holes through the C in "Congratulations" and the R in "Peter." The arms scissored, effectively slicing the paper down the middle, and a woman's head and torso burst through the opening.

"Oh, crap," someone muttered. Ken understood why as soon as he saw that thick mass of chestnut-brown hair, held in a loose clasp at the nape of her neck.

Pamela Bradford, who had obviously heard every word uttered since she'd been pushed into the room, emerged from the remains of the cake like a vengeful goddess.

PAMELA WASN'T THINKING, wasn't quite coherent and probably wasn't even completely sane when she burst out of the cake. She was acting on instinct, driven by rage-induced adrenaline. Thought played no part. She'd certainly never have made the conscious decision to emerge from the cake, dressed as she was, in front of a roomful of men.

When the drunken fool who'd found the cake had brought her in, Pamela had sent up every prayer she knew that her bridesmaids would come to her rescue. She'd stayed snug inside, peeking through the holes left by the man who'd tried to coax her out, wondering how darn long it could take them to find a bar in a beachfront hotel in a party town like Fort Lauderdale!

Seeing her fiancé holding a blond hooker had started her blood temperature rising. But she'd waited, giving him the benefit of the doubt, knowing it was his bachelor party. The woman had probably just planted herself on his lap.

Then he'd begun groping her.

She'd been furious, watching in sick disbelief. Her fiancé was feeling up some woman less than twelve hours before he was set to marry her. The fingers that had never once touched a single part of Pamela's body,

other than her hands or a casual squeeze around her waist, had been buried in the plump folds of flesh exposed by the blond floozy's leather miniskirt. She'd begun to have major doubts about the whole wedding thing even before the stupid fathead had opened his mouth.

Once he'd done that...well, Pamela's blood had gone from simmer to raging boil in a matter of seconds. She'd been no more able to stay inside that cake than a volcano full of molten lava could keep from erupting. And erupt she did.

"Pamela," Peter exclaimed as she burst through the top with enough force to shatter the tack-wood cake frame into tiny pieces. Peter pushed the blonde off his lap so fast she landed in a heap at his feet.

"Shut up, Peter. Just shut up," Pamela ordered as she pushed her way through the paper and sticky icing, feeling it matting in her hair and smearing onto her thighs. Her foot got stuck under the cart shelf where she'd been sitting. Pamela had to tug it free, silently cursing the shoes, her fiancé, her father and her life.

Peter reached out a hand. "Pamela, let me explain."

"Touch me and I'll rip your arm off," she snarled, feeling it was entirely possible she could do just that.

"Darling..."

"I'm not your darling!" Pamela finally got her foot free and stepped over the legs of the blonde, who watched with wide eyes from her position on the floor. "I was never your darling. And I'm not my father's princess. So you can go tell the king the wedding's off! I guess that makes you the jester, huh, Peter?"

She glared at every man in the room, noting that most of them dropped their eyes, ashamed to meet her stare. She didn't suppose a single one of them had been too ashamed to look away when she'd first gotten out of the cake. No, she imagined they'd gotten quite an eyeful. Her face flushed scarlet and she tugged the filmy pink shirt tightly around her body, crossing her arms in front of her chest.

Slowly, the men began turning away. Some reached for coats, some left the living area altogether, going toward another room in the suite. She ignored them and began walking toward the door.

"Please, Pamela, don't be rash. You misunderstood."

"I heard you perfectly well, Peter," she replied as she reached the foyer. "My father hired you, coached you on how to get me interested and promised you a big payoff for pretending you were madly in love." Her voice broke, and she forced herself to straighten her shoulders. "What's not to understand?"

He took a step toward her. "It wasn't like that."

Pamela pointed her index finger at him. "Ah-ah. I meant it. Don't you come near me. Maybe it won't be your *arm* I rip off."

Peter visibly gulped. Hearing one of the men chuckle, Pamela swung her gaze toward them. Most were still huddled in the back corner, near the interior hallway. There was also apparently some kind of kitchen area that she couldn't see, and she figured more of the weasels were huddled in there, listening to every word, peeking around corners or through archways like the nasty little vermin they were.

She'd never forget their laughter, the way they cheered Peter on, seemingly proud of him for his plan. She'd never forget their faces, knowing they probably derived some sort of satisfaction in her humiliation, since so many of them had made a play for her at one time or another. Yes, she imagined they were enjoying seeing her brought down to size.

Tears filled her eyes. She blinked them back, determined not to let a single one fall free of her lashes—at least not until after she got out of this room, away from their knowing faces, far from the echo of Peter's sickeningly self-satisfied voice.

From where she lay on the floor, the blonde cleared her throat. Forcing herself into a surreal sense of calm despite the raging intensity building inside her, Pamela met the woman's eye. "You have something to contribute to this conversation?"

"Them are Nona's favorite shoes you got on," the woman said matter-of-factly as she stared at Pamela's legs.

Not pausing, Pamela bent down and slipped one then the other of the glittery red spike-heeled pumps off her feet. She gently tossed one into the center of the room. The heel caught in the remnants of the cake and hung there, dangling inches above the floor. The other shoe flew out of her hand with a bit more speed and precision. It caught Peter right in the middle of his gut. He bent forward, gasping for air. Pamela was unable to stop a snort of satisfaction as she reached for the door handle.

Pamela opened the door, but before she stepped out

of the suite, she paused and looked back at her former fiancé. Peter looked unsteady. He still breathed deeply, swaying and blinking hard, as if unable to believe everything he'd worked so hard for was collapsing around him in a matter of ninety seconds. His shoulders slumped, and he raised a hand to cover his eyes. The hooker watched from below. The cowardly men still huddled in their corners.

"Oh, Peter?" Pamela called sweetly.

He immediately lowered his hand and looked toward her, a faint light of hopefulness in his beady little eyes that had once seemed so truthful and gentle.

Once she was sure she had his full attention, Pamela gave him a wicked smile. Uncrossing her arms, she tugged the filmy shirt open, flashing him. His jaw fell open.

"You're an idiot," she said as she ran one flat palm across the curve of her hip, concealed only by the thin red strap of her thong panties.

"And I'm definitely *not* a virgin."

THOSE IN THE SUITE remained silent after Pamela slammed out, as if the reverberations of the door had frozen them where they stood. In the kitchen, Ken was as shocked by her sudden appearance—and disappearance—as everyone else. Her parting shot hung in the air, though Ken knew he, Peter and the prostitute were the only ones who could have seen her last defiant gesture.

It took a half minute before Ken could breathe again. He'd only caught a glimpse of Pamela through the

leaves of an artificial plant hanging in an arched opening between the kitchen and living room. But he'd never forget the sight of her. Never.

She was, quite simply, glorious. The tawdry costume that should have appeared cheap had been heart-poundingly enticing instead. There was too much class in the woman, from her proud shoulders to the line of her jaw and the arch of her brow, for her ever to appear less than a lady.

He didn't think he'd ever seen a more beautifully shaped woman—not in magazines, not in the flesh. The full curve of her hips begged for a man's hands, while the sweet indentation of her belly cried out to be kissed. And the long line of her thighs invited hours of delightful exploration.

But it was the pain in her eyes that spoke to Ken's soul.

"Screw the coat," he muttered as he stepped out of the kitchen to go after her. No way was he going to just stand there while she ran through the hotel, dressed like that, devastated and alone. He might not know her. He did, however, know hurt when he saw it, and the woman needed someone to help her deal with what had happened.

As he stepped by, the blond hooker slowly rose from the floor. "She a workin' girl? She sure got the body for it."

Peter looked stunned. "How could this have happened?"

Ken gave him a frown of disdain. His fingers curled into a fist; he itched to slug the man in the jaw, even if

Pamela wasn't here anymore to need protecting. Though sorely tempted, he refrained, wanting nothing more than to get out of the suite.

When he glanced at the chair where Peter and his ladyfriend had been sitting, he spotted his jacket and grabbed it.

"You sure she don't dance? Gawd, she could be making some big bucks," the blonde said.

Peter shook his head. "Why didn't I *do* her when I had the chance?"

This time Ken didn't listen to any inner voice of reason. He answered Peter's question with his fist.

AFTER PAMELA slammed out of the suite, she had to stop for a moment, in the empty, silent hotel hall. She leaned her forehead against the wall as the tears built in her eyes, the sobs choked her chest, and the hot rage completely gave way to pain and humiliation.

She gave herself no more than a few seconds to wallow. Then she dashed down the empty corridor. Ignoring the elevator, she burst through the door to the stairs instead. There, safe for the moment from prying eyes, she hugged her arms tightly around her body and gave in to tears.

"You rotten bastard," she muttered. Only she didn't know who she was talking to at that moment. Peter? Or her father? Which one had hurt her more? Which one had thrust the knife into her heart, and which had turned it?

She didn't have to think about it for long. Her father was the one who really loved her. So he was the one

who'd really betrayed her. And she was never going to forgive him for it.

Nor would she ever forgive herself. Stupid! She'd been such a fool to let Peter get away with his scheme. God, she'd almost *married* the man!

Amazingly, there was no emotional pain at the loss of her fiancé yet. There was pain, oh, yes, but it was pain at being used, at being made a fool of. Mostly at being betrayed by her father. There was also anger, embarrassment and shock.

But did her heart hurt? Was she emotionally devastated? Not yet. At least not as much as she'd expect to be upon learning the man she was pretty doggone sure she loved had been using her.

Maybe that would come later. Or maybe she wasn't so doggone sure after all, and it wouldn't. Whatever the case, the one thing she *did* feel was humiliation.

After several minutes, Pamela descended the stairwell, wondering where Sue, Wanda and LaVyrle were. She didn't want to see them; she didn't want to see anyone who might demand an explanation. Pamela just wanted to find something to pull on over the ridiculous stripper's outfit and go home. Since she'd left her purse, money, clothes and car keys in the locked trunk of LaVyrle's car, she didn't see much chance of that happening anytime soon.

The stairwell ended near a back elevator, not far from the lobby. Nearby, Pamela heard the sounds of laughter and tinkling glasses from the hotel bar, and she wondered if her bridesmaids—ex-bridesmaids—were there. Doubtful. They'd probably already gone up-

stairs, discovered the cake cart was missing, and were wondering where she was.

Pamela took a few seconds to indulge a fantasy of how LaVyrle would react if she went into the suite and heard what had happened. "Wonder if Peter's health insurance is paid up," she whispered with an evil grin. Thinking of his pride in his big, white, flashy smile, she hoped LaVyrle went for the mouth.

The lobby was nearly deserted, but she had to assume someone was working behind the check-in counter. That person would be unlikely to miss a half-naked woman running toward the exit. Pamela avoided the lobby.

She also steered clear of the bar. As much as she would have loved a good stiff drink, she couldn't exactly see going in and ordering one. Nor could she have paid for it. "Bet someone would buy me one," she muttered sourly.

Instead, she made her way out the back door of the hotel, which obviously led to the pool area and the beach. Sending up a silent prayer that some careless tourist had forgotten an old T-shirt or cover-up, she prowled around in the darkness.

"Bingo!" she chortled when she found a colorful beach towel lying forgotten near the kiddie pool. It was better than nothing, and she wrapped it around herself, covering the obscenely thin shirt and spangled undergarments.

With no one around, no money and no means of transportation, Pamela knew she was going to have to call for help. But who to call? Her best friends were

somewhere inside the hotel. Her ex-fiancé was probably consoling himself in the arms of the hooker.

That thought sent another chill through her body, and Pamela realized she wasn't ready to see anyone she knew yet. She needed to be alone, to think, to absorb what had happened and what she was going to do about it.

"Well, the wedding's off, first of all," she muttered aloud.

Stepping away from the pool, she glanced at the wooden steps that led down to the beach. The gently lapping waves and the glimmer of moonlight shining on the surface of the water offered peace and seclusion, a way to soothe her turbulent emotions.

Without even hesitating, she walked down the steps onto the beach. The sand, cooled by the night air, felt sharp against her bare feet. Closing her eyes, she inhaled deeply, trying to remember the relaxation techniques Sue had taught her when her friend had been going through her "female empowerment" stage. That had been between Sue's stages of "I'm going to astronaut training school" and "I'm going to get artificially inseminated and raise a baby by myself".

"Focus on the sensations of each moment," Pamela reminded herself. "Think about nothing but the salty taste of the air on your lips, the froth of the waves lapping your feet, the churning surf filling your ears."

She closed her eyes, trying to focus. It worked for about six seconds. Then she snorted in disgust because all she could think about was her lying, cheating bastard of an ex-fiancé.

"You rotten louse!" she shouted to the sky, knowing no one was nearby to hear her. Shouting made her feel better. Punching something would have helped, too.

Pamela didn't realize she wasn't alone on the beach until someone spoke.

"Have we met?"

Shocked, she opened her eyes and jerked her attention over her shoulder. A man stood behind her, a few feet away on the beach. He watched her, nearly hidden by the shadow of the nearby dune crossover.

"No," Pamela said, casting a quick look around to see if she could spot anyone else. This wasn't exactly a safe situation. She stood, nearly undressed, on a dark beach, late at night, and a strange man was behind her. *Uh-oh.*

"How can you know I'm a louse then?" he asked.

She frowned. "I wasn't talking to you. I was having a private moment."

"Looked more like a private meltdown," he said.

As he stepped closer, out of the shadows and into the light cast by the streetlamp above them in the parking lot, Pamela got her first good look at him. She sucked in a breath, more concerned than she'd been before.

He wore the south Florida businessman's summer uniform. A white dress shirt, with sleeves rolled up, revealed thick, tanned forearms. He wore no tie, and his shirt collar was undone, displaying a neck corded with muscle and the hint of dark hair at the hollow of his throat. Though he also wore light-colored trousers, and carried a matching suit jacket slung over one shoulder, Pamela knew this was no normal happy-hour executive

out for a late-night stroll. The blasé businessman clothes lied.

He was all dark intensity. From the thick hair—likely black though she couldn't be sure in this light—that curled past his collar, to the piercing darkness of his eyes, he defied the image of polished executive that her ex-fiancé had cultivated. The strong line of his determined jaw warned of a man who wouldn't be easily coerced. The thickness of his arms and the breadth of his chest told of his strength.

He looked like a cop, or a soldier.

But as those amazingly well-defined lips curled upward into a teasing smile, she realized he did *not* look like an ax-murdering rapist. She managed to smile a little in response.

"Okay, I'm having a private meltdown. The key word being private."

"I take it you want me to take a hike?"

"If you please," she said, tugging the beach towel tighter around her body and turning her attention toward the surf.

She sensed his hesitation and glanced at him. He pointed toward her head. "Did you know you've got a clump of white stuff in your hair?"

Pamela reached a hand up and dug a fistful of icing off the top of her head and threw it into the surf.

"Rough night?"

"Beyond belief," she said with a snort.

"Anything I can do?"

"Not unless you're a hit man."

The man didn't seem shocked. "Sorry," he said with

a rueful smile. "Forgot my assassin gear. I guess you're out of luck."

"Now there's an understatement! Tonight has been just about the worst night I've ever experienced. All I want is my bed and a good stiff one."

The man laughed out loud, obviously hearing a sexy submeaning in her innocent comment.

"I mean a good stiff drink!"

"Yeah, I knew that," he said, trying hard to keep a straight face. The grin on his lips begged for a response, and Pamela's own smile widened.

"I'm not trying to flirt with you," she said, trying to sound stern, but laughing instead.

"Good thing, because you'd be doing a pretty pathetic job," he said. "I mean, first the louse thing, then you basically told me to get lost."

"Which you didn't do."

"Touché. Do you still want me to go?"

For some reason, though she'd come down to the beach to be alone, she found herself wanting him to stay. There was something so appealing about his crooked grin, the self-deprecating laugh and the warmth of his stare.

A few minutes with a stranger on a dark secluded beach. She could think of worse ways to spend what should have been the night before her wedding.

"You'd probably be better off leaving," she muttered ruefully. "I'm not great company right now. As a matter of fact, I'm pretty miserable."

"Not thinking of pulling a *Jaws* scene, are you?" he

asked, looking at her bare feet, then at the surf lapping closer toward them on the sand.

"No. I'm not going for a late-night swim. I'm, uh...just thinking. It's been a pretty bad night and, to top it all off, I now find myself stranded, without my purse, real clothes or a buck to buy a beer I can cry into."

Surprisingly, the man didn't ask about the clothes comment. Instead, he reached into the pocket of his sports coat and drew out a few minibottles of whiskey. "Would this help?"

Though she wasn't ordinarily a drinker, Pamela grabbed for a bottle, unsealed it and took a hefty sip.

"I hate this stuff," she said between choking coughs after she swallowed. The rush of warmth descended from her throat to her belly, and Pamela took it in, needing it to calm her nerves. Another sip brought the same reaction. This time, as she bent over in a small coughing fit, the towel came untucked and fell open. She snatched it back up, covering herself, looking at the man to see if he'd noticed.

He didn't comment on her clothes—or lack thereof. Instead, he took his suit jacket off his shoulder and held it out to her. "Here. At least it won't fall off."

Pamela stared at his hand, and the jacket, wondering why his simple, chivalrous offer brought tears to her eyes. She looked up at him, trying to find an indication of his thoughts in his expression. She saw only kindness. Concern. A gentle look of tenderness in eyes that she sensed could sometimes be as cold as a gray winter's sky. But tonight, under the light of the glowing

moon and what seemed to be a million stars reflecting off the water, they were infused with warmth.

"Thank you," she whispered, taking the jacket from his hand. He turned slightly, so that he faced the ocean. When she saw him avert his gaze, she knew he was offering her privacy. She took it, dropping the towel and slipping the jacket on over her shoulders. "You really are a gentleman. Unlike every other man I've run across this evening."

From where he stood, silently watching the surf as she donned his coat, Ken cringed. She'd sounded very bitter when she talked about the other men she'd spent the evening with. He had to imagine she was never going to forgive Peter's friends, the men who had witnessed what had happened in the suite.

How the hell could he tell her he was *one* of them?

"I don't know about that," he murmured finally. "But at least I know I'm not a louse."

Which she should feel pretty damn lucky about. Standing out here at almost midnight, dressed as she was, the lady could have found herself in some very serious trouble if the wrong kind of man had happened by.

"No, the louse...or is it lice?" she said with a bitter laugh, "would be my ex-fiancé and his friends. Plus my father."

"So it's not all males you're hating at this moment?"

"No. Just a handful," she admitted as she took another drink from the small bottle, draining it.

He took the empty bottle from her and watched as she popped open the second one. "Easy there."

"I'm entitled. You can't imagine the night I've had."

Actually, he could. But he wasn't about to tell her that. Pamela's embarrassment was already easy enough to see. If he told her he'd witnessed her entire humiliation, she'd stalk away from him. Now, after she'd had a drink, she would probably be even more vulnerable than she'd been before! He was thankful he'd been the one to find her after he'd left the party, leaving Peter laid out on the carpet behind him.

Ken flexed his hand, thankful he hadn't broken any fingers. Whatever bruises or stiffness he had tomorrow would be well worth the satisfaction he'd gotten knocking Peter on his arrogant ass. He hadn't stuck around to see how long it took the other man to get up. He'd been totally focused on finding Pamela.

She hadn't been hard to locate. How many places were there in a beachfront hotel for a half-naked female to hide? Certainly not the bar or the restaurant. He'd doubted she'd booked a room. There had been no place she could have possibly concealed any cash, ID or keys in that getup she'd been wearing, so he didn't imagine she'd hopped into a cab or her car.

Putting himself in her shoes, er, her bare feet, he'd figured the beach was where he'd have gone. He hadn't been surprised that was where he'd found her. "So, want to talk about it?" He looked back at her, raising a quizzical eyebrow.

She shrugged. "My name's Pamela Bradford. Tomorrow was supposed to be my wedding day."

"And what, you and the groom argued over the wedding cake and started throwing icing around?" he said,

trying to make her laugh, trying to avoid letting her know that he knew all about the cake incident.

"That's not so far from the truth," she muttered glumly.

Ken didn't know Pamela very well—heck, he didn't know her at all. But he had three younger sisters. Growing up, all three of them had considered him the representative for every male on the planet, heaping all the praises—but, more often, all the sins—of his sex right on top of his head.

One thing he'd learned—aside from never going near his sister Diana's chocolate stash around the time of the full moon—was that in moments of emotional crisis, females needed to get things off their chest or they'd explode. Not wanting his boss's daughter blown to a million bits on a Fort Lauderdale beach, he urged her on. "So tell me all about your wedding plans."

She snorted. "They're off!"

"The wedding's been called off?"

"Well, unofficially, yes. I guess I'll leave it to Peter to explain to all our guests why the bride couldn't make it."

Ken glanced at his watch. "He's going to have to come up with a reason pretty quick...or will he tell them the truth?"

"That he's a womanizing jerk who basically accepted a bribe from my father to get me to marry him?"

Ken winced at the anger in her voice. "Guess not."

Suddenly, without warning, Pamela was spilling out the whole story. Her childhood. Her relationship with her parents. Her dedication to her job, which had her

interacting on a daily basis with teenagers the city of Miami seemed disinclined to help. She even told him about her disillusionment with her fiancé.

Ken listened, finally understanding why Pamela would ever have gotten involved with a guy like Peter Weiss. The man had played her like an instrument, using her father's advice on her likes and dislikes to appeal to her. How could any woman resist a man who agreed with every word she said, who was completely supportive and anticipated her every need?

"Didn't that get boring? A guy who never said no to you?"

"It wasn't like that," she retorted. "There was security in knowing we were so much alike."

"Sounds like a yawnfest." Ken shrugged. "Stepford Groom."

"So what would you know about it?" she retorted, her fist on her hip. "Are you a relationship expert or something?"

"Nope. My relationships have basically blown lately."

She raised an eyebrow.

"But I do know I would never be able to stand being with a woman who agreed with every word I said!"

"As if that'd ever happen," she muttered, seeming to forget her own problems for the moment.

"Are you saying I'm difficult to get along with? And here I thought I'd been the soul of cordiality."

She suddenly looked contrite. "You have. I'm so sorry. You've been wonderful, and I don't even know

your name. I didn't mean to be critical. It's just that the men in my life have been less than sterling lately."

Ken knew without her saying it that she spoke more about her father than she did about Peter Weiss. Ken was not surprised to realize she seemed even more devastated by her father's involvement than she did by Peter's actions.

"My name's Ken."

A wicked grin crossed her face. "My Barbie dolls always preferred G.I. Joe."

"My G.I. Joe always preferred Wonder Woman," he retorted without missing a beat.

She laughed out loud for the first time since they'd met on the beach and Ken felt the sand shift under his feet. Odd. But it happened. The ground moved a bit, his breath grew heavy in his lungs, and he couldn't tear his stare away from her wide, smiling mouth. *This* was the Pamela he'd longed to meet.

"I once traded my scooter for a G.I. Joe doll. My father caught me playing 'G.I. Joe beats the crap out of Ken for trying to force Barbie to be a model rather than an astronaut.'"

Ken grinned. "And how did your father react?"

"He flicked my Ken doll's head so hard it flew off," she said with a sad smile that segued into a look of pain. "He used to tell me there was nothing a girl couldn't do."

Ken moved closer, tempted to take her arm, to stroke a stray wisp of fine, dark hair, dancing in the night ocean breeze, off her smooth brow. Instead, he said softly, "But now he's let you down?"

She tightened her arms around the front of his jacket, hugging it against her body. "He's been saying one thing but doing another. Sure, there was nothing I couldn't do—as long as it was something of which he approved."

"And you're sure he helped your fiancé a little bit?"

She snorted a laugh and tossed her head. "A little bit? Good grief, an Olympic coach probably wouldn't have done as good a job preparing Peter for the Pamela games!"

Her brief spurt of humor fled. Her face was again dark and troubled, and Ken regretted the change. She was thinking about her father, and Ken wondered how she'd ever be able to deal with what she viewed as his betrayal.

Jared Bradford loved her. Ken knew that perfectly well. But he couldn't reassure her of that. He couldn't ask her to admit that while her father's actions might have been reprehensible, they weren't malicious. Admitting he knew her father would mean telling her why he was at the hotel.

"Getting chilly out here. Do you mind?" He pointed toward the whiskey bottles in the pocket of his own jacket, which she still wore. He didn't really want a drink. But it seemed wise to reduce the supply so Pamela wouldn't drown her sorrows by drinking every single one of them.

Since the jacket pocket was just about even with one of her curvy hips, he did *not* reach out to help himself. *Touch her and you're a goner!*

"I think I've had enough," she finally said, studying the empty container in her hand.

Considering she'd downed two by herself, he thought she was right.

"But help yourself," she continued, pulling one of the remaining miniatures out of the pocket and handing it to him.

Ken took it from her fingers, noting the coolness of her smooth, pale skin against the slick glass. He took a quick step back, then busied himself opening the bottle.

"So, Peter pretended to be the perfect guy...but why on earth did you feel the need to show up at his bachelor party and jump out of his cake?" Ken asked, still not completely clear on what had led up to this evening's performance.

She sighed. "I don't know. The way it turned out, it would have almost been easier to accept if Peter was gay."

Ken almost choked on a sip of the whiskey. "You thought your fiancé was *gay?*"

"No," she insisted. "I didn't think so! My friends wondered if he might be, though, when I told them that I'd never...that he'd never...uh..."

"You weren't lovers," he stated, still feeling like a slimeball for not admitting that he'd witnessed the entire awful scene in the hotel.

"No," she replied, a note of defiance in her voice. "He seemed to think that I was destined to be pure as the driven snow on my wedding night, and my father insisted I remain that way. Thank God he did—at least I never slept with the creep!"

Ken nearly echoed the sentiment.

One thing Pamela hadn't mentioned during all her explanations was her one final, defiant gesture as she'd left the party. Not that he was surprised. He didn't know many women who'd have had the nerve to do what she'd done—and then talk about it!

"So," he asked as he put the cap back on the miniature bottle, "you going to give your father a chance to explain?"

"Nope," she replied succinctly.

"Are you going to at least tell him there's not going to be any wedding tomorrow?"

She scowled, looking as though she wanted to do just that. Then her shoulders drooped. "Do you have a cell phone?"

"Right-hand pocket."

He watched her pull his phone from his jacket and dial some numbers. She took a few deep breaths, looking up at the stars overhead while she waited for an answer. Ken watched, knowing the pain this phone call would reveal—and the pain it would inflict. Though he hated what Jared had done to his daughter, Ken knew how much the man loved her. This was gonna be bad.

"Hello, Daddy? No, no, I'm fine. Yes, I know what time it is." She looked at her wrist, but she wore no watch. Ken held his arm toward her and showed her his.

"No, please listen," she continued. "I want to tell you I hope you and your five hundred friends have a wonderful time eating the surf and turf tomorrow afternoon at the club. Hope it'll be worth it. Unfortunately, I won't

be there so I'll have to count on everyone else to tell me how the reception goes. Be sure to have someone save me a piece of *cake*."

She laughed, a desperate sound that held no joy. "Oh, Peter called, did he? So you understand, of course, why there will be no wedding."

She shook her head. "No. Dad, I don't want to hear it. I don't want to hear a single word you have to say." Her voice caught with unshed tears. "You betrayed me— Peter used me, but *you* betrayed me."

She cut the connection, turned off the phone, and promptly burst into tears.

3

MOST MEN didn't know how to react when a woman burst into tears right in front of them. Ken, however, had a little experience. Resorting to basics, he grabbed her by the shoulders and pulled her into his arms.

She cried until his shirt became warm and damp with her tears, but she made no move to step away. He ran a consoling palm down her back, cupped her head with his hand and tried to ignore the rush of physical pleasure he got out of holding her in his arms.

She fit very well against him. Since she was nearly as tall as he, her cheek brushed against his neck as she cried. His pants and dress shirt provided a layer of fabric between them, but he felt her curves against his body. The delicate perfume she wore competed with the lingering sweet scent of icing. With her head tucked into his shoulder, Ken found his lips next to her temple and was unable to resist placing a soft, consoling kiss there. His fingers tangled in her hair as he held her and he finally started to feel her relax.

Comfort gradually segued into something else. She drew in a few deep breaths. He felt the pulse in her temple beat faster as she acknowledged the intimacy of their embrace. Anyone watching from the crossover above would have thought them passionate lovers.

"I'm sorry," she muttered against his shoulder. "I can't believe I'm sobbing in the arms of a complete stranger."

"Well, in the absence of a beer to cry into..."

She pulled away from him and took a step back, wiping her cheeks with the backs of her hands. Her makeup was smeared under her eyes and her face was puffy. "I'm usually not a cryer."

"It's okay, really. I'm glad I was here."

"You won't be when you see the black circles my mascara made on your shirt," she said glumly. "If you give it to me, I'll be happy to have it cleaned."

She looked miserable. Ken wanted to see that smile again, wanted to move past the sudden moment of intense awareness that had flashed between them while she remained in his arms. "You're just determined to get all my clothes off me, aren't you?"

She raised an eyebrow, obviously hearing the teasing in his flirtatious remark. Her reply, however, wasn't quite so teasing.

"Is it working?"

That surprised him. Ken wondered if she heard the blatant suggestiveness in her own voice. He doubted it. Even if she did, he certainly wouldn't take it seriously. The woman was right smack-dab in rebound territory—and Ken had already had his one experience with a woman fresh from a breakup with someone else. It had ended with a *Dear Ken* letter. He'd vowed never to put himself in that position again. She needed a friend? Okay. She needed a sounding board? He could be that, too.

She needed a warm and willing pair of arms to make her forget her miserable love life? *Been there, done that. Pick another guy, lady.*

He gave her a noncommittal smile. "I think I can manage to wash the shirt."

She shrugged. "That's about how my love life's been lately. Can't get a man to even want to take off his shirt for me."

Ken almost barked out a laugh. Then he realized that while her tone was light, her expression was very serious. "You can't honestly still be thinking your fiancé didn't want you. Not now that you know why he was staying away from you."

She turned slightly, facing the water and looking down at her hands. "I obviously didn't offer much temptation." Apparently seeing his confusion, she hurried on, "Not that I'm not very glad we never went any further! It's just..."

"Yes?"

"Well, let's say my track record with men isn't so great. Not many guys are too hot for a five foot ten former basketball jock who now fights and claws through bureaucratic b.s., dealers, gangs and absentee parents every day in her job."

"Only men with brains to go with their...libido," he said.

She crossed her arms in front of her chest. "I've learned to accept the fact that I'll never be mistaken for a femme fatale."

Remembering what she looked like under that jacket, Ken had to bite his tongue to hold back a retort. As he

watched, Pamela reached into the pocket of his jacket and drew out the last small bottle of alcohol. "You're sure you want that?"

She opened the bottle and lifted it to her lips. "Hey, it's my wedding day. Doesn't the almost-bride deserve a toast?" Without pause, she drained the small bottle. This time she didn't collapse into a coughing fit, though she gave one shudder and blinked her watery eyes.

"So, I guess your father's going to be out a small fortune, hm?"

She nodded. "Guess so. It's not like he can't afford it. I didn't want the country club wedding, anyway."

"What did you want, Pamela?" Ken asked, studying her profile as she watched the surf.

"Just an awesome honeymoon."

He laughed.

"You think I'm kidding? After dealing with Peter's, uh...lack of interest, I wanted to go somewhere alone and make sure we were really compatible." Pamela took a step back, wobbled a little on her feet, then bit her lip. "Do you mind if I sit down?"

"Go right ahead." He grinned, wondering how uncomfortable the sand was going to feel against the huge amount of bare skin exposed by her underclothes. Just thinking of that sent a burst of heat rushing through him. *Don't even go there!*

"So, where were you going on this honeymoon?" he asked as he sat next to her in the sand.

Pamela glanced over at him, wondering why he didn't seem to care that his trousers were probably going to be ruined by sitting on the beach. Then she re-

membered she was wearing his jacket. While it didn't entirely protect her fanny from the damp ground, it would more than likely be in pretty bad shape by the time she got up.

Remorseful, Pamela leaned over, holding his jacket down over her backside with the flat of her palm, and grabbed the beach towel. She spread it out and moved over to sit on it.

"Might not be too late for this suit," she offered with a grin. She patted the other half of the towel, inviting him to join her. When he did, she realized exactly how small the kiddie beach towel was. While it had wrapped once around her torso, it certainly didn't provide enough width to keep their bodies from touching, shoulder to hip, bringing every one of her senses roaring to life.

"Uh, now, what did you say?" she asked, focusing on wiggling her toes into the sand to avoid staring at the well-defined shoulder just inches from her cheek.

"I was asking about your honeymoon. Where were you going?"

"Lake Tahoe. To a gorgeous couples-only honeymoon resort called The Little Love Nest."

She heard him chuckle, then he said, "Sounds pricey. Guess Daddy's going to be out some cash on that deal, too."

His words reminded Pamela of the truth. No, her father wasn't going to be the one losing out on the small fortune her honeymoon trip had cost.

She leaned back, dropping her elbows to the sand and reclining on them, frowning in disgust. "Nope, that

was all mine! Peter didn't even know about it. I paid for everything and had planned to surprise him tomorrow when we got there."

"No trip insurance?"

She snorted and cast an incredulous look at him. "Gee, do they offer insurance against jerk-off fiancés who cheat and lie?"

"Guess not."

She didn't even want to think of the amount of money she'd spent on the trip. Actually, she couldn't really think about it, because her head was a teensy bit spinny. From the alcohol. From the stress. From the nearness of this stranger whose cologne made her want to bury her face in his neck, and whose warmth made her long to crawl back into his arms.

She shook her head once, hard, trying to clear her brain. "I think maybe I shouldn't have had that last drink," she whispered as she tried to focus on sticking her toes into the damp sand. "I also think I'm going to wake up tomorrow and wonder if this whole thing was a nightmare."

"I think you'll be glad you found out tonight that your fiancé is a cheat and a liar," Ken replied, "rather than after tomorrow."

She sneaked another glance at him, liking the strength of his jaw, the quirk of his brow as he cast a knowing grin at her—not to mention the muscular neck, the broad shoulders, the long legs stretched out next to hers against the damp sand.

Pamela suddenly realized there was more than alcohol making her feel sort of funny, like she had butter-

flies in her stomach. She was responding to him physically. More than that, though, she found she liked him, this stranger who'd found her on the beach and somehow made her laugh on what was turning out to be the worst night of her life.

She liked his eyes, and she liked his laugh. She liked those big strong hands that had held her with such gentleness when she'd cried. *Yeah right. As if that's all she liked.*

She'd also very much liked the look of his lips and wondered if he used them for kissing as well as he used them for grinning.

The fact that they were so close together fueled her feelings. The elemental churning of the waves, and the moisture in the air brought forth a response deep within her. She suddenly found her mind filled with the most vivid picture of her and this man lying in the surf in a passionate embrace.

Now she knew she was tipsy. She was having sexual fantasies about a complete stranger! She tried to force them out of her mind, but they stayed, making her pulse beat faster, her breath come harder, and making her legs shake, though she told herself that was only because of the strong ocean breeze blowing across her. Looking at him out of the corner of her eye, she again noticed the strength of his face, the long lashes hooding his expressive eyes, and his hard body, hidden under the dress shirt and slacks.

She wanted him. "How crazy is that?" she muttered out loud, ignoring his questioning glance.

It was true. She wanted this gray-eyed man, wanted

his hands on her breasts and his mouth on her throat. Wanted him on top of her. Beneath her.

Inside her.

"Oh, goodness, I definitely had too much to drink," she whispered.

Knowing she had no business even thinking such things did not halt the thoughts. They did, however, remind her of that last scene with Peter up in the suite. She wondered where on earth she'd found the courage to do what she'd done, to say what she'd said. Because she was a big, fat liar. She'd taunted Peter that she wasn't a virgin. Whoops! Not exactly true.

As ridiculous as it seemed in this day and age, Pamela, at twenty-six, *was* a virgin.

Some people might wonder how she could have remained basically untouched all her life, but Pamela knew her upbringing and her job were the reasons. Growing up, she'd listened when her parents had talked about their respect and love for one another. Subconsciously, she'd wanted that for herself.

Considering that she was taller than nearly every guy she went to high school with, and could generally humiliate them on the basketball court, they weren't usually lining up to ask her out. The fact that her father used to like to greet the few who did dressed in old Army fatigues—sometimes while cleaning his antique gun collection—had helped too. The few guys she'd dated had been too scared to make a serious move on her. Any father was intimidating. One with lots of money probably more so. But one with money, guns and a military background? Pamela would've had a

better shot at winning the lottery than graduating high school *sullied*.

College had been about study and basketball, and not necessarily in that order. Not much time for guys. Then, once she'd started working in the inner city, her job had reinforced the lessons her parents had instilled. She interacted with troubled families on a daily basis. So many of their problems involved teen pregnancies, heartbreak, divorce. She'd seen what casual sex did to young girls, and her heart ached for them as they struggled to find their way through school, career and home life while trying to raise their babies.

Pamela's mind had simply erected an invisible chastity belt around her underwear. No, she hadn't set out to remain a virgin until marriage. Nor, however, had she ever intended to let sex trap her into a life she wasn't ready for and didn't want.

That was why Peter's disinterest had so devastated her. For the first time in her life, she'd let a man know she was his for the taking—and he hadn't taken!

Okay, so Peter's kisses hadn't overwhelmed her. They'd been pretty darned interesting though. Interesting enough to get her thinking about what would come *after* the kisses.

She was ready to move on, forge ahead, experience everything a woman possibly could in terms of sensual pleasures. That was why she'd jumped on the chance to go to The Little Love Nest resort at Lake Tahoe. Not so much to encourage Peter as to give her the chance to finally revel in the sexuality she'd kept bottled up for the past twenty-six years of her life!

There was so much she hadn't done. So much she'd assumed she'd learn with her husband. Her body was crying out to experience and do all kinds of things she'd only ever fantasized about. Pamela wanted to feel feminine, sultry and seductive for the first time in her life. She was ready to give in to heady desire and lust and love and passion. She wanted to do everything lovers did. Do everything she'd dreamed about and everything she could imagine.

Only now she was short one bridegroom.

"So, what do you want to do?"

The mouthful of air Pamela had just inhaled turned into a lump of sand in her throat, and she choked on it. *Had he read her mind?* She sat up, coughing and hacking into her fist, noticing Ken's worried expression as he patted her back.

"Are you all right?"

"Yeah, I'm fine," she muttered. "Just deep in..." *lust* "...thought."

"You trying to think of a way to get your money back on your honeymoon trip?"

She shook her head, scrunching up her brow. "Not exactly. More like trying to think of a reason not to go ahead and go by myself!"

She hadn't really considered it until she'd said the words, but now couldn't imagine why she shouldn't do it. Why should she lose out on her single vacation of the year? It was paid for, wasn't it? Her time off was scheduled. What was she going to do, sit around and wallow for the next week?

He laughed for a moment, and then obviously real-

ized she was serious. "I thought it was a honeymoon resort. Wouldn't that be kind've a downer?"

Rising to her feet, a bit unsteadily, she shrugged. "It's a spa. Relaxing. Rejuvenating. I'm sure there are lots of people I could meet."

The more she talked, the more she liked the idea. Seven days at Lake Tahoe, far from anyone who knew her, far from her job and her family and the self-imposed restrictions. Most particularly, far from her father, who couldn't scare off or try to buy a man for her.

Maybe she would meet someone amazing. Someone who had no conflicted loyalties, no knowledge of who her father even was!

She had seven days to test these physical desires that she'd buried for so long—desires that she thought would choke her if she didn't find a way to relieve them. "Lots of interesting men...people," she repeated under her breath.

"Lots of *married* men," Ken retorted as he stood up next to her and began brushing the sand off himself.

"I wouldn't be tied down to the resort," she said stubbornly. "I'll bet there are lot of places to go and people to meet."

People? Men! Men who might actually want her, not what her father offered them. What the heck, why *shouldn't* she?

Of course, there was the minor problem that the resort was vehement about being for couples only. They might frown on a swinging single bride. Maybe she could say her fiancé had been delayed and would join her later. A smile of pure evil crossed her lips. Maybe

she could tell them he'd fallen out of an airplane over the Great Salt Lake.

Her smile widened and she closed her eyes. She'd meet someone there and indulge in a decadent honeymoon with a completely delicious stranger. She'd bring the outfit she was wearing, confident that he'd be unable to breathe when he watched her undress for him. Her confidence would grow under the approval in his gaze as his gray eyes darkened with desire. His big, warm hands would cup her breasts the way he'd cupped her head while she'd cried, and his mouth would sip of her skin, indulging in the flavors of her body until she begged for mercy.

This stranger would desire her completely, seduce her thoroughly. Wash away every bit of pain, anger and self-doubt Peter had caused...and teach her everything there was to learn about physical pleasure between a man and a woman.

What a lovely fantasy.

When she opened her eyes and glanced over at Ken, she saw him watching her, his eyes wide, a tiny smile playing about his much-too-kissable lips. Another realization darted across her mind. There was no stranger from Tahoe. She'd been fantasizing about the sexy-enough-to-cry-for stranger standing right in front of her. The moments they'd spent together on the beach, the heat he'd built in her with one sweetly tender embrace and a few flirtatious words, made her wonder just what he could make her feel for a week in a resort that promised the "fulfillment of every sensual urge."

Would he come? The innuendo in her own thought

sent another rush of warmth through her body. *Oh, yes.* And so would she.

She closed her eyes again, feeling an insane pressure in her body, feeling sparks of heat shoot down her torso to pool between her legs. She was left shaking at the power of her fantasy.

"I think we should get you home," Ken said, his voice low and heavy in the silence. "You're obviously still overwhelmed."

Pamela lifted a hand to her brow, wondering how long she'd been standing there, thinking those thoughts. About him. Them. "Stop," she muttered out loud.

At least, she thought it was out loud. Or had she merely thought it? She wished she hadn't had that last drink. Her head was seriously spinning now. She was a large bundle of sensation, unable to think straight, her mind filled with images and positions she wasn't even sure were humanly possible. But, oh, how she'd love the chance to find out!

Ken's piercing eyes locked with hers. Beneath the fabric of his dress shirt, she saw his shoulders tense. He rubbed his hand against his jaw, looking uncomfortable, as if he knew what she was thinking, had heard her thoughts and was reacting to the blatant need in her.

God, had she been talking out loud?

Impossible. He was merely reacting to her obvious tipsiness. He didn't want to be stuck on a beach with a drunken, pathetic stranger! She drew in a shaky breath. "What time is it?"

"Nearly one."

"Hm...only ten hours 'til the wedding," she said, suddenly reminded that today was, indeed, her wedding day. So why couldn't she even remember her former groom's name? "My dress was very pretty."

"I'm sure you would have looked gorgeous in it," he said, still talking in that low, controlled voice that told her his mind was somewhere else.

Her shrug and heavy sigh seemed to shake him out of the mood. A gentle smile crossed his lips and he reached out to smooth a few strands of hair off her face. His fingers against her skin sent the awareness factor up another notch.

"And I'm sure you'll have another chance to wear your dress—for the right man the next time."

"Nope," she said, shrugging off the warm lethargy his touch had brought. "Won't be able to wear it."

"Why not?"

She looked at him like he was stupid. "Cause I'm gonna burn it when I get home." *Duh.*

"No, you aren't."

"Who's gonna stop me? I live alone."

"I will," he said as he took her arm to steady her on her feet. "You're in no condition to go home by yourself. I'll drive you. And while I'm there, how about I take your dress away until you're feeling better and you can decide what to do with it?"

She narrowed her eyes flirtatiously. "You're just trying to get into my apartment. Trying to get me alone."

"We're alone now," he said, a rueful laugh in his voice.

Some inner demon made her ask, "So why haven't you kissed the bride yet?"

He shook his head and made a *tsking* sound. "I try not to make a habit of kissing women who were engaged to another man two hours before. Especially not ones who've had a bit too much to drink."

"I'm not drunk," she said, aghast. "I've never been drunk in my life!"

"All the more reason why you shouldn't have drained more than four ounces of whiskey in the past hour."

"Is that why my head feels like it's three feet above my shoulders all of a sudden?"

"Could be." Ken tried to turn her toward the crossover, obviously intending to take her home.

Pamela's feet felt leaden in the sand, and the tears which hadn't fallen for the past hour or so gathered again in the corners of her eyes. "I'm such a loser. A bride who can't even get kissed on her wedding day."

Pamela wasn't feigning her sudden misery. She knew all those self-doubts, those unfulfilled desires and needs were shining clearly in her eyes. Fantasies were lovely. But they weren't going to keep her warm on her wedding night.

He must have seen her sudden sorrow. He leaned closer, touching her chin with his index finger, tilting her head up. Her breaths grew choppy and her tears dried. Pamela felt her heart pick up its pace in her chest as his lips moved toward hers. And when they met, a silent sigh rose from her body at the sense of rightness and overwhelming pleasure.

He didn't take anything she didn't offer in the kiss. When he started out gently, she sensed his restrained passion. She leaned up on her toes, fitting herself against him and sliding her arms up over his shoulders to encircle his neck. His lips were warm and firm on her own. Tasting, sipping, not invading. She tilted her head, parted her lips, deepened the kiss, knowing this one embrace would live in her memories for a very long time. It would give her something lovely to remember of this awful night.

His restraint eased, the awareness between them grew. He slid his hands down her body, tugging her tighter against him and cupping her hips. His tongue slipped into her mouth and another sigh rose from Pamela's throat. There was no frantic thrusting, no hard pulsing demands. Just sweet, languorous strokes of his tongue against hers, his lips on her mouth. She tasted him, breathed him, gave herself over to him and understood, for the first time in her adult life, what real desire was.

"Now," Ken said as he ended their kiss and took a step back, "let's get you home."

PAMELA WOKE the next day with a pounding headache, a pasty mouth that tasted like she'd eaten five bags of cotton candy, and a distinctly empty bed. "The bride might have gotten kissed, but she sure didn't get laid," she muttered as she tugged her pillow over her face to block out the morning sunlight.

She was thankful she'd made it home, at least. She vaguely remembered telling Ken where to find her

spare key under a potted plant on her apartment balcony. And she remembered something about him climbing up the bannister, swinging himself over the second story railing to her patio with his powerful arms, and finding the key in the darkness. She'd been so fascinated by the flex of muscles in his arms and shoulders, the way his pants had pulled so tight across his thighs, that she'd nearly forgotten to step out of his way as he swung back down. The two of them had barely escaped falling to the ground together.

One thing she did remember was that she'd had nice dreams. Yummy dreams. Dreams about a man on a beach who'd kissed her and aroused her...then taken her home and tucked her into bed. Alone.

"A gentleman," she said with a snort, then winced as her headache intensified.

She hadn't dreamed the kiss, though. At least, she thought she hadn't! Since her head felt like someone had bounced it around a basketball court, she wasn't too sure about anything.

But, no, she couldn't possibly have dreamed anything as delicious as that kiss, that wonderful interlude with a gorgeous stranger. How many women got to experience something like that? An anonymous hour on a beach with a handsome man who truly seemed to care about her, offering her comfort and support, and a kiss that had left her almost unable to walk?

Though she probably should have been lying in bed crying about the day she was supposed to be having, she instead closed her eyes and kept thinking of him. Ken.

She didn't know his last name. But she'd memorized his face. His arms and his mouth. The crinkle in the corner of his eyes when he laughed. The hands, so big, so tender when he'd cupped her head and tenderly stroked her face while they'd kissed.

The fact that he was all she was thinking about on this her wedding day gave Pamela a shocking dose of reality. Either she was one shallow social worker, or she really hadn't loved Peter. "Good Lord, maybe I didn't," she whispered out loud, the sound of her own voice sending another shard of pain through her skull.

She'd liked the *idea* of being in love. But when it came right down to it, Peter had never made her feel, in the entire six months they were together, the way a stranger had made her feel in their single hour on the beach.

It wasn't just attraction. It was the kindness, the humor...the laughter in his eyes. She grinned, suddenly remembering the look on his face as he'd triumphantly carried her wedding gown out of her room the previous night.

She wouldn't have burned it. Really. There was a perfectly nice Goodwill shop a few blocks away.

Glancing at the clock, she saw it was noon. The afternoon reception should have been starting right about now.

The blinking red light on her answering machine caught her eye. Pamela glared at it, figuring it was a darn good thing she'd turned off the phone's ringer. She imagined it would have been ringing off the hook all morning, otherwise. A sick sense of curiosity made

her push the play button. She fast-forwarded through three messages from Peter and two from her father, then turned the thing off with a shrug.

As she got up, Pamela heard a knocking coming from the front door of her apartment. Ignoring it, she headed for the bathroom and took a forty-minute shower.

Then she got ready to leave for her honeymoon.

By SIX O'CLOCK that evening, Pamela was sitting in a window seat on a jet on the runway of Miami International Airport. She wore dark sunglasses since her head still hadn't stopped pounding, despite an afternoon filled with caffeine and aspirin. She'd ended up gathering all her luggage and leaving her apartment early in the afternoon, knowing sooner or later Peter or her father would come knocking on her door and wouldn't give up until she answered.

She had called LaVyrle and asked her friend to meet her and bring Pamela her purse. LaVyrle had demanded full details of the previous evening and had told Pamela that by the time she, Wanda and Sue had gotten up to the suite, Peter and most of the partygoers had already left.

LaVyrle, at least, understood Pamela's need to get away. "You forget about him, honey. Forget about everything here. Go be wild and be happy and deal with this mess when you get back."

After they'd parted, Pamela had spent her last bit of spare time like any bride going on a honeymoon trip. She went shopping. She hoped whatever mystery man

she was going to meet and seduce in Lake Tahoe liked itty-bitty bikinis. She'd bought two of them.

Though, of course, in the cold light of day—well, the hot-June-in-Miami light of day—she didn't know if she'd be able to follow through on her grand scheme of seducing some gorgeous stranger. Last night? With that particular man? Yes, that had seemed entirely possible. Wounded feelings, raw emotions, powerful whiskey and a moonlit beach had conspired to make her think she could do that, actually have an affair with a stranger. Today she was less sure.

But, she wasn't ruling *anything* out!

Leaning back in the narrow seat on the plane, Pamela was thankful that at least she wouldn't have to make small talk with anyone. She had, after all, paid for the seat next to hers. When the flight attendant walked by, offering blankets, pillows and magazines, Pamela asked, "When do you begin beverage service?"

"Shortly into the flight," the woman said with a perky smile that grated on Pamela's nerves. "We wouldn't want anyone spilling hot coffee during take-off, now would we?"

Under her glasses, Pamela rolled her eyes. "Tell you what, the minute you start, please bring me the biggest Diet Coke you've got. And I don't mean a little plastic cupful, I want the whole can. Or a six pack." *Plus a handful of aspirin to go down with it!*

The woman's smile didn't fade. "Oh, someone's had a rough day, I can tell. I'll make sure that caffeine's on your tray table as soon as the captain gives us the all clear."

"Okay," Pamela said with a sigh. "If I'm asleep, just open up a vein and give it to me intravenously."

She hoped she'd be asleep! Since she hated flying with a passion that almost seemed like a phobia at times, she gave one silent moment of thanks for the hangover that would likely let her doze throughout most of the trip.

Pamela closed her eyes, not even watching as the flight attendant walked away to greet other passengers. She didn't realize anyone was sitting down next to her until she felt an arm brush her own.

Startled, she sat up, opened her eyes and turned. "This seat's..."

"Taken? I know. Gee, Pam, you're not in a great mood for someone leaving on their honeymoon. You almost ripped that nice little stewardess's head off."

She gasped. Him? Here? "What's going on? What are *you* doing here?"

Ken gave her an impossibly wide grin that accentuated the laugh lines around his gray eyes. "You invited me, sweetheart. Don't you remember?"

4

THE LOOK on her face nearly made this entire ridiculous situation worthwhile, Ken decided in the next few seconds. Pamela's already pale complexion went a shade closer to ghost-white. She grabbed at her sunglasses, yanking them off her nose and crunching them between shaking fingers. Leaning closer, she blinked a few times, obviously trying to ensure that it really was him. Her look of shock almost brought a laugh to his lips. Almost.

"You're insane." She shook her head slowly. "Truly. Insane."

He shrugged. How could he argue with her when he'd been telling himself exactly the same thing for the past ten hours? He'd been calling himself a complete idiot ever since he'd agreed to go on this "honeymoon" with his client's daughter.

Here he was, a successful software engineer with his own company—a company gaining an international reputation for innovation and excellence—acting as a stand-in groom. A convenient shoulder for a very gorgeous, very vulnerable woman to cry on.

Some guys probably would have been rubbing their hands together in glee. Ken just felt sick. But he'd given his word.

"You really were wasted last night, weren't you? Don't you even remember offering me the plane ticket as I was leaving your apartment?"

She sucked in her bottom lip and leaned back in her seat, looking angry and sheepish all at once. Then her eyes narrowed in suspicion. "Even if I had, you couldn't have used it. It was in Peter's name and they wouldn't have let you on without ID."

Busted!

"You're right. Frequent flyer miles."

She slumped back in her seat and he saw her wince as her head hit the rough upholstery. "Headache?"

"Somebody wake me up—I'm still asleep," she muttered, closing her eyes and shaking her head. She gave a little grimace with every movement.

Ken mentally echoed the sentiment, feeling like he was sleepwalking himself. He couldn't actually be sitting here, on an airplane, next to a woman he'd met eighteen hours ago, about to take off for a honeymoon trip to Lake Tahoe, could he? He sighed. "It's not a dream."

"Correction, it's not a *nightmare*," she retorted tartly.

A reluctant smile crossed his lips. Damn she was adorable, even when oozing headache-and-hangover-induced hostility. "That either."

"So maybe I did invite you. I'm not ruling anything out at this point," she said as she pressed her fingers into her temples. "Judging by the ferocity of the jackhammer pounding at the inside of my skull, I had a little more to drink than I should have last night. That doesn't explain why you took me up on

my...invitation." She slowly opened her eyes, turned her head, and stared at him.

Ken caught her gaze, saw the beauty in the high curve of her cheek, the sweep of her dark hair against her temple. His breath caught, then he felt a smile tug at his mouth. He contemplated answering her question with a question of his own: *Which invitation was she talking about?*

Because she'd issued two invitations to him the previous night. One subtle, mumbled—expressed as a whispered fantasy involving seduction, erotic pleasure and a passionate affair with a stranger. *That* one had nearly rocked the sand on which he'd been standing. He'd felt certain she hadn't even realized she was speaking aloud, nor that he'd heard. But she *had* said it. And he had *definitely* heard it.

Kissing her after hearing those whispered, heated comments had been a *huge* mistake! Okay, so she'd looked very much in need of a kiss. Hell, if he was honest with himself, *he'd* very much needed to kiss *her* at that point. He shouldn't, however, have actually done it. His interest in Pamela Bradford had gone from a reasonable attraction to a beautiful, intelligent woman, to a raging case of hormones inspired by the feel of her slim body against his, her arms around his neck, and her mouth opening against his lips. Stepping back after only one kiss had taken every bit of willpower he owned.

"Maybe I couldn't resist?" Ken finally answered, knowing she could see the small grin he couldn't quite hide. "Maybe the mental image of you going all the

way out to Reno, arriving at this Nest of Lust place and being turned away because you were alone just broke my heart.''

She glared. ''The Little Love Nest.''

''Uh-huh. Whatever. So let's just say I didn't want you to lose out on your wedding *and* your honeymoon in the same weekend.''

As she opened her mouth to argue, the stewardess began giving instructions on airplane safety. Ken, who flew so often he didn't even listen to them anymore, watched as Pamela sat up and turned to watch the flight attendant. She clutched her seatbelt and tightened it, drawing his attention down to her white-jean clad hips and long-enough-to-wrap-around-him-twice legs. That brought back all sorts of images that had raced through his head the night before after they'd kissed. Her bare thighs around his hips. On the beach, in his car, in Pamela's apartment. Hell, up against a wall.

He'd wanted her so bad his teeth hurt.

''I need a glass of water,'' he muttered. He swallowed hard, then forced himself to look at Miss Perky Stewardess with the too-wide-smile and the too-red lipstick. Her demonstrations with floating cushions and oxygen masks, and two-fingered pointing at the emergency exits, didn't hold his attention.

He did, however, hear Pamela muttering to herself. Noting her clenched hands on the armrest, he wondered if she was nervous about flying. ''You okay?''

''Shhh!''

Ken grinned as she cast him a quelling glance, obviously annoyed that he'd distracted her from the instruc-

tions every American who'd ever flown could recite by heart. "You're cute when you're nervous," he whispered.

She was also cute when she was tipsy. And downright adorable when she was curled up in her own big, soft, bed, drifting off to sleep, as she'd been last night when she'd issued her *second* invitation to come along on this trip.

Closing his eyes, Ken thought about it, remembering the softness of her voice in the shadowy darkness of her room.

Doing anything next week? Pamela had asked with a sleepy yawn as she curled into the big bed, just about the only piece of furniture in the bedroom of her apartment. The woman lived simply, he'd noticed that as soon as he'd entered her home.

"Working," he said cautiously as he edged toward the door. He needed to get out, get away from the sight of her, tousled and vulnerable, wearing the oversize Miami Heat T-shirt she'd donned while he took her wedding gown out to his car a few minutes before. "Why?"

"Wanna come to a honeymoon with me?"

He nearly tripped over the small mountain of suitcases in the corner of her bedroom. "Excuse me?"

"They won't let me in if you don't. Honeymoon Nazis."

Ken almost chuckled at the disgruntled tone in her voice. "I'm sure they'll let you in if you've paid."

She punched her pillow, rolled over and muttered, "No groom, no room. So, take the ticket on the dresser

and come, okay? You don't have to talk to me or anything, you know, just have a honeymoon."

He closed his eyes, almost laughing at his vision of what she offered. A honeymoon with no talking? A gorgeous woman, hot sex, a luxury resort and no conversation. Throw in a big-screen TV with a 24-hour sports channel, plus an unlimited supply of beer and chicken wings, and it sounded like the male version of heaven.

Only a few minor problems. He wasn't the groom. They weren't married. And no way in hell was he getting involved—delicious hot and wild sex or anything else—with a woman who'd planned to marry someone else in a few short hours!

"Sorry, sweetheart," he said before leaving the room. "Can't do it. But, hey, maybe you could ask me again in six months or so." After she'd recovered from Peter "The Slimeball" Weiss. Oh, yeah, he could definitely picture taking her up on her invitation, in one way or another, after her fiancé was well and truly out of her system.

She mumbled something unintelligible as she fell asleep. Ken stood in the doorway, the light from the living room shining in on her face. He stared at her for one more moment, then left, locking the doorknob to her apartment behind him, telling himself he'd get to know her better later. *Much* better. *Much* later.

Knocked from behind as the passenger in the next row accidentally kicked his seat, Ken forced the memory of the sleeping, innocent, sweet-faced Pamela out of his mind. Glancing over, he saw the bleary-eyed, frowning, suspicious-looking Pamela staring out the

window with her nose nearly pressed against the glass. Their plane was sitting on a runway, their takeoff delayed due to the long lineup of planes waiting to depart. Pamela looked as nervous as a retail store clerk the day after Thanksgiving.

"Are you going to be okay?"

She nodded too quickly, causing her dark hair to flop down over her eyes. Not thinking about it, Ken reached over and pushed it aside, noting the silky smoothness between his fingers. His breathing slowed, and he watched as hers sped up. Her lips parted and a slow flush spread across her high cheekbones.

Her own hand rose from her armrest, moving slowly until her fingers rested lightly against his. Her eyes never breaking their stare, a slow, very gentle smile spread across her lips—the kind he'd dreamed about during his few restless hours of sleep the previous night.

He shouldn't have touched her. Shouldn't have put the kindling to the banked fire that had existed between them since the previous night when they'd kissed on the beach. Yet here he was, with his fingers tangled in her hair, touching the soft skin at her temple, breathing in the sweet lemon-tinged scent of her shampoo and hearing the tiny sigh that escaped her lips.

She continued to touch him, too. Uncertainty shone in her eyes, along with something else. Wonder at first, then heat. The fire was starting up all over again. He felt it. She felt it, too. But she didn't pull away.

"What's your last name?" she finally whispered, as if

trying to break the heady silence that had fallen between them in a few sexually charged moments.

"McBain," he said as he finally pulled his hand away. "My name's Ken McBain."

He watched, waiting for a spark of recognition, wondering if her father had ever mentioned him to her. Apparently not.

She gave a slow nod, as if coming to some great internal decision. "Yes, you can come with me, Ken McBain. I don't know why you decided to, but you can come."

She didn't know why he'd decided to? Hell, *he* had no idea what he was doing here! Any idea that this would be okay, that he could handle it, could put aside the attraction he felt for Pamela had evaporated the minute he'd touched her.

He was in serious trouble. Ken struggled to find the resolution he'd felt last night. The memory of what a stupid sucker he'd been for getting involved on the rebound with Liz, his former girlfriend, had made it easier to convince himself he'd be able to avoid allowing anything to happen between him and another heartbroken woman. But those protestations weren't going to do him a damn bit of good if he let himself get caught in the web of raging need he felt whenever any portion of his anatomy connected with any portion of Pamela Bradford's.

"I guess I haven't quite kicked off my role as protector," he finally said, noting that she waited for some kind of reply. "Not to mention I could use a vacation!"

She smiled, but her eyes still shone with confusion.

Then, resigned, she leaned back in her seat. "I need some rest."

"Go ahead. We can save the sparkling conversation for the honeymoon," Ken said. "Oh, no, I forgot. No talking, right?"

She gave him a confused look, obviously not remembering her promise from the night before.

"Forget it. Get some sleep, Pam."

Ken watched her for a moment, noting the way her long lashes brushed her pale cheeks as she tried to nap. The dark circles under her eyes could have been caused by tears, or sleeplessness. He wanted them gone. Wanted her unhappiness gone. He was going to make that happen during this trip.

She moved closer, dropped her head on his shoulder, trusting him to be her pillow. Then she moved her hand over his on the armrest. Lacing her fingers through his own, she mumbled, "Thank you, Ken."

For the first time, he was glad he'd decided to come.

That surprised him, since he'd figured there was nothing that could make him happy after he'd told her father he would do this.

The previous night, Jared Bradford had used his caller ID to track Pamela's call from Ken's phone. He hadn't wasted time asking dumb questions—like why his daughter had used Ken's phone when the two of them didn't know each other. He'd just pleaded with Ken to make sure she was okay, make sure she didn't do something dangerous or rash.

Ken hadn't been very tactful when confronting Jared about his involvement in Pamela's love life. He had,

however, paused to listen to the man's explanation. Somehow, he'd found himself almost believing Jared when he said he'd never conspired with Peter Weiss. Knowing from their brief working relationship just how much he loved to talk about his stubborn but much-loved daughter, Ken thought he could see how Jared could be sucked in, thinking Peter's questions about her likes and dislikes meant he truly wanted to make her happy.

Jared certainly hoped to do whatever he could to ease Pamela's pain, going so far as to practically *insist* that Ken go with her on the trip to Lake Tahoe to make sure she was all right. Hearing Jared talk about his daughter's "innocence" Ken had begun to believe he understood why Peter had been operating under the false assumption that Pamela was, er, *inexperienced*.

Ken had refused, of course, telling Jared he felt sure Pamela would be okay. Even as he'd said the words, though, he'd questioned them. Would she? Would she really be okay? Were all those whispered, heated fantasies she'd uttered on the beach just alcohol-inspired dreams that wouldn't amount to anything?

Peter's betrayal had to have left Pamela questioning her own appeal. She'd said as much on the beach, mumbled about needing to act on the physical desires she'd suppressed during her relationship with her detached former fiancé. Would she really go find a warm, willing body to play substitute groom? To drown her misery in a spontaneous, anonymous affair that would soothe her emotions and make her feel like a desirable woman again?

Like hell she would! Not while there was breath in his body would Ken stand aside and let another man take what she broken-heartedly offered.

He didn't even try to kid himself that he was being purely self-sacrificing. Okay, maybe it was part chivalry, part loyalty to her father, even partly the thought of his own sisters. But it was also a big part self-interest.

He didn't want her getting involved with *anyone* while she got over Peter. Once she was over the bastard, Ken hoped the only man she'd be interested in getting involved with was *him*.

Selfish? Maybe. Determined? Absolutely. There had been some amazing chemistry working between them last night and he was determined they'd find out what it meant. But that wouldn't happen if she went out to Tahoe, took up with a stranger and got her heart trampled on some more. She'd likely come back swearing off men altogether!

It would be tough enough to make her understand why he'd deceived her, lied by omission about the fact that he worked with her father. Even though it was only a short-term project, in essence, her father was his boss for the next couple of months. Ken had felt more than one serious pang of guilt when he thought about that. Damn, the woman had been deceived enough!

When she found out he'd been at the party, she'd likely explode; he just hoped he could make her understand. She needed someone. She deserved to have someone looking out for her interests, making sure she was okay. And if he had to deceive her to do that, then

he'd have to live with the guilt—and pay for it later when he begged her to forgive him!

So he'd said yes.

He was stepping in merely as a substitute for her dear old dad—the one she pretty much hated right now. He'd run interference between Pamela and any smooth-talking user who might spot the loneliness in her eyes and try to take advantage of her sadness. That was it. A big-brother type. Forget about their kiss. Forget about the attraction. Forget about those long legs mere inches from his own, and the sweet smell of citrus rising from her hair.

Yep, he could do it. He'd just be standing there, a solid wall between Pamela Bradford and anything even remotely resembling sex.

There would be no torrid affair. No sweet, smooth legs wrapped around anyone's hips. No hours and hours of languid kissing and stroking. No frantic thrusting into her writhing body. No warm oil massages and mirrors and...

Ken shuddered. "Forget water, I think I need a scotch."

As THE PLANE began to move again, Pamela's eyes shot open. She became so distracted by her utter terror of flying that she nearly forgot about the man sitting next to her. Thankfully, his thick forearm, into which she was digging her fingers hard enough to make him wince, reminded her that at least he wasn't a stranger—well, not entirely, anyway.

Thrusting all confusion, humiliation and growing ex-

citement at his presence out of her head, she concentrated on willing the wings of the plane to stay connected to its body.

As she mentally chanted the words, *Don't let me die a virgin*, she forced aside the deep-down gut belief that if man were meant to fly the whole gravity thing wouldn't have happened!

"Are you sure you're okay?" Ken asked.

Pamela darted her eyes toward him, noting his genuinely concerned expression. "I, uh, don't fly too well," she told him in a loud whisper.

"No, really?" he teased. His grin faded when she glared at him. "I'm sorry. I'm not making fun of you. But you do know that statistically there's nothing to worry about. More people die in car crashes every year than plane crashes."

She winced. "Did you have to bring up the '*c*' word?"

His eyes positively twinkled. "Car?"

A tiny giggle escaped her lips, but turned into a groan as the plane picked up speed and roared down the runway.

"Don't you ever travel?"

She tilted her head toward him, but kept her eyes glued to the window. Casting quick, anxious glances between his face and the outside, where the long stretch of pavement passed beneath the wheels of the plane with growing speed, she said, "Boats."

"Boats? You travel by boat?"

She nodded. "Usually."

"You don't mind being in the ocean in a boat for days

at a time, rather than hopping on a plane and getting to where you're going in a matter of hours?"

To Pamela, there was no comparison. "Of course not."

"Remember the *Titanic?*"

She snorted. "Remember the Coast Guard?"

"Seems like a roundabout way to travel."

"My mother doesn't like to fly either," Pamela said with a shrug, finally tearing her attention away from the window to focus entirely on him. "Because once when I was a little girl we had a serious problem and an emergency landing. I remember sliding down the big rubber slide, hearing people scream, holding my mother's hand until our fingers became separated on the way down, being caught by a fireman at the bottom."

He remained silent. As they started to lift off the ground, the pressure pushed her back into her seat, and she jerked her attention to the window, wanting one more sight of land. Finally, when they were high enough that she was seeing clouds instead of treetops, she banged the window blind shut. Glancing over at Ken, she saw a look of understanding on his face.

"That must have been awful. No wonder you prefer boats."

"Mother won't fly at all. I do when I can't avoid it."

"No boats to Reno, huh?"

His sympathetic grin actually brought a smile to her lips. "Nope. And the snake didn't want to go on a cruise."

"So the Tahoe Den of Desire was worth the risk of flying?"

Pamela narrowed her eyes. "Ya know, no one said you *had* to come along on this trip!"

"But I'm here."

"And I still haven't figured out why," she said, leaning closer to him to avoid letting the flight attendant, who was passing by, hear their conversation.

His eyes, inches from hers, narrowed as he studied her face. Pamela inhaled slowly, getting lost again in the strength of his jaw, the blue-black sheen of his thick hair. And his eyes...yes, definitely a silvery-gray color that had her thinking of a newly minted coin.

Her gaze lowered to his mouth, his incredibly well-defined lips, and she remembered their kiss. Pamela slowly released the breath she'd been holding, and sucked in another between her teeth, wondering why her heart suddenly picked up its beat.

So they'd kissed. He'd held her. He'd comforted her. He'd cared for her like no one else other than her parents ever had in her life. Did it mean anything beyond the fact that he was one heck of a nice guy?

Or maybe he wasn't. Maybe he'd come for one reason—because he wanted her, too. That thought sent another rush of excitement through her body, leaving her reeling. Confusion and nervousness warred with the same thrill of pleasure she'd felt when he'd touched her face earlier.

That intensity in his eyes, the way he was clenching his fists in his lap, the coiled restraint in his tightly held body, all told of some great struggle going on within

him. Was the flirtatious, smiling image merely a pretense?

"Why did you come?" she asked, her voice low and needy, demanding the truth.

She waited, wanting to hear him admit it, *needing* him to admit that he wasn't just a nice guy. He was coming to act on the unspoken invitation he'd obtained from her the night before.

She'd been wanton in his arms during their one kiss, she remembered that much. And he wanted more. Was that it? She held her breath, hoping it was the truth. Wondering if she could go through with it, this reckless, passionate affair with a man she'd known for mere hours.

When she remembered the way he'd covered her with his coat, the sweet smile on his face as he'd taken her wedding gown away, the way she'd felt in his arms, she realized the truth. Yes. Yes, she could. With him, she could.

"Tell me." *Tell me you're going to bring me to life.*

He shifted, looking uncomfortable. "I liked you last night."

She nodded, encouraging him.

"I was worried for you."

"There's got to be more to it than that." She leaned closer, so their shoulders nearly touched and her breast brushed against his arm. He looked down, a bead of sweat breaking out over his upper lip.

"I had to go out West anyway?" he offered weakly, still staring down as if he'd never seen the bright shade

of pink of Pamela's shirt before in his life and had to memorize it. He shifted again, straightening his legs.

A strange sense of power shot through Pamela. He wanted her. She didn't need him to say it. His body made it clear—his labored breathing, the sheen of sweat on his brow, the tense way he held his arms. He was holding back, controlling it, but it was there. She nearly laughed with delight.

"You don't have to explain," she said. "I know how you're feeling. I've been the same way since last night."

He raised one eyebrow. "You do? You *have?*"

Pamela slid her tongue out to moisten her lips, noting that his eyes immediately shifted and he watched, very closely. She dropped her voice a bit lower. "We don't have to make excuses, don't have to justify it."

He crossed and uncrossed his legs, still looking at her mouth. "No excuses?"

Pamela shook her head and leaned closer. "We're two adults. Two mature, consenting adults."

"Uh, Pamela, listen..."

"Ken, look, we're strangers, that's obvious. But something's happened between us. The attraction is undeniable. We're on our way to spend seven days at a luxury resort that promises to indulge every sensual urge." *Where on earth had she found the nerve to say that?*

"Sensual urge?" This time his voice shook. He ran a hand across his mouth. "Pamela, I don't think..." Before he could finish his sentence, his seat was again jolted from behind. Pamela watched as he turned to peer through the crack between their seats, glaring at the elderly man behind him.

"No, don't think," she said when he turned his attention back toward her. "Neither one of us has to think about this. There's been something happening between us since the minute we met. I'm tired, Ken, so tired of letting other people decide what I'll do and when I'll do it. Lately, my career is about all I've had the energy to fight for. Somewhere along the way I started letting other people run my personal life."

First her father, then Peter. Well, no more. It was time for Pamela to take charge of her own sexual identity. And the man sitting next to her was the one she wanted to identify with!

"So let's take this moment. Spend a glorious week teaching each other how good a purely physical relationship can be between two people who want each other so badly." Her belief that she was doing the right thing carried her through the shock of saying something like that out loud to a relative stranger.

Pamela did hear the shakiness in her voice, though, and wondered if he noticed. Did he know the effort this took her? Or did he think she was some oversexed, experienced woman who was used to having casual flings? Maybe it was best to let him think that. If he knew her actual level of experience—basically none— he might turn her down.

"Well, what do you say, Ken McBain? Seven days of physical pleasure with no one to answer to and nothing to stop us except the limits of our own desire." She heard a purr in her own voice as she continued, "Are you up for it?"

She watched him swallow, hard. Glancing down, Pa-

mela noticed the sudden tightness of his khaki trousers, which he could no longer disguise by simply shifting his legs. God, they hadn't even touched and he was magnificently *ready*. Her mouth went dry and she got hot and achy down low, deep inside. Her own jeans felt tight and wonderfully uncomfortable. Pamela knew she'd made the right decision.

"Yes, I *definitely* think you're *up* for it," she whispered.

He groaned. He literally groaned out loud. Pamela wanted to clap with delight.

Finally, Ken ran his hands through his own hair, leaned back in his seat and took a few deep breaths. "No, Pamela, no." He cleared his throat. "I like you. I'm attracted to you. I want to get to know you—but in a *platonic* sense."

She froze.

"I'm sorry," he continued, his voice growing more forceful. "But this honeymoon is going to involve absolutely *no* sex."

5

JERKING BACK, Pamela sat straight up in her seat, then stared at him. He meant it. The look on his face—kind yet resolute—told her he was serious.

For the second time in twenty-four hours, she'd basically offered herself to a man and once again she'd been left feeling rejected and humiliated. Pamela willed the tears gathering in the corners of her eyes not to fall. Glancing in panic toward the front of the plane, she noticed the Occupied sign was lit, and decided not to leap over him to escape to the tiny bathroom.

She wanted to hide her face in mortification. More than that, she wanted to call him a liar, and then hit him.

As it turned out, she didn't have to, because the elderly man in the seat behind Ken took care of that. Before Pamela realized it was happening, he'd leaned over the high-backed chair and bopped Ken on the top of the head with his rolled-up newspaper.

"Ow," Ken exclaimed, shifting to look at the other man.

The man shook his index finger toward Ken. "What are you, crazy? Are you insane? Or didja get your parts blown off in a war or something?"

Pamela, still reeling at Ken's announcement that he

would not be making love to her during their "honeymoon," found herself waiting for Ken's answer. Then she blushed as she realized the elderly gentleman with the shock of thick white hair and the bright blue eyes had been listening to their conversation.

"Could you please mind your own business?" Ken said between gritted teeth.

"Not when you're being a damned idiot." The man glowered fiercely as he stood and leaned over the back of Ken's seat. "No sex? Are ya blind? Or are ya one of those namby-pamby girlie-boys? This babe wants ta have wild sex with ya on your own honeymoon and you tell her *no?*"

A heavyset woman sitting across the aisle, who, Pamela noticed, had been pretending to read the upside-down paperback in her lap, turned with a big smile. "Honeymoon? Oh, goodness, they're newlyweds having their first lovers' quarrel! Isn't that adorable, Stu?"

A balding man with red-rimmed eyes, wearing a Hawaiian shirt and pale blue Bermuda shorts, leaned forward to look past his wife's girth. "You got it backward, son. It's the wife who says no sex whenever you get in a fight." His wife playfully smacked his hand. The husband gave Ken a long-suffering look that said, *See what you have to look forward to?*

Pamela sucked in her lip to contain a laugh as Ken's face went a dark shade of red. He muttered a curse while others on the plane began turning in their seats to look toward them.

"Don't you worry about him," the wife said as she leaned across the aisle to catch Pamela's eye. "You put

on one of those pretty lacy white nightgowns I'm sure you got at your bridal shower and he'll be raring to go!"

Pamela managed a weak nod.

"And if that doesn't work," the older woman continued in a matter-of-fact tone, "try black leather."

A screech of laughter rose up in Pamela's throat, but she clamped her lips shut. Beside her, Ken's eyes went wider, and he looked around at the attention they were drawing from the entire front section of the plane.

Though it seemed things couldn't possibly get any more embarrassing, the perky flight attendant came back to up the humiliation factor another notch. "Did I hear someone say we have a honeymooning couple with us? Oh, my, is that why you were cranky when you got on board, honey? You and your new hubby had a tiff after the wedding?"

Now it was Pamela's turn to blush.

"We have complimentary bottles of champagne available. How about I get some glasses and we toast your happiness?"

"I'll toast to a man having sex on his wedding night, that's what *I'll* toast to!" the elderly man said with a belligerent thrust of his jaw.

Biting her lips didn't help. Covering her mouth didn't help either. Pamela suddenly erupted into laughter, almost snorting in hilarity as she took in the entire scene. Everyone on the plane was watching, lecturing Ken on how to be a good husband and her on whether white lace or black leather was appropriate wedding night attire. And they weren't even married!

She saw Ken's shoulders start to shake, then he was

laughing, too. He nodded at the old man as he agreed to make love to his "bride" that night, and agreed with Mrs. Red Dress that while black leather was indeed titillating, it was maybe best to keep the actual wedding night all white lace.

While the stewardess went off to fetch the free champagne, and others on the plane offered congratulations on their marriage, Pamela said under her breath, "We'll talk about the *terms* of our vacation later, okay? I know you're a wonderfully nice guy, and I somehow suspect you're trying to be chivalrous. But don't. Wait until you hear what it is I need and want before you make any decisions, okay?"

He didn't reply, didn't say no—just stared at her, weighing her words. He released a heavy breath, then glanced around, apparently to ensure no one was listening this time. "Pamela, there's no question there's something between us. Once you're over your ex-fiancé, maybe something will even come of it—*then*. In the meantime, we can certainly get to know each other better."

Well, at least he'd admitted the attraction! It wasn't quite the lustful declaration she wanted, but it was a start. "So you admit it. You feel the same way. You want me, too?" Hearing the hesitation in her own voice, she wondered if he knew how much his answer meant to her.

Leaning closer, Pamela tried to block the old man's view between the seats with her body. Pressing against Ken, she prodded, "It's not one-sided? You're not *pretending* you're interested?"

Her breath caught in her throat as she waited for his reply. Finally, he reached out an index finger to touch her chin and tilted her face up.

The sweet intensity in his stare shocked her. "Pamela, I want you so bad I don't know if I'm going to make it off this plane without spending a good ten minutes alone in the bathroom to, uh, *ease* the pain."

"Ease the...oh my," she whispered, realizing what he meant.

He continued with a throaty chuckle, "Like I nearly had to last night after I took you home."

She clenched her fist in her lap. "Last night?"

"Yeah, Pamela. Last night." He leaned closer, so that his lips were close enough for her to feel his exhalations against her skin. His breath smelled of mint, his cologne of the sea, and she shivered, aching with pure, undiluted need.

"Do you think it was easy for me, taking you home, walking away from you after one kiss? When what I really wanted to do was tear our clothes off, carry you into the water and make love to you while the waves pounded us both into oblivion?"

Her mouth went dry and Pamela had to clench her legs together, wondering why she'd started this torture for which she was now going to suffer. "I didn't realize..."

"You were whispering about a honeymoon and all I could see were your thighs wrapped around my hips, me buried so deep inside you that you'd scream at how good it felt."

Pamela whimpered as the sensitive flesh between her

thighs grew hotter, wetter. She wanted to cry out, to tell him to stop, that she couldn't take the sound of his voice and the look of passion on his face.

She said nothing.

"I wanted to taste every inch of you. To lick away those tiny bits of icing you had on your arms...your thighs. To put my mouth on you and watch your face as you came apart."

"Oh, please," she managed to mutter, helpless as her thigh muscles began to shudder. She pushed her clenched hands down to her lap.

"Yes, to hear you say that—please—hear you tell me you were ready for me. Then thrust into you so hard I could push every painful memory of that bastard you were engaged to right out of your brain, Pamela."

Someone passed by in the aisle, heading toward the front of the plane, and Ken suddenly seemed to realize what he was saying. He muttered a curse and pulled back. "I'm sorry."

"Don't be," she said hoarsely once she was able to draw enough breath into her lungs to be able to speak. "You can't know how much I *needed* to hear that."

"Yeah, well, I didn't mean to say it."

The raging hormones practically rolled off him; Pamela could feel his desire coming toward her in heat-laden waves of energy. Her body arched closer to him, still quivering.

What on earth could this man make her feel if he actually *touched* her? Considering she'd come close to having a screaming orgasm on a crowded plane just at the sound of his voice, she had a feeling actually mak-

ing love to him would be beyond the realm of her imagination.

"I came on this trip with you certain that I could control the way I feel when we're together." He shook his head, obviously still angry with himself. "I'm not some teenage kid—I can enjoy getting to know a woman without having to take her to bed right away."

She paused for a heartbeat. "What if that's what she wants you to do?"

He met her stare evenly. "Then she's going to be disappointed. That's not why I'm here."

"Yeah, I've got it," she muttered. "You're here strictly to be my friend, Mr. Protector."

"Don't make me out to be some white knight, sweetheart. I have my own motives."

She tensed, waiting for the other shoe to drop, knowing all about men with their own hidden agendas. "Motives?"

"I've said I'm not going to get involved with you while you're suffering a broken heart over your ex. But I'm also here to make damn sure no one else does either."

Not understanding at first, she lifted a brow.

"No other man is going to see that look in your eyes and give you what you've been begging for since we met last night." His tone was confident, verging on arrogant. "I'm the only man who's going to give you that, Pamela—when you're ready, not before. Then I'll make you forget Peter ever existed."

Another wave of excitement rolled through her at the certainty in his voice. "Promise?"

He nodded slowly, a small smile on his lips, utter confidence in his stare. His intensity spoke of heat. Passion. Everything she wanted—not later—now.

"I promise," he finally said. "Will you promise me something?"

"I'll try."

"Give it time, Pamela. Let it happen naturally. Take this chance for your heart to heal. I'll be there to make sure you don't do anything you'll regret in the future, like any friend would."

"Friend?"

"That's all I'm offering right now, Pamela. That's all I'm willing to be. Can you live with that?"

Could she? Be merely a friend to this tender, charming, sexy-as-pure-undiluted-sin man? He'd made her laugh, made her nearly have a shattering orgasm in the middle of a crowded plane, and was fighting his intense attraction to her for *her* own good. Could she give up any more heated, whispered words? Kisses like the one that had rocked her world the night before?

Not bloody likely.

"You can be my friend, Ken," she said with a gentle smile. She saw his tension ease. "And I can do my damnedest to change your mind."

Before he could reply, the flight attendant returned, carrying the free minibottle of champagne. Shooting Pamela a look that promised their conversation would continue later, Ken poured them each a serving while everyone watched. Lifting his glass, Ken looked around at other couples in nearby rows and said, "Here's to all

successful marriages, and to a happy, fun-filled honeymoon."

Pamela caught his eye, heard the unspoken message in his toast. Happy? Fun-filled? In other words, platonic.

Uh-uh. No way, mister. No way.

"I have a toast of my own," she said, lifting her glass again. "To white lace *and* black leather—both of which I happen to have in my suitcase."

KEN WONDERED how long it would take for the oxygen to be sucked out of his lungs if he leapt out of the plane somewhere over the northern part of Florida. Would he freeze to death or suffocate first? It didn't matter, he supposed, even if he survived screaming all the way down to the ground. Anything seemed preferable to sitting here with a record-setting hard-on while all around him people laughed and toasted his marriage to the bright-eyed temptress in the seat next to him.

White lace. Black leather.

"God help me."

He mumbled several silent prayers for mercy over the next few hours while they proceeded across the country on what he was now calling "the honeymoon-from-hell plane." It seemed everyone on board, including the pilot, felt the need to congratulate them...and to comment on their "lovers' tiff" during the flight.

One young man with a pierced nose and long dirty-blond hair swept back into a ponytail, offered to lend them his copy of the *Kama Sutra*. Ken somehow managed to refrain from asking him why he felt the need to

travel with a text on the Hindu art of lovemaking. Pamela had no such forbearance. The young man spent several minutes happily explaining why he worshipped women and wanted to do anything to please them.

The young man's lighthearted flirtation with Pamela made her smile, so Ken allowed it. Briefly. He didn't consider himself a caveman type, and Pamela definitely needed a shot of confidence after the night she'd had with her fiancé. Besides, they weren't *really* a newly married couple going on their honeymoon. He didn't have any claim on Pamela. And there wasn't much the blond stud could do on a crowded plane. Still, Ken felt a strong urge to knock Mr. *Kama Sutra* to the back of the plane when he started talking to Pamela about his *lingam*.

When she reached out to accept the book the young man offered, leaning farther out toward the aisle, she again pressed her breasts into his upper arm. Ken gritted his teeth.

"I'm sure this'll be fascinating," she told the man.

Ken only caught a glimpse of the cover but instantly recognized that it did, indeed, contain the ancient Hindu sexual teachings. He held his hand out, blocking her from taking it, and stared at the blond young man. "If you value your *lingam*, I suggest you go back to your seat," he said, knowing he probably sounded like a jealous moron, and not giving a rat's ass.

The other man nodded. "Okay. No harm, no foul."

After he left, the old man behind him cleared his throat and muttered, "'Bout time."

"What's a *lingam?*" the woman in the red dress asked her husband. He didn't seem to know; Ken did not offer any answers. He was not at all inclined to start discussing the male sex organ with strangers. Not when *his* was causing him such excruciating discomfort every time Pamela touched his thigh as she leaned over to talk to the other couple, or whispered into his ear, or let her soft hair brush against his cheek. When Pamela got up to use the restroom, insisting that he remain seated while she wiggled her sweet, jean-clad backside right in front of him in order to exit the row, he hissed.

She heard, took no mercy, leaned close and whispered, "Wanna join the mile-high club?"

"Pamela..." he warned.

She grinned, then, instead of walking toward the bathroom, sat in the vacant aisle seat next to him. "I know this flight hasn't been pleasant for you. You've been a very good sport."

"Oh, yeah, I so enjoy looking like some kind of modern-day eunuch who won't have sex with a gorgeous woman," he muttered.

She kissed his cheek, whispered in his ear, "I know the truth. Thank you for admitting you want me, even though it made for a rather, er, uncomfortable plane ride."

Ken tried to focus on the sincerity of her words, and to ignore the softness of her hair against his face and the curve of her lips just inches from his own.

"Remember, it's completely mutual, okay?" she continued, her eyes holding a look of tender understanding. "I feel everything you're feeling. And whenever

you're ready to shrug off your protector jacket and see that I am a grown-up woman making grown-up decisions, you can help me put us *both* out of our misery."

He started breathing again about sixty seconds after she slipped away, then whispered, "Will this flight never end?"

IT DID, of course, finally end, and by that point Pamela was on a first-name basis with the old man behind them and the couple in the seats across the aisle. Mrs. Red Dress seemed to enjoy instructing Pamela on wifely duties from the other side of the plane. Her harried hubby Stu rolled his eyes so often Ken was surprised they didn't get stuck up inside his head.

She charmed them all. Her quick smile, genuine laugh and the twinkle in her brown eyes charmed him as well.

Though deadly when she was flirting with him, he found her even more disconcerting during their long, casual conversations throughout the flight. She talked about her job and her dreams, about her past and her relationship with her parents.

They debated politics and sports. She told him she could whup his butt in a game of hoops and he suspected she could, particularly after learning that she'd been courted by the WNBA during her college years.

He liked her. Truly enjoyed her company. That, combined with the physical attraction he'd felt for the woman since the first time he'd seen her, made the guilt factor even worse. He was lying to this wonderfully

down-to-earth, charming, beautiful woman—a woman he probably could go nuts over given half a chance.

He wouldn't be given half a chance, however, if he couldn't make her understand why he hadn't told her who he really was.

When they landed in Reno, Ken was up, pulling his carry-on from the overhead compartment, before the plane even came to a complete stop. That earned him a frown from the flight attendant, who was not so perky after five hours in the air, and a nod of approval from the old geezer, who seemed to take Ken's anxiousness as a sign that he couldn't wait to be alone with his new bride.

"Are you ready to go, Pamela?" he asked as she continued chatting with others onboard, making no move to exit.

"Oh, he's so anxious," one of the older ladies in the front section of the plane said with a sigh. "Isn't that sweet?"

As they left the plane, Ken paused every few feet to accept congratulations, noting the happiness on Pamela's face. Remembering the tears he'd seen in her eyes the night before, he acknowledged that the humiliating plane ride was worth one of her bright smiles.

Her mood had definitely improved after he'd been stupid enough to confess how badly he wanted her. Ken realized he'd made a very serious tactical mistake. Her femininity had been rocked by her fiancé; now he'd practically tossed a gauntlet at her feet, almost challenging her to make him act on the attraction between them. Telling her he wouldn't had been a line drawn in the

sand. She'd already begun to cross it. He didn't know if he had the strength to draw another one.

As soon as they got to the spa, and had some privacy, they were going to have to have another serious talk. No way was he sticking around if Pamela had made it her mission to seduce him.

Ken wasn't stupid. It wouldn't take much effort at all and would be breaking his rules against getting involved with a woman on the rebound, and taking advantage of a woman who was hurting and vulnerable. So, he'd need to lay down some ground rules for this vacation. Number one, no white lace. Numbers two through ten, no black leather. Numbers eleven through twenty forbade the heated looks, sultry glances and all those innocent touches she'd managed to torture him with during the flight.

They'd just have to move past the sexual tension so thick between them he could spread it on toast, and try to enjoy their vacation like any two strangers in a honeymoon resort would.

How tough could that be? They'd be at an exclusive hotel with lots of things to do. There'd probably be horseback riding, kayaking, lots of activities that did not involve giving in to his overwhelming urge to throw her onto the nearest flat surface and take her in every way humans had ever discovered—and then some.

As the old man from the plane followed them to the gate, muttering wedding night instructions under his breath, Ken sighed in resignation. Pamela, who'd looped her arm in his, leaned close to whisper, "Almost

over. We'll be another anonymous vacationing couple in a few minutes."

"Thank goodness."

He took one or two more steps, not noticing at first when Pamela stopped moving. Glancing over his shoulder at her, he saw the color draining from her face. Her mouth hung open and her eyes were wide.

"No. Please, nothing else," he muttered out loud, almost afraid to turn and see what had sparked her reaction. Had Peter come to find her? Or was it her father?

Resigned, he followed her stare, searching for a familiar face. His gaze at first moved right past the burly, gray-haired man who wore a pale blue tuxedo and held a huge horseshoe of red, pink and white roses over his shoulders. Then he caught sight of the banner the man was carrying. It was almost enough to make a grown man cry.

Pamela somehow managed to avoid giving in to her first impulse, which was to run in the other direction and hide, and her second impulse, which was to burst into hysterical laughter. Instead, she tugged Ken behind her, and marched up to the flower-bearing man holding the banner that said, The Little Love Nest Welcomes Newlyweds Pamela & Peter!

"We're here."

A huge smile spread across the man's face. She wondered how much he'd paid for all the gold caps.

"Ah, the happy couple has arrived!" he boomed, drawing the attention of everyone nearby. "On behalfa da Little Love Nest, welcome ta Reno."

If there had been cameras around, Pamela would

have sworn someone was filming a Godfather-type movie. Because this guy was like every cinema image of a mafia enforcer she'd ever seen. His gray hair was cropped close into a blunt crew cut that hugged his square head. Though a genuine smile creased his lips, Pamela saw that his friendly blue eyes glanced in every direction, as if watching for a hit man...or a Fed. The only thing that would have completed the image would have been a black Italian suit. Somehow, his pale blue tuxedo and ruffled shirt—fresh from a 1970s prom night—didn't fit the mafia image. "Thank you so much for the welcome," she finally managed to say.

"My name's Al, and it's my pleasure. These would be for you," he said as he took the horseshoe of roses off his own shoulders. "Better let hubby carry them, though." He hung the roses over Ken's shoulders, obviously not noticing the way Ken's jaw tightened.

"Let's go get yer bags, then we'll be on our way. We got about an hour's drive, across the state line, to the southwest shore of the lake."

"Giddyap," Ken muttered between clenched teeth as Al walked away. "Looks like I won the Derby."

Pamela couldn't resist. "And you haven't even *rid-den*—not yet, anyway."

His eyes narrowed at her suggestive taunt. "I think I forgot my spurs. Guess that's okay...I won't be doing any riding on this vacation anyway."

She heard the challenge and responded to it. "I might have something in my suitcase you could borrow... black leather, metal—oh, no, that'd be the handcuffs."

She watched him swallow, hard. Then he obviously shook off the sexual image and gave her a knowing look. "Don't tell me Peter was the kinky type."

"I have no idea, remember?"

Ken nodded in male satisfaction. "Oh, yeah, that's right. I remember now."

He looked too pleased with himself. Could he really be glad, for his own sake, that she hadn't consummated her relationship with Peter? Out of what? A sense of protectiveness? Or jealousy?

She hoped it was the latter.

"Hm, I just hope you're a distance rider," she finally continued, unwilling to let him have the last word, "not one of those jockeys who finishes the race in under a minute."

"It's not the speed of the race that counts," he said, his voice low and confident. "It's all in the technique."

"And not falling off the horse," she said with a grin as she turned to follow Al toward the baggage claim.

Ken fell into step beside her and gave her a look of wounded male pride. "I've never fallen off."

"Never been thrown, either?"

"No way."

"Not even if the mount was particularly, um, aggressive in her movements during the race?"

He paused, taking her arm. "That makes the ride more exciting." He leaned closer, ignoring the passengers who continued to walk by them in the terminal. "Two bodies moving together like one, pure instinct taking over as they strive toward the finish line, reaching for that big payoff."

Now it was Pamela's turn to swallow hard. She almost regretted taunting him. "Big payoff?"

"Oh, yeah," he said, his voice silky, his eyes now a dark gray as he held her gaze. "Straining toward it, going for it with every bit of physical energy they possess, then reaching that final moment when they cry out with triumph."

Her mouth dry, Pamela muttered weakly, "Sounds like you've had a lot of experience."

"Some. And believe me," he continued, his voice as seductive as a caress, "nothing feels as good as being deep *inside* that winner's circle, achieving the *ultimate* prize."

"Oh, good grief, you did it again," she muttered as her legs weakened beneath her. She shuddered, rubbed a hand over her eyes and shook her head. When she looked at him again, Ken was watching, a knowing smile playing about his lips.

"Do you know what you're doing to me? Right here, in the middle of a public airport? Jeez, you ought to register that voice of yours as a lethal weapon."

"Don't start playing sexy word games with me, sweetheart, unless you expect me to play along."

"Well, heck," she said in confusion, "isn't that the problem? You not wanting to play along?"

"Don't ever think it's a question of wanting or not, Pamela. There's no doubt about what I want." He lifted his hand and brushed his fingers against her cheek, burning her, making her ache even more. "It's all about the timing."

He turned to catch up to the driver and Pamela fell

into step behind him. Noting the amused looks he was getting from passersby, she had to give him credit for not pitching the flowers into the nearest trash can. Al, the driver, who'd apparently just noticed that they hadn't immediately followed him, waited for them to catch up. When they reached his side, he gave them a rundown on the weather and local activities, most of which seemed to involve gambling. He appeared to be an expert in that area.

When they reached the baggage claim area, Al asked them for a description of their bags, then left to retrieve them. As soon as he was out of earshot, Ken asked, "Exactly how much do you know about this resort, Pamela?"

She shot him a worried glance. "Their brochures were nice."

"Do you actually know anyone who's ever stayed there?"

Biting her lip, she shook her head. "I'm sure it'll be okay, though. This area's very exclusive. Maybe the resort has some liberal hiring policies?"

They stared as Al reached for one of Pamela's bags, elbowing everyone else waiting near the conveyor out of his way. Ken winced. "Or maybe they support the local work release program!"

She didn't reply.

Al rejoined them, pushing a cart loaded with Pamela's bags and one unfamiliar one, which she assumed was Ken's. "Okay, we're all set." Giving them another toothy grin, he grabbed the flowers, draped them over the top of the suitcases on the cart and led

them toward the exit. Everyone waiting in the baggage claim area stepped out of his way.

Outside, the air was damp with a recent rain. Low-hanging, murky clouds hid any sign of stars in the night sky. Pamela's internal clock forced her to emit a huge yawn. Though it was only about nine here, her body thought it was midnight. She was more than ready for a good night's sleep. Tomorrow, she decided, would be soon enough to begin the *real* honeymoon.

Now, after twice experiencing his verbal powers of seduction, she had to wonder what Ken was capable of with his hands, his lips, his...oh, how she wanted to find out!

He'd definitely paid her back for teasing him throughout the flight. Glancing at him as they walked, she hid a smile as she remembered his discomfort on the plane. He'd been positively oozing restrained sexual need! She'd done what she could to push every lustful button he had. Maybe not fair, given his insistence on a platonic honeymoon, but she didn't really care about fair right now. Peter certainly hadn't been fair with her, nor had her father. So maybe it was time for Pamela to be the taker, to get what she wanted.

And, oh, she so very badly wanted Ken McBain.

Since Pamela wasn't, by nature, a selfish person, she'd felt more than one moment's concern about using him to soothe her own heartbreak and self-doubt. When she thought about it, however, she acknowledged the truth: she didn't want him because of what had happened with Peter, nor because of the fact that she'd

never made love with anyone and feared being the world's oldest living virgin.

She wanted him because of that smile. Those eyes. Those hands that had held her so tenderly while she'd cried. She wanted him because of that kiss. The feel of his lips on hers, the sweep of his tongue in her mouth that had stolen her breath, her will and her self-control. She wanted him because of his laugh. Because of his sense of humor. Because of the way he looked in his pants...

She wanted him because he had covered her with his jacket. Because he could make her thighs weak with a single heavy-lidded look. And, oh, heavens yes, because of the way his whispered words had made her lose control, had filled her mind with images she'd only ever dreamed about—and some she hadn't.

Mainly she wanted him because she knew she would wonder for the rest of her life what might have been if she didn't take a chance and fully experience the joy she felt sure she could find with him. Physically. Emotionally. In every way possible.

Okay, they hadn't met under ideal conditions. But the sparks firing between them would have happened no matter where they'd met. She knew it.

She also knew, without question, that he wanted her as much as she wanted him. He'd admitted it. So he'd decided to be chivalrous, act the part of protector? She admired him for the gesture. But chivalry wasn't what she needed from him.

She needed passion, soul-stirring desire and physical fulfillment. She needed to laugh with him some more,

to make his silvery eyes darken to gray when he looked at her. Needed to kiss him senseless, as he'd done to her the night before on the beach. She needed to know him, to memorize his smell and the way his skin tasted after a shower. Needed to know what sounds he made when he made love. Needed to look into his eyes, be mentally connected with him as he exploded inside her when they finally came together.

Yes, those would be her terms for their vacation.

Pamela smiled, casting another look at him as they walked outside on the still-wet pavement. She looked forward to bringing him around to her way of thinking, knowing he might not be easy to persuade. He'd adopted the mantle of protector and it might take some serious persuasion to get him to change his mind.

Persuasion? *Seduction!*

A strong sense of purpose—and anticipation of the payoff—overcame any question in her mind that she could do it. Maybe Peter hadn't wanted her enough, but that was because his greed had been interfering with his libido.

Ken was nothing like Peter. He was honest, for one thing. He had no idea who she was, who her father was. And while he fought valiantly to suppress it, he felt the same physical draw toward her that she felt toward him.

Yes, seduction could work. Pamela suddenly found herself very thankful for those bikinis she'd bought in Miami earlier in the day—not to mention some of the other surprises LaVyrle had given her at her bridal shower. She hadn't been joking about the handcuffs!

"Oh, God, please tell me there's a Mary Kay convention in town," she heard Ken mutter. Startled out of her very pleasant musings, she followed his horrified stare.

They had reached a loop with spaces reserved for buses and limousines. The spots were full, for the most part, with tourists boarding shuttles to the various casino hotels in Reno, or to the Lake Tahoe resorts. One car stood out.

"It's pink," Ken said.

"Very," she agreed.

Her faint hope that Al would pass right by the bright pink boat parked in one of the spaces near the end of the row was quickly dashed. He cut between the nightmare and a lovely black Mercedes limousine and tossed their luggage into the trunk of the cotton-candy-mobile. He then unceremoniously dumped the flowers on top of them and slammed down the lid. "Hop in, folks!"

Ken didn't think he'd ever entered a car faster in his life. Giving a quick glance around, and noting that no one appeared to be looking in their direction, he yanked the back door open, pushed Pamela into the back seat, and dove in after her. Maybe no one had seen. *Please, let no one have seen!*

Al got into the front seat and turned to face them. "There's champagne in the fridge. Remember, we've got a whole hour until we get to the resort." He gave them a somewhat lascivious smile. "I'll give you two lovebirds some privacy. The windows are impossible to see through...and that includes this one." He pushed a button and a solid black sheet of glass slid up from be-

hind the front seat. Before Al's face completely disappeared, he gave Ken a very obvious wink.

Then they were alone. In the semidark. Cocooned from everyone else in the entire world. For the next sixty minutes.

Pamela sat so close to him that her body touched his from knee to hip. He moved away, toward the door, trying to ignore her sweet scent and the memory of what those long legs had looked like last night on the beach—trying to forget their conversations, both on the plane and in the airport, when he'd been foolish enough to let her hear his need for her.

She scooted closer until they were touching again. *Uh-oh.*

Al's voice interrupted from an overhead speaker. "How about some music, folks?"

Thankful for the distraction, Ken nodded, then remembered Al couldn't see him. "Yes, music," he ordered. "Anything." *A marching brass band, a rap song— just nothing low and sultry!*

Then he heard the music start and knew his wish had not been granted. Donna Summer's voice, moaning orgasmic oohs and aahs as she sang "Love To Love You Baby," slid out of the stereo speakers and completed the atmosphere of raw sexual tension.

Feeling his self-control skid away in huge chunks, Ken muttered, "It's a conspiracy!"

6

"WHAT IS?" Pamela asked.

Ken looked at her out of the corner of his eye, knowing she knew what he was talking about. The innocent expression on her face couldn't hide that her body was moving...just barely...to the sexual sounds. Every gesture was a blatant invitation, designed to be impossible to refuse.

"Forget it," he muttered, trying again to move away, gain some distance. "I guess the 1970s disco music works as well as everything else has so far."

She reached into the ice bucket sitting atop the small refrigerator and glanced at the champagne bottle. "Looks like they have good taste in champagne at least." Then she slid across the roomy leather seat until her hip once again came in contact with his. "Want some?"

His mouth went dry. "Uh, is there any bottled water?"

She leaned over to open the fridge, her pink shirt pulling free of the waistband of her jeans. Ken stared at the long, pale strip of skin, the indentation of her bare waist revealed below her shirt. His gut clenched.

It took her forever to root around in the tiny refriger-

ator, particularly since she insisted on wiggling lower, pushing her sweet rear end against his thigh.

Conspiracy.

She finally sat up and shook her head. "'Fraid not."

He gave a helpless shrug, wondering if she knew how the soft lighting emanating from the amber bulbs in each door cast hints of gold on her hair.

Did she also know she was killing him? Could she imagine the restraint it was taking to avoid accepting the invitation at her every move? Did she know how much he wanted to press her back onto the long leather seat and explore every bit of her?

He waited, noting the sparkle in her eyes and the curve of her lips. Pamela handed him two fluted glasses that had been sitting on top of the bar, then held up the bottle of champagne.

When he reached to take the bottle from her, she waved his hand aside, popping the cork herself. Some of the pale golden fluid spurted out of the top, bubbling down over Pamela's hand. He heard her gasp, then watched as she drew the bottle toward her mouth, to lick away the moisture from her own skin.

"Lovely," she whispered throatily as she tasted the champagne. The smooth, unhurried strokes of her pink tongue on her long fingers nearly had Ken begging for mercy... *Which was what she'd intended.*

He saw the mischief in her tiny grin, combined with a look of physical pleasure. She was enjoying the sensuality of the moment—the darkness, their closeness, the music, the taste of the liquid on her own flesh. Pamela

Bradford was reveling in sensation. That gave him another insight into her character.

But her provocative teasing ended when she saw what he was certain was an explosion of answering heat in his own eyes.

"Let me," Ken murmured, not knowing where the words came from, only knowing he had to taste her or go mad. He pulled the bottle free of her hand and set it in an ice bucket on the bar, then tugged her fingers toward his lips.

Excitement widened her eyes and Ken never let their stare break. He moved closer, until his mouth was a breath away from her fingers. Only after her hand shook in his own did he slide his lips over the tip of her pinky.

She moaned, rose off the seat.

Ken moved his mouth down her finger, licking off the sweetness, tasting her with his tongue and his teeth. When he'd licked off every bit of moisture from that finger, he released it and moved to the next, taking his time, dipping his tongue to taste the tender flesh between.

"Ken..." she said on a sigh, her voice holding both an invitation and a plea.

Her hands weren't enough. He wanted to kiss every inch of her—every delectable, sweet-flavored inch.

Her mouth, however, would do for a start.

He caught her lips with his, hearing her soft groan as she parted them invitingly. He felt her hands slide behind his neck as she tilted her head to the side to deepen the kiss.

She tasted sweet, warm, her tongue meeting every stroke of his own until they were both moving to the same rhythm.

"Got to touch you," he muttered, telling himself it was crazy but unable to stop. "I have to touch you, Pamela."

She pressed closer, arching her back and sliding lower into the leather seat. He moved over her, covering her body with his own. Moving his hands to tangle in her hair, he cupped her head and continued to kiss her, deeply, endlessly, losing himself in her completely.

Then, unable to resist, he slid his hands lower, caressing her neck, her shoulders, the pale curve of her throat, her high, lovely breasts.

"Oh, please," she said, her hips jerking in reaction as he passed his flattened hands over the front of her pink cotton shirt. He felt her rock-hard nipples beneath the fabric and simply had to bend lower to taste them, making her shirt wet and warm as he sucked one tender tip into his mouth.

His hands were tugging her pink top up before his mind even had a chance to order him to stop. Her skin was hot, throbbing and vibrant beneath his fingers. He drew the shirt up slowly, peeling the tight fabric off inch by agonizing inch, relishing each strip of flesh as it was revealed.

She lifted her arms above her head, and he tossed her shirt aside. Ken heard her cry out as he moved lower to press a hot kiss on her stomach, and he paused, savoring her sweet fragrance, taking tiny tastes of her, sliding

his mouth lower until he was breathing onto the front of her white jeans.

"Ken," she muttered hoarsely, "please..."

"Please what? Please relieve the pressure?" He moved back up her body, knowing the way she twisted beneath him that she'd wanted him to stay where he was. "Or should I let you suffer the way you made me suffer on that plane?"

"I need, can't...*please!*"

He moved higher, until his mouth was scraping the lace of her bra. His breathing grew ragged as her nipples puckered and hardened beneath the white lace. He nudged one strap off her arm, kissing a path along the high curve of one breast. When he slid his tongue beneath the fabric for just a taste, a simple taste of her sweet skin, she jerked so hard they nearly flipped off the seat.

"You like that."

"That's going to kill me," she muttered hoarsely. "Don't you dare stop."

Stop? Hell, he'd sooner stop drawing breath.

Finally he pulled the bra down, cupping her breast with his hand, teasing her sensitive nipple with his fingers. She grabbed his hair, pulled him closer, demanding more. When he sucked her nipple deep into his mouth, she cried out beneath him.

She was writhing now, moving wildly on the seat. Her flushed cheeks, thrashing head and audible cries told him that, incredible as it seemed, she was close to finding her ultimate release with nothing more than a few kisses and caresses.

"Please, please," she cried out, arching into him, thrusting her pelvis up against him, rubbing herself against his raging erection until his frenzy nearly matched hers. "I can't, I've never..."

She'd never had hot pounding sex in the back of a limousine? Never driven a man so out of his mind that he'd abandon all good intentions and come close to pulling her clothes off and thrusting into her now, *right now*, heedless of the driver in the front seat?

He wasn't quite that lost. But no way could he pull back. No way could he take her that far and not see her go right over the edge of the cliff. "Go with it, sweetheart, go ahead and fall. I'm right here," he muttered hoarsely.

Keeping up the heated kisses to her breasts, he moved one hand down her body in a smooth stroke until he reached her hip. Then lower, circling her thigh.

When he cupped her sex he found her jeans hot, the fabric damp. She squirmed against him, "Yes, oh, please," and jerked up harder, forcing herself against his palm.

He stroked. Once, twice. Moving up to catch her cries with his lips, he kissed her deeply but never stopped touching her, using his hand to bring her higher. Until, finally, beautifully, she cried out his name and came apart right before his eyes.

PAMELA COULDN'T MOVE. Though she imagined she made quite an interesting picture, she couldn't even bring herself to care.

She lay there beneath him, wrapped around him, try-

ing to control her ragged breathing. He was having the same problem. Even over the sound of Marvin Gaye's voice singing about "Sexual Healing" through the car stereo speakers she could hear Ken's choppy breaths.

Lying with him, legs splayed, weak and trembling, one bare breast just inches from his mouth, she tried to come to terms with what had happened. Her entire body was sensitized, throbbing with pure electric energy. She felt something like wonder as she realized it was true—for the first time in her life, a man had brought her to orgasm.

It wasn't that she was a complete stranger to orgasms. She'd made friends with her Shower Massage at a young age, just like many other young women with inexperienced boyfriends who never knew exactly where to touch. Not that she'd usually even dated guys long enough to let them progress to any real touching!

But she'd never experienced more than that, never shared the amazing body-rocking sensations with anyone else. Until now. Him.

She couldn't imagine what it was going to be like when they went beyond touching. Though she still quivered from the aftereffects, still shook with the intensity of the pleasure he'd given her, she wanted more. She wanted him buried deep inside her.

Finally able to move, she shifted slightly, tugging him with her. "I think you almost fell off that time," she said, not trying to hide a laugh.

"Slippery seats," he muttered against her neck.

When she slipped one of her thighs between his legs, she found him rock hard against her. "Oh, my."

"Don't move," he bit out. "Just don't move."

She heard something akin to pain in his voice. "Why did you stop?" she asked, knowing the effort it must have taken him to bring her to release without finding any for himself.

"Why did I start?"

"Don't. Please don't apologize; don't try to take it back. I know all about your noble ideas, know you didn't plan to let anything happen between us. But I'm glad. I confess it. Does that make me wicked? A bad person? That I can be glad I'm here with you, like this, feeling these things I've never felt before, when I was supposed to marry someone else this morning?"

He pressed a kiss on her temple, smoothed her hair away from her brow. "You're not a bad person, Pamela. But you're very, very vulnerable. You needed someone to make you feel better and tonight that someone was me."

"*Someone?*" She stiffened beneath him. Was he saying anyone would have done as well? Suddenly angry, Pamela pushed at his chest, slipping out from under him. "That's bullshit," she muttered as she tugged her bra back up, covering her still-sensitive breast.

He sat up, eyeing her warily. Either he was shocked by her language—which she doubted—or he'd noticed the fire of anger in her eyes. "Is that what you think? That I would have let any guy with good hands and a sweet mouth make me feel what you just made me feel?"

"I didn't mean it like that," he said, his tone reasonable, which made her madder.

"Well, how did you mean it then? Do you think I'm so desperate I would've picked up someone on the plane, or Al there in the front seat, just to get my jollies and make me feel better about myself after what Peter did?"

He didn't reply for a moment, and Pamela pushed away from him, hard, shoving at his chest and sliding across the smooth leather seat. She yanked her shirt on over her head, then reached to turn down the speaker, which had moved past Motown and was now playing Madonna's "Like A Virgin."

"Look, last night you were talking about coming out here and finding some stranger to indulge in an affair with."

"You heard that?" she asked in a weak whisper.

He nodded. "All of it."

"Oh." She pushed her hair off her face, trying to deal with all the emotions still coursing through her. "And you believed it to the point that you felt the need to come with me and make sure I didn't go through with it?"

"Something like that," he admitted.

He'd said as much on the plane; it made sense now. "So you are here to stop me from having sex altogether?"

"Right."

"Including with you," she said, hearing the skepticism in her own voice.

"That's the plan."

She thought about it, tilted the tip of her index finger

against her lips, then looked at him out of the corner of her eye. "You'd better keep your day job."

He raised an inquisitive eyebrow.

"I don't think you'd make much of a living making plans for anybody. Because you suck at sticking to them."

"Pamela..."

"Hey, I'm not complaining. You've definitely made this ride more interesting. But if you think that's going to make me forget my idea of a sensual honeymoon with a sexy-enough-to-die-for stranger, you're dead wrong."

He stiffened, leaned closer and said, "Forget it, Pamela. No way in hell are you going to pick up some guy at this resort and shack up with him for a week."

He'd misunderstood. Pamela debated being honest with him. Should she admit she had absolutely no intention of shacking up with anyone but *him* for the next week? By kissing her the way he had, bringing her to the ultimate level of fulfillment without doing much more than touching her, he'd only fueled her certainty. They were going to go all the way to the end of this sexual roller-coaster ride they'd been on since last night. No question about it.

"You going to stop me?" she finally said, hearing the challenge in her tone.

"You bet your sweet ass I am."

"That might take some maneuvering that you're not quite prepared for. It might require some sacrifice on your part."

"Sacrifice?"

She nodded, meeting his eyes, noting his confusion, knowing he never saw it coming. "If you want to make sure I don't end up in someone else's bed...you might just have to keep me in yours."

KEN SOMEHOW MANAGED to avoid either strangling or jumping on Pamela again during the remainder of the drive to the resort. It took a lot of self-control—which really had long since dissipated—to ignore the sultry invitation in her smile. She flirted, cajoled and silently seduced him with each heavy-lidded glance.

He tried talking to her, insisting that she was raw from her breakup, didn't know what she wanted yet. She shrugged and said nothing. But her knowing looks told him she knew he would never be able to *not* make love to her before another day or two had passed.

He also knew she was goading him with her "affair with a stranger" plan. She wouldn't have gone through with it. Okay, he hadn't known her long, but he felt certain he knew her well. She wouldn't have been able to pick up some guy, have mindless sex and then walk away. So her threat—and outrageous solution that he keep her in his bed—had been unnecessary...but definitely effective.

She'd set her sights on him. She wanted him with an intensity matched only by the depth of his desire for her.

Damn, this was getting complicated!

He could only hope that when they arrived at the resort and were surrounded by other people and lots of activities, they'd be able to dilute the sexual tension still

raging between them. There had to be distractions that would somehow get his mind off what he'd been thinking about since the first time he'd seen her in her father's office: being with her, knowing her, kissing her...making love to her for hours.

It was a lucky thing she didn't know how he really felt. If she had any idea that he'd been seriously attracted to her since before they'd ever met, she'd be even more determined. Either that, or she'd never speak to him again because she'd know who he was—and who he worked with!

Ken was mercifully saved from his musings when the car pulled off the highway onto a twisty mountain road. Every hundred feet or so, he was able to spot well-lit signs advertising their destination. The Little Love Nest seemed to have a strong affinity for the color pink. They also appeared to love hearts—judging by the shape of the signs—and nauseatingly cute little bare-ass cupids complete with arrows.

"I am having a very bad feeling about this," he muttered under his breath as they rounded the final bend and saw the resort in all its glory.

"Oh, boy," Pamela whispered when she saw it too.

The building was impressive. Sprawling, three stories, with columns, balconies and balustrades lining the front facade. It stood at the foot of a steep hillside, facing the lake. Ken imagined that in the light of day the vista would be tremendous.

"Nice view," Pamela offered weakly.

Yeah. Nice view. Which was required when the building itself was painted a hideously awful shade of

pink that hurt the eyes. It was like someone had poured a mountain of melted raspberry sherbet over the stucco, then trimmed it with dark red strips of licorice. "All we need are Hansel and Gretel to tell us if the witch is home," Ken muttered.

The floodlights on the front lawn illuminated small groups of topiaries, cut into heart and cupid shapes. Ken thought he saw a swan dozing near a small pond, which was framed by three vine-covered gazebos. A romantic swing, the perfect size for two, hung from a towering tree. They passed a small wishing well and Ken was able to make out a sign on it, which read, Wishes Cost A Kiss. Wishes That Come True Cost A Thousand Kisses.

He rolled his eyes and grimaced. The whole place was so cheesily romantic he found himself wishing he'd grabbed an airsick bag from the plane!

A woman stood at the bottom of the front steps, obviously waiting to greet them. As the car pulled to a stop, she opened Ken's door. "Welcome to The Little Love Nest. We're so pleased you've decided to share the most special vacation you'll ever enjoy right here with us."

Ken stepped out of the car, getting a good look at the woman under the lights, and watched Pamela to gauge her reaction as she did the same. Probably in her early sixties, their hostess wore a white spandex jumpsuit, trimmed with pink rosebuds at each cuff and around the neck. High spike-heeled shoes gave her a few extra inches of height. Somehow, in spite of her age, she managed to carry off the ensemble. "I'm Miss Mona, the owner of this establishment," she said, her voice a

husky purr, "and I am here to make certain you have the most sensual and deliciously erotic time of your lives."

Sensual? Deliciously erotic? Oh, hell!

"Believe me, I'm an expert in male-female relationships, having been in the field all my life. And what I've created here is the perfect atmosphere for newly married couples to kick off their lives together with a veritable explosion of delight."

"In the field? Are you a marriage counselor?" Pamela asked.

The woman gave a light laugh. "Oh, no, no, my experience has been much more *hands-on*, you could say. I've owned establishments like this in the past, but they were for couples who were, uh, less *committed* to each other than my clientele here."

Ken suddenly understood what she was talking about. Pamela still looked confused. He hoped she didn't ask any more questions. In case his suspicions were correct, he didn't really think he wanted Miss Mona talking about her days in the bordello business.

"Al will bring your bags, let me show you to your rooms. Tomorrow is soon enough for the full tour."

They fell into step behind Miss Mona, Pamela looking around wide-eyed as they entered the hotel. The place was quiet, eerily so. Ken didn't even spot anyone working behind the check-in desk.

"More swans," Ken muttered, noticing two of the birds reclining near a huge fountain that dominated the center of the courtyard-type lobby. Faux Grecian statues of well-endowed naked men and buxom women lined the fountain, spilling water from plaster

urns...not to mention bodily orifices. Ken just shook his head. Then he saw the statuary lining the hallway past the fountain.

"Oh, my goodness," he heard Pamela whisper as she paused to stare goggle-eyed at a statue depicting a naked couple making love. The pose was a little too familiar—with the man's mouth on the woman's breast, and her head thrown back in ecstasy as she kept her legs tightly wrapped around him. "They're..."

If she said it, he thought he just might have to punch a hole in the wall. Grabbing her arm, he tugged her along, nearly causing her to stumble, but not caring. The very last thing he needed was for Miss-I-Need-It-Now to get any more ideas!

His own steps slowed when he saw the next statue standing in a discreet alcove set into the wall of the corridor. This one showed a couple engaged in *oral* activities. *Simultaneous* oral activities.

There was no dragging Pamela past it.

"Oh, my gosh, are they doing what I think they're doing?"

"Can we please go to our room?" Ken bit out between tightly clenched teeth, wondering how she managed to make him even hotter with this innocent act than she had on the plane with her blatant suggestiveness.

"How can her back arch that far?"

"It's a statue, Pamela."

"But is it possible?"

Miss Mona paused in front of them, watching over her shoulder in amusement.

"Pamela, please," Ken muttered.

"I mean, that looks painful!"

"Oh, my dear, this *is* going to be a special honeymoon," the hostess said. "And don't worry, you're tall."

Pamela gave her a puzzled expression. "Tall?"

Miss Mona gave her a nod and a mysterious smile. She met Ken's eye, raising one brow as if to ask if he knew what she was talking about. Hell, yes, he knew what she was talking about! As soon as Pamela had stopped to gawk at the statue he'd had a mental image of just how perfectly matched their bodies were for certain intimacies.

Ken mumbled a curse word under his breath. When he finally managed to get Pamela moving again, he sent up a silent prayer that there would be no more statuary between them and their room. No such luck. But at least she didn't start asking too many questions about the next one. She gave it one shocked stare, obviously recognizing what the couple—both on all fours—were doing, and walked on.

Miss Mona finally stopped a few feet before they reached another statue alcove, leading Ken to think that maybe his luck was changing. He didn't know if he could handle another blatantly sexual exhibition, nor Pamela's reaction to it!

"Are you ready?" Miss Mona asked, pausing dramatically with one hand on the doorknob. Ken nearly had a heart attack on the spot when he noticed their room number. *Sixty-nine? Could things get any worse?*

"I am *so* ready," Pamela said, her voice shaking.

Yeah, Ken was *so* ready too. So ready to get the hell out of here and hightail it back to Miami before all his

good intentions fled and he showed Pamela what Miss Mona had meant about her being "tall." *Yes, they'd fit together very well.* She damn sure wouldn't have to arch her back too far if they got a little oral.

Thrusting that numbingly erotic mental image out of his brain, he watched as their hostess opened the door to their room.

"Ah, ah," Miss Mona said as Pamela moved past him. "Haven't you forgotten something?" They both stared. "Isn't it customary for the groom to carry the bride across the threshold?"

The woman obviously wasn't going to take no for an answer. Gritting his teeth, Ken grabbed Pamela and picked her up, ignoring her start of surprise. For such a tall woman, she didn't weigh much. He willed himself not to notice how perfectly she fit in his arms.

"Much better," Mona said with a nod.

The woman reached around the door to flip on the light. Ken paused to force a surreal sense of calm to descend as he prepared for whatever he was going to find in their suite. Then he stepped inside. It was a good thing he'd paused to prepare himself. "It's a bordello," he muttered, standing just inside the door with Pamela still in his arms.

The pink cupids and hearts were gone. All the sickeningly sweet romantic trappings had faded away just past the lobby. Here, in this room, the atmosphere screamed one thing: raw, sexual need. He could only wonder what Miss Mona was thinking as she watched the two of them staring around the place, their eyes wide, their mouths hanging open.

"I'll leave you two alone," she said with a pleased,

knowing smile. Before she left, Al arrived with their luggage, placed it inside the room, and followed Miss Mona out without saying a word.

The click of the door echoed loudly in the silence, reminding Ken of the firing of a starter's pistol. *Let the games begin!* After all, that's what this room was entirely about.

Games. Adult games. Erotic, sexual games.

From the rich burgundy carpeting to the heavy golden drapes on the windows, the suite was bathed in deep sensuous color. Lying before a huge double-sided fireplace, a thick, white rug provided a splash of brightness. It was, of course, the perfect size for two. He couldn't stop a mental picture of Pamela's thick dark hair against that white rug, knowing how much she'd enjoy the sensuality of her naked skin against the soft faux fur. Shaking off the image, he continued to look around.

Next to the rug rose a circular staircase. Ken slowly allowed his gaze to travel up it. The steps wound around a tall champagne-glass shaped bathtub.

Bubbles and firelight. Mood music and rich colors. Erotic paintings on the walls.

Yes, things had definitely gotten worse.

Then he spied the chaise lounge, complete with velvet ropes discreetly draped across the curved headrest, and visualized the possibilities of *that* particular piece of furniture.

Mental images of cold showers and wrinkled old people getting it on were not stopping his body's reaction. He kept holding Pamela in his arms, knowing if he

let her down she'd be *sure* to notice his physical response.

Besides, she was too busy taking in every inch of the room, with her mouth hanging open, to demand that he release her.

"Guess I'm going to get to look at that after all," she said softly. He followed her gaze. A huge hardcover edition of the *Kama Sutra* stood prominently on one of the side tables, right next to a room service menu, which was opened to a page displaying the various sex toys for sale in the gift shop.

They both continued to look around, their eyes falling almost in unison on the sensuously draped bed. The sensuously draped *round* bed. Right below the mirrored ceiling.

Pamela finally looked up at him, her face flushed. "Wow."

Ken muttered, "Welcome to the best little whorehouse in Tahoe."

A seductive smile curled across her lips. "Ken, remember that platonic honeymoon idea?" Her arms tightened around his neck and she pressed closer until he could feel the jut of her pointed nipples against his chest.

He nodded warily. "I remember."

"Sorry to tell you this, darling. But you are *totally* screwed."

7

AFTER HER audacious proclamation, Ken dropped her to her feet. Grabbing his suitcase, he marched across the room and tossed it in a corner. "I'm taking a shower," he growled as he grabbed some clean clothes.

"Want me to scrub your back?" she offered, laughing throatily as he glared at her from across the dimly lit suite.

Once he was gone, Pamela began exploring the room in earnest. There was no question that this was a rather *unusual* honeymoon resort.

There was no television, though she noticed a sign saying that TV's and VCR's could be requested, along with a complete stock of erotic movies. "No, thanks," she said aloud, dropping the card back onto the table.

The brochure of special amenities offered by the hotel was certainly interesting. Massages. Herbal wraps. Naked Jell-O Twister in a rubber-floored room. "Might have to try that one."

Mirrors graced every wall. Heady, musky incense was provided on a bedside table. Outside was a very private covered patio, with screens laced with fragrant vines that made it seem like a completely secluded forest grove. A two-person spa stood in one corner. It looked warm and inviting, particularly in the cool night

air. A sign beside it read Due To The Delicate Balance Of Moisturizing Oils, No Clothing Of Any Type Is Allowed In The Spa.

"Convenient," she said with a grin, hoping she was going to be soothing some aching muscles in that hot water before too many days had passed. She hoped she had some *unusual* aches—from muscles that hadn't been given a very vigorous workout thus far in her virginal life.

The bed fascinated her. She'd never in her life seen a round bed, didn't even know such things were made. But somehow Madame Mona—she imagined the title madame suited her—had found one. When she pulled back the crushed velvet burgundy bedspread, trying to figure out how on earth one would find bedding to fit, she immediately noticed the black satin sheets. "Slippery," she mused, her mind filling with delicious images of rolling around on the bed. Naked. And definitely *not* alone.

Okay, Pamela, you got him here. Now it's time to put your money where your mouth is. And your body where your mouth wants to be!

Knowing she couldn't count on Ken remaining in the shower much longer, she grabbed her suitcase and dug through it until she found the nightie she was looking for. Black leather wouldn't be quite as dramatic next to the black sheets, though she imagined it would be quite interesting another night, perhaps against the backdrop of the thick white rug in front of the fireplace. Tonight, however, white would do the trick.

By the time she heard the shower turn off, she'd

brushed her hair, touched up her makeup, donned the so-sheer-it-was-nearly-invisible nightgown, and somehow managed not to throw up in terror.

She wouldn't have to *do* anything, would she? He was a guy. He was dying for her—she knew that much. Just seeing her like this, would he need any further incentive to forget his silly ideas of a platonic relationship? She hoped she wouldn't have to talk him into it, for heaven's sake. Frankly, Pamela didn't know if her ego could take it.

No, they couldn't talk about it. Either he would see her, want her, act on it, or she was going to throw her hands up in surrender and go to sleep.

She waited, standing beside the bed, hardly breathing as she wondered which it was going to be.

KEN SHOWERED for as long as possible, leaning against the white and black tiles and letting an ice-cold stream of water subdue the raging hormones he'd been dealing with for hours.

"Let her be asleep," he muttered under his breath. "She has *got* to be asleep."

Finally, when he knew he was on the verge of hypothermia, he got out, toweled off and grabbed the clean sweatpants he'd brought in from his suitcase. Hopefully, Pamela would be dressed in a similar fashion! After all, she barely knew him. She was probably suddenly feeling very uncertain and uncomfortable, and would back off the seduction routine now that he was in a position to call her bluff. At least, so he hoped. So he prayed.

When he walked out of the frigid bathroom into the suite, and saw her standing beside the bed, bathed in the golden glow of a dozen candles she'd lit around the room, he knew heaven had not heard his prayers.

The nightgown didn't cover her, it merely floated around her. Wispy. Sheer. Seductive and inviting. As sinful as only the color white could be when draping the form of a beautiful woman.

The tiny spaghetti straps barely held the top up over her breasts, and he saw her dark, tight nipples only a centimeter below the fabric's edge. Remembering the taste of her, his breathing slowed, his heartbeat increased.

The silky material gathered tightly at her waist, then fell in sleek undulating folds to the floor. But there were no sides. At the sight of her bare hip, her long, slim legs, the dark patch of hair at the top of her thighs, Ken almost gave in. He almost reached for her, almost pulled her to the bed. He almost buried himself so deep inside her body that he didn't know if he'd ever find his way out again.

Sanity intruded. "You. Get that off." He pointed toward the gown.

A slow, knowing smile curled across her lips. "My, my, so much for foreplay," she murmured as she reached to tug one minuscule strap off a shoulder.

"No! I mean, put something else on!"

"Oh, I intend to. There's something I very much want on me."

"Clothes," he managed to hiss. "I meant other clothes."

"So you prefer the black leather after all?"

"Only if it's a belt so I can spank you with it," he muttered under his breath.

Her head cocked back and her eyes widened in innocent misunderstanding. "Now who's the kinky one?"

"Pamela..."

She leaned forward, dropping to the bed on hands and knees. He had to close his eyes as she began to crawl toward him, the gown gapping away from her breasts and her hips. He remembered the last statue in the hall. Knew she remembered, too.

"You've got to be exhausted," he said hoarsely. *Get that look off your face—I am not going to do this!*

"You, too. So come to bed," she purred.

"Come on, Pamela," he finally managed to say, trying hard to sound reasonable and not on the verge of carnal meltdown. "You're overwhelmed, emotionally, physically. Go to sleep, okay? Take a big, huge T-shirt out of my suitcase, change into it and just go to sleep."

Please. Please just go to sleep before I climb on there with you, grab your hips and drive you into the headboard!

Did she see him shaking? Did she notice that the elastic waistband was no longer needed to hold his sweatpants up? There was no way in the universe they'd be able to fall down, considering that the record-setting hard-on he'd finally managed to subdue in the frigid shower was back with a vengeance.

"You don't want me?" It wasn't a question. It was a verbal challenge. She'd crossed the width of the strangely shaped bed and reached his side. Rising to

her knees, she managed to slide her silk-covered form against every inch of his bare skin, from waist to shoulder, as sinuous and sensual as a cat. "You're *sure* you don't want to do this?"

What are you freakin' insane?! Hell yes...do it! a mental voice screamed.

Then her hands moved across his skin, cool, fleeting, building the fire. "I've been wanting to touch you since the minute we met," she said with a sigh. She dropped her head back, closed her eyes, smiling as she continued to drive him mad with her smooth, pale hands.

She moved her touch lower, sliding the back of her fingers down across the front of his pants, letting out a groan of pleasure at finding him so hard for her. That needy sigh, accompanied by a shudder that ran through her long, curvy body, brought him to the brink—and very nearly over it.

"Let me," she whispered, sliding her hand into the waistband of his sweatpants and moving her body lower to nibble on his chest, his stomach. Then she scraped her teeth along the edge of his sweatpants, making him shake.

Then she was *there*—breathing hotly through the fabric, cupping him with her hands as she teased him with her mouth, much as he'd done to her in the car.

"Let me give you some of what you gave me," she said with a throaty purr as she began pushing the waistband down, her sweet, wet lips curved into a sultry smile that promised pleasure beyond description.

He would have. He was that gone, that powerless as he looked down at her, watching her dark hair against

his stomach, needing her—her kiss, her touch, oh, damn, her mouth!

Then came the knock. And reality.

"Room service."

Pamela had never wanted to let out such a scream of frustration as the one she choked on when Ken pulled away from her and turned toward the door. "No!"

He groaned. "No is right."

Then he walked away. At least his legs were shaky—she saw him grab the back of the chaise lounge to steady himself as he passed on his way to answer the door. She threw herself down on the bed, lying on her stomach, shaking her head back and forth. So close! She'd been so close—and so had he!

Hearing mumbled voices, she listened as Ken thanked someone, then watched as he turned around carrying a bottle of champagne and two glasses. She saw the uncomfortable look on his face and knew what he was thinking. If he offered her a drink instead of the sex she was dying for, she might just have to crack the bottle over his head.

"Champagne. Compliments of Miss Mona," he said, still standing across the room by the door. "Good timing."

She snorted in disgust. Reality, in the guise of what appeared to be a bottle of Dom Perignon, had shaken him from his sensual lethargy.

"Why don't you leave it right there?" she asked, rising to her knees on the bed, knowing it was useless but not quite willing to give up yet.

He couldn't have missed the heady invitation in her eyes.

"Uh, actually, I think I'm going to take a shower."

"You already *took* one!"

"I think I need another one." He bit each word out from between clenched teeth.

"You are a coward, Ken McBain!" she called as he walked toward the bathroom. "And since you just took a half-hour shower, I hope you run out of hot water!"

He paused, his hand on the doorknob, and looked over his shoulder. "What on earth makes you think I used any hot water the *first* time?"

When he entered the bathroom, he slammed the door behind him with such force that a painting—depicting a couple in a position Pamela doubted was humanly possible—fell right off the wall.

Rolling over, she punched the mattress, cursed the champagne bearer and wished to heaven she'd gotten to the shower first. She could definitely use some strong jets right about now!

"That's it, Ken McBain. You have lost out. The Pamela express has passed you by and is heading on down the tracks," she muttered as she yanked off the stupid white negligee and went over to dig her own T-shirt out of her suitcase. She didn't want anything of his touching her body.

Well, that was a big, fat lie. She wanted every inch of *him* touching her body. Forsaking that—as he obviously had—she wasn't in the mood for any T-shirt substitute!

As she changed, kicking the sexy nightgown under the bed in disgust, she grew more and more angry.

What was with her lately? Dammit, she was no door-mat. Peter didn't want her as much as he'd wanted her father's money? Well, to heck with him. Ken wanted her but wouldn't take her? Well, to heck with him, too!

She wasn't going to beg. She wasn't going to try any more seductions that left her shaking and empty and so horny she wanted to pull her own hair out.

And she was going to tell him so—right now. Then she was going to demand that he get out of the bathroom so she could take her own shower! Or else go out on the patio and see if that damn whirlpool had seat jets!

Marching across the room, she pushed the bathroom door open and stepped inside, her eyes immediately going toward the double-size shower. It was huge, obviously built for two, with shower heads at head and waist level, plus a sturdy-looking bench seat that extended from one side to the other near the back wall. That made her angrier.

Reaching for the handle, she yanked open the misty glass door. "You just lost your best chance, mister. I'm through. Finished. Don't ever expect me to try to seduce you again."

He stood frozen, staring at her, his face a picture of sexual torment. Pamela's tirade ended as her breath exited her lungs and her last thought flew from her mind.

"Oh, my," she whispered, unable to look away.

His body was perfect. She had already seen his beautiful bare torso, complete with a light matting of black chest hair into which she'd wanted to bury her fingers. Earlier she'd longed to have a chance to nibble his thick

arms, and press more hot kisses against that flat stomach so rippled with muscles.

Now she saw the rest of him—the lean hips, the long, powerful legs, and, oh, the *rest* of him.

He was fully aroused. Thick, heavy, hard. Pamela's legs went weak thinking of him, of that part of him, inside her.

Would he really fit? "Ken..."

"Ever learn how to knock?" he asked, his voice a low, husky drawl. She began shivering, from the air moistened by the cold jetting water, from the liquid desire pooling between her legs with hot, wet insistence.

She finally raised her eyes to his. "I am through playing games," she said, hearing a slight quiver in her own voice. "I know what I want. I know *who* I want."

He listened but said nothing.

"I want *you*. Ken McBain. The man who found me on the beach. The man who offered me his coat. The man who took my gown away so I wouldn't burn it. The man who showed up on that plane so he could be certain I didn't get myself hurt anymore." Her voice quivered and softened. "The man whose whispers go from my ears right through my body and make me *crazy*."

"Pam..."

"Shh," she said, holding up a hand, palm out. "I'm not a little girl. I'm not someone you need to protect. I'm someone who's about to walk out of your life because I truly can't handle this game you're playing."

"Game?" he asked, his voice low, his eyes narrowing.

She nodded. "You want me so bad you can barely walk. But instead, you'll...how did you say it? *Ease the*

pain all alone. Well, maybe I need someone to help me ease my pain," she gave a bitter laugh, knowing no shower jets were ever going to make her feel what Ken could with just a whisper.

"I want that someone to be *you*. No one else. For no other reason than that for the first time in my life I know what it's like to be out of my mind wanting a man's hands on me. *Your* hands. *Your* lips. Every part of *you*, Ken. But I can't stand any more of this back and forth. Your nobility is killing me."

He wasn't looking terribly noble now. Actually he was looking terribly magnificent. She crossed her arms, holding them tightly against her body as another shiver of need coursed through her. "So take me. Or leave me. But don't expect me to ask you again."

Ken braced one hand on the tile wall and reached the other toward the spigot to turn the temperature from cold to hot. The last of his resistance dissipated under the warmth of the jetting water and the sweet need in her voice.

Leave her? He didn't think he was *ever* going to be able to leave her.

He'd been able to resist her on the plane and in the car. Been able to somehow walk away in spite of how she'd looked in her white nightgown.

But he could not hold back against the look in her eyes now. Simple, dignified honesty and heady desire combined to cast away all his doubt.

"Grab one of those, would you?" he said, nodding toward a basketful of condoms on the bathroom counter. She didn't appear any more surprised to see them in

this place than he had been. Her eyes widened in understanding as she did what he asked.

Slipping one hand across her hip, he pulled her into the shower with him, bringing her tightly into his arms. Catching her mouth in a kiss that held up every bit of pent-up longing he'd ever felt for her, he was barely cognizant of her moan of pleasure. He only knew he had to have her. Had to be in her. Now. For as long as he could keep her. For as long as it lasted.

"Please, Ken," she said on a moan as she tugged her T-shirt off over her head and tossed it to the shower floor. Then she stood before him, dripping, wearing only a tiny pair of white nylon underwear that did nothing to hide the dark curls he'd been wanting to touch since he'd seen her in that nightgown. "Please don't make me wait anymore," she said softly, so softly, her voice floating over him like a caress.

He couldn't wait if his life depended on it. Taking a single pleasureful moment to move his mouth to her breast, he sucked one warm nipple between his lips. Then he pushed the tiny nylon underwear off her hips and down to the floor. Encircling her waist with his hands, he pushed her against the tiled shower wall.

"Yes," she said with a drawn-out sigh. One slim thigh rose along the outside of his legs as she leaned back, her jutting breasts irresistible. He bent for another taste, stroking her fullness, lifting it in his hand, sucking and giving her tiny love bites until she started to shake with need.

He wanted to do everything with her.

But not now. Now he just needed to be inside her.

They'd had over twenty-four hours of foreplay and if he didn't feel her wrapped around him soon, he knew he was going to erupt all over the floor of the shower like some teenage kid.

Just because he was ready, though, didn't mean for certain that she was. He had to touch her, had to make sure. Slipping his hand down her back, he caressed her hip. He felt her shudder in reaction as she lifted her leg higher. Her parted thighs invited him on and she pressed back against his hand, taunting him with the slickness of her skin, the curve of her buttocks.

Bending to kiss the hot skin at her nape, he pulled her closer, higher. Then he slipped his finger between the backs of her taut thighs, liking how she hissed, loving how she rocked against his hand and pleaded, low and incoherent.

Her flesh was swollen, wet, and his fingers sunk into her easily, causing them both to moan.

"I need...please, Ken, now!" she ordered.

He didn't need any further encouragement, pausing only to tear open one of the condom packets and sheathe himself. She reached to help, but he grabbed both of her hands in one of his and lifted them high above her head, knowing if she touched him he might just lose his mind.

She squirmed against the wall, arching her back, thrusting her breasts toward him and he couldn't resist. He kissed one perfect dark nipple, then the other, and she shuddered and whimpered, twisting her body beneath his mouth.

"Now, please, Ken. Please take me now," she urged.

She hooked her leg behind his knee, tilted farther, rubbed herself against him. She was wet everywhere. Hot, wet, completely ready. And he simply couldn't wait.

Releasing her hands, he picked her up. He wrapped both of her thighs around his hips, pressed her back into the wall, and pulled her closer, nudging her dark curls apart with his erection. Catching her mouth with his in another breath-stealing kiss, he pushed into her.

She hissed when he entered her, but kept her arms wrapped in a death grip around his shoulders.

"Tight," he muttered, not believing how good she felt, how wet, warm, and unbelievably *tight*. He wanted to go slow for her, wanted to slide into her inch by inch, but his body was urging him to plunge in, make her his, make her scream and then make her come over and over again.

Pamela must have sensed his restraint. She pushed against him, tightened her legs, grabbed his hair with both hands and caught his mouth in a hot, carnal kiss. "Now," she ordered against his lips as she pressed frantic kisses against his face. "Now."

He couldn't wait. Ken drove home with a hard thrust and brought their bodies as close together as it was possible for two adults to be. He was so deep inside her he could feel her flesh spasming against him as shudders wracked through her body. He didn't move at first, just savored the wet heat, wondered if he'd ever experienced anything even close to the physical pleasure engulfing him now—and knew he hadn't.

"Yes," Pamela whispered, kissing the side of his neck

and keeping her face buried there. She clung to him, feeling tears in her eyes as she acknowledged that it had finally happened. He was inside her, completely inside her body.

There were no fireworks, no instant orgasmic explosions. In fact it was awkward. She felt stretched, a little uncomfortable. But she also felt so close to him. Cherished. And so deliciously filled. She didn't want him to stop, didn't want it to end.

He drew back from her, and Pamela pulled his face closer, keeping her own buried against his neck, not wanting him to see her tears. He kissed her neck, slid his tongue along her collarbone, gave one tantalizing nip to her shoulder. The water continued to pound on them, warm and steady, and slowly Pamela felt her body relax, her skin stretch and accept.

His kisses helped. He moved lower, tasting, sipping of her, starting those crazy sweet love bites on her breast. The pain continued to fade and she felt herself growing more restless. Wanting more. Wanting what was next.

As if sensing her anxiousness, Ken slowly pulled back, then slid into her again. She sucked in a breath, a little scared, a lot excited. She wiggled her behind against his hands, saw how her every movement affected him. Tentatively squeezing him deep inside, she loved how his eyes flew open and a groan escaped his lips.

He stared down at her, a ragged smile on his handsome face. "You keep doing that and I can't guarantee this is going to last much longer."

She smiled and did it again.

"Witch," he muttered.

Stepping toward the back of the shower, Ken lowered one of her legs until her foot rested on the bench seat. She'd wondered, when she first saw it, why it was connected only to the sides of the shower, not to the back. Now, seeing the possibilities, she thought she understood. It would be very easy to sit with her legs on either side. A thrill of excitement went through her as she thought of straddling him, being in control.

He slowly drew almost all the way out of her, and Pamela leaned back, keeping her eyes closed as the water continued to pelt them. Then he stopped. Didn't move. Didn't plunge into her as she'd expected.

Opening her eyes, she saw Ken staring down at her upraised thigh. His eyes were narrowed, and he slowly shook his head. As he lifted his gaze to her face, she saw his confusion and realized he'd seen flecks of red on her skin.

"Tell me this wasn't your first time."

She said nothing.

After a few seconds, when he saw she wasn't going to deny it, he pulled his body completely out of hers, let go of the one leg he still held around his hips, and stepped back. "You're a virgin?"

"Not anymore," she whispered.

He groaned. "Why didn't you tell me?"

"Does it matter?"

"Yes, it matters. Hell, Pamela, I sure would have gone about this a different way if I knew you'd never done it before!"

She raised a challenging brow. "Gone about this a different way? Like no way at all?"

"So you didn't tell me because you knew I wouldn't make love to you if I knew you were a virgin?" She remained silent, daring him to tell the truth. Finally, he ran a hand over his brow and said, "You're probably right." He gave a heavy sigh and leaned on the opposite wall of the shower. "Damn."

"Don't. Please, don't feel whatever it is you're feeling. Don't say anything to try to explain it away or pacify me. I wanted this. I wanted this with you. Now. Tonight."

Staring at her, he reached out to brush some wet strands of hair away from her brow. With one thumb, he wiped moisture away from the corner of her eye and smiled at her tenderly. "I know. I'm sorry, sweetheart. I'm so sorry I hurt you."

She bit her lip, feeling tears rise again at his tenderness, wondering how on earth a man so big, so handsome and strong, could know exactly what to say to leave her weak-kneed and quivering. "I'm all right."

Reaching for a washcloth that hung on a rack behind them, he soaked it, then gently pushed her toward the bench. "Let me take care of you," he whispered.

Pamela let him lower her to the bench, twisting her body so her back rested against the shower wall. He lifted one of her thighs, parting her, exposing her. Pamela watched, feeling the excitement rise again as he knelt on the floor of the shower in front of her.

"So sorry," he whispered as he took the cloth and gently, tenderly, washed away the small amount of

blood from her skin. Then the cloth was gone, there was no barrier between the warmth of his hand and her own achingly tender flesh.

A moan escaped her lips as he touched her. He slid his fingers through the slick folds of her body and expertly stroked her right where she needed his touch most. "Yes," she whispered, closing her eyes as she gave in to sensation.

He built the heat again, not merely with his hands, but with his mouth. Ken pressed kiss after kiss on her arms, her neck, her lips. Then he moved lower, paying lavish attention to her breasts, sucking a nipple deep into his mouth just as he slid one finger deep into her body.

She jerked up, thrust against his hand, restless and wanting more. He knew. Kept stroking, kept kissing. Moved lower. And then his mouth was there, sweetly tasting her.

"Oh, please," she muttered hoarsely when she felt his tongue slide into her.

He didn't stop. Drawing her thighs farther apart, he used his mouth and his hands to bring her to the edge, bring her to a quivering mass of sensation.

But it wasn't quite enough.

"I need you inside me when you make this happen again," she whispered, her voice thick and demanding. "Please, don't make me fall alone this time."

He didn't hesitate. As he rose to stand next to her, Pamela saw that he was still as thick and erect as before, and her mouth went dry. She wanted him inside her when he made her explode.

She pulled him down so he sat facing her, both of them straddling the bench. Instinct told her what to do and his eyes darkened as she moved over him.

"Take your time, sweetheart," he whispered as he cupped her face. "You are in control here."

That thought thrilled her. In control. Of this luscious, caring man. For a few minutes, anyway, he was giving her the power to do what she wanted, take what she needed.

She needed everything.

Moving closer, she slid her thighs over his and pushed him into a reclining position on the bench. Then she slid up his wet body, kissing his chest, nibbling on his neck and finally catching his mouth with her own. "I'm in control," she whispered against his lips.

Then she lowered herself onto his erection, noting how smooth it was, how his caresses had made her so wet he slid into her with ease.

He groaned as she engulfed him. Pamela closed her eyes, taking him deeper until he was fully inside her. She remained still, noting that there was no pain this time. Still the fullness, but now only pleasure. Then she began to move, to ride him, sighing with every stroke.

Ken held her hips and moved below her, matching her pace. Their movements grew more frenzied until Pamela began to gasp with the intensity of it all. Then Ken moved his hands to her stomach. And lower.

He parted her curls with his fingers, and began to stroke her, matching each sweet flick of his finger to each strong thrust inside her. He brought her to the

precipice again until she was shuddering with the pleasure of it.

And this time, when he brought her to that shattering convulsion of pure physical energy, he fell right along with her.

AT SOME POINT, after their bodies had become pruney, Ken turned off the shower and carried Pamela out of it. He toweled her off with one of the thick, fluffy bath sheets, then wrapped her in it while he dried himself.

She didn't even try to speak. A languorous smile curled across those gorgeous lips and her eyes were heavy—tired, but filled with pleasure. He liked that he put that look on her face. Correction, he *loved* that he put that look on her face.

Her every movement was lethargic, boneless and sated. When he picked her up to carry her into the bedroom, she curled against him as if they were two halves of a whole.

Tomorrow reality would intrude. Somehow he'd have to deal with the guilt that was already wracking his brain. He'd made love to her, a beautiful, needy virgin he hardly knew. A woman who'd been set to marry someone else. A woman who didn't even know why he was really here with her.

There was no changing what had already happened, however, and plenty of time to worry about it later. So, for tonight, he simply allowed himself the pleasure of holding her sweet, sleeping body in his arms.

8

KEN WOKE UP the next morning certain the person who'd invented the round bed was a sadist. Probably worked for the Spanish Inquisition in another life.

"Pure torture," he mumbled, knowing he'd never had a more restless night.

There was no way to sleep apart on the round monstrosity. If he moved away from Pamela toward his side of the bed, either his feet fell off at one end, or his head the other. The insidious thing was designed to keep two people firmly in the middle, spooning, or wrapped around one another, all night long. Which was probably fine and dandy for most people staying in this room.

But not for him.

"Damn," he whispered as streaks of light began to sift in from the heavily draped windows. Though it was barely seven, there was no sense remaining in bed. He wouldn't be able to go back to sleep. Nothing *else* was going to happen either.

During the night, when he'd rolled over several times to find Pamela's naked body curled up against every inch of his own, he'd been sorely tempted to kiss her awake. He wanted to show her what languorous late-night lovemaking could be like. Wanted to take his

time, caress and stroke every inch of her, to make up for what had happened earlier.

Her first time *ever* making love and he'd shoved her up against the wall of a shower. *Stupid, McBain!* Exciting, yes. Amazingly fulfilling, too. Still stupid, though.

She deserved more. So much more. And he was dying to give it to her. But he wouldn't.

Ken gently moved her arm from across his chest and slid out from under the silky black sheets, wondering how many people had rolled over and fallen onto the floor in this place. Behind him, Pamela sighed and snuggled deeper under the covers, probably missing his body heat. He had to force himself to turn away and pull on some clothes. Then he escaped to the patio.

Though the middle of summer, compared to Miami, where he'd been living for the past month, the morning mountain air was downright chilly. The climate was even cooler than at home in northern Virginia. He thought about going back inside but needed to be alone, to think about what to do next.

Go back to bed.

No, that was out. He couldn't get close to her again, as much as he wanted to.

There was no longer any question of staying away from her in order to protect his own emotions. Yes, he'd used his failed relationship with Liz as a mental barrier, sticking by his mantra of "no women on the rebound" even when he knew Pamela was nothing like his ex. Somehow, however, that concern no longer applied. Frankly, having spent hours talking to her yesterday

and the night before, he was having serious doubts about how much Pamela had cared for Peter anyway.

"Pamela and Peter." He stretched out in a lounge chair, shielded from view all around by the thick vine-covered trellis encircling the patio. "How could you even stand the sound of your names together?" he mused aloud.

No, he truly didn't believe, deep down, that Pamela was mourning the end of her engagement. Nor did he think less of her for that. He'd seen the confusion in her eyes more than once when she'd discussed Peter's whirlwind courtship, which had seemed too good to be true. She'd seemed anything but devastated. Embarrassed? Yes. Humiliated? That, too. But her heart wasn't broken. Not by a long shot.

Ken no longer felt he had to keep her at arm's length until she got over Peter. She didn't have to get over him. She'd never been *under* him, emotionally or physically.

"Thank God," he muttered, still glad to know she'd never completely given herself over to her ex.

Or to any man. Until last night. With him.

And that was exactly the problem. It had been bad enough when he feared she was a vulnerable woman on the rebound. Now he knew the truth. Okay, maybe she was emotionally accessible. But the fact that she had never been involved in a physical relationship increased the stakes a hundredfold.

Standing to peer through the thick hedge, he caught a glimpse of the morning sunlight shimmering on the surface of the lake at the bottom of the hill, and his breath caught. He wanted to share it with her. The

morning. The sunrise. Many more nights like last night. Lots and lots of showers.

He'd been half gone on the woman before they'd ever met. Now...well, now he felt something like a cliff diver who'd leaped off a mountainside in Hawaii into the cool blue waters of the Pacific—over his head and sinking fast.

If he wanted any kind of chance at all of letting things develop between them, he had to be honest with her. He wasn't much better than Peter in that regard. No, he didn't work directly for her father, wasn't using her as a stepping-stone. Ken's contract with Bradford Investments to update the entire corporate software system had been signed and sealed before Ken ever knew Pamela Bradford existed.

That didn't change the fact that he worked *with* her father. That he'd seen what had happened at the hotel. That her father was the one who'd pleaded with him to go with her to Tahoe.

Once she found out the truth, she wouldn't stay around for more than the ninety seconds it would take her to slap his face. The only chance he had of making her stick around for longer was to show her how good they could be together—and not just physically. That was a given. They'd proven it last night—proven it beyond all doubt—to the point where he got the shakes even thinking about it. Being with her. Being *in* her. How her eyes darkened and her lips parted when he touched her. That sweet little sound she made in the back of her throat—a tiny helpless cry as her body shook in orgasm. *Snap out of it!*

He had to get past the physical and make her know him, trust him, so that when he told her the truth maybe it could be a beginning for them...rather than the end.

Until then, he couldn't make love to her again, though that might be the death of him. The guilt wouldn't let him. Not while he wasn't being honest with her.

That was the plan at least. But like she'd said in the car last night...lately he really sucked at sticking to his own plans.

PAMELA AWOKE to an empty bed and at first wondered if last night had been a dream. Had she and Ken really made heated love in the shower? Had he truly held her in his arms until she fell asleep? Rolling toward the other side of the bed, she caught the warm, masculine scent on the other pillow and hugged it close. *Not a dream.*

Getting out of bed, she retrieved the silky robe that matched the white nightie she'd worn briefly the night before. It did nothing to keep out the chill but was all she had. Then she went looking for Ken. "Good morning," she said when she found him sitting on the patio.

He gave her a lazy smile and held out a hand for her to join him. "Good morning yourself." He scooted over, making room for her on the lounge chair. She sat down and curled up against him, resting her arm across his chest and her head in the crook of his arm, finding warmth in his embrace.

"You okay this morning?"

She heard the real question he was asking and knew

he was still thinking about the fact that she'd been a virgin until a few hours ago. "I'm fine." Sliding one thigh over both of his, she curled closer and pressed a soft kiss against his neck. "Better than fine."

"Good," he said softly as he stroked one hand up and down her back, making her shiver. Not from cold. She was feeling very warm, verging on hot.

"So what do you want to do today, on this first official day of our honeymoon?" Ken asked.

"Stay in bed?" When he didn't respond, she asked warily, "Ken, what's wrong?" Pulling away to look up at him, she noticed a slight frown on his face. "Please don't tell me you're having regrets."

"No regrets, Pam," he assured her. "You?"

"Not on your life."

He chuckled at the obvious vehemence in her voice.

"So what's the problem? Why can't we go back inside, order pancakes with whipped cream for breakfast, then save the whipped cream for later instead?" She wagged her eyebrows suggestively.

A rueful smile crossed his lips. "Pamela, I don't regret last night. But I still don't think we should be jumping into anything here. Maybe we should slow down, take our time."

She wasn't prepared for that. "Isn't that kind of like shutting the barn door after the mare already got out and partied all night with the stallion down in the far pasture?"

"You and your horse analogies," he muttered.

"Ya big stud." He laughed and hugged her closer to

his chest, but she noticed the laughter didn't quite reach his eyes. "Why? What's holding us back?"

He took a deep breath and looked like he was about to speak. Then he sighed and glanced away.

"Ken?"

"I just don't think either one of us is ready for this," he finally said.

"Speak for yourself."

"Okay, I will," he said, his tone serious. "I spent three months last year getting involved with a woman who, it turned out, was definitely *not* over her ex. And I've sworn that I'd never put myself in that situation again."

Pamela didn't quite know what to say. Part of her ached for him, part of her wanted to slap whoever the woman was who'd dared to hurt him. Another part was relieved. *Her idiocy...my gain!*

"I'm sorry you were hurt."

He shrugged and shook his head. "Not hurt, at least not long-term. I hadn't lost my head—or my heart. And Liz ended up with the right guy, although there's no denying my pride was hurt."

"I know a little something about that one."

He squeezed her shoulders. "Mostly it was a wake-up call. It definitely made me more cautious about the women I date. No one wants to be used."

She heard his next thought, though it remained unspoken. *You of all people should understand that.*

True. She did understand that. Remembering the devastation she'd felt when she'd learned Peter had merely been using her to get ahead with her father, Pamela tilted her head down and bit her bottom lip.

Since the minute she'd met Ken on the beach she'd been selfish. First wanting him to ease the hurt of Peter's actions, then wanting Ken to help her explore all the pent-up passion buried deep inside her. She hadn't taken a moment to think about his feelings, though he'd voiced them several times.

"I've been pretty awful," she whispered.

"That's not true—"

She cut him off. "It is. You're right. I used you, Ken. You told me how you felt and I completely ignored what you wanted and thought only of myself."

She'd been as selfish as his ex—to this wonderful man who'd been nothing but good to her since the moment they'd met. It wasn't a pleasant realization.

"You're right," she murmured. "You're right, and I'm sorry."

"Don't be sorry. Hey, maybe last night had to happen. The two of us have been striking sparks off each other since the minute we met."

She couldn't contain a smile. "True."

"So maybe we needed to act on them," he continued, "to douse the fire before we sent this whole place up in flames."

"And now that we've doused the fire, is it completely out?"

He must have heard the uncertainty in her tone because he tipped her chin up with one finger and looked deeply into her eyes. "Not by a long shot, Pamela. Just banked for a little while. I know it could burn out of control in a heartbeat, if we let it."

"And you don't want to let it?" It wasn't really a question.

"Do you?"

"Do you want me to be honest, or do you want me to lie?"

He laughed out loud and shook his head. "You are a joy, Pamela Bradford, do you know that? I don't think I've ever known a woman as relentlessly honest and forthright as you."

"Okay, so being totally honest...yes, I'd love to make you burn, Ken McBain."

His eyes darkened, his jaw clenched. Beneath her fingers, she felt his heart begin to pound in his chest and knew that if she pushed him, she could change his mind.

But where would that leave her? Satisfied in the short term—very satisfied, if last night was anything to go on. Yet what about later? She sensed this man could mean much more to her than a week of all-out passion and erotic indulgence. A week was nothing. Because somehow, some way, she sensed he could mean a lifetime of happily ever afters.

Crazy, given their short-term relationship. Crazy, perhaps, but true. She knew to the depths of her heart, in a way she'd never been completely certain of with Peter, that in Ken she might have found someone with whom she could fall head over heels in love. She'd known it from the very beginning. From the moment he'd handed her his coat.

"But I also understand that we've gone a little too fast," she admitted softly, confused still by the emo-

tional floodgate coursing through her mind. How could she be so sure? After the fiasco with Peter, she should have been questioning her own judgment, but she wasn't.

Somehow, deep down, she knew something very special was happening with her and Ken. Like all good things, that was worth waiting for. "I'm willing to take it down a notch, if you are. After all, we have a week here."

"And I'm sure there's a lot to do."

"Oh, absolutely. Horseback riding, kayaking, naked Jell-O Twister."

He choked out a laugh. "You're kidding me."

"Nope. They have an entire game menu."

"I think I missed that," he said. Almost looking afraid to ask, he said, "What kind of games?"

"I didn't go down the entire list. But it appears they have lots of role-playing games, complete with costumes."

A grin quirked his lips. "See anything interesting?"

"You could be a Texas Ranger and get those spurs you were talking about."

"I don't think I'll need them."

"No, you definitely didn't fall off," she said with a giggle.

"Ha."

"Okay, at least *I* didn't fall off. They also have lots of board games."

"Board games? Sure, we'll sit around and play Clue for six days."

She cast him a sideways glance through her lowered

lashes. "Mr. McBain did it in the shower with his very big lead pipe."

He responded by tickling her until she almost fell off the lounge chair. "No, no," she squealed, trying to wiggle away. "No fair. I'm way too ticklish!"

He relented and tugged her back down to lie across his chest. "Anyone ever tell you you've got a wicked tongue, Pamela Bradford?"

"Wouldn't you like to know?" she said, giving him a sultry, moist-lipped grin.

His eyes darkened. "Oh, yeah," he replied, the heat factor intensifying. Then he sighed. "But not today."

"Right," she agreed, pretending she wasn't disappointed.

"Anyway I should have said 'smart mouth,'" he continued. "I bet you drove your parents crazy when you were growing up."

She nodded and cuddled closer, her body seeking his warmth. "Pretty much. My mother says 'why' was the first word in my vocabulary. Quickly followed by 'no.'"

"My mother taught my sisters that 'no' should be the first word in *every* girl's vocabulary."

She grinned. "How many?"

"Three. All younger."

"Bet they loved having your friends around."

"It took almost a whole year for me to figure out why all my buddies on the football team always wanted to hang out at my house after practice, and never anyone else's."

She curled her fingers around his neck and gave a wistful sigh. "Sounds wonderful."

"How about you?"

"Only child. Which I always regretted. I guess that's why I like working with kids now."

"You talked about your job on the plane," he said, smoothing back a lock of hair from her brow. "You work with troubled teens, right?"

She nodded. "At a recreation and counseling center in downtown Miami. That smart mouth comes in handy sometimes. It's hard to know the right thing to say to even your normal, all-American teenager. Trying to help the kinds of kids I meet on a daily basis, I have to be able to talk on their level, to give as good as I get, to make sure they know I'm not going to put up with any of their bull. Then, slowly, they'll start to open up to me."

He tucked her hair behind her ear and pressed a soft kiss on the top of her head. "I'm sure they're crazy about you."

"Not usually," she said with a rueful grin. "Not at first, anyway. It generally takes a while to break through. I always try to find some common ground. Being able to kick some butt on the basketball court helps. I sometimes play the kids for talking points."

He shook his head. "Not following."

"We'll play one-on-one," she explained. "For every shot I get on them, they've got to open up, to talk, to listen. It's a way of maintaining a dialogue with some teenagers who would otherwise never dream of interacting with an adult."

"Smart idea."

"You've got to use what you've got. My friend La-

Vyrle gets the girls to talk to her by doing their nails. The longer the acrylic, the longer the conversation."

"Sounds like you're a good team."

They lay in the lounge chair as the sun rose higher, casting warmth inside the shadowed, sheltered patio. Pamela didn't know when the last time was that she'd spent so much time just talking to a man. Certainly she'd talked to Peter. But now, when she looked back on it, she acknowledged that he'd merely done a lot of nodding and agreeing with whatever she said. Ken didn't. He baited her, teased her, challenged her. They got into a ten-minute debate on whether or not Michael Jordan could stage yet another comeback—which she was firmly convinced could happen.

He opened up, too. Making her smile when he reminisced about his sisters, making her frown when he told her about his ex-girlfriend. He discussed his company and, for the first time, she realized how successful a man he was. He and the half-dozen software engineers he employed worked on the kind of contracts that had to be raking in some big bucks. Very big. And yet he'd still walked away from it to come on a spur-of-the-moment trip with her. To protect her. To get to know her.

To make her fall in love with him.

Well, maybe that hadn't been what he'd set out to do. But she had a feeling it might be the end result.

She found warmth, solace and strength in his arms. She loved his laugh, loved the way his silver eyes sparkled in the sunlight. Their laughter eventually led to

kisses and slow, tender caresses. Nothing more, even though she knew they both wanted more.

Finally, as if knowing if they remained wrapped around each other exchanging warm, lazy, open-mouthed kisses, they'd go further than either of them meant to, he moved away from her. "You hungry? It's almost lunchtime."

"Starved," she said. "I hope they serve more than oysters and champagne in this place."

He nodded. "Food. And if it's all oysters and champagne, we'll find the game room and go for some of that Jell-O."

THE RESORT, as it turned out, had a fantastic restaurant. In keeping with the rest of The Little Love Nest, the tables in the small, intimate café were secluded, screened with palms and white trellises. The décor wasn't nearly as garish as in other parts of the hotel, and the food was to die for. Pamela ate like she hadn't eaten in days, leaning over to steal some of the seasoned fries from Ken's plate after she'd polished off her own.

They saw a few other couples passing by and seated at tables around the room. The clientele provided an interesting opportunity for people-watching. "Now, do you think they're celebrating their fiftieth wedding anniversary, or are they really on their honeymoon?" Pamela gave a surreptitious nod toward an elderly couple, neither of whom probably stood taller than five feet. They were utterly engrossed in one another and she saw the man lean over to pinch the woman's thigh more than once during their lunch.

"Probably swingers. Shameless strangers on a hot, sexual honeymoon together. Like us," Ken replied with a grin.

"Now there's a picture," she said with a rueful grin. "But that's not us anymore, remember? Unless you want to change the game plan." Pamela heard a teeny hopeful note in her own voice and quickly shook her head. "No, no, I didn't mean that."

He shrugged. "Yes, you did."

"Okay, I did," she said as she lifted a glass of water to her lips and sipped from it.

Before he could reply, they were distracted by the arrival of another couple. A young man in a black leather jacket and his obviously pregnant dining companion took a seat at the next table, and immediately began making out over the bread basket. Pamela had to bite the inside of her cheek to prevent a laugh as the two of them exchanged loud, slurpy kisses and called each other nauseatingly cute pet names.

A mischievous twinkle shone in Ken's eyes as he asked, "Ready to go honey bunny?"

"You bet, cootchie-pie."

THEY NEVER DID make it to the game room that first day, instead finding things to do outside. Though he'd never been on a horse before, Ken let Pamela talk him into going for a guided ride up some of the trails near the resort. He hadn't wanted to, mainly because he was a city boy and didn't at all understand the appeal of getting his nuts crushed on the back of a bouncy animal. But

her grin and the sparkle in her brown eyes were so engaging, he relented.

The hotel even provided a picnic snack, complete with champagne and caviar. Their guide presented the basket to them in a secluded wooded area an hour into the ride. The man told them he'd give them time to eat in private, and left.

"I think we're supposed to believe he's really gone and get naked," Pamela said as she passed over the caviar and nibbled on some crackers.

"Bet he had a video camera in that saddle bag."

"And I'll bet he's standing about fifty feet away hiding behind a tree."

"Poor guy. Just his bad luck to get us for his customers today," Ken said.

"Yeah, if only he'd had Mr. and Mrs. Geriatric. They'd probably have given him quite a show."

He grimaced. "I think I've lost my appetite."

"Hey, I think it's wonderful that they're obviously so mad for each other, even if they are pushing one hundred."

"You're right," he conceded. "But it's not exactly something I'd like to visualize."

No, if he was going to visualize anyone rolling around naked on the soft carpet of pine needles and old leaves beneath them, it was he and Pamela. He'd like nothing more than to pull off her clothes, uncovering her pale body in the bright sunlight. Then he'd make love to her for hours under the canopy of trees and glimpses of bright blue, cloudless sky.

It had been a grand total of about six hours since

they'd decided to back off on the physical feelings they had for one another. Six agonizing hours of heightened awareness, reaction to her smile, her laugh, her warm, sweet, citrusy scent and every breath she took.

How in heaven's name was he going to be able to stand days of it? Falling deeper for her, getting caught up in her infectious laugh, liking her more and more...yet not touching her the way he really wanted to? He wasn't a damn saint. He did, however, have a feeling that after a few more days, he was going to be completely insane.

That night they went to Reno and discovered they shared a disinterest in gambling. They lost about thirty bucks between them playing slot machines, grew bored and went to a show instead. Afterward, they discovered a great Thai restaurant, both relieved to finally eat a meal that didn't, in some way, include an aphrodisiac.

They spent the next few days in much the same way. Boating, swimming, hiking or bicycling during the day. Discovering the charm of nearby small towns, with their quaint shopping areas, restaurants and friendly residents. They laughed and held hands, talked endlessly, sometimes kissed with a sweetness that left Pamela breathless and slightly teary-eyed.

By unspoken consent they left the hotel in the evenings. Neither thought they needed any more of the carnal atmosphere at The Little Love Nest just before the uncomfortable moments when they went to bed for the night.

"I'll take the chaise lounge," Pamela said the first

night. Ken had just pulled a pillow and blanket off the round bed and prepared to sleep on the chair.

"I'll be fine," he insisted. "Less chance of falling off this thing than those silk sheets."

She gave him a sultry smile and pointed toward the velvet ropes attached to the chaise. "You could always tie yourself down on that, too."

He glared.

"I'd be happy to help."

Then he threw the pillow across the room at her.

Laughing, she tossed it back and pulled down the covers on the bed. "We could share the bed," Pamela said. "I mean we had a long, busy day. We both know the ground rules. We've gone at least the past twelve hours or so without any serious groping."

He gave her a look that was purely incredulous. "And you really think we could get through the night together in that torture device without anything happening?"

She thought about it, pictured their limbs wrapping around each other in the night, their bodies acting on instinct and suppressed desire, doing what their minds had been denying them all day. "Guess not," she said, her voice barely a whisper.

He slept on the chaise that first night and the two that followed, finally allowing her to insist that he take the bed the fourth night.

And throughout every long, sleepless minute of each long, sleepless hour, Pamela wished she had the nerve to sneak across the room, slide under the covers and co-coon herself in his arms.

It wasn't supposed to be this way. "It's too good to be true," she whispered to herself in the dark as she tried once more to count sheep in a vain effort to find sleep.

This trip was originally supposed to be about sex. It was meant to be a carnal interlude, easily indulged, joyously decadent. Sex with a stranger, fulfillment of every sensual urge, a hot-blooded affair to long remember and never regret.

It wasn't supposed to be about laughter. And friendship. Bright smiles and shared memories. Whispers and entwined fingers. Though she'd sensed she could care for the man, when she'd set out on this trip with him she hadn't imagined she would truly fall in love with him. Even the other morning, when she'd agreed to take the heat down a level and let them get to know each other, she hadn't imagined how helplessly, crazy in love with him she'd be just a few days later.

She was, though. She tried to analyze that love, tried to understand how she could be certain of it, given her history and her relationship with Peter. It was just... there. In the smile that crossed her lips when she said his name, in the pounding of her heart when he took her hand. In the delight she got watching him sleep, the low red embers of the fireplace casting shadows across his body in the bed a few feet away.

She loved being with him, admired his intelligence, loved hearing him talk about his sisters, and his business. Loved debating sports and politics with him. But it was deeper than that. She trusted him, physically, mentally, emotionally. She sensed he would be incapable of hurting her. And she knew deep in her heart that

she would never be able to do anything that would hurt him.

So was that love? Yes. She truly believed it was.

Not that being in love meant she didn't mind sex being out of the picture. On the contrary, the harder she fell for him, the more she wanted him! Late Saturday night had been about pure heat. Maybe love had been blooming somewhere deep inside even then, but it hadn't been much on her mind. Emotion didn't have as much to do with those intoxicating moments in the shower as pure, undiluted lust. And it had been utterly fabulous.

So, with her emotions engaged, how might he make her feel *now*? How deeply might she lose herself in him now that he had her heart as well as her body?

She wanted to find out. Very, very soon.

9

"READY FOR BREAKFAST?"

Pamela had just exited the bathroom and was toweling her hair dry Thursday morning. As usual, they were both up early. She wondered if his night had been as sleepless as hers.

"Gimme ten," she replied.

He nodded, obviously knowing she meant it. Ken had told her more than once how much he admired her nongirliness. If she said she would be ready in ten minutes, she was. He liked that she was opinionated, told her it was refreshing that she went with her gut instincts more than her brain most times.

Peter had never told her that. Actually, no one had ever told her that.

As she finished pulling on some clothes and putting on a little lipstick, her minimum makeup requirement for being seen in public even at 8:00 a.m., the phone rang.

"It's LaVyrle," Ken said after he answered the phone.

She wondered why her coworker would be tracking her down at Lake Tahoe. Knowing LaVyrle would want an explanation as to why a man was answering her phone, Pamela shrugged. "Why don't you go ahead to

the restaurant without me? I'll meet you in a few minutes, okay?"

Nodding his agreement, Ken pressed a quick kiss on her lips. "Coffee, cream no sugar. Fruit plate, wheat toast, one scrambled on the side."

She grinned. "Okay, so I'm predictable. Maybe I'll go for the English Muffin today instead!"

"No, you won't." Ken winked as he left the room, giving her privacy to take the call. She was still smiling at how well he already knew her as she answered.

"Okay, who's the dude?" That was LaVyrle. No beating around the bush.

"Uh, would you believe the bellhop?"

"Uh-uh."

"Waiter."

"Try again."

"A gorgeous hunk of male that I picked up on a beach, talked into coming with me on this trip and have fallen head over heels, madly, passionately in love with?"

A ten-second silence was followed by a bellow of LaVyrle's warm laughter. "I'll take number three."

"Me, too."

Pamela gave LaVyrle a quick rundown of her meeting with Ken, answering her friend's suspicious questions to assure her that, no, Ken was not a psycho serial killer nor a gigolo trying to con her for money. Finally, she convinced her friend that she'd simply had the great, incredible fortune to meet that rarest of breeds: a truly nice guy. A hunky, sexy, kissable, well-endowed adorable guy who loved long, slow kisses and shatter-

ing sex in hot, steamy showers. Not that she actually went into the well-endowed part. Or the sex in the shower part.

But LaVyrle could read between the lines.

"You using protection?"

Pamela didn't take offense, since that was a standard question where the two of them worked. "That's not really necessary, at this particular time, but yes, we did when it was required."

"What do you mean *not* necessary? You having a hot and wild affair or not?"

"Well, yes. But there's no sex involved."

Though LaVyrle dropped the phone, Pamela still heard her shriek of dismay. When the other woman picked up the receiver again, she said, "Tell me you did not end up with another man who doesn't like sex."

A warm smile of memory crossed her lips. "Oh, there's not a doubt in my mind that he likes sex."

He'd have to in order to be so darn good at it!

"Then tell me you didn't end up with another man who's making you doubt yourself. Honey, you have been there, done that and sent back the postcard."

She chuckled. "Don't worry, LaVyrle. There's no question of the attraction, really. There are other, uh, issues. We're slowing it down."

"Well, don't slow down too far, missy. You're coming home in two days."

"I know." A smile crossed her lips as she glanced at the thick, white rug, the tub, the round bed and the mirrors. "It'd be a shame to leave here without really experiencing all this place has to offer."

She hoped she and Ken would have at least a day or two at the end of the trip to take advantage of the possibilities. She knew she wasn't going to be able to go much longer without having him again. And she could tell by the way his dark, heavy-lidded eyes devoured her lately—her lips, her throat, her body—that he couldn't wait either.

"So was there a reason you called this morning? Is everything okay there? You haven't heard from my father, have you?"

"Not a peep here," LaVyrle replied. "Your friend Sue stopped by and asked if we'd heard from you, though. She said your father has phoned her once or twice to ask if you've called. Since Sue knew I'd seen you before you left for your trip, she told him that much, that you were okay and you'd gone out of town for a while. That's it."

"Good."

"Maybe not so good."

"Why not?"

"Well, Peter's been working on Sue, too."

She groaned. "Peter?"

"He's gone to see her, certain she knows where you are. She hasn't told but, you know, that friend of yours has a big ole heart, but not much in the way of backbone."

Pamela thought about it. "Not a huge deal, LaVyrle. Even if Sue told Peter I'd come to Tahoe, he wouldn't be able to find me. He had no idea where we were staying."

"Okay, just wanted to warn ya. So far, it's not a problem, Sue swears she won't tell. But I thought you should

know that the snake's tearin' up Miami looking for you, telling everyone he needs to straighten out the big misunderstanding." LaVyrle snorted in disgust. "I'd like to straighten that boy out—with a tire iron."

Pamela chuckled in spite of herself. Though, thinking about it, she really didn't wish any harm on the man. She felt nothing as she thought about him. Nothing but relief. He'd been a bastard and a louse, but she'd escaped from their relationship unscathed, even the better for it. Because if it hadn't been for Peter, she'd never have met Ken that night on the beach. So, while she wasn't nearly ready to forgive and forget, she didn't feel the need to expend energy in hating him, either.

After chatting with LaVyrle for a few minutes about how things were going at the center, Pamela ended the call and left the room. She took her time walking to the restaurant, pausing along the way for a closer look at some of the statues in the corridor. Ken had hurried her past them every other time they'd walked by.

Damn, before they left this place, she was determined to figure out what Miss Mona had meant when she'd said it was good that Pamela was tall.

As soon as she entered the restaurant, she spotted Ken sitting at a table in a corner. He saw her, stood, waved, then froze.

"Ken!"

Pamela hadn't said his name. Someone directly behind her had. A female someone. Slowly, Pamela turned on her heel and looked at the woman standing there.

"My gosh, Ken, is that you?" the other woman said as

she pushed past Pamela and walked across the restaurant to give Ken a big, friendly hug.

Pamela watched as Ken held himself stiff beneath the woman's embrace. He caught her eye over the blonde's head, and she almost chuckled at the look of horrified helplessness on his face. Okay, so he wasn't entirely glad to see this person. That was a good thing, considering she sure seemed enthusiastic about seeing him!

Taking her time, Pamela crossed the room to join them, studying the newcomer as she approached. She was little. Teeny, bubbly and blond. Just the kind of rah-rah-cheerleader twit Pamela had so disliked in high school. The kind of female who always made Pamela feel huge and Amazonian, who'd always brought curling irons to keep in their gym lockers at school so they could look perfect after an icky, sweaty, nasty old game of softball.

"What a surprise! I was just thinking of you the other day," the woman was saying as Pamela stepped up behind her. "I never expected to run into you *here*, of all places."

"Hello, Liz. Yes, this is a surprise for me, too."

Liz? As in ex-girlfriend Liz? Pamela's teeth clenched even tighter in her jaw. What were the odds they'd run into his ex-girlfriend in this place? There had to be a million other honeymoon resorts in the country. Okay, so maybe The Little Love Nest was showing up in feature ads in the back of every bridal magazine on the planet, but couldn't Liz have chosen the Caribbean? The French Riviera? The moon?

As if it wasn't bad enough that Ken's ex had shown

up here—did she really have to look like the same kind of Kewpie doll cutie that always made Pamela feel huge and bumbling? *Well, doesn't this just stink!*

"Dave and I went around in circles for months planning our wedding. Finally we got tired of it, hopped a flight to Vegas and got married." The woman laughed, the sound grating on Pamela's nerves like nails on a chalkboard. "We'd seen all the ads for this place, found out they had a last-minute cancellation, and came up last night."

"Small world," Ken said weakly as he finally pulled away and disentangled Liz's arm from around his waist. He took a single step back, unable to go farther since he was blocked by the table. Shooting Pamela a look that promised an explanation, he crossed his arms and turned his attention toward his ex.

"So why are *you* here?" Liz asked, completely oblivious to the fact that Pamela was staring down at the top of her head, noting that her dark roots were within a week of needing a color job. "Goodness, Ken, you didn't follow me, did you? I mean, we broke up months and months ago!"

Kewpie-face might not have noticed, her being so low to the ground and all, but Pamela definitely saw Ken roll his eyes. His lips twitched, and she wondered at his good humor, considering the woman had implied he was stalking her.

"Liz, I've been here since Saturday. I had no idea you'd turn up. Congratulations on your marriage. Where's the groom?"

"He's making arrangements for a hiking trip this afternoon."

For the first time, Pamela heard a bit of the chirpy good humor fade from the other woman's voice.

"Still a real outdoorsman, hm?" Ken asked, his tone sympathetic.

"That's why we had such a problem planning the wedding," the woman admitted. "Couldn't interfere with hunting, skiing or boating seasons. Anyway, why are you here? Are you doing a software project for the hotel?"

"What makes you think I'm not here on my honeymoon?"

The woman laughed again. "Oh, you big silly, I know you haven't been dating anyone since me. I bump into Diana occasionally. She keeps me updated."

Diana? Oh, one of his sisters. Well, maybe Ken could afford to be magnanimous, amused in the face of her sweetly spoken put-downs, but Pamela had had quite enough.

"Darling, I'm *so* sorry I kept you waiting. It took forever to shower and get all that body paint off from last night," Pamela said as she stepped around Ken's ex. "That Cherry Jubilee flavor might have been tasty, but it leaves bright red stains in the most *embarrassing* places!" Ignoring his widened eyes, she slipped her arms around his neck and planted a long, wet kiss on his parted lips.

She sort of forgot about Liz at that point. So did Ken, apparently. Because for several long moments he kissed

her senseless, coaxing needy shivers out of her with his lips and the slow, sweet strokes of his tongue.

Oh, it had been too long since he'd kissed her like this! They'd both tried so hard to avoid physical contact in the past few days. That had done nothing but banked the fire! Time certainly hadn't doused it. Because now, in his arms, with his mouth on hers, she found herself jolted back to that steamy shower, feeling the water pelt her, smelling his hot desire, experiencing his kisses clear down to her toes.

"Ahem."

She was the one who ended the kiss. It hurt, but she did it, knowing they had an audience. Not that most of the patrons in The Little Love Nest's restaurant were going to be too shocked by a couple kissing. She and Ken had seen even more intimate moments, particularly between the eight-and-a-half-months pregnant bride and her Rebel-Without-a-Clue hubby, who seemed to have made it their mission to play tonsil hockey in public at least ten times an hour.

"Sorry," Pamela whispered against Ken's lips as she finally ended the kiss. "I couldn't resist."

His breathing was almost as ragged as hers, his eyes glazed. "Forgiven."

"I've missed you," she said softly, knowing he understood what she meant. *I've missed this.*

"Me, too."

Before she could ask what they were going to do about it, Liz interrupted. "Are you going to introduce me?"

Pamela finally glanced at the blonde, who watched

them with a speculative look on her face. "Hello, I'm Pamela." She did not offer any last name. She certainly wasn't going to introduce herself as Ken's wife. Not when this woman was obviously a friend of Ken's family. She could only imagine the kind of turmoil that would cause if word got back to his sisters or parents that he'd gotten married without telling anyone!

"How nice to meet you," the woman said, sounding confused but not malicious. "I didn't realize Ken was *with* someone."

Pamela heard the woman's real meaning—she didn't realize Ken was *seeing* someone—but feigned ignorance. "It'd be kind of a bummer to stay here alone," Pamela commented. She heard Ken's chuckle.

"So, the two of you are, uh..."

"Vacationing," Ken supplied.

Pamela could tell the woman was dying to ask more questions. She waited, expectantly, but didn't pry. Pamela had to give her credit for that. Okay, so she wasn't a complete bimbo. She did have a little tact.

"Well, I'm very happy to meet you," Liz finally said when she realized no explanation was forthcoming. "You're lucky—Ken's an amazing man."

She again caught a note of wistfulness in the other woman's voice and wondered at it. Perhaps she had regrets? From the sound of things, her husband wasn't exactly the type to sweep a girl off her feet with grand romantic gestures—unless they involved camping gear or fishing poles.

But Ken...well, Ken was the kind of man who'd cover a woman with his jacket. Kiss her within an inch of her

life. Tuck her into bed alone. Rescue a bound-for-the-fireplace wedding gown. Go on a honeymoon with a stranger. Make love to her until she nearly fainted with pleasure. Then gently insist they get to know each other better.

That was Ken. *Her* Ken. She curled closer to him, sliding her hand around his waist and resting her head on his shoulder. When he pressed a soft kiss to her temple, she sighed with pleasure. Not for Liz's benefit. No, the pleasure was all Pamela's.

The other woman watched for a moment, then glanced away.

"Well, I'd better see what's holding up my husband," Liz said as she turned to leave. Just then, a good-looking, beefy blond man entered the room and waved. Liz smiled and waved back.

"Here he is now! I have been wanting him to meet you," she told Ken.

Pamela heard Ken's nearly inaudible groan. Great. First the ex, now the guy the ex had dumped him for. She wished they'd had breakfast in their room. Actually, she wished they'd had breakfast in bed. The same bed. Together.

"Tomorrow," she murmured, deciding right then and there that the platonic part of their honeymoon was *over*.

Four days. She'd given him four days, more than half their vacation. She'd suppressed the desires and the needs, given them the chance to get to know one another. Now she was certain, one hundred percent convinced that she was crazy about the guy, would have

been crazy about him even if Peter Weiss had never been in her life. This was no rebound. This was not about wounded feelings, nor about a virgin dying to be deflowered.

This was about her, Pamela the woman, wanting to be with Ken, the man she'd fallen in love with. Period. And it was about damn time she let him know that, too. But first...there was the ex to deal with.

If Dave knew Liz had been dating Ken the previous year, he certainly didn't appear to hold a grudge as he joined them and extended his hand in greeting. Somehow Liz managed to get them all to agree to have breakfast together. It should have been a miserably uncomfortable meal, but Liz actually proved to be a nice, blond Kewpie doll. Okay, she wasn't someone Pamela would normally have wanted for a friend, but she was funny and warm. She seemed genuinely happy that Ken had moved on with his life, though Pamela couldn't help noticing how closely she watched every time Ken took Pamela's hand or pushed an errant lock of hair off her brow.

Dave was a blustery, big-hearted, down-to-earth guy. He and Liz had apparently been high-school sweethearts. While he obviously adored her, it was equally apparent he was not exactly skilled in romance. Here he was on his honeymoon discussing the best fishing tackle, the weight room, and inviting Ken and Pamela to come along on their five-hour hike that afternoon.

"No, thanks ever so much, Dave, but I think I feel a bit of a cold coming on. I'm counting on Ken to *take* care of me today. In our room."

She heard him suck in a breath and knew he was fully aware of what she was really saying.

"You will take care of me, darling, won't you?" she asked, glancing at Ken. He met her stare, held it, incinerated it. Then he smiled that slow grin and looked away without saying a word. But his hand tightened in hers, his body shifted closer.

He hadn't been touching her any more during breakfast than he had been in the past few days, but every brush of his fingers sent shivers down her spine. She couldn't stop thinking of that kiss. The awareness was back, thrumming between them, as vibrant and alive now as it had been Saturday. He felt it too; she could tell. His posture was relaxed, but his body was tense and alert next to hers. When she shifted on the bench seat and brushed her hip against his, he hissed and jerked upward.

Oh, boy.

"Besides," Pamela continued, knowing Ken was listening intently, "Ken and I only have a few more days before we have to return to Florida. And I think I'd rather stay here and experience more of the hotel's *amenities.*"

"Sounds lovely," Liz said softly.

"Nah, boring," Dave said with a laugh. "We can laze around at home. We're on vacation—we've gotta go do stuff!" Liz's sigh turned into a smile when her husband threw his arm around her shoulder and tugged her close to nuzzle the top of her head.

As they finished breakfast and lingered over coffee, Pamela began itching to get away. She wanted nothing

more than to return to their room so she could see if Ken was as ready to end this platonic situation as she was. "You know, I just remembered I have to make a call. Sweetie, why don't you finish your coffee and come back to the room when you're done?"

The other two were oblivious to the undercurrents running between them, but Ken's eyes brightened and a slow smile crossed his lips. "Okay. But, uh, after you finish your phone call, there's something we need to talk about."

Giving him a distracted nod, she leaned over to press a quick kiss on his cheek. She had to give him credit. He didn't so much as wince when she nibbled his earlobe.

She wasn't quite so controlled. When he responded by slipping his hand between her thighs, she gasped. He smiled as he gently caressed the bare skin along the hem of her khaki shorts. Finally noticing the other couple watching them curiously, she stood up on shaky legs.

"It was great meeting you. Maybe we'll see you again before we leave," she said, trying to sound normal, trying to hide the fact that Ken's touch had stolen every thought from her brain and the breath from her lungs.

"Oh, sure," Dave replied. "Let's plan on doing lots of things together. It's more fun with another couple. You know, when your cold's gone."

"We'll see," she replied. Then she gave Ken a purely evil look. "We might be pretty *tied up* these next few days."

This time she got a reaction. Ken cocked his head to the side and narrowed his eyes, obviously remember-

ing the velvet ropes in their room. ''Yes, absolutely. Though I do find I've developed a real desire to do some *riding*.''

As her legs turned to jelly, Pamela grabbed the back of the chair she'd just vacated. She wondered if anyone noticed the wobble in her walk as she exited the restaurant. She didn't really care. Nor did she care that a passing maid watched as she danced a little jig around one of the cheesy sex statues in the lobby, then dashed toward their room like she was doing a full court press.

Minutes. She only had a few minutes until Ken arrived. She wanted to be ready. Everything had to be just right.

KEN DIDN'T WANT another cup of coffee. He could have left when Pamela did. He certainly didn't feel the need to sit here and make small talk with Liz and Dave. No, sitting across from his ex-girlfriend and her new husband wasn't the worst breakfast he'd ever had, but he couldn't say it was high up on his list of fun things to do on one's honeymoon. Not that he was really on his honeymoon.

So no, it wasn't the company, nor was it the coffee that kept him from returning to their room. It wasn't Pamela's phone call, either, which he suspected she'd made up.

He was stalling. Somehow, he felt like a kid preparing for the last week of school, with final exams to get through before a long, glorious summer filled with decadent freedom.

Only, he didn't have a final exam, he had a conver-

sation to get through. An explanation. An apology. Hopefully it wouldn't be a *final* in any way. Then, if he was very lucky, they could proceed to the long, glorious part.

The past four days had been delightful, filled with laughter and smiles, deep conversations and a growing sense of emotion. Definitely emotion. And he wanted more of that. Much, much more. Beyond this week, beyond this month. Enough to last a lifetime.

Ken tried to work up some anger at himself for doing exactly what he'd sworn he would not do—falling in love with Pamela Bradford. Too late.

As he'd suspected the first time he'd seen her, the first time her father had spoken of her, he found Pamela Bradford irresistible. She was funny and tough. Sexy and vulnerable. Thoughtful and outrageous. A beguiling blend of temptress and virgin.

He'd planned to wait until they returned to Florida to tell her the truth about why he'd come with her—that he'd been at the bachelor party and her father had asked him to look after her. Now, however, he knew he couldn't wait. Because he sensed he wasn't alone in his feelings. Pamela had fallen, too. Fallen damn hard. He felt sure she knew him enough, trusted him enough, that she would believe him when he told her how sorry he was for not being honest with her. The longer he delayed, the worse he felt.

Truthfully, he also didn't think he could wait until they were back in Miami to make love to her again. Not now. Not when he knew how he felt about her, and was certain she returned his feelings.

So, the time had come to wipe the slate clean—which was why he lingered over an additional cup of coffee he didn't want, chatted with an ex-girlfriend who bored him, and listened to Dave's explanation of the benefits of ice fishing to a man's prostate.

He hadn't noticed that an hour had passed until a waiter handed him a note. "From your room," the young man whispered.

Ken glanced at it, noted Pamela's writing, and opened the page.

Come *now* unless you want me to start without you.

His hand shook and he dropped the paper, watching it flutter to the floor. Time to go.

Quickly saying goodbye to Liz and Dave, he made his way out of the restaurant. He didn't know what to expect. The virgin? The seductress? The basketball nut? He was still asking himself that question when he entered their room, pushed the door closed behind him, and spotted her.

The vamp.

"Black leather," he murmured, his voice caressing the words as his gaze traveled over every inch of her.

She lay on the thick white rug, bathed in the morning sunlight that spilled forth from the half-opened patio blinds. Her hair was loose, falling in a mass of waves to below her bare shoulders. Her chestnut curls were rich

and vibrant against the rug and the thick fluffy pillows on which she reclined.

When he'd gathered the strength, he dropped his gaze lower. Down the long, smooth column of her neck, the gentle, kissable flesh of her nape. To the soft pale curves of her breasts, pushed temptingly high by the black top she wore. He thought it was called a bustier. One of those Madonna things with leather and metal loops. It cinched tight around her midriff, tighter beneath her full breasts, leaving them exposed almost to the nipples. A shiny black ribbon laced up the front, holding the whole thing together.

He wanted to undo it with his teeth.

He also wanted to explore that tempting strip of skin between the bottom of the bustier and the elastic band holding up the ridiculously tiny black panties she wore.

Her bare legs went on for days, from sweetly curved hips all the way down to a pair of spiked black high heels that adorned her feet. She shifted under his stare, moving restlessly against the fur. He saw her mouth open on a sigh at the physical sensations bombarding her and marveled at Pamela's sensuous nature.

He took a deep breath, shuddering with the effort. "You didn't start without me?" he finally asked as he made his feet move across the room toward her.

She answered in a sultry purr. "Did you want me to?"

That would be lovely to see. Pamela pleasuring herself, touching her body, showing him what she liked. "Another time. Definitely."

She smiled a slow, knowing smile, obviously aware

that his restraint was nearly gone. If she so much as lifted her hair off her bare shoulder he might just lose it then and there.

She held out a hand for him to join her on the rug. "It took you long enough."

He could hardly remember why. Why on earth had he delayed coming here to find her like this? Then he remembered. Their conversation. The big one. He'd completely forgotten it the second he'd spotted her. "I really did want to talk to you." He cleared his throat and tried to focus. "Have a serious talk with you."

She shook her head. "No talking. We've talked enough over the past four days."

"Pamela..."

"Later, Ken. We'll talk later. About anything you want. Right now the only talking I want is you telling me how much you want to be inside me and me telling you that if I don't feel your naked body against mine soon I'm going to go completely insane."

As Pamela rose to her knees in front of him, giving him a clear view right down the top of her minuscule black leather outfit, he gave up all thought of conversation. There was only now, only this. For the first time in his life he was going to make love to a woman he really loved.

Everything else would come later.

She dropped her head back, looked up at him with a smile full of mystery and promise. "Now, *you*, get that off," she said, pointing to his shirt.

Remembering ordering her to do much the same thing Saturday night, Ken grinned. His grin faded as

she reached for his belt buckle. She brushed his hands
aside when he moved to undo it himself, so he pulled
his shirt off instead. He had just dropped it to the floor
as Pamela undid his trousers and pushed them down
his hips. She gave a throaty little sigh of approval as she
trailed her fingers across his erection, which strained
against the front of his tight boxer-briefs.

"As I recall, we were interrupted Saturday night,"
she said huskily. Before he could reply, she'd freed him
from his briefs and moved her sweet wet mouth over
him.

Pamela was acting on instinct and desire, becoming
the sensual person she'd kept buried all her life. Certainly she'd never done *this* before. She worried for an
instant that she'd be clumsy, but could tell by the way
Ken's breath grew choppy and hoarse that she was doing all right. She liked the musky taste of him, the feel of
his hands tangling in her hair, the sounds he made. But
he wouldn't let her go on too long.

"Can't take much of that, sweetheart," he said as he
gently pulled away from her and kicked off the last of
his clothing.

She still knelt below him, certain she'd never seen a
more perfect man, a more beautiful male body. All deliciously hers. Every ounce of pent-up passion and desire she'd ever experienced rushed through her with the
speed and velocity of a freight train. She tingled down
to her fingertips. Like a starving person at a banquet,
she wanted to try it all, sample everything.

Mostly she wanted his mouth. His sweet-talking
mouth. When he dropped to his knees and knelt before

her, catching her lips in a kiss that went on forever, she almost cried at how right it felt.

"I'm in love with you. You know that, don't you?" he said against her lips as he lowered her to the rug.

"I know," she managed to say, through her sighs and her tears and the pounding of her heart. "I'm in love with you, too. I think I started loving you the moment you handed me your jacket that first night on the beach."

"It's crazy," he whispered. "This is exactly what I swore wasn't going to happen. But I've never felt anything was more right in my life."

He moved his mouth lower, pressing hot kisses on the curves of her breasts. But not low enough. She arched her back, offering herself to him. Wanting more.

He took what she offered, tugging at the satiny lace between her breasts with his teeth. Untying her. Exposing her. Then he stared down at her, his eyes getting heavy and dark before he lowered his head again to take one nipple completely in his mouth. He moved lower, pressing kisses across her chest, her belly, paying careful attention to her other breast.

Pamela shrugged the bustier completely off. Running her flat palm across her stomach, she noted the way his lips parted as he watched her touch herself. He couldn't tear his gaze away as she moved her hand lower, brushing the edge of the tiny black panties. The nylon fabric slipped down, revealing the dark curls between her legs. Ken groaned at the sight.

She liked this sense of intimate power, this sensuality

she was able to share with him. She knew she was safe to explore anything. Everything.

Reaching over to the fireplace hearth, she retrieved a small bottle. "I found these in the bathroom," she said with a purr. "This mountain air has dried out my skin. Would you mind?"

The hotel had provided a variety of scented oils, guaranteed perfect for sensuous massage. She could think of nothing more pleasureful or sensuous than the feel of Ken's hands touching every inch of her. As she fully intended to do to him.

Giving him an innocent smile, she handed him the plastic bottle, then settled back on the rug. She stretched against the faux fur, the softness bringing heightened awareness to her already electrified skin.

"It would be my pleasure," he said throatily as he took the bottle and opened the cap. He lifted it and sniffed. "Nice."

"It's called 'New Orleans Evening.' Plumeria. And the tiniest bit of sandalwood. It says that's an aphrodisiac."

"I don't think we need it," Ken said as he poured a small amount into his hands and lowered the bottle to the floor.

Then he moved his hands to her shoulders, smoothing the liquid over her skin. The warmth of his fingers and the slickness of the light oil made his every movement a seductive delight. His hands didn't so much touch as glide across her, heightening her anticipation, bringing her nerve endings roaring to life. The sweet scent filled her brain and made her think of lying in a

garden courtyard, under an endless navy-blue night sky, surrounded by the fragrance of heady flowers and by warmth. And by love.

His hands touched every inch of her, making her want to weep with the pleasure of sensation. Looking up at his passion-filled face, surrounded by his scent, the jagged sound of her own breathing and the rapid staccato beat of her heart, she felt more in tune to her senses than she ever had in her life.

"I could touch you for days."

"I want you inside me," she said hoarsely. He slipped his hand between her thighs, pulling the panties off and tossing them aside. Stroking her expertly, he slid one finger into her body as he lowered his mouth to hers for another of those deep, wet kisses. When he flicked the pad of his thumb higher, against her most sensitive spot, she cried out, her hips bucking up in response. "Now, Ken, please."

He grabbed one of the condoms she'd left near the massage oil, put it on and moved over her. Her body was still slick; not greasy, but moist and fragrant. Open and ready for him. She cupped his face in her hands as he slid into her, filling her up. No pain this time. Just sweet, gentle possession.

If Saturday night had been about elemental need and soul-consuming lust, this was about all the other aspects of lovemaking. Desire, yes. Physical arousal, oh, absolutely. But there was such tenderness, such passion. Each of them moved together like two parts of the same person, anticipating each stroke, tailoring every movement to suit one another. Climbing higher, build-

ing the pleasure, until Pamela simply had to cry out with it.

He caught her cries with his lips, then increased the pace. Pamela wrapped her legs around him, not even noticing at first when he pushed one leg higher, so it slid over his shoulder. When he plunged back into her, she gasped at how deep he was. She caught his movements, met them, danced to the crazy-sweet rhythm only the two of them could hear.

And as they came together, she knew this man was a part of her in every way. Not for a week. Not for a fling or a mindless sexual release. This man was her soul mate.

She knew it. In her heart she'd always known it.

"SHOW ME WHAT Miss Mona meant when she said it's good that I'm tall."

If Ken hadn't already lowered Pamela into the hot bubbly water of the whirlpool, he might have dropped her. Instead, he shook his head and eased himself in next to her. "We'd drown."

She splashed water in his face, then curled her wet naked body up against his. "I meant later."

Though it had only been a half hour since they'd made love on the white rug inside, he found himself reacting physically to her suggestion. No question, Pamela was open to exploring her own sexuality, and he looked forward to showing her what she wanted to know. He'd been thinking of exactly that when she'd taken him into her mouth earlier. The thought made him groan. "Later."

Pamela shifted on the seat, dropping lower until her shoulders were covered, obviously enjoying the heat and the bubbles swirling around them in the fragrant spa. "I can hardly wait," she murmured. "For everything."

"I think I've created a monster," he said with a chuckle. "I don't know if I'm going to be able to keep up with you."

"You're doing okay so far," she said as she slid closer. When she turned to face him, then moved one thigh across his lap to straddle him, she obviously felt his renewed interest. "I'd say you're doing just fine."

Unable to resist the sweet, sultry challenge in her voice, he slipped his hands into her hair, pulling her closer. Her eyes widened as he caught her mouth in a hot, wet kiss that left them both panting.

"Do you want to go back inside now?" he asked, his voice husky. Though the hot tub was relaxing, he wanted nothing more than to take her to bed and make love to her again.

"This patio is *very* private. I think that's the point— we can do anything we like," she said as she tilted her hips closer.

She was on top of him, her flesh teasing his beneath the water and Ken *so* wanted to slide up into her swollen heat.

"Might be nice to make love in a bed for a change," he said hoarsely. "Besides, we didn't bring anything from inside. For protection."

A tiny pout pulled at her lips. "You're right. But it's just so nice out here. So warm and wet."

He groaned as she wiggled again. She moved closer, taking the tip of his erection into her body, but no more. Bracing her hands on the back of the hot tub behind his head, she held herself just above him. Ken couldn't resist her bare breasts, inches from his mouth, and allowed himself a pleasureful kiss. His body was screaming at him to thrust up into her, filling her completely,

but he resisted. "Pamela, let's take this inside. I want to protect you."

"Have you had many lovers?" she asked, looking down at him with both curiosity and dread.

"That's a helluva question to ask at a time like this," he managed to grit out, holding on to the thin thread of his sanity as she swayed just above him.

"You know I haven't," she prodded. "I'm safe. And I have the feeling you're not the type to play the field, so I suspect you're healthy, too."

He knew what she was getting at. "Don't worry, Pamela, I'm fine. There are, however, other issues. Small, screaming, diaper-wetting ones."

She chuckled, lowered herself a little, drawing a groan from his mouth. "You're killing me," he muttered.

"Don't you like babies?" she asked, her tone growing more serious.

Babies? Their babies? Somehow, while the idea should have left him feeling *deflated*, he felt warmly confident instead. "Yes, sweetheart. I do. But how about we finish the honeymoon, then maybe go on a date or two before we think about naming our children, okay?"

She sighed and lifted herself off him. "All right. You win." She smiled gently. "I'm glad, though."

"About what?"

"That you like children. I do, too."

He knew she was referring to the future. Their future. Their happily ever after future. "We're talking the SUV and the two-point-five here, aren't we?"

She nodded.

"You sure you're ready for that?"

"We can date for the next year and I won't be any more certain than I am right now about my feelings for you." She spoke simply, her words coming from her heart.

Her honest assurance awed him. He remained silent, staring at her, wondering how on earth his life could have changed so miraculously, so fulfillingly, in just a matter of days.

Were there really such things as perfect soul mates? Had he somehow known she was his from the first time he'd seen her? Why else would she have consumed his thoughts, appealed to him so completely, brought out every protective instinct he owned from the moment they'd met?

It was as if something inside had been telling him all along that they were meant to be together. She obviously felt it, too. How rare was that? How many people had the fortune to not only meet their perfect match, but to also understand and recognize the real thing when they stumbled upon it?

"I'll be right back," she said with a flirtatious smile. "Don't you go anywhere."

She stepped out of the hot tub, gloriously naked and glistening in the morning sunlight. Grabbing a fluffy towel off a nearby chair, she wrapped it around her nude body, moving slowly as if she knew he watched.

"You sure you don't want me to come inside, too?" he asked, unable to tear his eyes from the line of her neck and the long strands of dark hair brushing the

curves of her breasts. "We have yet to fool around in that round bed."

She paused, her hand on the patio door handle and raised her index finger to her mouth. Nibbling on it thoughtfully, she finally said, "That's very tempting. But how about later tonight? For now I want to be out here with you, hearing the birds, breathing the cool fresh air. There's something terribly decadent about being outside, naked, in the broad daylight, isn't there? Even if no one could possibly see?"

He nodded his agreement.

"Then again," she said with a grin, "I was practically naked on the beach the night we met."

The night they met. On the beach. He closed his eyes, remembering the conversation they were supposed to have. "Pamela, wait a minute. Before you go inside, before we, uh...well, there's something you should know about the night we met. I want to wipe the slate clean between us."

She paused, waiting.

"That first night, the night of the bachelor party. Well, it wasn't *completely* a coincidence that I found you on the beach," he said.

She raised an eyebrow, then laughed softly. "Well, of course it wasn't, silly."

He froze, wondering if she knew the truth, if she'd known all along.

"It was fate, Ken," she finally continued with a heart-breakingly sweet smile that shot through him with the power and intensity of a lightning bolt.

Her sweetness, trust and unadulterated joy touched

him someplace deep inside. Here he was, about to repay that trust by admitting he'd deceived her, even if it was out of a desire to protect her.

Ken wanted to make it up to her. Wanted to make her understand, even though he, himself, didn't fully comprehend how he could have had such strong feelings for her since before they'd even met. But it was the truth.

"It was more than fate," he finally said. "Do you believe in love at first sight?"

"Of course," she said. "Didn't I tell you that earlier? That's exactly what happened when you handed me your coat."

She bent forward and pressed a sweet kiss on his lips. "Fate." Then she ducked into the room, leaving him alone before he even had a chance to tell her.

Love at first sight and fate. Plus a bachelor party for a guy he couldn't stand with a bunch of other guys who had seen the woman he loved in a G-string and pasties.

It was time to come clean.

PAMELA PAUSED in the bathroom to brush her hair and pull it up off her face before retrieving the condoms. She'd grabbed a handful, mentally laughing at the expression she knew she'd see on his face when he saw the seven foil packets.

She'd stepped out of the bathroom, preparing to go back outside, when she heard a knock on the door. "Oh, great," she murmured, wondering who'd be bothering them, specifically since she'd hung the Do Not Disturb sign on the knob when she came back from breakfast.

The hotel did enjoy bringing little surprises to the rooms, however. Like the champagne that first night, and a decadent chocolate raspberry truffle another evening. Tempted in spite of herself, she called, "Just a minute," then grabbed a pair of Ken's sweatpants and a long T-shirt to pull over her naked body.

It was a good thing, too. Because when she opened the door and saw who stood there, she froze on the spot. If she'd been wearing nothing but a towel, she might have been startled enough to drop the thing!

"Peter?!"

"Hello, darling,"

"You are *not* here. This can't be happening."

"Can I come in?"

"No."

"Pamela, we need to talk, and I'd rather not do it out here in the hallway."

She pushed the door toward his face. "There's nothing to talk about."

He kept his foot between the door and the jamb. "Please give me five minutes."

"I'll give you a broken foot. I can't believe you followed me here."

"How could I not? Knowing you were here alone, heartbroken about our misunderstanding. I had to come, just as soon as I found out where you were."

Misunderstanding? Yeah. Sure. Right. "How did you find out?"

His eyes shifted. "Sue."

She didn't believe him. "Sue couldn't have told you where to find me because she didn't know where we

were supposed to be staying. You're not very good at lying anymore, are you?"

"She told me you came to Tahoe," he admitted. "And I found out where you were staying when I found the brochures for this place." He looked around, peering around the door to the room, his eyes widening when he saw the tub, the rug, the bed. "Thinking of you here, alone, miserable and depressed, I couldn't stand it."

"The brochures? Which brochures would those be? Surely not the brochures in the desk drawer in my apartment?"

Again the eyes went down.

"That's called breaking and entering."

"No, it's called desperation. I had to find out where you were so I could explain everything."

"No, you didn't. What you have to do now is get back on a plane to Miami and never come near me again."

"Pam, baby, I can see how unhappy you are. You're a mess. Moping around in your room, looking like that."

She shouldn't have cared about his opinion, but she still crossed her arms, offended. "Looking like that?"

"You know, like you're so upset you can't even get dressed in the morning. Lying around all day, crying, not seeing anyone. It's not healthy."

"Peter, I'm going to give you one more chance to remove your foot from this door before I scream for someone to come help."

"Don't be silly. I would imagine this place is sound-proofed for screams." He gave her a lecherous look, which she supposed he intended to be sexually titillat-

ing, amusing or charming. She found it faintly disgusting.

"If I scream, it won't be a bellman who comes running. It'll be the guy in my hot tub."

He gave her a patronizing smile. "You don't have to try to save face. I already know what a fool I was to not make you see how I really feel about you. It isn't necessary to try to make me jealous."

Just then the patio door opened. She heard it from behind her, and watched as Peter's eyes widened. "Who's that?"

"The guy in my hot tub," she explained matter-of-factly.

She should probably have felt an instant of satisfaction at the look of stunned dismay on her ex-fiancé's face. Frankly, she didn't care enough about him one way or another to muster up the energy. She just regretted his intrusion, knowing if he hadn't knocked, she and Ken would have been enjoying a delicious daylight interlude right about now.

"What's keeping you, Pamela?" she heard Ken call. Turning, she saw him walk into the room from outside. Naked. Wet. Glistening. Utterly glorious. Then he noticed her standing at the door and cocked his head in confusion. When he spotted Peter, she saw him tense from several feet away.

Peter just looked stunned. He stared at Ken, shock and confusion written all over his face. Pamela had to hide a grin, knowing Ken was the kind of man who made other men feel *small*.

"McBain?" Peter said, his voice barely a whisper. "Ken McBain?"

She didn't understand. Glancing back and forth between them, she watched as Ken grabbed for a towel from the patio and slung it around his hips. Peter still looked dazed.

"What the hell are you doing here with my fiancée?"

"I'm not your fiancée," she retorted mechanically, still not quite following the conversation. These two *knew* each other?

"Pamela, what is he doing here? You're not—you didn't...." he looked around the room again, then at Ken, who still stood just inside the patio door. "Just how long has this been going on? Were you cheating on me with him even before we broke up?" Peter looked more stunned than angry. "I didn't even know you two knew each other!"

Finally, it sunk in. "I didn't know *you* two knew each other, either," she mumbled. Glancing over her shoulder at Ken, she saw a look of pleading on his face. "Ken?"

"Pamela, just shut the door and come back outside so we can talk."

"So you've been here all week?" Peter interrupted, glaring at Ken. "Of course you have. No one's seen you since the night of the party. And Jared obviously knew it. That's why he acted so funny about you being out of the office this week."

Jared? There was no denying the implication. Pamela sucked in a breath, not wanting to believe it. *Ken worked for her father?*

"Tell me it's not true," she whispered.

"Of course it's true," Peter retorted.

"You shut up," Pamela and Ken both snapped at the same time.

"Pamela, I can explain," Ken said. "Just shut the door so we can talk."

Frankly, she was getting a little sick of men telling her they could explain things away. First Peter. Now, oh, God, now Ken. She shook her head, slowly, trying to take it in.

She thought about what Peter had said, still trying to make sense of everything. Ken hadn't been seen since the night of the party. *The party? That* party? "You were there? You saw?"

He gave a single, regretful nod. "Sweetheart, my heart was breaking for you."

"What a crock. You were a wreck and he saw a chance to get into your pants," Peter said with a sneer.

This time, Pamela didn't even give him a warning. She slammed the door, hard, probably crunching a few of his toes, but at least getting rid of him. He pounded on the door a couple of times, then gave up. For all she knew, he might have been waiting right outside, listening, waiting for the argument he must have anticipated.

She couldn't argue. She couldn't muster the energy to tell Ken off, to tell him where to go.

Peter had hurt her.

Ken. Well, Ken had devastated her.

"Pamela, you've got to listen to me."

"I want you to leave me alone," she whispered.

"Pamela, it's not what you think. Yes, I was at the

party. I barely know Peter, or any of the other men who were there. I'd only been in Miami a few weeks. I was leaving as you came in. And once I saw you, saw what happened, I only wanted to help you and make sure you were all right."

He reached for her, trying to take her hand, but she yanked it away and curled her arms tightly around her body. "That's why you conveniently found me on the beach," she said softly, still reeling, feeling the same sense of betrayal she'd felt as she sat inside that stupid cake listening to her fiancé talk about why he was marrying her.

"I just wanted to make sure you got home okay."

"As a favor to my father? Your boss?"

She heard him groan. "It wasn't like that."

"Well, what was it like? Which part do I have wrong? You saw me at the most humiliating, vulnerable moment of my life. You tracked me down and took me home, then came on this trip with me. You made me fall in love with you," her voice broke and he reached for her again. Again she stepped away. "But there's one thing you didn't do. You never once bothered to mention the truth."

"I tried to tell you a little while ago."

"Better a week late than never, huh?"

"I was afraid if I told you sooner, before you got to know and trust me enough to know it *killed* me to be dishonest with you, that you'd lash out and refuse to let me help you."

"Don't you mean I'd refuse to let you into my bed?"

He cursed and ran his hands over his brow and

through his hair, still devastatingly gorgeous in nothing but the white towel, his powerful body tense and sinewy. "Don't you understand I was afraid you were going to come out here and get taken advantage of all over again?"

"Isn't that *exactly* what happened?"

He froze, looking hurt by the accusation, but she didn't relent. "Please just go away."

"Pamela, we can get past this."

She shook her head slowly. "I don't know that we can. I just want you to answer one question for me, Ken. Please, just be honest with me about one thing."

"Anything."

She caught his eye and held it, so he'd understand how important this moment was to her. To them.

"Did my father ask you to come with me on this trip?"

She saw the answer in his eyes long before it crossed his lips. And her heart broke even more, if that was humanly possible.

"Pamela, that's not why I came. He might have asked me, but..."

"Don't say another word to me. I need to be alone right now. Just please go away and let me be by myself for a while, to think about this, to try to absorb it." She was crying now, unable to stop the tears pricking the corners of her eyes. She blinked rapidly, not wanting him to see, just wanting to hold it together long enough to get him to leave her alone with her thoughts.

"Pamela, I'm in love with you," he said, a heartbreakingly tender expression on his face. "You know that.

This doesn't change how we feel about each other. I couldn't be honest with you up front and I so deeply regret that."

She shook her head, so confused and tired and overwhelmed. He was in love with her? Maybe he thought he was. Or maybe he, like Peter, was in love with the idea of a wealthy father-in-law. She just didn't know right now. It was too raw, too sudden and unexpected. She'd been on a roller-coaster ride of emotions for a week now and she honestly didn't trust her own instincts.

In a low, weary voice, she said, "Please, give me some time." Not waiting for his reply, she walked across the room and entered the bathroom, locking the door behind her.

She listened for a few minutes while he apparently got dressed, then heard the clicking of the door to their room as he left it.

He still hadn't come back a half hour later after she'd packed all her things and walked away from The Little Love Nest for good.

11

FOR THE NEXT six weeks, Pamela threw herself whole-heartedly into her job. The teens at the center probably would have preferred that she'd wallowed at home and left them alone, but she needed an outlet for her energy. So she nagged. She cajoled. She counseled, listened and tried to be a friend to some of the kids who hadn't had an adult friend in their lifetime.

She didn't see Ken. She thought about him once in a while—okay, constantly. But she didn't see him.

He called once, leaving her a message on her machine telling her he'd be waiting for her when she was ready to talk.

She wasn't ready yet. She didn't know if she would ever be. She had recognized over the weeks that Ken had probably been completely right in thinking she had been all set to go out to Tahoe and get herself hurt again. That didn't mean she'd forgiven him for deceiving her in order to help her. Nor for doing it because her father had asked him to, though her father had told her he didn't believe that's why Ken had gone on the trip. He couldn't, however, offer any better explanation. So she'd had to believe the worst for the past month and a half.

"You going to stay here until after dark again to-

night?" LaVyrle asked as she came back into the small office the two of them shared at the recreation and counseling center. "Or am I finally going to be able to get home and have dinner with my honey-pie?"

"You don't have a honey-pie," Pamela retorted.

"I do now. He's on channel eight at six-thirty and, girl, I have never seen a weatherman who can make the humidity go up so high so fast! Me 'n' Wanda have decided we need to study up on our weather-ology and then arrange a field trip for some of the kids down to the TV station. Oh, my, I think I see some cumulus clouds on my horizon." She fanned herself, rolling her eyes, obviously trying to make Pamela smile, just as she'd been trying to do for weeks.

Pamela chuckled in spite of herself. "Well, I hate to tear you away from dinner with your TV lover. You don't have to stay with me, you know. I can lock up by myself."

LaVyrle snorted. "I am not leaving you here by yourself until all hours of the night!"

"She won't be by herself." They both jerked their heads toward the door, shocked as a male voice interrupted them. "I'm here."

"We're closed, mister," LaVyrle said, putting her hands on her hips and glaring suspiciously at the intruder. "The kids have all gone home."

"Ken," Pamela whispered, knowing it was him, though he stood in the shadowed hallway outside her door. She would have known it was him even without recognizing his voice. Her whole body went on high

alert, tingling with anticipation just because he stood a few feet away.

Drat the man for still being able to affect her like this!

LaVyrle looked between Pamela's face and Ken's, obviously recognizing the name. She couldn't have missed Pamela's immediate tension. "Oh, boy, I'm leaving."

"Don't go," Pamela pleaded.

"Weatherman's waiting, honey. I will see you tomorrow. Or maybe I won't. Depends on how the weather holds up around *here*, I suppose." With a stern stare at Ken, she maneuvered around him, coming chest to chest in a blatant attempt at intimidation. He held her stare, nodded his head as if to say yes, he'd gotten the message and wouldn't be hurting Pamela anymore. LaVyrle studied him for a moment, then left the room, a small smile playing about her lips. Obviously, she liked what she saw. *The traitor.*

The walls of the cramped office closed in around them with a deep, heavy silence. Pamela busied her hands, locking her desk drawers so she could leave, not even looking up at him.

"Have you talked to your father?" he finally asked.

She shrugged, knowing she didn't have to answer yet wanting to anyway. Just so he didn't think he intimidated her, standing there all dark and intense and gorgeous in the doorway. "Yes."

"You've made your peace?"

"I suppose so," she admitted, her tone grudging. "I've lived twenty-six years of my life ruing the fact that

my father likes to sing my praises to pretty much any-one who'll listen. I guess Peter was a good listener."

"So you've forgiven him."

"For the most part."

"But not me."

She stood, grabbed her black nylon gym bag and stepped out from behind her old scarred-up metal city-issue desk. She held her head up as she walked the few steps across the room, waiting for him to move. He didn't get out of the way, merely stood there, blocking the door. Since she was nearly as tall as he, they came nose to nose. Pamela ignored the sensations *that* brought—the minty-sweet smell of his breath, the flicker of energy that passed between their bodies, held so rigidly, mere inches apart.

"Will you excuse me?" she finally managed to bite out. "I'm ready to go home now."

He muttered something under his breath, something that sounded suspiciously like "stubborn as a mule," but finally stepped aside to let her pass. She flipped off the light switch as she left the office, leaving him standing in the darkness. "Are you going to come out or am I supposed to lock you in there for the night?"

He finally exited, watching while she locked the office door and dropped her bulky key ring into her bag.

"Can we go have dinner somewhere, just to talk?"

"I'm not hungry," she said as she turned away and marched purposefully down the hall toward the building's exit. He followed, of course. When they reached the gymnasium, she entered the double doors to ensure the overhead lights had been turned off. They had.

Ken stepped in behind her, again blocking her path when she turned to leave. His nearness was disconcerting, distracting. Devastating.

She hadn't forgotten, in the six weeks since she'd seen him, just how strong the physical attraction had been between them. She'd never experienced anything like it before. She doubted she ever would again.

"Please, Pamela. Let's go somewhere and talk. I've missed you so much," he said, raising his hand to brush his fingers against her cheek.

"I said I'm not hungry," she finally managed to say, her words ending in a near croak as he stepped closer. She took a tiny step back. "Now, I have to go. Goodnight, Ken."

He muttered something again, then said, "Play me."

She paused. "What?"

"Play me, Pam, for talking points. Isn't that what you call them? Come on. You scared?"

"Of you? Get real, McBain, you computer-obsessed couch potato. I would whip your ass all over the court."

He chuckled. "So put your money where your slam dunk is. Play me. For every point I score, you listen to me—*really* listen."

"And for every point I score?"

He paused, considering. "I'll listen to you."

"Nope," she said with a snort. "I don't have anything to say to you." She tried to push past him and exit the darkly shadowed, cavernous room.

He caught her arm. "Wait a minute,"

"Have you got something better to put on the table?"

she asked, cocking her head to one side and putting her fist on her hip in an unspoken challenge.

He glanced around, as if searching for an answer in the silent, sweat-tinged air of the gym. Then he grinned. "Maybe. How about cash? For every point you score on me I'll donate a thousand dollars to the center. Win or lose, a thousand bucks a point. What do you say?"

Her mouth dropped open.

"We'll play single point one-on-one," he cajoled.

"To eleven or twenty-one?" she asked, still not quite believing he was willing to spend thousands of dollars just to get her to listen to him.

"Twenty-one. I have a feeling it's going to take until at least twenty for you to admit you love me."

She snorted at his arrogance, then threw her gym bag on the floor. Shaking her head, not quite believing she was going to do this, she flipped on all the light switches lining the wall by the exit. The overhead fluorescent fixtures buzzed, then flashed on, bathing the room in a brilliant white, letting her see him clearly for the first time that evening.

He looked tired. His face was a shade paler than she remembered, and she noticed a frown line on his brow. The man was still devastating, of course, even dressed casually in a gray cotton T-shirt and jeans. Tight jeans.

She mentally ordered her pulse to stop pounding and hardened her heart. Grabbing a worn, dirty-orange ball from a rack on the side of the gym, she muttered, "A thousand bucks a point, McBain."

He scored the first one. She couldn't believe it, blaming herself for being caught unaware when he stole the

ball and made a nice shot that barely kissed the rim as it sailed through the net. She muttered a swear word, drawing a grin from him.

"I don't work for your father."

"That's one," she said as she stole the ball, dribbled, and countered with a point of her own.

"I owe you a thousand bucks."

"I know that. You don't get to tell me. No talking unless you score."

"No *scoring*," he said, his tone making his sexual meaning clear, "unless I talk enough to convince you I'm crazy about you, either, I guess." His frustration was evident.

He distracted her, darn it. That sexy little comment cost her another shot. He took full advantage, aimed and scored again.

"I was working on a contract for your father's company that was signed, sealed, delivered and well underway before you and I ever met. You had absolutely *nothing* to do with me getting that work. And I am *not* his employee."

"That was more than one point's worth," she said, even as she thought about his words. Her father had told her something similar, so she wasn't entirely surprised to learn that Ken did, indeed, own his own computer software consulting firm and wasn't an employee of Bradford Investments.

Then she thrust the thoughts aside and concentrated on keeping the ball out of his very quick hands. She scored three more points, but they weren't easy. He was

better than she'd expected. Better than the teens she usually played with here at the center.

"You're up to four grand now," she muttered, trying to taunt him into making a mistake.

He hadn't so much as broken a sweat as he guarded her. Then he stole the ball and sunk another one from the top of the key.

"Yes, your father asked me to go with you and make sure you were okay. But that wasn't why I went. I went because I had half-fallen for you before we ever met, from the first time I saw you at his office."

She listened in spite of herself. He took advantage of her interest and scored again.

"That night on the beach just cemented something that was already growing in my heart every time I saw your picture or heard your father talk about you, Pamela. I was falling fast and hard, half-gone on you before we met. And then, that night, I wanted to protect you, to make sure no one else ever hurt you again. That's why I agreed to go with you."

She sneered. "That's all?"

"Hell, no, that's not all," he retorted as he swiped the ball out of her hand, dribbled and landed a nice lay-up. "I wanted you for myself, dammit. I did not want you to go out to Tahoe and hook up with some loser."

Somehow, though he'd said it before, hearing it again like this, she started to believe him.

"And it didn't occur to you to be honest with me from the beginning? You couldn't just tell me you'd seen that awful cake incident?" That was on *her* point, but he didn't quibble.

"You wouldn't have given me the time of day. If you knew I'd been there, you would have refused even to speak to me on the beach, much less invite me to come along on a honeymoon with you."

She frowned. Yes, she had invited him, after all. He paused on the court, obviously hoping she was softening toward him. She took advantage and scored again. "There goes another thousand. I hope that contract with my father is a lucrative one."

"I'm finished with the job, Pamela," he replied as he snagged the ball and dribbled toward the basket. "I've been working sixteen-hour days, seven days a week, wanting to have the project finished. So you can't use that as an excuse between us now. I have nothing to gain by being here—except getting you to admit you love me. And to believe I love you."

She hesitated, her feet almost stumbling even as her heart tripped at his words.

She hadn't known he was finished. No wonder he looked so tired! Her father had told her Ken's project was scheduled to last for three months. He'd obviously completed it in much less time than that.

"My business is flexible, I can work from anywhere in the country. I want to stay here in Miami, permanently, with you."

"You said you were in love with me," she said softly, still not ready to forgive him just yet.

"So?" he asked, taking the ball and holding it behind his back. She grabbed for it, reaching around his waist, trying to knock at it with her fingertips.

She succeeded only in jerking her whole body against

his. They stood chest to chest. Panting. Lips parted and eyes wide. The intensity roared between them.

"Being in love with someone isn't the same as loving them," she finally said. "'In love' is a temporary condition brought about by cupids and round beds and sweet massage oil."

He smiled gently. "So what's love? Is it this? Is it sweaty basketball courts, a thousand bucks a point and a deserted rec center?"

She didn't answer.

"I *love* you, Pamela. I've loved you for longer than I've been *in* love with you."

She stared into his eyes, testing the truth there, seeing it, starting to believe it.

"I resisted it because reason and logic told me it couldn't happen. That I couldn't have fallen so hard, so fast. That you couldn't reciprocate. That it was a rebound romance."

He dropped the ball. She glanced down as it bounced away toward the middle of the court. Then he tilted her chin up and stared at her. "None of that matters. The truth is you're the other half of me, the part it took me thirty years to find. Now I've found you. You're my mate. I know it. And I'm willing to wait, or play basketball or donate a thousand bucks a point until you are ready to admit it, too."

She looked down, scuffed her toe against the floor. "I'm better than you are. You'll go broke."

"Quit stalling."

She smiled at the mock-threat in his voice. "I'm not stalling."

"You're cute when you're nervous."

"The last time you told me that I was afraid our plane was going to crash and I was going to die a virgin."

He shook his head and a wicked grin crossed his lips. "Oh, no, indeed. Too late for that, love."

"Thank goodness," she said with a tiny, heartfelt sigh.

She finally believed it, finally accepted it, finally took it all in. He loved her. Truly. With the forever kind of love that outlasted games or honeymoons or software projects.

"You still interested in the SUV and the two-point-five?"

His eyes glittered with satisfaction. "Only with you." She slipped her hands over his shoulders, circling his neck. "I love you, Ken McBain. And you're not crazy. It did happen. We were both fortunate enough to see it, feel it and recognize it instantly. You're the person I've been waiting for all my life."

His kiss was tender, sweet, gentle and laden with restrained passion. He held her tightly, as if he'd never get tired of holding her in his arms, and she sank against him, feeling complete again for the first time in more than a month.

Finally, when he tipped her chin with his index finger and tilted her head back for another kiss, she gave him a wicked smile. "This still doesn't let you off the hook. I believe the score is six to five," she said.

"We still playing to twenty-one?"

"Only if you tell me you love me for every one of your talking points."

"How about every other?" he asked as he scooped up the ball and took a long shot from half court. He landed it. She couldn't believe he landed it.

"Why every other?"

"Well," he replied as they walked hand in hand to the end of the court to retrieve the ball. "I figured the other half of the shots I'll be telling you everything I plan to do with you when we get back to The Little Love Nest for our *real* honeymoon."

They paused, Pamela raising her eyebrow, her heart beginning to pound. Then he beckoned her closer, gesturing with his index finger until her face was inches from his.

"Starting," he said with a sultry whisper as he nibbled on her earlobe, "with telling you why I'm so very happy you're tall."

Harlequin truly does make any time special. . . . This year we are celebrating weddings in style!

To help us celebrate, we want you to tell us how wearing the Harlequin wedding gown will make your wedding day special. As the grand prize, Harlequin will offer one lucky bride the chance to **"Walk Down the Aisle"** in the Harlequin wedding gown!

There's more...

For her honeymoon, she and her groom will spend five nights at the **Hyatt Regency Maui.** As part of this five-night honeymoon at the hotel renowned for its romantic attractions, the couple will enjoy a candlelit dinner for two in Swan Court, a sunset sail on the hotel's catamaran, and duet spa treatments.

To enter, please write, in, 250 words or less, how wearing the Harlequin wedding gown will make your wedding day special. The entry will be judged based on its emotionally compelling nature, its originality and creativity, and its sincerity. This contest is open to Canadian and U.S. residents only and to those who are 18 years of age and older. There is no purchase necessary to enter. Void where prohibited. See further contest rules attached. Please send your entry to:

Walk Down the Aisle Contest

In Canada	In U.S.A.
P.O. Box 637	P.O. Box 9076
Fort Erie, Ontario	3010 Walden Ave.
L2A 5X3	Buffalo, NY 14269-9076

You can also enter by visiting www.eHarlequin.com
Win the Harlequin wedding gown and the vacation of a lifetime!
The deadline for entries is October 1, 2001.

PHWDACONT1

HARLEQUIN WALK DOWN THE AISLE TO MAUI CONTEST 1197
OFFICIAL RULES
NO PURCHASE NECESSARY TO ENTER

1. To enter, follow directions published in the offer to which you are responding. Contest begins April 2, 2001, and ends on October 1, 2001. Method of entry may vary. Mailed entries must be postmarked by October 1, 2001, and received by October 8, 2001.

2. Contest entry may be, at times, presented via the Internet, but will be restricted solely to residents of certain georgraphic areas that are disclosed on the Web site. To enter via the Internet, if permissible, access the Harlequin Web site (www.eHarlequin.com) and follow the directions displayed online. Online entries must be received by 11:59 p.m. E.S.T. on October 1, 2001.

   In lieu of submitting an entry online, enter by mail by hand-printing (or typing) on an 8½" x 11" plain sheet of paper, your name, address (including zip code), Contest number/name and in 250 words or fewer, why winning a Harlequin wedding dress would make your wedding day special. Mail via first-class mail to: Harlequin Walk Down the Aisle Contest 1197, (in the U.S.) P.O. Box 9076, 3010 Walden Avenue, Buffalo, NY 14269-9076, (in Canada) P.O. Box 637, Fort Erie, Ontario L2A 5X3, Canada. Limit one entry per person, household address and e-mail address. Online and/or mailed entries received from persons residing in geographic areas in which Internet entry is not permissible will be disqualified.

3. Contests will be judged by a panel of members of the Harlequin editorial, marketing and public relations staff based on the following criteria:

   - Originality and Creativity—50%
   - Emotionally Compelling—25%
   - Sincerity—25%

   In the event of a tie, duplicate prizes will be awarded. Decisions of the judges are final.

4. All entries become the property of Torstar Corp. and will not be returned. No responsibility is assumed for lost, late, illegible, incomplete, inaccurate, nondelivered or misdirected mail or misdirected e-mail, for technical, hardware or software failures of any kind, lost or unavailable network connections, or failed, incomplete, garbled or delayed computer transmission or any human error which may occur in the receipt or processing of the entries in this Contest.

5. Contest open only to residents of the U.S. (except Puerto Rico) and Canada, who are 18 years of age or older, and is void wherever prohibited by law; all applicable laws and regulations apply. Any litigation within the Province of Quebec respecting the conduct or organization of a publicity contest may be submitted to the Régie des alcools, des courses et des jeux for a ruling. Any litigation respecting the awarding of a prize may be submitted to the Régie des alcools, des courses et des jeux on for the purpose of helping the parties reach a settlement. Employees and immediate family members of Torstar Corp. and D. L. Blair, Inc., their affiliates, subsidiaries and all other agencies, entities and persons connected with the use, marketing or conduct of this Contest are not eligible to enter. Taxes on prizes are the sole responsibility of winners. Acceptance of any prize offered constitutes permission to use winner's name, photograph or other likeness for the purposes of advertising, trade and promotion on behalf of Torstar Corp., its affiliates and subsidiaries without further compensation to the winner, unless prohibited by law.

6. Winners will be determined no later than November 15, 2001, and will be notified by mail. Winners will be required to sign an return an Affidavit of Eligibility form within 15 days after winner notification. Noncompliance within that time period may result in disqualification and an alternative winner may be selected. Winners of trip must execute a Release of Liability prior to ticket and must possess required travel documents (e.g. passport, photo ID) where applicable. Trip must be completed by November 2002. No substitution of prize permitted by winner. Torstar Corp. and D. L. Blair, Inc., their parents, affiliates, and subsidiaries are not responsible for errors in printing or electronic presentation of Contest, entries and/or game pieces. In the event of printing or other errors which may result in unintended prize values or duplication of prizes, all affected game pieces or entries shall be null and void. If for any reason the Internet portion of the Contest is not capable of running as planned, including infection by computer virus, bugs, tampering, unauthorized intervention, fraud, technical failures, or any other causes beyond the control of Torstar Corp. which corrupt or affect the administration, secrecy, fairness, integrity or proper conduct of the Contest, Torstar Corp. reserves the right, at its sole discretion, to disqualify any individual who tampers with the entry process and to cancel, terminate, modify or suspend the Contest or the Internet portion thereof. In the event of a dispute regarding an online entry, the entry will be deemed submitted by the authorized holder of the e-mail account submitted at the time of entry Authorized account holder is defined as the natural person who is assigned to an e-mail address by an Internet access provid online service provider or other organization that is responsible for arranging e-mail address for the domain associated with submitted e-mail address. **Purchase or acceptance of a product offer does not improve your chances of winning.**

7. Prizes: (1) Grand Prize—A Harlequin wedding dress (approximate retail value: $3,500) and a 5-night/6-day honeymoon trip Maui, HI, including round-trip air transportation provided by Maui Visitors Bureau from Los Angeles International Airport (winner is responsible for transportation to and from Los Angeles International Airport) and a Harlequin Romance Package, including hotel accomodations (double occupancy) at the Hyatt Regency Maui Resort and Spa, dinner for (2) two at Swan Court, a sunset sail on Kiele V and a spa treatment for the winner (approximate retail value: $4,000); (5) Five runner-up priz of a $1000 gift certificate to selected retail outlets to be determined by Sponsor (retail value $1000 ea.). Prizes consist of on those items listed as part of the prize. Limit one prize per person. All prizes are valued in U.S. currency.

8. For a list of winners (available after December 17, 2001) send a self-addressed, stamped envelope to: Harlequin Walk Down Aisle Contest 1197 Winners, P.O. Box 4200 Blair, NE 68009-4200 or you may access the www.eHarlequin.com Web site through January 15, 2002.

Contest sponsored by Torstar Corp., P.O. Box 9042, Buffalo, NY 14269-9042, U.S.A.

PHWDACONT2

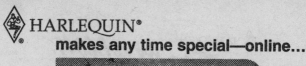